RYANN FLETCHER

Storm Signal

Cricket Chronicles book 3

Copyright © 2021 by Ryann Fletcher

All rights reserved. No part of this publication may be reproduced, stored or transmitted in any form or by any means, electronic, mechanical, photocopying, recording, scanning, or otherwise without written permission from the publisher. It is illegal to copy this book, post it to a website, or distribute it by any other means without permission.

This novel is entirely a work of fiction. The names, characters and incidents portrayed in it are the work of the author's imagination. Any resemblance to actual persons, living or dead, events or localities is entirely coincidental.

Cover art by Sarah Holmes. https://Tumblr.com/ANebulousPurpose

First edition

ISBN: 978-1-9163750-4-8

*This book was professionally typeset on Reedsy.
Find out more at reedsy.com*

To all those who fight for justice – keep fighting.

Contents

CHAPTER ONE	1
CHAPTER TWO	11
CHAPTER THREE	20
CHAPTER FOUR	28
CHAPTER FIVE	38
CHAPTER SIX	49
CHAPTER SEVEN	57
CHAPTER EIGHT	66
CHAPTER NINE	72
CHAPTER TEN	86
CHAPTER ELEVEN	95
CHAPTER TWELVE	108
CHAPTER THIRTEEN	113
CHAPTER FOURTEEN	118
CHAPTER FIFTEEN	123
CHAPTER SIXTEEN	136
CHAPTER SEVENTEEN	140
CHAPTER EIGHTEEN	152
CHAPTER NINETEEN	163
CHAPTER TWENTY	172
CHAPTER TWENTY-ONE	181
CHAPTER TWENTY-TWO	190
CHAPTER TWENTY-THREE	200
CHAPTER TWENTY-FOUR	210
CHAPTER TWENTY-FIVE	219
CHAPTER TWENTY-SIX	229

CHAPTER TWENTY-SEVEN	241
CHAPTER TWENTY-EIGHT	255
CHAPTER TWENTY-NINE	269
CHAPTER THIRTY	280
CHAPTER THIRTY-ONE	291
CHAPTER THIRTY-TWO	304
CHAPTER THIRTY-THREE	312
CHAPTER THIRTY-FOUR	319
CHAPTER THIRTY-FIVE	328
CHAPTER THIRTY-SIX	340
CHAPTER THIRTY-SEVEN	351
CHAPTER THIRTY-EIGHT	362
CHAPTER THIRTY-NINE	374
Epilogue	381
End of book three	385
Sewing Deceit preview	386
About the Author	392
Also by Ryann Fletcher	394

CHAPTER ONE

Georgie wrinkled her nose at the full waste bin in the conference room, piled high with half eaten fruits and used tissues. It never ceased to anger her that Coalition higher ups would waste food when so many here in Skelm were starving. Janitors like her were routinely fired for picking through the trash, as it was deemed *unseemly* by the well-dressed rulers of this rock.

Skelm was dirty, covered in thick layers of grime that settled in your lungs at the first opportunity. The cleaning solvents were harsh and made Georgie feel like she couldn't get enough air. She wasn't allowed to wear a mask, because that was considered *unseemly* too. She dumped the contents of the overflowing basket into her wheeled bin, and swallowed back a gag at the fruit, not long in the trash, but brown and slimy from the hot sunlight that beat down through the windows that spanned from the floor up to the ceiling. Whoever designed this building was a mindless fool, and the conference rooms were never anything other than unpleasantly warm.

She tugged at the neck of her orange jumpsuit and felt sweat drip down her back. An unfortunately familiar feeling for Georgie, who had worked as a janitor in the Skelm administration building for nearly five years, ever since she managed to escape the factories. Despite the chemicals that settled at the back of her throat when she scraped away the unending muck that settled on every surface in this settlement, her job was a far sight better than working at one of the many factories on Skelm. That was a death sentence. She thought of her mother, sick and struggling to breathe, and her jaw set firm. Someday she'd get her family off this rock.

It had been nearly two months since she helped the pair of pirates escape the city, and they'd promised to come back for Georgie's family. "We're the Paynes," she'd said, before creating a diversion for them by way of a chemical explosion. Nearly all the windows in the building had shattered, sending shards of glass spiraling through the air and settling on the streets like ice. The windows had been replaced within the week, and already they were covered in Skelm scum.

"Amaranth, honestly, no one can understand you like that!" a flustered man said, rustling papers at the long, oval table. "Why don't you just write it down instead?" The man was a visitor in the city, probably some higher up Coalition manager who wanted to be sure that production was flowing at the factories.

The woman he addressed scribbled furiously on a pad of yellowing paper, splashing ink across the varnished wood. *Great*, Georgie thought to herself, *something else I'll have to clean up later.*

"Amaranth, we're just going to let someone else take point on this one. We understand your predicament and that you've not healed quite yet, but we need someone who can command and train a team of new investigators, and I'm afraid you're not up to the challenge. Don't worry, you'll get your opportunity with the next batch of recruits."

"Uh, she's writing that she's completely capable, and that her jaw will be unwired within the fortnight," said a small man, dressed in a deep green velvet jacket. His voice was squeaky and unsure. "She says that she won't have this posting taken from her on account of not being able to speak, as the most effective interrogation efforts don't require speech."

The first man sighed and rubbed at his temples. "I realize you are very capable at what you do, Amaranth, but we cannot delay these recruits any longer. The Coalition has great need of them! Have you even seen how high the prisoner files are stacked these days? What do you expect me to do, interrogate them all myself?" He paused and gave another exasperated sigh when the woman began scratching at the paper with her pen once more. "No. No, enough. I'm not going to debate this with you,

CHAPTER ONE

Amaranth, we have neither the time nor the resources to drag this out any longer." He straightened the papers in front of him and stood up. "We will revisit this when you are better equipped to teach a class. Until then, you will be reassigned to desk duty, where you will review and file completed confessions."

The woman bared her teeth, covered in silver wire, and grunted loudly, something Georgie imagined would sound like "No" if she was able to open her mouth. The woman slammed her fists down on the table and glared at the man. The other participants at the table shrank back in their seats, intimidated by the aggressive display. After all, most of them were here for a visit, not stationed here, and preferred to be much further away from witnessing the violence of an interrogation first hand. Georgie tipped the second wastebasket into the bin and gently pushed down on papers to create more room in her wheeled bin. The delicate crunch of the papers drew the attention of everyone in the room.

"Don't you think you could do your job a little *quieter*?" a woman dressed head to toe in vibrant purple silks scoffed. "Surely that's achievable?"

"Yes ma'am," Georgie replied, and plastered a grin across her face. "My sincerest apologies."

"A verbal response was not required," the woman in purple said, her ire palpable. "I shall report this to your supervisor."

"Come now, Rowena, we don't have time for such frivolities. We have to get back to the transport within the hour or we'll have to wait until tomorrow."

"Charles, it would be inappropriate to ignore a breach in etiquette from a member of staff, even in a backwater like this."

The man sighed again and slid his papers into a polished leather briefcase. "Very well, then. But make it quick, I don't want to be late for our next meeting."

Georgie backed against the wall as Rowena passed, the silks of her skirts rustling noisily. She nodded politely, her eyes fixed on the gleaming marble floor, shot through with flecks of gold and sparkling granite. She couldn't risk being written up for any further infractions; if she lost this job, then her family would end up back in the tenement they'd started in. No, she couldn't go back to that. Her mother and sisters deserved better than to be crowded into bunks with hundreds of strangers, all fighting for scraps of clean linen for their beds.

"Amaranth, my decision is final. Stop writing, I won't read it," Charles said, his voice flat and disinterested.

The woman thrust the papers at his face and gestured to her jaw, grunting.

"Absolutely not. It's no longer up for discussion. We will return in six months, and we will reinstate you then, if you are fit for the position. In the meantime, we will have Johnson fill in for you. As I said, we have no time to spare in these matters. We cannot wait for you to be ready to do your job." He strode from the room, briefcase in hand, his footsteps even and sure on the marble.

The woman glared at him as he left, her fists clenched in fury. The small man looked at her apologetically and shuffled to the door, papers in hand.

Georgie moved to the windows and dumped a scoop of the waxy white cleaning beads into a bucket of cold water in preparation to scrub the windows clean and prevent the yellow build up of grease and smog that would thoroughly offend the visiting Coalition management. Georgie began to scrub at the grime, now accustomed to the insistent burning of the cleaning solution as it ran down her arms. Gloves weren't allowed either, as it might make people think the cleaning solution was dangerous.

The angry rustling of papers made Georgie look over her shoulder at the woman, who was shuffling through files looking for something. "Did you need any help?" Georgie asked. It was an infraction to not offer help to someone with seniority and position over her.

The woman stared at Georgie, a close-lipped smile spreading over her face as she dumped the entire well of ink out over the desk, making sure to shake the last drops free. She stood, leaving scraps of paper littered over the desk and floor, and swept out of the room, a silk top hat under her arm.

When the door closed behind the woman, Georgie swore under her breath. The entitlement of these Coalition suits was just breathtaking. She began to mop up the ink, knowing that the longer it sat, the harder it would be to

CHAPTER ONE

clean. The sticky black ink was already beginning to set, drying into a shiny mess atop the varnished wood. Water dripped from the bristled brush onto the table as she scrubbed. The cleaning agent they used on the windows, walls, and floors would strip the paint from the wood in a heartbeat. She didn't want to think what it was doing to her lungs day in and day out, and whatever harm it was doing wasn't as bad as the emissions from the heavy machinery at the factories. Coal dust filled the air there, a result of the huge boilers that powered the city.

The crumpled page that the woman had thrust at Charles soaked in the water from the brush. The words, *"My name is Inspector Allemande"* blurred and disappeared into the soaked paper.

* * *

"Did you have a good day at work, Georgie?" her mother asked when she came through the door.

"Sure."

Her mother looked at her with suspicion. "Are you positive about that?"

"Yeah." Georgie grinned and hung her bag on the hook. She didn't like to complain, not when her mother spent years almost working herself into an early grave to provide for her and her sisters. They were better off than many in Skelm; they had a one-room apartment all to themselves. It was more privacy than anyone who lived in the tenements could ever dream of. Her sisters shared the bed, and her mother slept on the makeshift sofa; Georgie slept on the floor with some thin blankets they'd managed to save up for.

"Were they nice to you?"

"Sure."

"You're late tonight, Georgina," her mother said, and coughed into a dirty handkerchief.

Georgie grimaced at the use of her full name. It meant that her mother knew something was going on. "Don't worry about it, Ma."

"Georgina," her mother repeated in a warning tone.

"It's not a big deal, I promise," she said, unlacing her work boots and leaving them as close to the door as possible. "Some higher up in a meeting wanted to show off to her superiors, ratted on me for answering a question and rustling some papers."

"What did your supervisor say?"

"Not much." That part wasn't a lie - her boss was a man of few words, and not only because the years of exposure to Skelm's toxic air and solvents had blistered his throat raw. "I can't get another infraction or they'll replace me."

"Georgie!" her mother gasped. "Georgina, you have to be careful. I don't want to see you working down in the factories. It's not safe. I'd go back to work there before I'd let you risk your health like that."

"Absolutely not, Ma. The mountains of Skelm will be crumbled to dust before I'd let that happen."

"There's some bread for you on the table here. Sit down and have something to eat."

"I'm not hungry."

At the warning look in her mother's eyes, Georgie sat down at the wobbly table and ripped a chunk of bread off the loaf. It was still a little warm, no doubt baked fresh by one of her little sisters. Her mother was too frail to stand for very long anymore. She mopped up what was left of the thin gravy and shoved it into her mouth. She tried to make sure there was always food left for them, so ate as little as she could at home. Sometimes she'd forage for scraps in the dumpsters behind the swanky Coalition cafe, but she'd never tell her mother that. If her lungs didn't give out, the shame of it would kill her.

"I worry about you, Georgie," her mother said when she finished. "I know you want to take care of us, but you have to stay healthy too." Her voice was raspy, weak from the extended coughing fits she suffered from. "Your father never would have wanted this."

"Yeah, well, he lost his right to have a vote when he died," Georgie replied, bitterness creeping in at the back of her throat. "Things are different now. Someone's gotta make sure Lucy and Emeline have a roof over their heads and go to school. He brought us all to this godsdamned place, and you and I both know we should have stayed on Gamma-3."

Her mother sighed and traced her calloused fingertips over the bare wood of the table. "It was supposed to be an opportunity. There was so much poverty on Gamma-3, so much pollution. If you'd have seen the broadcasts, Georgie, it looked like this was a paradise. We were promised homes, a safe place to raise our children, parks for them to play in. It was too late when we realized the lie, that happiness was only for the wealthy and the social climbers. Your pop and I, we tried our best. I'm just sorry it wasn't good enough."

Georgie softened and took her mother's hand. "Don't say that, Ma. You made a better life for us here than most have managed. We'll find a way off this rock someday soon, I know we will." She thought of the promise that Evie Anderson had made her weeks prior, a tiny glimmer of hope that got smaller every day. It's possible those pirates would never come back for them. She wouldn't, if the situation was reversed. She'd get far away from this place and never return. They'd have to kill her first. "Where are the girls?"

"They went for a walk, I'm sure they'll be back soon."

"Ma, you can't let them go wandering the streets! Don't you know what's going on out there?"

"They aren't babies anymore, Georgie. They'll be alright."

The yellow light of the street lamps flooded the pavement outside their building, with no sign of her little sisters. Lucy was just eleven, she still loved braiding her doll's hair over and over, so often that the hair had started to fall out. Georgie had wanted to get her a new one for her birthday, but there just weren't any spare credits for presents this year. Or any year, for that matter.

"They aren't babies, but the folks in the tenements are desperate and angry. They won't hesitate to take out their aggression on a couple of girls on their own. Besides, haven't you seen the flyers Emeline has been coming home from school with? It's rebel propaganda! I don't want them getting mixed up in all that."

Her mother stared. "And what of that explosion two months back? Do you expect me to believe your cock-and-bull story about how you took the long way home from work that day for some fresh air? I saw that ash on your face, Georgina!"

"Do you want someone to hear you, Ma?" Georgie hissed. "I told you, it wasn't me. I was nearby. They say it was a boiler explosion." It had been a boiler explosion, but not due to a fault in the construction. Georgie had dumped canisters of the caustic cleaning agent on the metal, releasing a highly flammable gas that was lit by the boiler's pilot light. An almost perfect crime, except for her mother's keen observation skills. The head of the maintenance department never even suspected foul play. Perhaps they should have hired her mother instead.

"Mm. A boiler explosion."

"Anyway, even if it was planned, *which it wasn't*, it was probably the rebel cell that started up recently. They're dangerous. And that's why I don't want Emeline and Lucy out in the evenings. Em keeps saying she wants to change things. I'd like to see change, too, but I don't want to see it at our expense."

"I don't know, they seem to have some good ideas. Maybe they can clean the place up, put some pressure on the management to make the factories safer."

"Oh, Ma," Georgie scoffed, "they'll never listen to any of us. There are too many eager replacements desperate for these jobs for them to care. Besides, I think all these rebels are going to do is set a few things on fire before they get themselves killed."

"Your pop would have kept fighting."

"His associations with the last rebel cell is what got him killed."

"You don't know that, Georgie."

"You should hear how they talk about us up in that administration building, Ma. We're expendable. Cattle. Cheap labor. That whole cell was wiped out in one night down on the docks. It sure as damn hell wasn't a coincidence."

"Emeline is just like him."

CHAPTER ONE

"And that's why I know I need to keep her safe. I'm going out to look for them." Georgie turned to tug her boots back on when the door slammed open and Lucy and Emeline tumbled in, giggling.

"Georgie, you're home!" Lucy shouted, and threw her arms around Georgie's waist. "Did you have some of the bread I made?"

"I did. Delicious, as always." Georgie looked at the taller of the two sisters, standing in the doorway in her shabby hand-me-down dress and corset, which was frayed at the edges of the steel boning. "And where were you two wandering around at this time in the evening?"

Emeline shrugged, a mischievous grin spreading across her rosy cheeks. "Nowhere important."

"Then why is the hem of your dress all muddy? Em, you weren't down by the docks, were you?"

"You're just like Ma, you know," her sister scoffed, closing the door behind her. "I'm grown now, I can take care of myself."

"You're sixteen," their mother chimed in from the table. "You're not grown yet, and until things are safer in Skelm, I want you home before the street lights come on."

"Ma!" Emeline protested, kicking off her buttoned boots, "That's not fair, you know I'll be careful!"

"There are things going on that you don't know about," Georgie said firmly, hoping her sister would take her seriously.

"Oh, and you do? Funny, I didn't see you down at the meeting tonight."

"So you *were* at a meeting! Em, what have I said about that rebel group? They're dangerous! You're going to get yourself killed, or worse!"

Emeline snorted. "What's worse than being killed?"

"You don't want to know what they do to rebel insurgents in the administration building. It *is* worse than being killed. And there's no way in hell I want that to happen to you." Georgie wriggled out of Lucy's grip and laid a hand on Emeline's shoulder. "Promise me you won't go back down there."

"What am I supposed to do, just sit around and wait for something to change? Pray to the gods that they'll find us a way off this base? It's not like they've ever listened before, and they sure as hell aren't now. Why not take a stand, show the Coalition management that we deserve to be treated better? What's the harm in that?"

Georgie bit her tongue. Her sisters didn't know the truth of how their father died, and believed he was killed in an accident on the docks. "Just promise me, Emeline."

"Fine, whatever you want, Georgina," her sister spat, and flopped on her shared bed angrily. "I hate it here."

"We'll figure it out. We just have to be patient," their mother said, and Georgie could only hope that was true.

CHAPTER TWO

Henry stepped off the transport and onto Skelm's dock, tugging her silk scarf up over her mouth and nose. "Gods, this place is even more disgusting than they warned me it would be."

"The sooner we complete our work here, the sooner we can get to our next assignment."

"Honestly, Roger, I never imagined it would look quite like *this*."

"Progress comes at a cost, it always has," Roger replied cheerily, his voice muffled behind layers of cloth tied into a crisp knot behind his head. "What can we do, other than our work? Who would study the native storms if not for us?"

"All I know is that I need a hot bath and a bed before I do any academic study of the storms beyond the terraformers." She stretched her arms out over her head, stiff from the long journey from Gamma-3. If they were lucky, they wouldn't be here long. This place was horrific, great clouds of smoke billowing from factories as far as the eye could see, obscuring the view of the administration building at the summit.

"Miss Weaver, is it?" a young boy said, tipping his cap. "I'm here to take your things to your apartment."

"Yes, that's me," Henry replied, and released her grip on her tan leather suitcases. "Are you sure that's not too much for you?"

"No, ma'am, you've got far less than most who come through these docks." The boy turned to Roger. "Did you need help with your bags, too?"

Roger furrowed his brow, offended. "No, I am quite capable of carrying my own things, thank you."

"Right then, follow me," the boy said, lugging the cases with surprising dexterity. "It's not far."

"Pity they couldn't send a steamcar for us," Roger grumbled, and Henry smirked beneath her scarf. Her colleague wasn't a man who enjoyed anything resembling manual labor. "Bloody cases are heavier than I remember packing them. Gravity must be high on this base."

"You know as well as I do that it's the same as Gamma-3," Henry laughed. "Pick up the pace, Rog, the faster we get to our apartments the quicker I can have a warm soak and scrub off the travel grit."

"Easy for you to say, you have someone carrying your bags!" Roger protested.

"It's just there on the corner," the boy said helpfully, and lifted one of Henry's cases to gesture at a tall, gleaming building with green tinted glass windows, nestled safely behind a razor wire fence and a magnetic steam gate. "I told you it's not far."

"It's no capital building," Roger sighed, "but it will have to do." He turned back to Henry and looked at her over his round, silver-rimmed spectacles. "I'm telling you, Weaver, you'd better have some more of your brilliant ideas percolating in that head of yours. I want to get out of here as soon as possible."

Henry nodded grimly. "Agreed." Her mentor had warned her about coming to Skelm, told her of the filth and the incredible pollution, how the Coalition broadcast advertisements painting the settlement as a place of endless opportunity were outright lies. The opportunity to study the native storms was too good to pass up, with a promotion and the promise of accolades when she would eventually publish her research. If she could observe the storms without human interference, it could have untold benefits for the people of Gamma-3. Storms throughout the Near Systems were rare within terraformed communities, disrupted by the fluctuations in gravity and atmosphere. But here, the storms continued apace, defying the slow march of human development as the city sprawled ever further to the

CHAPTER TWO

south and east.

The magnetic lock released when the boy waved up to a security drone, hovering just beyond the door, its propellers flapping noisily. He led them past the wire fences, topped with blades sharp enough to sever an artery if anyone ever tried to climb over them. Henry swallowed hard and followed the boy into the foyer of the building. The lamps that hung from the ceiling were filled to the brim with algae imported from Gamma-3, sent here to cleanse the air of pollutants and keep buildings habitable amid the dozens of factories that belched smog into the atmosphere outside. An ingenious solution to a problem that shouldn't exist, Henry always thought. They cast an odd greenish glow over the white marble floors, giving the vestibule a kind of underwater feeling that was both imaginative and suffocating. Henry tugged the scarf down over her chin and took a deep breath.

"This is as far as I go," the boy said. "I'm not allowed upstairs."

"Of course," Henry said, and tipped the boy a few credits for his trouble. "Thank you for your help."

"My pleasure," the boy said, and tipped his hat again. "I'll be down at the docks if you need my help again."

Henry nodded politely, and the boy scuttled back out the door and into the street. A shame that such a nice boy should have to work instead of pursuing his education. What exactly was going on here in Skelm, anyway?

"Two apartments, booked under the names Weaver and Beauregard." Roger leaned on the granite desk, winded from the short walk.

"Maybe you should pack lighter next time," Henry smiled wryly, and received a disgruntled huff in return.

"This is all necessary!" Roger retorted.

"Then perhaps you should have accepted help when it was offered?"

"Henry, please. I have *some* pride."

"Your rooms are in the east wing," the receptionist chirped, her smile plastered across her face. "There are no other rooms there, so you shouldn't have any trouble finding them."

"Thank you, my dear," Roger replied with a winsome grin. "You've been very helpful."

Henry rolled her eyes as they turned their backs on the woman and lifted their bags onto a baggage trolley. She gripped a bar on the trolley and pulled it, the wheels sliding silently across the marble floor. "You don't have to flirt with every receptionist we meet, you know."

"I'm just being polite!" Roger pulled on the other side of the cart, and they began to cross the large open foyer of the building. Light streamed in through the skylights, yellow from the smog before it filtered down through the algae chandeliers. "She is very pretty, though."

"Roger, don't be ridiculous. She's far too good for you."

"Oh, and I suppose she's not too good for you?" he teased.

"Please, she's not my kind of woman," Henry winked. "Look, here are our doors." The foyer led into a stunted corridor with two doors, one on either side. "East wing, sure. Don't wings usually have more than two rooms?"

"At least they managed to get us these rooms at all, if there hadn't been a cancellation we'd be sleeping on the transport."

Henry shuddered at the thought. There were no baths or proper beds on the transport shuttles, that was for sure. "Perish the thought," she mused aloud, slipping the key into the lock on the left-hand door. "I assume these rooms are identical?"

"That's what our very helpful and attractive receptionist implied, yes."

The door swung open into a moderately sized room, with a sitting area consisting of a small sofa and a matching armchair. "I'll see you in the morning, Roger," she said, swinging her luggage from the trolley. "Eight sharp. Don't be late, either, I hear they expect punctuality in the administration building."

"Enjoy your soak," Roger replied, taking his own bags from the cart and pushing it against the corridor wall. "Make sure you don't skip breakfast."

Henry let the door latch closed behind her and locked it for good measure. One could never be too careful, even in a highly protected estate like this. Skelm seemed to be rife with poverty and desperate people, and that was almost always a recipe for trouble. She pulled off her white gloves and laid them on the table next to the door before lifting her suitcase off the floor and sweeping through to the bedroom. She sighed at the bed, a third smaller

CHAPTER TWO

than hers at home on Gamma-3. It would have to do for now. Roger was right - without someone's last minute cancellation, she wouldn't even have that.

She hung her dresses in the wardrobe and slid the suitcase under the bed. With any luck, she'd be packing it back up in a few weeks' time to head home to Gamma-3 with research in hand. The bathroom, across from the bedroom, was lit with the odd algae lamps, the verdant glow reflecting off the full-length mirror. Henry stripped off her corset and dress, followed by her underthings, and ran herself a steaming hot bath.

*　*　*

The Skelm administration building was impressive, a goliath building with striking architecture, with high tinted windows and a courtyard connecting the two wings. Henry loosened the knot on the silk scarf tied around her face, letting it drape around her neck. It was a challenging, early start, but she was eagerly anticipating a trip outside the terraformers to witness the legendary Skelm storms in all their terrifying glory.

"Miss Henrietta Weaver, I take it?" asked a short man in a squeaky voice.

She grimaced at the use of her full name. "Henry."

The man wrinkled his nose. "What an odd name for a woman."

Henry stared at the man with a cold glare until he looked away. "A pleasure," he said stiffly. "My name is Lawrence Tripp."

"Mr. Tripp, I have to say I don't want to waste a single moment here, and I'm ready to get to work on my research."

"Yes, of course," he muttered, and turned his attention to Roger. "Mr. Beauregard, I'm told you've already begun your research on the Skelm storms?"

Roger shifted uncomfortably. "I think you'll find that Miss Weaver is the primary researcher on this subject. I am the *second* named researcher on those findings, and as such I am thrilled to be here as her second."

"If you'll just follow me to the laboratory, we can get you suited up for the next expedition, which leaves in an hour sharp," Lawrence sniffed. "We don't tolerate tardiness here on Skelm, and I know what kind of lackadaisical schedules you keep on Gamma-3."

Henry bristled and opened her mouth for a retort when she felt Roger poke her in the ribs and shake his head almost imperceptibly. They'd been told that things were harsher, more rigid here on Skelm, but she certainly hadn't expected blatant disrespect from the head of the science division here.

"As you may know, we don't have a meteorological team stationed here. We graciously allow scientists like yourselves to rotate in and out." He gestured down a long, dimly lit corridor. "Though in my humble opinion, none of you Gammas could last longer than a fortnight here, anyway." He let that jibe hang in the air, where it did not dissipate. "The laboratory is on the left at the end of the hall. You will have the lab to yourselves, as the other on-staff scientists are working in the larger lab on some more pressing research."

"Thank you, Mr. Tripp," Roger said quickly, and Henry knew it was a desperate attempt to keep her from insulting the man. She bit her tongue and gave a tight-lipped smile. "We'll be sure to keep to ourselves and alert you if we uncover any phenomena that may be of interest to you and the other scientists."

"I doubt that very much, Mr. Beauregard. If you need me, I shall be in my office." Lawrence Tripp turned on the heels of his polished shoes and disappeared behind his office door, which rattled when he slammed it.

"Pleasant fellow," Roger said, and Henry snorted a laugh. "No wonder Gammas don't stick around this settlement for very long."

"I think he's possibly worse than the smog," Henry said, pushing open the door to the lab. "Oh, gods." Whoever last used this lab, they'd left it in total disarray. Beakers and glassware stacked haphazardly on dusty, grime encrusted tables, stained lab coats thrown into a heap in the corner, and scattered piles of paperwork strewn all over the floor.

"And they say I'm a messy technician," Roger mumbled, stepping over folders that had long since spilled their contents. "This is going to take days to get back into shape."

CHAPTER TWO

"We don't have days to spare," Henry said, frustration building at the base of her spine. "I find it very difficult to believe that scientists are allowed to behave like this here, to leave the lab in such a state. I'm going to go talk to Mr. Tripp."

"Do you think that's a good idea, Henry?" Roger asked her retreating silhouette, his voice muffled behind the door that had already closed.

"Mr. Tripp?" Henry called through the heavy oak door, knocking intently. "Mr. Tripp, I need to speak with you."

The door flew open. "What is it, Henrietta?"

"Henry. Mr. Tripp, the lab was left looking like a disaster by the previous scientists. How are we supposed to—"

"How you get on with your research is not my concern, Ms. Weaver. Other Gamma-3 scientists have been capable of settling in, getting through their rotations here, and returning home without needing my assistance with their work. Are you saying that you don't think that's achievable for someone like you?"

"Of course I can do my work, it's just—"

"Then I suggest you do that," he said, and slammed the door in her face.

Henry huffed angrily and swallowed back the urge to burst through his door, threatening to report him to the Coalition Science Agency for gross misconduct and apathy towards workplace safety protocols. Instead, she smoothed a hair back into the twist she'd set it in that morning, and popped her head back into her lab. "Roger, I'm going to go find something to clean all this up with. Mr. Tripp doesn't seem very keen to help us with this."

"I hate to say I told you so, but—"

"Perhaps you could make a start on finding where they've hidden the protective equipment? I'll be back in a flash."

"Henry, we have to meet the expedition in under an hour!"

"Back in a flash!" she repeated, calling over her shoulder. She couldn't bear seeing a laboratory in such a condition. It wasn't efficient, and it wasn't a good environment to work on her research. Most importantly, it was unsafe. While most Gamma-3 scientists that rotated in and out of this base were studying weather patterns like she was, there was no telling what some may have been up to. This far from the Capital, one could indulge in all manner of unofficially approved projects. She was suddenly feeling very grateful that weather patterns and meteorology was her field of study, and not infectious diseases or illness. She cringed at the thought of studying bacteria and analyzing symptoms, and caught a glimpse of her soured expression as she passed a mirror. She smirked at herself and tucked a loose brunette hair back behind her ear.

The heels of her buttoned boots echoed against the marble floor, and then were swallowed up by the elaborate fountain in the courtyard, with spurts of sparkling water arcing through the air and cascading back down to the pool with a splash. Skelm's citizens might be impoverished, but you wouldn't know it by the interior of this building, with doors inlaid with steel and gold, quartz flecked through the marble floors, and this obscene fountain at the center of it.

She saw a janitorial cart pushed against a wall, and she made a beeline for it. She'd just quickly clean up in the lab, and then head out on the expedition, the first of several, she hoped. Henry rummaged through the cart, pocketing several rags and a scrub brush with bent, overused bristles, yellow from the grime that coated the city walls, kept at bay inside the administration building by a team of silent workers.

"Can I help you?" a voice asked in a smooth, honey-sweet drawl.

Henry jumped at the interruption and turned to see the most attractive woman she'd ever seen in an orange jumpsuit with tall black laced boots and a tawny colored ponytail swishing over her shoulders. "I, uh..." Henry mumbled, taken aback. "It's just that — uh—"

"What's the matter, you lost?" the woman asked with an eyebrow cocked.

"No, I'm a scientist."

The woman snorted. "Okay, and?"

"Oh," Henry replied, chastising herself for sounding like a complete fool. "No, I um, I'm a visiting scientist here, rotating in from Gamma-3, and my lab is in total disarray, and—"

"Did you put in a janitorial request?" the woman interrupted. "No one will go into the science labs unless there's an official request. We aren't allowed in case we interfere with experiments or research."

"Right, sure, that makes sense."

"So did you?"

"Did I what?" Henry asked, wondering how someone's eyes could be that green.

"Put in a request."

"Oh... no. I just got here. I have an expedition in an hour and I thought I could tidy the lab before we left."

"Ma'am, I mean no disrespect, but it isn't customary here for the scientists to be scrubbing down the science labs. That's left to us to do."

"I just thought I could get it done faster if I did it myself."

The woman laughed. "You trying to put me out of a job? That's no way to treat someone you just met."

"Of course not! In fact I was trying to help, lighten the load a little maybe—"

"I'm Georgie."

Henry smiled and felt a deep blush creep up her neck. "Henrietta Weaver. Henry, for short."

"Miss Weaver, I'd be more than happy to clean your lab while you're out on assignment with the expedition team. I'll have it shining brighter than my mama's silver on Sunday."

"Thank you, Miss...?"

"Georgie is fine for me ma'am, I'm just the janitor." She leaned against the cart with a nonchalant attitude, one arm resting against the handle and her other hand thrust into her deep pockets. "Is there anything else I can help you with?"

Henry clasped her hands in front of her to keep them still. "No, that will be all, thank you. I appreciate your efforts. After all, a clean lab is a safe lab!"

"Have a good expedition, Miss Weaver," Georgie said with an effortless charm, and tipped an imaginary cap. "In the future, I recommend against rummaging through a janitorial cart. If you're not careful, they'll think you're one of us."

CHAPTER THREE

Henry hopped into the back of the monorail that was going to take them to the boundary of the terraformers. There, they'd be able to see the storms up close and witness how they behaved in a natural, unimpeded environment, away from the manufactured atmosphere that kept them at bay. The Skelm bubble was its own ecosystem, with quiet rain that was more like condensation, and light that was magnified down into the city's center by huge mirrors. It made for a similar experience to living on Gamma-3, outside the shifted day lengths. Days were shorter here, and the nights longer, but people worked the same hours they would at home.

"Roger, are you ready to go?" she asked.

"Of course I'm ready to go, I'm not the one who was off gallivanting around the building looking for cleaning supplies."

"I can't believe they won't let us go outside the boundary today. That's what we're here for!" Henry pouted, still annoyed they'd be witnessing the storms from a safe, civilian distance.

"I told you not to lock horns with Tripp. No doubt that's where this order came from."

Henry turned her sights on a burly, balding man in green coveralls. "You there, sir, what is the reason we won't be traveling past the boundary today?"

"New orders," he replied in a gruff, uninviting voice.

"From whom?" Henry pressed. "From Tripp?"

CHAPTER THREE

"Look, we aren't privy to the whys and the whoms. We're the engineers at this settlement, and you get to accompany us when it's convenient to the work manifest." He turned back to the panel of knobs and flashing lights. "Gods know no scientist ever lifted a finger to help us with a job," he grumbled.

"When will you next be going beyond the boundary?"

"When the work manifest dictates it. A week, maybe two."

"A week!" Henry said, exasperated. "That's far too long. We're only here a short time, and—"

"I'm failing to see how that is my specific problem to manage," the man retorted. "Repairs need to get done, we—" he gestured at himself and the other two engineers, "do the repairs. We aren't responsible for your scheduling conflicts, yeah?"

"My good man," Roger started, turning the charm on full blast, "I'm *so* sorry that we have inconvenienced you today. I'm also sorry on behalf of the other scientists you've been forced to contend with, they sound like absolutely ghastly and inconsiderate rats." The man softened, and Roger continued to barrel along, taking the engineers along with him. "In fact, we are embarrassed by their negligent behavior. Engineers are who keep this settlement alive! Why, without you, there'd be no opportunity for us here at all."

"You're damn right about that," one of the other engineers said, her unruly hair wrangled into a frizzy braid. "It's about time someone appreciated us around here."

"Yes!" Roger agreed, throwing his hands to the sky. "If we can't see beyond the boundary, then that's no fault of yours. After all, you have your own jobs to contend with, we're just hangers-on as far as you're concerned. Keeping the boilers heated and the ventilation shafts clear is far more important than indulging a pair of visitors in their scientific whimsy, even if it is research that could potentially shape the way new settlements are formed, and prevent further catastrophic storm damage back on Gamma-3."

"I miss Gamma-3," the burly engineer said, and Henry could almost feel his heartache. Though the Near System was populated from core to the Outer Rim, almost everyone had been born on Gamma-3 until very recently. Most settlements weren't set up for children and schools, it just wasn't possible. If anywhere had achieved that kind of structure, it would be very impressive indeed.

"Aye, you're always going to miss home. We won't be back home for years."

Henry raised an eyebrow at this very obvious lie, but the engineers seemed to buy it. "The longer we're away working on this research, the greater the chance the storms on Gamma-3 will keep getting worse," she added.

"Listen, friend, we can't take you beyond the boundary today. It's just impossible with the work we've got on our docket. No way we'd make it back to the monorail before dark. And you don't want to be out there after dark."

"Why wouldn't we want to be out there after dark?" Roger asked.

"It's blacker than black out there after the mirrors go in," the engineer with the braid piped in. "You'd never find your way back to the monorail, not even with kinetic flashlights. The darkness just swallows up all the light." She cast her eyes down at the ground. "We lost three good engineers out there last year. I don't want to lose anyone else."

Roger held up his hands in defeat. "I completely understand, and far be it from me to even dream of requesting something that would put any member of your team in jeopardy. If it's alright with you all, we'll ride with you to the boundary, and do our observations from there. Maybe next time we'll get the chance, eh?"

"We uh, might be able to move around some of the scheduled work," the burly man said, looking at the rusty clipboard in his thick fists. "Maybe get you out there next week on a transport. We'll see what we can do for ya's. Least we can do."

"That is absolutely *splendid* news, isn't it, Henry?"

"Yes, thank you," she said, irritated that Roger's bullshit charm had won over another stranger. She just didn't know how he did it. It was like mind control to see him change people's minds with an overly familiar air and

CHAPTER THREE

a touch of tugging on their heartstrings. It was his secret weapon, and it always made her look like she was being unreasonable. "Shall we get a shift on, then?"

The burly man grunted in affirmation and pushed a red lever forward. The monorail car began to ease forward on the track, smooth and silent. It was almost amazing that it even existed here on Skelm, which was more or less a Coalition backwater outside the administration building. The only reason people came here was for research, or to monitor productivity levels at the factories. There was no reason to stay in a place like this.

Grey concrete buildings faded into the distance as the monorail picked up speed, carrying them further and further from the relative safety of the city. Henry watched the administration building, the pinnacle of the settlement, sparkle in the morning's reflected rays, and her mind settled on the janitor she'd met. If they had to stay longer on this rock, maybe that wouldn't be all bad. After all, it wasn't every day you'd meet a woman with eyes that sparkled like emeralds. The thought made Henry feel off balance, and she instinctively reached out, grasping a hand railing to steady herself.

"You alright there, Hen?" Roger asked. "Not motion sick, are you?"

"No, no, I'm fine. Just a little distracted."

"You'd better pull your head back down to terra firma, because we're nearly there."

Henry craned her neck to look out the wide windows and take in what was a breathtaking panorama. The sharp skyline was built of jagged rock, and even the smallest mountain was bigger than any on Gamma-3 by at least half. The light here was different, cast in an eerie, greyish-blue haze, far from the warm glow of the city. The mirrors were far away now, at least a couple of hundred kilometers. Without the advanced speed of the monorail, it would take days to traverse on foot, and it would be dangerously cold in the long night. She could see the flicker of lightning against the crests of the mountains, heavy beneath clouds of acid rain so potent it would burn exposed skin.

"The storm is so close I can almost taste it. Do you smell the petrichor, Roger?"

"Aye, I do," he said, his voice cloaked in awe. "Just a shame we can't get beyond the barrier today. That storm looks absolutely fascinating."

"You people have lost your marbles," the engineer with the braid said, flipping it over one shoulder. "Those storms are incredibly dangerous. I've never understood you scientists who would beg, bribe, borrow, or steal in order to get in the middle of it. You'd be better off staying the hell away from it, in my opinion."

"Ah, but don't you find the awesome power of a storm humbling?" Henry asked, her hand pressed against the cool glass of the window. "It reminds us how small we are, how little we matter on a cosmic scale. We can't control weather, it controls us. We're totally at its mercy."

"Yeah, that doesn't fill me with awe," the engineer retorted, rolling her eyes. "Makes me want to stay *inside* the barrier, more like." She gave a warning look, and Henry knew it was meant for her. "Don't let me catch you trying to sneak outside the border. We won't bring you back out here with us if you do." She unhooked a clipboard from the wall and ticked off a box on the paper. "Ever."

Henry nodded. "We understand."

"Our repairs will take us up until lunch to complete. You have until then to observe, research, make sketches, do whatever the hell it is you people do. Don't be late back on the monorail. We don't want to leave anyone behind, but our asses will wind up in the factories if we don't keep to the schedule. So don't be late."

"We will be sure to return on time," Roger assured her. "Good luck with your repairs!" he called to the engineer's retreating figure.

* * *

"Gods, Roger," Henry breathed, staring up at the darkened sky that streaked with lightning. "It's so much more than I ever could have imagined."

"Do you ever think it strange that we do this?" he asked.

"Do what?"

CHAPTER THREE

"This," he gestured, "chasing storms. Like that charming engineer said, it isn't an activity most would partake in."

"It's important work, you know that." Henry opened her leather-bound notebook, worn with age and use. She pulled at the frayed ribbon bookmark, dingy from tea spills, to flip to the current page. "If we weren't out here surveying this, deciphering patterns in the storm's creation and growth, who would?"

Roger shrugged. "Sure. But you can't say you don't enjoy it."

"Of course I enjoy it, just look at it!" She looked up just as a cluster of flashes brightened the highest mountain peak. "It's exhilarating."

"Did you see the way that bunched up there?"

"Yes, I'm sketching it. Later, back in the lab, we can work on an analysis. I know other meteorologists who have cycled through have some theories, but I think we can dig into why these storms never cease here. Why, sometimes there are flares that cause cyclones. It's most unusual, given the exceptional amount of vertical air flow."

"Mm," Roger agreed, scribbling in his own notepad. His was crisp and new, the sign of a man who bought a new book for every project. Henry couldn't blame him - the allure of a new leather-bound book was too tempting to ignore, sometimes. She had her own stack of unused, pristine notebooks back home on Gamma-3, but this one was her favorite. In some ways, it felt like it was lucky.

"Did you record the temperature and barometric readings?"

"I did, of course."

"Any anomalies?"

"Nothing out of the ordinary for this location, it matches up with the predicted result."

"Hmm." Henry looked from her sketch back to the sky and watched lightning repeatedly strike one of the mountain peaks. "Rog, I wonder if we could get a balloon up there."

"In that atmosphere? It would get torn to shreds, surely."

"But what if we reinforced it somehow? Used a different material, something to keep it safe until it descended back to ground. I bet there's something interesting about the air pressure up there, something that doesn't usually happen on Gamma-3." She jotted down a note. "Or something to do with the ground here being more positively charged? Something that would cause this many lightning strikes?"

"What does that have to do with Gamma-3? I thought our research was meant to reduce the risk of storms back home, to anticipate the superstorms and find a way to dissipate them."

"Do you really think we'd have gotten our funding for this trip if it wasn't to benefit Gamma-3? These storms are incredible, I just want to know what makes them tick. Why here, and why they cause such destruction outside the atmospheric barrier."

"You'd better find a way to make it relevant to our grant proposal, or we'll never get another one, ever again."

"So the balloon, Rog."

He tapped his fingers on the rocky ground. "How would we make sure we can get them to ascend, gather data, and descend in time to catch the monorail home? We can't leave them out here, even if they were better prepared for the elements."

"Maybe you could convince your new engineer friends to hold off on heading home before dark for once."

"Didn't you hear them? There's no way they'd do that, no matter how thick I laid on the charm. No, if you think the balloons are our best bet at obtaining new information, then we'll have to alter their flight patterns to be more efficient. That's a difficult ask in only a couple of weeks."

"What if we stayed longer?"

"In that tiny shack of an apartment? Absolutely not."

"But we could be sure we'd get new data! Our research could change the face of Gamma-3, of all the Near Systems!" She gave him her best pleading smile while simultaneously taking detailed notes on the fork patterns of the lightning. "We could be famous scientists, Weaver and Beauregard, the meteorologists who saved millions of lives!"

"Why does your name go first?" Roger grumbled.

"Because I'm the brains of the operation." She stretched her legs out in front of her, the soles of her boots scraping across the rock. "Besides, it sounds better that way."

Lightning streaked across the sky, casting light over the ground and illuminating the never ending kilometers of gravel. The thunder, usually muffled by the atmospheric barrier and distance, cracked so loud that Henry felt her heart leap into her throat. Despite her years of storm chasing, piling in steamcars with packs of other scientists to observe dangerous superstorms, she still jumped at the sound.

"That was much closer that time."

"Too close," Roger agreed. "What's drawing it? It should be limited to the peaks, not striking the ground near the barrier."

"Strange." Henry felt her shoulders tense with excitement and danger. "If it continues, the terraforming generators could be in danger. They wouldn't be able to sustain that kind of damage without an automatic shut down. The city would suffocate."

"I don't like this at all. We need to report this to Tripp, get some safety protocols in place."

Henry nodded. "We need to get back to the monorail, they're leaving soon. With that storm out there, I don't want to get caught if it crosses the boundary. We'd freeze to death before we ever made it back to the city."

CHAPTER FOUR

The lab was sparkling when Georgie finished with it, and it was no small feat to get it in that condition. The attractive, confident scientist - Henry - hadn't been exaggerating when she said the previous group left it in an awful state. It had taken her three hours just to scrub the mysterious grime out of the corners of the pans, her nose and mouth covered with the thin fabric of her undershirt. There was no telling what they got up to in these labs, and Georgie didn't want to risk inhaling any mysterious chemicals or pollutants. If she got sick, her mother and sisters would starve. She couldn't take the chance of having to stay home sick. The thought of her mother going back to work at the factories made her stomach turn.

   She wiped down the countertops and tossed the soiled rag into the small laundry bag that hung on her cleaning cart, and pulled a fresh one from the folded stack below to tuck into her front belt loop. At least cleaning the lab had kept her out of the line of fire of Inspector Allemande, whose unadulterated fury at being silenced was flaring up at every underling in her path. After Georgie had spent hours scrubbing ink from the conference room table, she had to wonder what the hell was in that stuff that made it so much more difficult to clean than normal ink. It sank into the fibers of the wood and stained them almost immediately.

   "You ready?" her coworker, Erin, said from the doorway. "We have to do the evening sweep." She looked around, her shiny black hair tied up in a severe ponytail. "What have you been doing in here, anyway?"

CHAPTER FOUR

"Special request."

"That better be the case, because we're not supposed to be in the labs, you know that."

"New scientists came in from Gamma-3, needed it cleaned."

"Was it logged?"

Georgie gritted her teeth. "I was on my way to do that before you came in."

"You should be logging the special requests before you start, and get them signed off by the person who requested it."

"I figured actually cleaning the lab before they returned from today's expedition was a higher priority than paperwork."

"Without the signature, they don't know if you were actually requested to clean this lab, or if you decided to have a quiet afternoon in a pristine lab having a nap. If this gets back to Mr. Jackson, there's no doubt he'll write you up for it."

"Yes, okay Erin, I hear you," Georgie relented. "I'll go log it in right now. I was just trying to be efficient."

"You know I care about you, right? I don't want to see you get fired and end up down at the factories. I know you've got your ma and sisters to look after." Erin ran a finger over the counter and inspected it. "You missed a spot."

Georgie rolled her eyes and laughed. "Yeah, well I'd like to see you do a better job. This place was a disaster when I got in here."

"I'm not surprised, that last group of scientists were barely out of school. Young, rowdy, disorganized. I couldn't wait to see the back of them. You should be thanking your lucky stars you didn't have to clean the bathrooms after they'd been in there. It was the tragedy of my life."

"Gross."

"Any plans this weekend?"

"Funny."

"You should get out more, Georgie. You're still young! You could meet the woman who'll sweep you right off your feet."

"I'd rather sweep myself and my family off this godforsaken settlement."

"Lower your voice! Don't let them hear you disparaging the Coalition, they'll send your mama right back to the factory so fast it would make your head spin."

"Come on, Erin, nobody likes it here, not even the big wigs with their huge steamcars and bathrooms that could fit our entire apartments in them. It's dirty, it's dangerous, and every single person here wants nothing more than to get the hell away as soon as they possibly can. You can't tell me you like it here, either."

"No, but it's not like leaving is an option. The transport fees are astronomical. Might be a safer bet to just find someone you can tolerate, settle down, try to make the best kind of life you can."

"No thanks."

"You could come out to the Twisted Lantern with us later."

"What, the speakeasy? I don't think so."

"You could have fun!"

"I have to get home after my shift."

"A little fun isn't going to kill you, ya know."

"It's *illegal*."

"Oh please, everyone drinks nowadays," Erin scoffed, looking at her reflection in the pans and smoothing back a stray hair. "I've even seen management in there sometimes."

"Bullshit."

"No, it's true! And besides, your mama and sisters can manage without you for one night. I know you've had to be the bread and butter since your pop died, but—"

"I'm not going."

"Suit yourself, spoilsport, but either way you'd better get that special request signed and delivered before Mr. Jackson starts to wonder where the hell you've been all afternoon."

"Yeah."

"If you change your mind, you know where to find us tonight. It would be good to see you there, Georgie. I'll cover the evening sweep while you do that paperwork, and hope that the extra time means you'll actually show up

CHAPTER FOUR

for once." Erin flipped her ponytail and dragged her cart out of the room, leaving Georgie to fill out paperwork in the empty, pristine lab.

***

Despite all her sense and good intentions, Georgie found herself exactly where she said she shouldn't be. Erin had been laying it on thick for weeks, and Georgie knew she wouldn't let up until she gave in. The Twisted Lantern wasn't easy to find, even with her sister's detailed instructions. She didn't want to know why Emeline knew where the speakeasy was, and so she had forbidden her from ever visiting it. Emeline was growing up too fast, and was too interested in the paltry rebel resistance in Skelm. If she wasn't careful, it was going to get them all killed, just like their father.

   The cobbled road came to a dead end surrounded by red brick, caked with yellowed smog. It hadn't seen cleaning agent in months. There was a faded sign with a picture of a book hanging over a green wooden door with the paint flaking off to reveal the untreated pine beneath. She hadn't even known a book shop was here, but with every book being censored and vetted, Georgie knew it would be no more than a place for the Coalition to prop themselves up with virtuous propaganda. She missed the stories she read as a young girl back on Gamma-3, daring tales of warrior princesses and powerful witches. Frivolous literature had been banned on Skelm, in order to keep the workers at their maximum capacity. No one dreaming of dragons and far-off lands was likely to meet the punishing efficiency targets.

   With a resigned sigh, she pushed open the door with a loud creak to reveal a dark, empty shop piled high with dusty books about the Coalition's achievements, and stories about people who achieved riches from following the rules. It was all bullshit. Georgie frowned at the books and hoped that one day she'd be able to buy her sisters all the books in the Near Systems. A lantern burned brightly at the cash register, illuminating the faded buttons and the bent bronze handle at the side. Emeline had told her the speakeasy was open when the lantern was lit. Georgie pulled on the handle, and a slit appeared in the wall behind her.

"Password?"

"Er – tarantula juice?"

The sound of locks unlatching dulled against the walls of heavy books. A panel slid into the wall, revealing a lively club with people draped across the long bar at the back. "Thanks," she said, stepping behind the wall.

"Hurry it up, lady, we don't have all night."

"Sorry." The woman operating the door was perched on a tall stool, smoking a pipe that filled the air with a green haze. The panel slid closed, and Georgie looked around for anyone she might know. Anxiety settled in her stomach, and she was already regretting her decision to ignore her instincts and meet with Erin and some others. This was reckless, and if she was caught, she'd be dismissed immediately from her job. Erin was nowhere to be seen, so Georgie sat at the edge of a deep, overstuffed chair covered in a purple damask print. None of the furniture matched, and seemed as though it had been pilfered, one piece at a time, from dozens of different establishments and homes.

"Can I get ya anything?" a tall, lean man in a tan leather waistcoat asked in a bored voice.

"What do you recommend?" Georgie had only drunk swill once, at a party when she was Emeline's age, but that was years ago now.

The man rolled his eyes. "I could get you tonight's cocktail special."

"Sure."

He wandered back to the bar and pulled bottles from beneath the counter. The walls in the Twisted Lantern were coated with layers upon layers of newspaper to deaden the sound from the outside, a strange collage of news stories from the past decade on Skelm. This speakeasy must have been around for some time, probably since the start of the alcohol ban soon after Skelm was terraformed. Books littered the low tables in small piles, well-worn spines showing their age and use. Georgie picked up one and flipped through it, expecting the same Coalition nonsense that filled the books store beyond the sliding panel. To her surprise, it was a daring tale of pirates on the open sea, in search of a mysterious treasure. Intrigued, she turned to the first page and began reading.

CHAPTER FOUR

"Here's your drink," the server said, setting down a smudged glass filled with a murky pale yellow liquid. "It's bathtub gin with some honey and lemon." He turned to another table and said to her over his shoulder, "By the way, books aren't allowed out of the room. Can't risk them being confiscated."

Georgie nodded, already immersed in the story, turning page after page as she sipped the sweet drink. There was a bite to it that hung at the back of her throat like the first prickle of a cold, but she liked it. The delicate haze of inebriation softened her edges, and allowed her to sink back into the chair with a relieved sigh. She felt like she had found an oasis in the desert. She finished her cocktail and waved for another one. It appeared on the table in mere moments, leaving a ring of condensation on the bare, unfinished wood. Chapter after chapter, Georgie read about thrilling fights and daring escapes, and yearned to stay up all night in order to finish it.

"Hey, it's closing time," the server said impatiently, a hand on his hip. "Come back tomorrow, I want to go home."

"Gods, what time is it?" Georgie asked, tearing her eyes away from the book.

"Ten past midnight."

She swore under her breath. "Sorry, er— thanks."

"You can pay your tab at the bar. We accept credits, trades, bribes, and blackmail."

"Blackmail?"

"How do you think we've managed to stay open this long? It's no accident we've never been shut down by the military police."

"Oh." Georgie racked her mind for any useful information, but everything she knew about the Coalition managers was common knowledge. "Just credits this time, I think." She leaned on the bar and yawned, rubbing her eyes as she signed her name on a dotted line for a credit transfer. The drinks weren't cheap, but they had been worth it to lose herself in that book. "Good night, then," she said, and ducked under the doorway back into the book shop, where the light from the lantern was casting long, dancing shadows over the dusty book covers. She'd have to wait until the next night to see what happened.

*　*　*

"Georgie?"

Light streamed in through the dirty, cracked window of their little apartment, and dust particles sparkled in the air.

"Georgina!"

"What?" Georgie covered her face with the pillow, her head pounding.

"Shouldn't you have left for work already?"

Her eyes flew open, and she sat up, grasping around on the floor for her work uniform. "What time is it? Why didn't you wake me up?"

"It's almost eight, and I *am* waking you up." Emeline sat perched at the edge of the empty sofa, her legs tucked under her skirts. "Where were you last night?"

"Nowhere."

Emeline's eyes widened with excitement. "Did you go to the Twisted Lantern? How was it? Did you have fun? Did the password work? Who was there?"

"None of your beeswax," Georgie grumbled, shedding her green button-down shirt and sliding into her orange coveralls. "I just overslept."

"I don't remember hearing you come in last night, love," her mother said, steeping yesterday's coffee grounds in boiling water. "You must have been out late."

"It's nothing!"

"You'd better hurry or you'll be late for work. You don't want to be giving Mr. Jackson a reason to write you up again."

"I am hurrying," Georgie hissed, yanking at the laces on her boots. "I'll be home late, don't wait up." She kissed her mother on the cheek and sped out the door, taking the steps two at a time. If she was going to make it to the administration building on time, she was going to have to run the entire way, up the steep hill that led to the side entrance for janitorial staff. Her head pounded a punishing rhythm, and her mouth felt like she had been sucking on a nightshirt while she slept. Her limbs felt heavy and useless as she willed them into action, and it became obvious why the Coalition had banned alcohol. The odds of making it into work on time were significantly reduced with a hangover.

Her boots thudded against the cobblestones, her legs sluggish. A glance at the clock tower informed her she only had a few minutes to get there on time, so she squeezed her eyes shut and pushed herself up the slope to the door to the janitorial storage room, where she bent double, desperate to catch her breath.

"Cutting it a little bit close, aren't we, Miss Payne?" Mr. Jackson asked, his voice rough from years working with the harsh solvents.

"Sorry sir, I... overslept... and..." she wheezed.

Mr. Jackson frowned so intently that it reached his humorless eyes. "Sit. I'm about to assign today's rota."

She flopped down on the uneven wooden bench, which squeaked under her weight. Erin was staring at her, probably wondering why she was nearly late for her shift. If there was anything the Coalition, and especially their boss, didn't tolerate, it was tardiness and a failure to be punctual.

"As you all may well know, we have welcomed some new management in recent weeks. With the tragic passing of Mr. Ralph Baker, the Coalition has been rotating senior management in and out of the city to keep things running smoothly. In addition to the mandatory memorial parade, we are also going to be required to submit to rigorous health testing, in order to avoid another cardiac death like his."

Georgie bit back a frown. She'd been the one to clean up that mess - blood was soaked all the way through the thick rugs into the floorboards below. She hadn't seen Mr. Baker himself, but she could only assume that the rebels she helped escape had something to do with it. She wondered when she would hear from them, if she ever would. They were her only real shot of getting out of Skelm alive, with her mother and sisters intact.

"Furthermore, there will be more stringent controls on solvents going forward. Your carts will be counted in at the end of your shift."

He didn't elaborate, but Georgie's heart dropped into her stomach. Maybe they knew that she sabotaged the boilers with the solvent, or at least suspected foul play from someone on staff. She felt like the net was closing in, ready to ensnare her for her crimes. She swallowed hard and pushed a weak smile across her face.

"Erin and Georgina, you'll both be cleaning the offices today." He coughed, and blood spattered the wrinkled white handkerchief in his hand. "The rest of you, business as usual. Dismissed."

Georgie breathed a cautious sigh of relief. If they suspected her, they wouldn't have her cleaning the offices, where sometimes important paperwork ended up in the wastebasket, would they? "Hey, Erin," she said, coaxing the tension out of her shoulders, "where were you last night?"

Erin's eyes grew large with surprise. "You *went?*" she hissed, pushing her cart through the storage room door. "I never thought you'd actually turn up!"

"Yeah, well I did, and you were nowhere to be found!"

"I'm sorry, Payne, I decided to stay home with John instead. If I thought you were really planning on going, I would have showed up!" She looked at Georgie suspiciously. "Are you hungover, Georgie?"

"Hush."

"You are! May wonders never cease. I hope you at least had fun last night."

"I found ways to occupy myself."

"Oh really?" Erin asked, wiggling her eyebrows. "And who did you occupy yourself with?"

"None of your business," she answered, letting her vague answer hang in the air. Maybe if Erin thought she'd met someone, she'd leave her alone about going out all the time.

"Oh ho ho! I guess I'll just keep myself to myself then!"

They pulled the carts up the back maintenance stairs, the tools and the bottles of cleaning solution rattling. The office wing of the building had doors lining every corridor, with the main hall ending in what used to be Mr. Baker's office. In the past two months, it had seen six upper managers come and go, rotating in from other bases and back out again. No one wanted to

CHAPTER FOUR

stay in Skelm.

"You take left side, I'll take right," Georgie said. They weren't allowed to work together, in case their chatting impacted efficiency. "We'd better get through all of them before the morning meetings let out."

Erin nodded. "Yeah, the last time I was late finishing a room, Mr. Jackson threatened to send me to the factories." She shuddered and pulled a clean rag from the folded pile, each of them bleached clean. "Race you to the end of the hall?" she asked mischievously.

"What does the winner get?"

"Loser buys lunch."

"Deal."

Georgie opened the door to the first room and allowed her mind to wander back to the book she'd been reading the night before. A thrilling story about pirates stealing from the rich to give to the poor, outrunning their would-be captors. Despite her near disastrous morning, she couldn't wait to get back to the Twisted Lantern to read more. A few more nights should do it, and then she'd never step foot in there again. It was just too dangerous, too much of a risk when she had her mother and her sisters to take care of. Maybe if Evie Anderson ever came back for them, she could indulge more in reading silly, fanciful stories. Once this book was done, that was it.

She wiped down the desk, polishing the mahogany to a beautiful shine before emptying the wastebasket and watching each crumpled piece of paper float into the cart's trash receptacle. Scribbled ideas, discarded. She didn't care what they said, it wouldn't be of much use, anyway. Most of the management lucky enough to have their own office in the administration building used a series of codes, anyway - to prevent people like her from gleaning any kind of information from scrapped plans.

The windows in the offices were smaller than the conference rooms, but dirtied just as quick, gathering grime from the smog that hung low outside. Georgie sighed and rubbed at her temples, before starting in on the filth with the caustic white powder and a damp rag. Just eleven more hours before she could pack it in for the day.

CHAPTER FIVE

"So as you can see, Mr. Tripp, if the storms get any closer to the city, the generators and terraformers would be in jeopardy."

"Hmm."

"More tests need to be run to determine the cause of the increasing frequency of the electrical strikes, and around-the-clock observation in a storm tower should be implemented going forward to protect the settlement. I've put together a formal request for funding—"

"That's not necessary, Ms. Weaver."

"But sir, if you'll just take a look at our research—"

"If memory serves, you were not sent here to oversee major projects. You are to complete your assigned research and observational tasks and rotate back to Gamma-3 in two weeks' time."

"I wanted to talk to you about that sir, we were blocked from going beyond the barrier in yesterday's expedition. The earliest we can go out is next week, and that means we'd only get one chance to carry out some very necessary tests. If we could just stay a little longer—"

"That will be unnecessary, Ms. Weaver, Mr. Beauregard. You will not be crossing the boundary in your time here due to crew restraints. I suggest you rework your research to allow for observations at a distance." Lawrence Tripp looked up at them from over his glasses, drumming his fingers on the smooth red wood desk. "You are dismissed."

"Mr. Tripp, if you please," Roger said, stepping forward. "These are matters of grave importance. The entire city could be in danger of suffocation and death if those terraformers and generators go down. There's no alternative safety protocols in place. Thousands would die."

"I believe I made myself clear, Mr. Beauregard. I am not interested in any further discussion on the matter. Leave your findings on the desk, you are dismissed."

Roger pressed his hands together in a politely pleading manner. "Sir, I beg of you not to ignore this."

"You. Are. Dismissed," Mr. Tripp annunciated, a dark look spreading across his face. "I don't want to see you in my office again for the duration of your rotation. Get out."

Henry opened her mouth to protest again, but felt Roger tug gently at her skirt. Enraged, she turned and marched to the door, yanking it open and glaring daggers at Mr. Tripp. Roger closed the door softly behind them.

"Let's talk back in the lab," he hissed. "I think there's something more to this than we realize."

She couldn't trust herself to speak without shouting, so she returned a terse nod and marched back towards the lab, located in the opposite wing of the administration building. Her pewter grey skirts swirled angrily as she walked, the sound of her boots echoing against the marble floors. The courtyard was all but empty at this time of day, with most of the staff and management on location holed up in conference rooms, having unnecessary meetings about improving efficiency and maximizing output. It was all pointless, useless chatter in the face of a major disaster. Those storm patterns were shifting, changing. Something was different, and Skelm was in major danger.

"What the hell does he think he's doing?" she huffed when they were safely back in their lab. "We presented credible evidence that those terraformers are susceptible to a strike, and he took our research and kicked us out of his office."

"Not to mention he's banned us from observing or testing from beyond the barrier," Roger added. "There's only so much we can learn from a distance."

"Does he *want* the entire city to die? What is he playing at?"

"I don't know, Weaver, but I think we should report this back to the CSA back on Gamma-3. These are important findings that shouldn't be ignored. I know that Skelm is far from being one of the most important settlements, but to ignore these structural concerns isn't just dangerous, it's against guidelines."

"Rog, I worry that reporting back to Tripp's superiors isn't going to earn us any favors. Going over your supervisor's head isn't smiled on by the science overlords, if you know what I mean."

"I don't think we have the luxury of hoping he'll come around. I think we have to act now."

Henry sighed, exhaling through the corner of her mouth. "If we do this, we won't ever get another grant approved."

"If we don't, people could die."

She sat down on a bench, her weight landing heavy. "We could lose our careers over this, regardless of what happens. If we report our findings over Tripp's head, no more grant credits for expeditions or research. If we don't, and those terraformers do get struck, then we will almost certainly be the scapegoats."

"You know what we have to do, Weaver."

"I know."

"We have to be sure our observations of the storm patterns are correct before we report. We need to get beyond the barrier."

"Yes, we do." She stood, straightening her skirts and smoothing her hair back. "Go talk to your engineer friends. I'll contact the CSA and request more time on base. Tripp can try to block the request, but it will at least buy us a couple of extra days here while it's processed."

"Good idea." Roger clapped a hand on her shoulder and grinned. "This is why I love working with you, Henry. Never a dull moment."

"Hold on to that feeling, because if this all goes wrong, it's going to be rather boring in the science library filing reports. We'll be lucky to even get that."

Roger nodded. "At least it will have been worth it, in the end."

CHAPTER FIVE

* * *

"What do you mean, Mr. Tripp has blocked our wire access?" Henry hissed, barely holding back her rage. The poor wire operator looked terrified.

"He has the authority to grant or deny any wire transmissions from the science division," the operator said in a small voice. "I'm sorry, there's nothing I can do."

"This is important!"

"I'm sorry, ma'am. If I go against his orders, I'll be fired on the spot."

"Can't you just say it's being sent from someone else? Why can't you send it?"

"All due respect, Ms. Weaver, but you're only here for a couple of weeks. I have to work here every day. If I went around undermining the management, I'd end up working in the factories before I knew it."

"The safety of the city could depend on this," Henry replied evenly, her eyes squeezed shut with all the concentration it took to not reach over the desk and yank the telegraph off the desk. "Please, if you could just send the transmission to the president of the CSA, that's the Coalition Science Association. All I'm asking is for some extra time here to confirm my findings."

"You'll have to ask Mr. Tripp to lift the ban on your wire privileges, then. Until that happens, I'm afraid there's nothing more I can do for you." The wire operator turned away from Henry, shuffling through cards scribbled with messages to be delivered to people in the building.

"Henry!" Roger shouted from the edge of the courtyard, out of breath. He was holding the weather balloon they'd been working on until late in the night under his arm. "Henry, come on. We have to go now."

"*Now?*"

"Yes, now!"

She picked up her skirts and ran across the gold inlaid floors that sparkled in the mid-morning light, following her colleague down a long, twisting corridor that was not meant for them. Here, the floors were cracked tiles, and the doors dented and dirty. This was the maintenance corridor, and she could hear the huge boilers gurgling. "Roger, what's going on?"

"They've been sent on a last minute expedition, but they're leaving in ten minutes. If we're not there, they leave without us." He threw open a door and waved her in. "Atmospheric suits are in that locker. We need to hurry."

"Tripp blocked our wire privileges," she said, unbuttoning her jacket.

"He *what?*"

"We can't get any messages to the CSA. We're on our own here."

"Fuck," he breathed.

Henry stripped off her skirts and boots and stepped into the suit, which was the same green as the maintenance coveralls. They were heavy and claustrophobic, but she'd grown used to them in all her time on non-terraformed settlements. She started on the tiny buttons that held the inner layer closed, flipping toggles closed on the overlayer as she went. She tugged the helmet free from the slightly too-small locker and held it under her arm.

"Hurry up, Roger!"

He looked at her, bewildered. "How did you do that so fast?"

"Sheer determination with a side of panic."

"Alright, alright," he said, fumbling with the buttons. "Okay, I'm good, let's go."

"Do they know this is against guidelines?" she asked, opening the door to the corridor.

"I don't think so. Seems like Tripp didn't anticipate us getting friendly with the engineers."

"Let's *go.*"

He nodded, and they trudged towards the monorail bay, located within the engineering block. Before, they'd caught the monorail from the loading dock. This time, they'd have to look like part of the team if they were going to fly under Tripp's radar. The engineering block was noisy with the roar of boilers and pipes, and Henry wondered how all of them didn't have extensive hearing damage. She pressed her shoulders to her ears in a futile attempt to block out the sound.

"Y'all ready?" the engineer with the frizzy braid shouted over the din.

CHAPTER FIVE

"We have to leave now if we're going to be back on the track by dark."

"We're ready!" Henry shouted back. "I'm Henry, by the way!"

The engineer nodded. "We know. Rog told us."

Henry turned to her colleague and mouthed, *Rog?* He returned a shrug and a grin, and she knew he'd secured this for them using his trademark wit and charm.

"I'm Jess, and the other fellow over there is Bale." She waved them onto the monorail and noted the time on a pad of paper. "We won't have much time once we get past the barrier, so you'd better do whatever you need to do, and fast."

"Is there a radio tower out there?" Henry asked, her voice innocent.

"Yeah. But you'd be better off sending a wire from the telegraph desk in the courtyard if you're trying to send a message. The towers out here are meant to boost reception signals, not to send communications. Notoriously unreliable."

"Oh, I was just curious, you know us scientists!"

Jess stared. "I thought your department was meteorology."

Henry laughed along with Roger, and she hoped that would be the end of the line of questioning. If there was a tower beyond the barrier, maybe they could send a message to the CSA, or at least get word back to a trusted colleague back on Gamma-3 that Tripp was endangering the entire city with his incompetence. Maybe it could save them.

The monorail slowed to a stop at the end of the track, farther than they had been before. From here, they'd have to walk out past the barrier; the atmospheric and meteorological conditions would be too much for a delicate transport like the monorail to handle. The rocky ground was dull and dry, safe from the acidic rainstorms that pounded the mountain tops.

"You have three hours. Do not be late," Bale said, his voice heavy with warning. "We won't come out looking for you. You'll just have to try to survive until morning."

Roger nodded. "We understand."

They disembarked and shuffled in their heavy suits as fast as their muscles would allow, towards the boundary. Beyond, the natural atmosphere wouldn't support human life, so they strapped on their helmets and the in-suit air filtration. The packs on their back held small boilers to power the suits, but they wanted to wait until absolutely necessary to begin draining the power reserves.

Distant light from the city's mirrors reflected against the edge of the barrier, sparkling with fluidity. The closer they got, the more the land beyond looked like a mirage, an oasis in the desert. They switched on their suits and stepped through, heading for the mountains. If they could get the weather balloon sent up, they could retrieve it in just enough time to make it back to the monorail. Henry looked around for the transmission tower and spied it far in the distance, away from where the balloon needed to be launched.

"Beauregard, you don't need me to launch that balloon. I'm going to head for that tower." Her voice sounded strange and flat inside her helmet.

"We should stick together," Roger replied, his own echoing through the speaker in her suit.

"There's no time for that, and you know it. Listen, launch the balloon and I'll meet back with you as soon as I send that message."

"I don't like this, Henrietta."

"Too bad," she grinned, and saluted him, marching away in a loping, comical manner thanks to the suit. The terrain was uneven, the rocks shifting beneath her every step with the soft grinding sound of shale crushing up against itself. The communications tower was at least seven stories high, twice as high as the administration building, but dwarfed by the behemoth architecture back home on Gamma-3. It had been years since she studied communications equipment, and at least a decade from the last time she took apart a radio and pieced it back together. She was a meteorologist, not an engineer, and she just hoped that technology hadn't changed much in the interim.

When she reached the tower, she craned her neck up, squinting at the spire far above her. Everything looked intact, down to the even taller spikes embedded in the surrounding ground, charged with positive particles to protect the communications array. They were built to withstand extreme weather and electrical surges, but it was better to mitigate the risk than to deal with the fallout if a strike occurred.

The fuse box was bolted shut, but not locked. After all, the odds that anyone would be outside the barrier at all were slim, much less a rebel insurgent. She pried a tool from the latch at her hips and removed the bolts one at a time until the door swung open. The wiring was exactly what she had hoped for, easy to splice into the radio in her helmet and replace without anyone knowing what she'd done. This communication tower had so many channels, many of them unused at this time of day. Most Skelm citizens couldn't afford to send wires, and they went quiet unless there was some kind of emergency.

She stripped one wire of its protective rubber casing, and then another, twisting them together and straining her ears to hear past the static. "Skelm meteorologist Weaver to anyone who can relay a message to the Coalition Science Association, do you read me?" She twisted a frequency knob left, and then right. "I repeat, this is a message for the Coalition Science Association." She flipped another switch and continued to repeat her call. "CSA wire desk, do you read me?"

There was no reply other than heavy static. Henry sighed angrily and jostled the knob. "Useless piece of crap," she muttered under her breath.

"Hello, we picked up a distress call from this location?"

"Hi! No, not distress, I—"

"Who are we speaking to?" asked a suspicious voice.

"This is Ms. Weaver, I am trying to reach the CSA to relay a message."

Static crackled. "We can relay your message. Transmit."

"This is Ms. Weaver for Jhanvi Jhaveri, I am formally requesting a continuance of my position here in the meteorology department on Skelm."

"Jhanvi?"

"Yes, Jhanvi Jhaveri, she works in the security sciences department. Can you get a message to her?"

"...yes." The line crunched and fuzzed. "Ms. Weaver, why not use the official wire line?"

"Er—" she had to think fast. She hadn't anticipated this line of questioning. Her status on Gamma-3 as a lead scientist meant she could request messages be sent without having to explain herself. Were things different here in Skelm, or could it be a rebel monitoring transmissions? "The main line is down," she lied. "This is a matter of utmost importance, can you please confirm you will relay the message?"

"Confirmed."

Henry wanted to know who was intercepting communications from Skelm. Who would even want to? It was no more than a manufacturing backwater as far as Coalition standards were concerned, and an unlikely target for espionage. "Who am I speaking to?"

"Evie—"

Another voice cut in, urgent: "Don't give her your real name!"

"Uh, Stevie, that is."

"Thank you, Stevie," she replied, the hairs on her neck prickling. "I trust my message will reach its intended destination."

"Over and out," the voice said, and the line cut out.

Henry was left pressing her ear up against the speaker in her helmet, unease settling in her gut. If someone *was* intercepting unofficial correspondence from Skelm, why would that be? Was there a rebel insurgence beneath the gritty surface of the city, waiting for the perfect moment to strike? She had to assume that her message would never reach Jhanvi back at the CSA, and she and Roger would have to find some way to convince Tripp to let them stay and gather evidence that the terraformers were in danger if the storms continued to drift further from the mountains.

She scooped up a handful of rock and earth and funneled it into a glass sample container. There was no harm in practicing a little creative geology in their quest to observe and predict the storms. Clouds began to gather overhead, the static charge crackling through the air. Henry basked in the danger of storms, invigorating in their unpredictability. There was something addictive about being able to predict the trajectory of clouds, assume the strength of the lightning and the speed of the winds, and it's what kept her laboring in the lab day in and day out, desperate to make a break in the mystery of nature. If they could control the weather, that would change millions of lives throughout the Near Systems.

The weather balloon was on the rise, a tiny blot against the immense rocky skyline that she had to squint to see. It would gather data on the air pressure, charge in the air, humidity, and drift, and when it returned to the ground, it would give them incredible insights on the storms here near Skelm. She needed to know why the storms were drifting after decades of staying up in the mountains, despite terraformed land and atmospheric shifts every time the city expanded further into the rocky desert. She plodded back towards Roger, keenly aware that night was beginning to creep in at the edges of her vision. They didn't have much time.

"Roger!" she shouted as she approached, out of breath and sore from stumbling over the unstable ground. "Rog, I think someone is intercepting all unofficial transmissions coming from that tower."

He looked up from his notebook with a quizzical look. "Really? Why?"

"I don't know, but I couldn't get past whatever it was to get a message to the CSA. They said they'd pass it on, but I have my doubts about that."

"Rebels?"

"Maybe. Or what if it's a Coalition security monitor, making sure no one sneaks around the wire protocols?" A knot settled in her stomach. That would be worse than rebels.

"You'd better hope that's not the case. Did you give them your name?"

"I had to, in case they might actually pass on the message."

"Who did you try to contact?"

"Jhanvi Jhaveri in security sciences."

Roger nodded. "Smart. She's unlikely to report you up the chain of command, and she's high enough that if some monitor reported you, it would stop at her desk."

"We used to have lunch together, before she transferred. I can only hope it was some bored radio hobbyist scanning frequencies on their flightpath."

"Either way, we need to prepare for the possibility that Jhaveri won't get the message, or that we won't be granted a stay. We don't know how high Tripp's influence goes."

Acid rain began to fall from heavy, dark clouds and sizzle onto the parched ground. "I only hope that balloon holds up," Henry said, watching the rain grow heavier in the distance. "We desperately need that data if we're going to make our case to the CSA about the dangers here."

"Shouldn't be long now before it starts back." He examined his pocket watch and snapped it shut. "It had better hurry up, I believe Jess and Bale when they say they won't wait for us if we're late."

Lightning flashed across the sky, striking some of the nearest peaks to the city. Henry frowned, willing them to stray back to the far mountains. "It's getting closer every day," she said. "I don't understand why Tripp wouldn't be concerned about that."

"Scum-sucking cretin," Roger huffed.

"I don't trust this place. Something feels off. Like there's some kind of seismic activity under the surface that's going to take us by surprise."

"Balloon's coming down."

Henry squinted up into the clouds, the ivory balloon narrowly skirting around a cliff. She'd give almost anything for a remote device in this storm, but they weighed too much for the balloon to carry along with all of the other equipment. The limitations of technology were a frequent frustration in their line of research. "Not long now," she agreed after a moment.

Their weather balloon descended to the earth, battered and beaten by the elements, but mostly intact. The sun was sinking behind the mountains, taking the light with it at an exponential rate.

"Looks like our adjustments worked, it survived!"

"Yes, but we have about ten minutes to get back to the monorail. Grab it and let's go, Beauregard. I'm not spending the night in a gorge."

CHAPTER SIX

"I can't believe I let you talk me into this," Henry muttered from the corner of her mouth. "A speakeasy, Rog? Really?"

"Relax, Weaver. I thought we might be able to get some ideas about that transmission interference from earlier."

"You *thought* you could get a lukewarm cocktail, is more like it."

Roger wrinkled his nose. "I should hope they aren't warm."

"Somehow I doubt the standards in Skelm will match the ones you're used to on Gamma-3," she said, pushing open the worn bookshop door to the sound of a gentle bell tinkling overhead. "You might have to get used to the idea of settling for some bootleg swill, rather than the top shelf contraband you prefer."

He harrumphed softly and followed her into the shop, unlit except for one flickering lantern on the table with a cash register, each key engraved with faded ornate flourishes that danced in the firelight. Though the stacks of books piled high to the ceiling were covered in years of accumulated dust and grime, the rug that lay between the door and the table was threadbare enough to see the drab grey painted flooring beneath.

"Password?" a voice asked.

"I'm not with the military police," Roger offered, giving the open slat in the wall a winning smile. "Just two friends looking for a place to relax for an evening."

"*Password.*"

"I can assure you, I mean no harm! We're visiting from Gamma-3, a short rotation into your lovely city, and we just wanted to experience Skelm the way that locals do."

"Anyone who describes this shithole as 'lovely' is definitely an MPO. We don't serve military police officers here." The slat slid closed, deadening the lively chatter within. "Unless they have a shitload of credits to burn."

"You don't know the password?" Henry hissed, leaning against the table. "I thought you said you had the correct information!"

"I did—that is, I do. I got us here, didn't I?"

"What use is that if we're stuck on the wrong side of the wall?"

Roger knocked on the wall, straightening his hat with the other hand. "Excuse me, miss—"

A rectangle of light appeared again. "Password?" A pair of eyes slid into view. "Oh, it's you again. You're not getting in without the password."

"What could I offer you that might convince you otherwise?"

"A million credits."

"A million—" he guffawed. "I'm a researcher, not an aristocrat."

"Looks the same to me."

"We're just trying to find some information out about a series of wire interferences, do you know anything about that?"

"No."

"Do you know anyone who might?"

She paused and leaned away from the window. "Maybe. But it will cost you."

"I told you, I don't have that much—"

"Give me your watch."

"My watch! But this is—"

"Are you going to give it to me or not?"

"Yes."

"Good." The wall slid open, revealing the speakeasy within, with people of all social classes draped over hodge podge, mismatched furniture. Certainly not the opulent gin tasting bars on Gamma-3, secreted away beneath museums and abandoned monorail stations.

CHAPTER SIX

"Thank you, miss, we—"

"Uh huh, whatever." The woman nodded her head toward the bar, worn wood cracked and stained deep from thousands of spills. "House special tonight is the gin volley, which is our finest bathtub gin, lime, and soda. Except there ain't no limes because this place is a bullshit backwater, and the soda is flat. Enjoy." She slid the panel shut behind them. "Stick around here long enough, you'll find someone who knows something about something."

"But when—" Henry started.

"You can go now."

"But the information?" Roger asked.

"Listen, Mr. Fancypants Researcher, we're not fools here. I'm not saying another damn word until I see you order a drink. Any moment before that, and this could be some kind of sting operation."

"We're already in an illegal speakeasy," he retorted. "How much more implicated do you want us to be?"

"Everyone knows about this place, even the visiting management. As long as we keep our noses clean and put on a good show of staying hidden, they'll never shut us down. And besides," she said, peering through the slot, "I already told you, you'll just have to hang around here long enough."

Roger turned to Henry and shrugged his shoulders. "We can at least ask around, I suppose," he offered.

Henry nodded and moved towards a pair of chairs that had just been vacated by a very amorous looking couple, headed for the lavatory. "Who should we talk to first?" she asked, sinking into the overstuffed, threadbare seat. "I don't want to question the wrong person and have this all come crashing down around us. Anymore than it already is, anyway."

"That gentleman over there looks like he might know something about wire interference."

"What makes you say that?"

"I have a hunch."

"A hunch." She sat back in the chair and smoothed the cerulean blue taffeta of her dress. "We have to be careful, Roger."

He winked at her and gave a broad, mischievous grin. "Without risk, there's no reward."

Henry watched him saunter up to the bar and order two house specials, along with another round for the man he wanted to question. She'd seen the act a thousand times, Roger acting as though he recognized them from their time working for the military police, or from a meteorology seminar, or an old childhood friend from back in the old days, in order to get grant money for their research, or a meeting with a reclusive scientist he heard someone knew. The lies never even had a grain of truth, but they always worked. He didn't need her for this. She wasn't even sure why she agreed to come.

"Your drink, ma'am," a bored looking bartender said, setting the drink down on the low table in front of her. It was sloshing over the side and dripping down the glass, pooling at the base and soaking into the bare wood where the paint had chipped away.

"Thank you," she replied, but he was already gone. The drink wasn't very good, but it might at least take the edge off. It was warm, the bitterness of the homemade gin puckering her cheeks before it struggled down her throat. She watched Roger give a broad smile to a gentleman in a black silk top hat, the edges frayed and the ribbon band missing. It was the look of someone who didn't have much to spend on vestments, but better off than a factory worker. She'd be surprised if she saw any of them in there at all, given their piss poor wages.

A bronze gilded clock behind the bar ticked the seconds by, and already Henry was feeling restless. She was regretting caving to Roger's big puppy-dog pleading eyes and wished she was back in the small apartment soaking in a hot bath. The storm's grit that scraped off the atmospheric suit was still plastered to her skin. A thick book with a faded blue fabric cover sat on the table in front of her, one of the pages folded down to mark someone's progress. It was one of her favorites from when she was younger. She rankled at the disrespect some would show to a book, even if it was a banned piece of literature. Could they not have found a stray piece of paper, or just memorized where they'd left off? It was almost blasphemous.

It was smooth in her hands, the worn fabric soft from years of readers. The binding was still taut, sewn at the spine with thread that matched the cover. She opened the book, noting the illegible writing on the inside. It wasn't any language she recognized, and she had studied several at university, including the ancient ones that were no longer in use, but were useful for writing coded messages during the last rebellion. Her parents had pushed her to become a Coalition investigator, but the skies were what held her attention. She had no interest in interrogating spies or mountains of paperwork to track a person of interest. Perhaps the inscription was a code. It wasn't unlikely, given its location and the subject matter: pirates on the high seas, stealing from the rich to give to the poor. Exactly what the Coalition would detest.

Roger was engrossed in conversation with the man in the top hat, so Henry turned her attention to chapter one. Pages seemed to turn themselves as the characters sailed from one ransack to the next, distributing piles of rubies and emeralds amongst the poorest in the land, using antiquated, one shot pistols to intimidate the rich nobles into giving up their wealth and their ships, marooning them on sandbars and sending up a smoke signal for the naval ships to rescue them. It had been a long time since she'd read a fictional story; they were all boring, identical tomes of thinly veiled Coalition propaganda now, and had been for at least fifteen years.

"Excuse me," an alto voice with a southern drawl interjected. "You're reading my book."

Henry looked up, and her breath caught in her throat at the sight of the beautiful woman she'd seen at work. Long, tawny hair tied back, a black wool waistcoat with a button missing at the bottom, her green eyes sparkling like emeralds in the dim light. "Hello," she finally managed to say, her voice cracking.

"Hello. Can I have it back, please? I was just getting to the good part." Georgie flipped her hair over her shoulder, her hands calloused and worn. "If I could just have it for tonight, maybe I can read fast."

"Won't you sit down?" Henry asked, gesturing at Roger's vacated chair. "I'm Henry. Henry Weaver."

The woman hesitated, looking around at the other patrons of the speakeasy, before perching at the edge of the chair with a reluctant sigh. "I remember."

"It's a fun read, isn't it?"

"Yes, that's why I came back for it."

"I only started it tonight, in fact, waiting for my lab partner to finish up some research at the bar."

"Mm."

"You don't talk much, do you?"

Georgie rubbed her palms on her faded trousers. "I'm a woman of few words. Too many will get you killed around here."

"Oh it's alright, I'm just a scientist," Henry said, leaning closer. "I'm only interested in the pursuit of information, of meteorological phenomena. You don't have to worry about me." She was babbling, and she knew it. She clamped her jaw shut with what she hoped was a charming smile, and not one that made her look unhinged.

"All due respect, ma'am, I have no way of knowing if that's true. Coalition investigators spy on folks all the time with convincing cover stories."

"Oh." Henry held the book out. "Here, you take it. Let's call it a gesture of good will."

"I'll just come back tomorrow." Georgie stood, tugging at the hem of her waistcoat. "Nice seeing you again."

"Wait!" Henry reached out and grabbed Georgie's wrist, and felt her own stomach jump with excitement. She couldn't let her just walk out, not when her heart was pounding at the slightest touch of skin. "I'll go, you can stay. After all, you were reading it first."

Georgie sat back in her seat. "It's alright. Don't go." She took the book in her hands and flipped through the pages expectantly, her brow furrowed.

"You're the one who folded the page down, aren't you?" Even the woman's desecration of a book couldn't sway Henry's attraction to her, which was an alarming thought.

"Yes, but I can't find it now."

"Page one hundred and forty two, just after the pirate and the queen swashbuckled their way out of certain death on the naval ship."

"Thanks. You've read this one before?"

Henry smiled. "*Pirates and Queens* is one of my favorites."

"I'll read a chapter or two, and then I'll hand it back. Is that a deal?"

"It's alright, I've already read it. You should finish it."

"Hey, no loafing in here without ordering drinks," the bartender shouted. "This isn't a library for waifs and strays."

"We'll have two more of these," Henry shouted back, lifting her water-stained glass. "My treat," she added, winking at Georgie. She couldn't figure out what had gotten into her. It wasn't in her nature to be quite so forward or flirtatious with someone she barely knew, and certainly not someone in a speakeasy on a settlement she'd be rotating out of before she knew it, especially if Jhanvi Jhaveri wasn't able to get them an extension. It was foolish. She wanted more.

Georgie was already leaned back in the overstuffed chair, her eyes darting back and forth over the surprisingly crisp printed text, turning page after page, oblivious to Henry's gaze. The drinks were shoved across the table, this time even less appetizing than the last, but Henry drank it down anyway, feeling the alcohol melt away the few reservations she had left over not immediately pulling this woman across the city, back into her apartment. It was gauche, not how she had been raised, and yet it was the only thing on her mind as she ran the tip of her index finger around the rim of the glass.

"Is it getting good?" Henry asked, pushing the other drink towards her.

"Yes. Sorry I'm not saying much." Georgie replied, taking the cocktail and draining the glass with a grimace.

"I don't mind. Just watching you read it is enjoyment enough." As soon as the words left her mouth, Henry turned away, her fair skin turning red. "I'm sorry, I—"

"They've taken the naval ship now, and forced the officers to walk the plank over shark-infested waters," Georgie said, one eyebrow arched in curiosity. "Do you want to hear more?" she asked, her voice lower now.

"Please."

"As the naval officers were about to jump to their doom, Mabel changed her mind and cut loose the dinghy to give them a chance to live, and threw them one flare to call for help."

"I've always wondered why. Why not just let them be eaten and pay for their crimes with their lives?"

Georgie tilted her head to the side, a piece of loose hair draped across her cheek. "Maybe she thought that everyone deserves a chance at redemption. Or perhaps she just didn't want their blood on her hands. Either way," she continued, flipping another page, while casting her eyes over Henry, "it makes for a compelling story."

"Are you going to keep reading?"

"Do you want me to?"

"What's the alternative?"

Georgie traced a fingertip across the back of Henry's hand. "We could get out of here, assuming you have somewhere to go."

CHAPTER SEVEN

It's too late to go home now, anyway, Georgie kept thinking to herself as she followed Henry through the streets of Skelm, up the cobblestone roads where the buildings stood firmer and the windows weren't broken or missing. She didn't want to risk waking her mother or her sisters, even if she had managed to sneak in undetected the night before. The girls had school, at least so long as she could keep paying for it, and her ma needed all the good sleep she could get in her condition. It was all just excuses. She wanted to follow Henry out the door. She wanted to follow Henry wherever she wanted to go.

"Where are we going?" she whispered, her fingers interlaced with Henry's.

"I have an apartment here. It's not much, but it's mine as long as I'm stationed in Skelm." Henry turned, her face lit by the warm glow of the street lamp. "Unless you'd prefer we go to your—"

"It's alright, we're already on our way." Georgie was proud of what her family had achieved, given their meager beginnings on this rock, but it was still a far cry from what Coalition scientists were used to. She had a feeling that this woman in her genteel dress and boots, without years of scuffs where the cobbler had repaired the heel, had never gone without. What passed for decent here was worlds apart from the rest of the Near Systems, and sharing a room with three others while you worked twelve-hour shifts every day of the week was all but unheard of for anyone not on the bottom rung of the societal ladder.

Henry nodded and pulled her past the docks, which were never quiet. Ships were always docking, loading, and leaving again. They had to, to keep up with the production levels of the factories here. Dock workers shouted to each other over crates stacked high, filled with ammunition, droids, and replacement parts. Anything that could be manufactured, it was probably manufactured in Skelm. They walked into a courtyard guarded with razor wire fences, the kind meant to keep people like Georgie out. A security drone chirped angrily, but stayed hovering above the door.

"This is where you're staying?" Georgie asked, marveling at the crisp beauty of the building she'd only ever seen from afar.

"I know it's not the best," Henry said, laying a hand on the small of Georgie's back to guide her into the building. "But at least we'll have more privacy than in the speakeasy."

They all but sprinted through the corridor, the heels of their boots echoing against the gilded marble floor and bouncing up into the rafters of the vaulted ceilings. Georgie had never seen anything like it outside of the administration building, and certainly not for temporary accommodations. Then again, the factory tenements were supposed to be that for the workers, but decades on, people were still crammed in there, sleeping two or three to a bed in a dorm of hundreds.

"This is mine," Henry said, a bronze key clicking in the lock. The door swung open into a beautiful room, with hand-woven rugs spread across the floor and a huge four poster bed with thick velvet curtains that hung to the floor.

"It's perfect." Georgie pushed her up against the closed door, running her hands over the smooth black corset above her hips. "I want you to know, I never do things like this," she murmured into her hair, kissing her neck.

"Me neither," Henry said, fumbling with the buttons on Georgie's waistcoat. One popped off and fell to the rug silently before rolling beneath the bed. "There's a first time for everything."

Clothing fell to the floor piece by piece: a tarnished belt buckle clattered against the bare marble between rugs, a dress rustled to the floor in a heap.

CHAPTER SEVEN

Stockings landed atop the warm radiator, and a shirt was tossed to the side, where it fluttered briefly like the birds on Gamma-3, before it perched silently beside the large cedar trunk, engraved with ornate twists.

Georgie hesitated, her hands hovering over bare breasts. "Should we? I don't want to make you feel like we have to, or—"

"I want this. I want *you*," Henry replied, leaning up and pulling her down into a deep, slow kiss, the anticipation of feeling skin on skin building and burning temptation into the space between Georgie's hips. The kisses were sweet, in spite of the bitter swill they'd shared, a gentle biting of lips and the suspense of tongue on tongue. It felt natural and easy, their bodies fit together as though they were carved from clay for each other, perfect and seamless.

Henry took Georgie's hand and led her down into the dark hedge of hair. She was slippery with anticipation, and the sound of her gasp when Georgie explored inside made her own core throb with excitement. In that moment, she felt like she had known Henry forever, as though they were lifelong lovers and not practically strangers. It was intoxicating and dangerous, and she could feel herself getting lost in Henry's embrace.

Smooth hands brushed over Georgie's hips, pulling her closer and begging for more. She obliged, pushing deeper inside and leaning down to kiss from Henry's shoulder to her collarbone and back, heavy, hot breaths against her ear. She smelled of sweet sweat and earth, the sandy rocks that made up the surface. It was surprising for a scientist who dressed and lived as Henry did.

She felt drunk, but not from the gin. It was a different kind of intoxication, one more thrilling and all-encompassing. All she wanted was more of Henry: more kisses, more skin against skin, more sharp intakes of breath and quiet, greedy cries of pleasure. She needed to taste Henry at her core, and kissed from her shoulder down across her rosy nipples, and lingered at the crease between her thighs before kissing deeply, drawing a sigh from Henry that turned into a moan.

Georgie kissed, and kissed, and kissed, feeling Henry tense with every press of her fingers. Her own body was primed and hungry, and she reached down to touch herself as she lost herself in Henry. They didn't need to talk. It was like each knew exactly what the other wanted, and they moved in perfect synchronization until they were both panting with exhaustion, laying next to each other covered in a fine sheen of well-earned sweat.

"That was…" Henry trailed off, her once tightly wound bun now loose, with stray hairs draped across the white linen pillow case.

"Yeah."

"I didn't expect that. I mean, I guess I…"

"I know. Me too." Georgie turned to face her and trailed a fingertip over her waist. "So what now?"

"I don't know. I don't want to think about how much time we have, I just want to lay here with you." Henry took Georgie's hand and interlaced their fingers. "Rough hands."

"Sorry."

"No, I like it."

"I have to work in a few hours."

"You're welcome to stay. The bed is certainly big enough." Henry yawned, her energy spent. "Please stay."

Georgie nodded, resting her hand on Henry's hip. "I'll stay." The bed was so soft, so tempting. A far cry from her place on the floor at home.

"How long have you worked at the administration building?"

Despite their connection, and despite how much Georgie wanted to stay at her side forever, for some reason, the question made her uncomfortable. She wasn't sure she could handle herself at work knowing Henry was there too, working away in the cramped lab writing reports on gods only knew what. "Oh, you know. A while. I'm just a cleaner. Nothing important."

Henry propped herself up on an elbow. "Of course that's important."

"So how long are you in Skelm for?" Georgie asked, desperate to turn the conversation away from what she did to make a living. She wasn't ashamed of her job as such, but she certainly wasn't proud that they all lived in one room, and that one missed paycheck would see her sisters kicked out of school and her mother back in the factories.

"I don't want to go into all that."

"Okay."

"Tell me about your childhood."

"No." Georgie was even less interested in talking about that than she was in talking about her job as a janitor. "Why don't you tell me about yours, instead?"

"I grew up on Gamma-3, but you probably knew that. In fact, I still live there really, when I'm not on a research trip like I am now."

"Where? On Gamma-3, I mean."

"Sector Eight. My parents were ambassadors for the burgeoning settlements before they retired, so we have a nice little house, nothing grandiose. Simple. It was typical, I suppose."

Georgie couldn't help wondering what a nice little house looked like, considering her whole apartment would probably fit into Henry's bathroom here. She resisted the vague urge to tell her that and instead traced circles with her thumb over Henry's hip. "What was your first girlfriend like?"

Henry barked a laugh. "We'd better not talk about her. Let's just say that she was the daughter of a rich merchant trader, and her family thought she could do better than me."

"Her loss is my gain, then."

"That was a long time ago." Henry brushed a hair out of Georgie's face. "We wouldn't have lasted, anyway. She said science was *boring*."

Georgie snorted. "Well, how dare she. The audacity!"

"Right?" Henry giggled, and then let out a long, soft sigh. "Last I heard, she'd run off with some pirate and got into a bunch of trouble. Messed with some salvage crews, they turned her in. It's only thanks to her family's position in the Coalition she didn't end up in a work camp, but she's definitely on house arrest."

"Wow."

"So, safe to say it's a good thing I didn't travel too far down that path." Henry laughed. "And besides, it was never as good as it was with you just now."

"Oh." Georgie felt a blush creep up her neck into her face. "Good?"

"Very good. The best, in fact." Henry yawned again and gave her a slow blink. "Should we turn off the lamp?"

Georgie kissed her on the forehead and leaned over her to plunge the room into darkness, and wrapped her arms tight around the woman she was terrified of becoming attached to, and even more that she would leave forever.

* * *

Georgie awoke at the first sign of light, the huge mirrors that hung over Skelm shifting into place to redirect what little sun there was all the way out here in the Near Systems down into the city. Henry was still nestled in her arms, sleeping peacefully, her eyelashes fluttering as she dreamed. As much as she dreaded the thought of leaving, she couldn't risk another close call at work. Mr. Jackson wasn't the kind of man to make empty threats.

She gently freed her arm and tugged the soft wool blanket over Henry's shoulders, setting a pillow behind her so she'd think Georgie was still there and not wake up. Goodbyes were too difficult. It was easier to leave in the darkness and start the impossible task of forgetting they'd ever met. There was no future for them, no possible happy outcome where they ended up together and safe somewhere far away from Skelm. No, as much as it pained her to her core, Georgie would just have to hope that the pain of separation passed quickly, and allowed her to refocus her efforts on getting her mother and sisters out of here, even if it meant she stayed. Unless Evie Anderson came through for them soon, that's exactly what would happen.

Her clothes were strewn around the room, evidence of a night of passion, not that she'd ever had one quite like that before. Her heart throbbed a faint ache in her chest at the thought of giving up ever seeing Henry again after she was reassigned to another base somewhere else. She'd have to avoid her at work, too - not only to cover up her lie, but because the more she saw her, the more she'd struggle to not run screaming to the docks the day her transport took off. No, that was out of the question so long as she had her family to think about.

Dressed in last night's clothes, she latched the door quietly behind her, and came face to face with a man exiting the door opposite.

"Well, well, good morning to you," he said, in a voice far too chipper for that time of morning.

"Mornin'," Georgie mumbled. Without the appropriate pass, she could get into serious trouble being in this building, and she didn't want to draw too much attention to herself. She tipped her hat and made for a quick exit, her head down, eyes on the imported marble floor as she approached the vestibule.

"Ma'am?" the woman at the front desk shouted after her. "Excuse me, I don't recognize you as a guest, do you have a pass?"

"No thank you!" Georgie replied, her pace quickening.

"Ma'am, it's procedure to—" the woman stopped. The chipper man was leaning over the counter, obscuring the receptionist's view and taking her attention. *At least he was good for something*, she thought, heading back into the street. It was a close call, and not one she was keen to repeat.

Mornings in Skelm were dreary affairs, the streets laden with workers shuffling to their jobs in the factories, some as young as fifteen years old, dressed in stained grey jumpsuits, too baggy for their small frames. It made her stomach turn.

She made it to the janitorial room in plenty of time to change into her orange coveralls and stash away her clothes before Erin saw and had too many questions she wouldn't want to answer. She'd have enough interrogation from Emeline and her mother later, that much was certain. She finished buttoning up her coveralls just as the others started to trickle in, followed by Mr. Jackson, a grim look on his face and stained paperwork on his clipboard.

"Morning, everyone. Please take your seats for today's work assignments." He waited as the small crowd of orange shuffled to the rusted chairs against the wall, the metal legs scraping painfully against the floor. "We have an announcement today. There's been a new governor assigned to Skelm in the wake of Ralph Baker's tragic demise. After interviews were concluded, it was decided by the upper management in the Capital back on Gamma-3 that the best person for the job would be Inspector Amaranth Allemande."

Georgie wrinkled her nose at the sound of the name. Rotten monster. She'd hoped Allemande would rotate out of Skelm soon now that her jaw was unwired, and back to whatever Coalition prison hell hole she'd crawled out of before being assigned desk duty here. It looked like they were stuck with her, now.

"As she is the ruling authority here in Skelm, any order you get from her obviously outranks anything else. Please plan accordingly and report back any anomalies in your scheduling. She has announced a new mandatory system with tracking devices," he said, gesturing at a box on the floor heaped with tracker cards on lanyards, "more effective than your standard issue Coalition chip. These will be able to pinpoint your location in the Administration building at any time during your shift."

Erin raised her hand. "Uh, sir? Who is going to be monitoring these tracking devices?"

He sighed. "Inspector – that is, Governor Allemande now, has assigned me the task of monitoring and marking the janitorial staff's locations at five minute increments throughout the day. This has been implemented in order to improve efficiency and cut down on idle chatter."

"We aren't allowed to work together as it is, who does she think we're talking to?" Erin asked. "And what, are our bathroom breaks timed now, too?"

"Due to the nature of the tracking lanyards, yes, that's correct."

Discontented murmuring spread through the room. Whispers gathered like cobwebs in the corners, hovering over the room like a bad omen. How much more could they be managed, before their jobs became even harder to accomplish with the timescales set out by the Coalition management? A room could only be cleaned so fast, if it was to be done right.

"In any case," Mr. Jackson continued, quieting the grumbles, "these new procedures will be implemented starting today." He picked up the box and began to hand out the tracking cards, each one suspended on a woven fabric lanyard that matched the orange janitorial jumpsuits. "If you have any questions or concerns, please come to me directly. Governor Allemande will be very busy catching up on over two months of backed up work from the late Governor Baker's desk, and we should all strive to not bother her with our trivial concerns."

"What he means is that he doesn't want to look bad to the new boss lady," Erin mumbled under her breath, passing a lanyard down her row of chairs.

"What I *mean* is that from here on out, we will be observing established Coalition hierarchy to the letter, which is what we should have been doing from the start. These methods have been tested and found to improve working conditions and efficiency, so that's what we are going to do." He passed the final tracking card in the box to Georgie, who was sitting at the end of the front row. "We should be more vocal in our pride for the Coalition. Without it, we'd all still be squabbling back on Gamma-3, with no space exploration in sight."

Georgie hung the tracking card around her neck and tucked it beneath the collar of her boilersuit. She was never one for talking much at work, but knowing there was yet another facet to the Coalition's surveillance lodged in her gut like a rock, especially given her near-miss at the hotel that morning. If they were ever required to wear them in their time off, it would have a severe impact on how people lived their lives.

"Let me be clear," Mr. Jackson said, empty box in hand, "anyone found to be concealing their location, or tampering with their device, or in any way obfuscating the location data, will be fired immediately and escorted from the Administration building. You will also be given no severance pay and banned from working for any Coalition property for the rest of your days."

Georgie sucked in a breath and touched the tracking card beneath the thin orange fabric of her uniform. The factories, the cafes, everything in Skelm was owned by the Coalition in some capacity. Being banned from employment would be a death sentence for most, with no way to access housing or food. It was a distinct and unsettling threat from their new overlord. If Evie Anderson didn't come through for her soon, she'd have to take matters into her own hands.

CHAPTER EIGHT

"The readings, Beauregard, what do they say?"

"I said give me a minute, I'm trying to get the damned panel off! In our admirable quest to further weatherproof the balloon, we made it almost impossible to get back into once it touched ground again."

Henry stood poised with a short, stubby pencil at the end of the lab table, the eraser completely worn away. "We don't have much time to launch a second balloon at the next expedition to support our findings if we don't get this data purged today."

"You don't have to tell me that, Henry, I know." He jammed a screwdriver into the hinge of the panel and pried it loose, sending the metal door to the floor with a loud clang. "Any word from Jhaveri?"

"No." She sighed and scribbled the date into the corner of her notebook. "I'm worried she never even got the message. If we don't get an extension, we're out of here in ten days and all our research will go to waste."

"What if you tried sending it again?"

"I suppose I could, but there's no guarantee that interference won't still be there." She peered into the open cavern of the weather balloon and pulled out the long string of paper, encoded with binary language from the small printer within. "Didn't you get any useful information from that man at the speakeasy last night?"

"Not as such, but it certainly sounded like he's got some kind of fluid connection to a rebel cell here. Strange. I didn't think there was much of that here in Skelm, after the last time."

A moment passed in amiable silence, but the quiet made her head spin. "I'm almost surprised that you haven't taken that receptionist to bed with you yet. She certainly seems taken with you."

Roger let loose a guffaw that rang the tuning fork perched on the counter. "Are we not going to talk about that very attractive Skelm resident I saw sneaking out of your suite this morning? Far be it from me to judge, but glass houses and all, neither should you."

She felt a deep blush burn across her cheeks. "I wasn't judging."

"There was a slight edge of annoyance, Weaver. I know you."

"I just don't know how you do it. Everyone listens to you, does what you want. When I ask for things, the answer is always a hard and fast no."

"Seems like that wasn't the case last night."

Henry threw her pencil at him from across the table. "Shut up," she said, laughing. "It's none of your business."

"I knew as soon as she sat down at your table that you were a goner. You went completely doe-eyed and practically floated out of the Twisted Lantern after her."

"You didn't see that from across the speakeasy."

He shrugged. "I saw enough." His fingers clumsy, he pulled the rest of the ivory colored tape from the balloon, raveling it neatly as he went. "How about those readings, then?"

"Right." Henry was simultaneously relieved and disappointed to turn the conversation away from Georgie. She wanted to relive every detail, every kiss, every whisper, especially as Georgie was gone when Henry woke up, usually a sign that the feelings weren't exactly mutual. Science was a welcome distraction.

"The readings, Henry?" he pressed.

"These can't be correct," she replied, scanning through the lines of code. "I must be interpreting wrong, this information is totally inconsistent with established weather patterns outside the terraformers."

"Could it be that the adjustments we made to the balloon impacted readings? Skewed them in some way?"

"I won't say that it's impossible, but it's improbable. We left the sensors unrestricted and unencumbered."

"What does it say?"

She smoothed the tape across the table and rotated it so that Roger could see. "These readings suggest an exponential increase in strike patterns outside the mountain range. If these are correct, then…"

"…then Skelm has less than a week before that lightning gets within range of the terraforming machines."

"I don't think Tripp will believe us, not when we only have one data set to go on."

"We have to get back out there." He compared the tape to his notes. "There's not another expedition planned until next week."

"We can't wait that long!"

"You need to get that message to Jhanvi Jhaveri. She needs to know what's going on here, and that Tripp is ignoring our research and the clear danger to the city. Surely his superiors would want to know what he's up to, and that he's endangering thousands of lives here."

"Our wire access is still blocked. Unless we can get beyond the boundary to the communications tower again, I won't even be able to try."

Roger ran his hands through his thick silvery hair. "I'm sure we can figure something out, we have to. Otherwise they'll have us on a transport the second Tripp knows what we've been up to."

"Shit!" Henry yelled, and tossed her notebook angrily to the desk. "That stupid old man is going to get us all killed, himself included. What's even the point? Why would someone do that?"

"Pride is a strange thing, unpredictable. Maybe he didn't like that we showed up and started questioning how they do things here, and whatever anomaly is going on past the barrier is unrelated. Either way, Hen, we've got to get the word to Jhaveri, or someone at the CSA."

"I know. I just don't like how we're going to have to do it."

* * *

CHAPTER EIGHT

Henry rubbed her temples, trying to ease away what was almost certainly a migraine. She'd been analyzing the data for hours, trying to discern any kind of pattern that made sense. Her initial analysis of the code had been correct, much to her disappointment and terror, though she'd compared every line of binary with the code processing book she kept in her briefcase, hoping her lack of sleep made her misread the data.

If they got these readings again, provided they were able to send up a second balloon, then Skelm was in serious danger. One strike from the superpowered lightning from the atmosphere would destroy the terraformers and slowly suffocate every living being in the city. And for some inexplicable reason, Lawrence Tripp was completely ambivalent to the danger. She could only hope he'd look over their research and change his mind, allow them to do emergency research, and call in a team of the best meteorologists in the Near Systems to help them prepare for the worst.

Roger had left long before, to try to talk his new engineer friends, Jess and Bale, into rearranging their maintenance schedule to accommodate a secret, emergency expedition beyond the barrier where they could try to replicate the findings from the first balloon. With any luck, it was a user error, and there was nothing out of the ordinary, just some strong lightning storms that were stable and remaining where they should, far away from the city and its life force.

A soft knock at the door roused her from her troubled thoughts. "Come in," she answered.

"Hiya," Georgie said, sidling into the room with her cleaning cart. "Someone requested a clean?"

"Oh!" Henry felt a grin spread across her face so broad, it made her cheeks ache. "I'm so glad to see you, when you were gone this morning, I thought—"

Georgie gave her a warning look. "What did you need cleaned here? A gentleman by the name of Mr. Beauregard caught me in the hallway and said you needed something in this lab." She pulled a clean rag from the folded pile atop the cart. "I think he's in the same hotel as you?"

Henry nodded. "My lab partner."

"So what needs to be cleaned?"

"Oh, nothing, I think he just saw you and put the pieces together, and—"

"I really can't just stand here in the doorway."

"Oh…" Henry trailed off. She was being so curt with her. Maybe she was a love-them-and-leave-them type. Was that why she'd left so early that morning without saying goodbye? "It's nice to see you, anyway," she added hopefully.

"If you have something for me, I'm happy to get started, but if not, then I'm afraid I have to get back to my assigned tasks." Georgie pulled a white card on an orange lanyard from beneath her jumpsuit. "Efficiency training."

"Oh, right." A part of her had hoped Georgie had made up an excuse to come see her, but now it seemed like she was making every excuse to get as far away from the lab as she could. "I guess I hoped that you just wanted to see me."

"I did want to see you," Georgie grinned, flashing that same impish grin she had in the speakeasy the night before. "But I can't stay. Every special request has to be logged and categorized."

"Seems like a lot of work."

Georgie shrugged. "Better than some jobs around here." She took a step into the lab and brushed her fingers against the back of Henry's hand. "Just too bad we're from different places."

"We're not so different, we—"

The tracker flashed yellow and beeped. "Gotta go," Georgie winked. "Be sure to tell them I cleaned up a spill or something, if anyone asks. Don't get me fired, okay?"

"Can I see you later?"

"It's… better if we didn't."

"Wait, Georgie—" Henry protested, but Georgie was already gone, leaving her to plead with the closed door of the lab. She couldn't decide if she felt better or worse, having seen who she was becoming convinced was the love of her life walk into her lab and then back out. Of all the backwater settlements in the Near Systems, she had to be living in this one, where it would be nearly impossible to keep in touch. It's not as though janitors and groundskeepers had access to the wire terminal in the courtyard. She felt her heart contract in her chest, an acute ache that left her feeling empty and alone.

CHAPTER NINE

The orange lanyard fell into the open box with a clatter, and she had never been happier to be leaving work. The persistent alarm that sounded every five minutes made everyone feel on edge, racing to complete each task so they wouldn't be analyzed as being too slow, or too lazy. No doubt some hadn't cleaned as thoroughly as they usually would for fear they'd get fired. She wondered if they'd ever get a reprieve from the damned things.

She looked in her locker and sighed at the sight of her nice clothes crammed into a small bag at the bottom. If life was different and fair, she'd be heading straight back to the Twisted Lantern to see Henry, to drink gin and read about people much freer than she was. Instead, she was heading home to her family and an inevitable inquisition.

"Heading home?" Erin asked, stripping off her uniform to change into a simple blue wool dress with a tattered grey corset over the top.

"Yeah."

"How did you find the new trackers today?"

"Same as everyone else, I expect."

"I wonder if they're going to hire someone to help Mr. Jackson with the data entry. He can't do his job and all of that, too."

Georgie knew that if a position opened up, Erin would be gunning for it. It was only her and John, who worked down in the factories, but credits were scarce on Skelm for those not born with them. "I guess we'll have to wait and see."

CHAPTER NINE

"Would you go for it, if there was a job?"

"I don't know. It depends, I guess." Georgie didn't want to discourage Erin, but the thought of taking a position that put her in line with the management turned her stomach. This is how they operated, allowing one or two token low line workers to achieve something other than squalor to keep the rest of them quiet, and she wanted no part of it. There was unlikely to be a significant raise, anyway - just the perk of having access to better housing and supplies than the rest of them. Tempting as it was to try to secure that for her family, she couldn't bring herself to be the one to shit on other workers.

"You could come out tonight," Erin offered, securing the brass toggles at the front of her corset.

"I'm not falling for that again. Last time you left me high and dry. Besides, I have to help my sisters with their school work, and my ma shouldn't be exerting herself too much with cleaning the place. Maybe I'll catch you next time." It was only half a lie, really. She did help her sisters when they were younger, but their education had since outstripped her own. She'd made sure of that. But the real reason she wouldn't be returning to the speakeasy any time soon was that she was in serious danger of falling desperately in love with a woman she could never be with. The less they saw of each other, the better.

Erin rolled her eyes and gave a halfhearted wave, and Georgie swung through the door and headed for home, shuffling along the crowded streets with everyone else who was doing the exact same thing. Dusty cobblestones kicked up clouds of dirt with every step, the sole of her worn boots allowing the rocks to press into her feet. The girls needed new shoes for school, and they took priority. She'd get new work boots in a few months when they'd saved enough.

Thoughts of Henry flickered through her mind's eye, and she got lost in her own daydream. She ached to feel her touch again. It had been so long since she'd felt something, since she had thoughts for her own future and not just her family's. They'd never save enough to get out of Skelm in her current job. There had to be some other way, some way to get them all out and run away with Henry, if she even wanted her like that. For all she knew, it was no more than a casual tryst, something Henry did in every posting she knew she'd soon rotate out of.

"Georgina, you never came home last night," Emeline teased, and it yanked Georgie out of her thoughts.

"Yes I did, you just didn't see me. I left early."

"Nuh uh, Ma said she hasn't seen you." Emeline jumped off the railing where she was perched outside their apartment and wrapped her gangly arms around Georgie's shoulders. "So where were you? Did you go back to the Twisted Lantern? Were your friends there? How come you were out all night?"

"So many questions, Em," Georgie laughed. "I was just with some friends, that's all."

"Friends, or," Emeline wiggled her eyebrows, "*friends*?"

"Friends. And don't worry about it."

"Ooh, Georgina's got a girlfriend!"

She clapped a hand over her sister's mouth. "Hush! Don't tell Ma!"

Her sister wriggled out of her grasp. "Why not? What's wrong?"

"It's nothing. She's leaving soon, and—" she sighed. "And it's nothing. Don't tell Ma, she's desperate to marry me off."

"She just wants you to be happy, George. We all do."

She gave her sister's arm a squeeze and climbed the steps to their door. "I know. But we've gotta get out of here first."

The door to their small apartment creaked when it opened, the rusted hinges screaming to be replaced. It wouldn't get replaced, not with the Coalition Housing Association as the landlord. It wouldn't even get replaced if the entire door came off.

"What if we stayed?" Emeline whispered, following her into the apartment. "What if we stayed and tried to make it a better place? Judy said that if we got enough people to stage a general labor strike, then—"

Georgie rounded on her. "Who the hell is Judy?"

"A friend from the commons, and—"

"Em, these are dangerous ideas. People have been killed for less."

CHAPTER NINE

"Nothing's ever gonna get better unless we fight for it!"

"Keep your voice down. I know you want to make things better for us and others here, but it's just not possible. Not now. Maybe not ever. Our best chance at a better life is getting the hell out of here on the first transport we can afford and never looking back."

"You never listen, Georgie! You never want to think about how things could be different here. You just hate it so much that you'd rather leave than fight. You're a *coward*."

"A coward?" she hissed, slamming the door behind them. "Do you really want to live here, after what this place did to Pa? After what it's done to Ma? She used to be a strong, healthy woman back on Gamma-3 when we worked in the fields. Now she can't even leave this godsforsaken apartment because her lungs are in such terrible condition."

"I barely even remember Pa!" Emeline shouted back. "But he wouldn't have been a chicken like you are!"

"Yeah, and it got him *killed*." When her sister clamped her jaw shut, her eyes filling with tears, Georgie continued. "He wanted to save this place too. He wanted to change the way people are asked to live and work around here. He got involved with the rebel cell, went to midnight meetings on the docks. One night, he never came home. None of them did. Fifteen people, gone just like that."

Emeline turned her face away, tears spilling down her cheeks. "I want things to be better. I don't want us to have to live like this forever."

Georgie enveloped her sister in a tight embrace. "I know, Em. That's why I'm trying as hard as I can to get us a way out of here. Maybe someday things will change, and this place won't be so toxic."

"It just feels impossible," her sister sobbed, her voice muffled by the fabric her face was buried into. "I want to do something to help."

"Leave it to me, okay? I'm working on a plan. I'll get us out of here, all of us." Georgie knew that last part was a lie, a sweet untruth to calm her sister. The reality was she had only made Evie Anderson promise to come back for her mother and sisters, not her too. There was no telling if she was going to come back at all.

"How?" Georgie hesitated, and her sister felt it. "Come on, tell me. I'm old enough. I'll have to work in the factories next year if my school doesn't place me in an apprenticeship."

"You have to swear on your own grave not to tell Ma or Lucy. Especially not Lucy, she couldn't keep a secret if she tried."

Emeline sprang back from the embrace and crossed her finger over her heart. "I swear."

"A while back, I helped some pirates escape from the city, and made them promise to come back for us," she whispered, not wanting her mother to overhear. She was nearly deaf from the years of working in the factory, but she could spot sisterly sedition from a mile away.

"Pirates?"

"Yeah."

"What makes you think that pirates are going to keep their word?" Emeline scoffed. "You might as well wish on a star for all the good that will do us."

"I don't think these are average pirates. I think they're involved in some serious stuff."

"And you say *I'm* being too dangerous going to labor rights meetings, when you're blowing up buildings and helping pirates escape after they did gods know what."

"I'm older than you." When her sister opened her mouth to protest, Georgie cut her off. "And it's my responsibility to keep you and Lucy safe, and make sure Ma can stay home, and carve out some kind of future for us all. When you're my age, you can make your own decisions. And I didn't blow up the building."

"Oh please, Georgina, you smelled like solvent for days after the explosion. Even Ma knows."

"I only blew up a boiler, actually," Georgie winked, "but don't tell Ma that either."

"Don't tell Ma what?" her mother asked, rounding the corner. "I'm hard of hearing but y'all forget I can still read lips."

"Nothing," Emeline said with a grin. "You'd have to ask Georgie." She gave a pirouette in her stocking feet and flounced off to the bed, where she sat down heavily on the thin mattress and pulled out her school books.

"Georgina, should I be worried?" her mother asked.

"Probably."

"Well, so long as you're handling yourself. I know you're a smart girl." Her mother patted her arm, and pulled her to the rickety table next to the peat stove, bubbling with a thin stew of whatever canned items had been left in the cupboard. "Lucy should be home soon. She's walking back with the neighbor's girls."

As if on cue, the eleven-year-old burst through the door, kicking off her hand-me-down buttoned boots caked with mud. "I'm home!" she shouted, tossing her worn leather book bag onto the floor with a thud.

"How was school, Honey Bee?" their mother asked, sitting down heavily on her chair, winded from the effort.

"Fine. Candace says she shouldn't have to be my lab partner. She said we're trash."

"Candace needs to learn to keep her big mouth shut," Emeline called from the bed. "She's the trash, Ma, she gossips about everyone."

Lucy shrugged. "I don't like her anyways."

"Good, you just stay focused on your schoolwork," Georgie said, stirring the thin stew, watching a lone chunk of carrot get caught in the current of her stained wooden spoon. "You're a smart girl, Lucy."

"Yeah, way smarter than I was," Emeline agreed. "By the time you're my age, you'll be a genius!"

"Alright, don't be giving her a big head now, she won't fit through the door when she comes home next," their mother said with a gentle chide, but it was clear from her beaming face how proud she was of her three daughters.

"Oh, Georgie, there's someone outside said she knows you."

"What?"

"Yeah, she was asking around where you might be."

Georgie stumbled to the small, dirty window and pulled aside the makeshift curtains to see Henry standing at the base of the stairs, illuminated by the yellow glow of the street lamp. "Luce, why didn't you say anything?" she shouted, tripping over the table to get to the door. "How long has she been out there?"

Lucy shrugged again. "I dunno."

"Who's out there, Georgie?" their mother asked, craning her head towards the window.

"It's no one," Georgie replied, shoving her feet into her boots and yanking the door open, leaving her laces untied.

Emeline leapt off the bed and skidded to the door in her stocking feet. "Is it her?"

"Is it who?" their mother asked again.

Lucy wandered over to the stew pot, disinterested in the commotion. "It's some fancy lady."

Georgie tumbled out the door and leaned against it to keep Emeline from following her out. "Ms. Weaver, why in all the gods' names would you be here at my home?"

"I, uh, found your button," Henry said, holding up a tiny black button. There was absolutely nothing special about it, just a standard, mass produced black button. "Under my bed," she finished, her voice now in a whisper. "I thought you might want it back."

"How did you find out where I live?"

Henry held the button out in the palm of her hand, still standing at the foot of the stairs. "Roger has a way with people. He asked around, found out what district you live in. I just thought I should return it, since you've been so busy at work, with those trackers and all."

"Oh, right." She leaned away from the door for just a second, long enough for Emeline to shove her way out and onto the stairs.

"Ooh, she's *pretty*, Mama."

"Emeline! Get back inside."

"Is this her? The one you were out all night with?"

"Emeline..."

"You told them about me?" Henry asked hopefully, leaning away from the street lamp in a futile attempt to hide her bashful smile.

78

"Georgina Payne, don't be rude! Ask your friend inside!" their mother shouted from inside.

There were many things she'd rather do than invite Henry inside in that moment, up to and including tap dancing alongside an angry rattlesnake. Their home was an achievement considering where they'd started from in Skelm, but it was smaller than Henry's temporary accommodation, and that shame ignited in her spine, tightening the muscles in her shoulders. "She's just returning something, Ma."

"In this home we are gracious to our guests. Invite her in."

"Would you like to come inside?" Georgie asked through gritted teeth, hoping against all hope that Henry would decline the invitation and be on her way.

"I would love to," Henry replied, taking the steps two at a time, and greeting Georgie with a kiss on the cheek, at which Emeline squealed with delight.

Georgie squeezed her eyes shut and waited for them to pile inside so she could close the door, the squeaky hinge screaming even louder than usual, the dried mud on the floor next to Lucy's shoes like an advertisement for how they lived. "You could have just given it back to me at work," she whispered.

"I wanted to see you," Henry said, reaching out for her hand and giving it a reassuring squeeze.

"Hello, I'm Georgie's mother," she said, struggling to get off the chair.

"Oh, don't get up on my account!" Henry said, crossing the room and shaking her hand. "I'm Henrietta Weaver, we... work together."

Georgie's mother looked her up and down. "You don't look like you work in the janitorial division."

"No ma'am, I'm just a meteorologist here on a temporary assignment from Gamma-3. I work in the labs in the Administration building."

"I'm going to be a scientist one day!" Lucy chimed in, her attention drawn from the savory-smelling pot. "I'm working real hard in my lessons, too. My name's Lucy."

"Well, that's excellent to hear, Lucy. I look forward to working with you someday."

Georgie couldn't help but smile at her youngest sister's beaming face. They didn't get much in the way of encouragement around these parts, but Lucy was a fighter nonetheless. If she could get them all out of here, her sister might just have a real chance at becoming a scientist.

"Won't you stay for dinner?" Emeline asked, a devilish smile spreading from ear to ear. "Ma, can't she stay for dinner?"

"Of course she can. Ms. Weaver, won't you join us?"

"I'm sure Henry has better things to do than to spend her evening with us," Georgie interrupted. "She is an important scientist, after all."

"I'd be honored to join you for dinner."

"I want to sit next to Henry!" Lucy shouted, dragging an upside down bucket to the table to function as an extra chair.

"Maybe we should let Georgie sit next to her," their mother said gently.

"It's alright Ma, it's not like it's a big table." Georgie turned back to the peat stove to dish out the meager rations, but saw that Emeline was already on the task, pouring thin soup into chipped, faded bowls.

"So this is where you live?" Henry asked, her tone innocent enough, but Georgie understood the underlying concern. *You live here, all of you in the same room*, was more the question, and it made Georgie bristle with defensiveness.

"Yes. And it's a far sight better than the factory tenements most live in. We're lucky to have this, and we've worked damn hard to achieve it. Ma nearly died working in those factories, inhaling who knows what for over a decade."

"I'm fine," her mother reassured the rest of the room. "I'm a tough old bird, it's going to take more than some silly old smoke to take me out."

"I think your home is lovely," Henry said, passing a bowl of stew to Lucy. It was earnest, and made Georgie soften just enough to give her a tiny smile from the corners of her mouth.

"Thank you."

"What do you do in the labs? How often do you get to go to other settlements? When will you know what causes the storms beyond the barrier? Who do you work with? Where was the scariest storm you've ever seen?" Lucy fired off in quick succession.

"Whoa, let her eat her dinner," Georgie laughed, sliding a spoon across the table with a scrape.

"Maybe someday you can come intern with me in the lab for a few weeks, after you pass your exams," Henry said. "It's not every day I meet a keen storm chaser."

"Can I?" Lucy shrieked, and Emeline flinched from the shrill noise. "Oh please, Ma, can I please go and intern with Henry after my exams?"

A grim look passed over their mother's face. "We'll see, Luce. Transports are expensive."

"Oh," Henry said quietly. "Well, perhaps we can find some kind of scholarship to cover the costs." She grinned at Lucy, her face brightening. "After all, we can't let a smart girl like you go to waste!"

"So," Emeline said carefully, slurping at her soup. "Do you intend on keeping our Georgina out every night?"

"Em!" Georgie hissed, pinching her sister's arm under the table.

"I mean, we do worry about her, we just want to make sure you're not going to break her heart." It was clear that Emeline had no intention of letting up on her embarrassing line of questioning, and their mother wasn't going to put a stop to it, either. More likely, she was just glad there were signs that Georgie was spending her time with someone other than her family.

Henry blushed a deep scarlet and ate another mouthful of soup. "I'm sure you worry about her," she finally said.

"And you're not going to break her heart?"

"Emeline!" Georgie scolded. "Enough!"

"I promise I won't break her heart," Henry said, answering Emeline but staring straight into Georgie's eyes. Georgie had hoped to keep the rapid deluge of emotions away with avoidance, but clearly that wasn't going to happen. Here she was, in her home, charming her family with talk of apprenticeships for Lucy and promises of a forever love. Every minute she was close, Georgie felt herself grow more attached to the idea of spending the rest of her life with Henry, and it was the most terrifying thing she'd ever experienced. Blowing up a boiler didn't even come close.

"Are you two heading out tonight?" Georgie's mother asked innocently, pushing her bowl, still half full with soup, towards Lucy. "Here Honey Bee, I'm full."

"No." Georgie drained the rest of the soup out of her bowl and stacked it neatly inside Emmeline's. "I have an early shift tomorrow."

"That didn't stop you last night," her sister teased, wiggling her eyebrows.

"Yeah, well, last night I didn't know they were going to be gifting us all with fancy new tracking devices to wear around our necks to improve efficiency in the Administration building. Courtesy of the new Governor."

"New Governor?" Henry asked, dabbing at the corners of her mouth with a napkin.

"Well, I'm surprised you haven't heard of her, given you're in the science department."

Henry shrugged. "I'm just on a temporary assignment. Maybe that's why they didn't think it was important."

"Anyway, Governor Allemande used to be an inspector. A real piece of work."

"Why do you say that?" Henry asked, and Georgie exchanged a look with her mother across the table.

"Henry dear, inspectors aren't exactly known for their magnanimity." Georgie's mother motioned for Emeline to clear the table and leaned back in her chair. "It's highly unusual for an inspector to be given a position of higher authority, at least here in Skelm. They usually come in for a teaching assignment and rotate back out to one of the prison colonies."

"Yeah, I think most people would choose prison over living here," Georgie snorted.

"Georgina, you shouldn't say things like that," Emeline argued. "If what Judy and Cole say is true, prisons are the worst places in the Near Systems to be."

"Oh, it's Judy *and* Cole now, is it? Who else has been filling your head with this dangerous nonsense?"

"It's not nonsense to want to make life better here."

"We're not having this argument again, and definitely not at the dinner table." Georgie stood and collected the dishes from the table, her hand brushing against Henry's for a second, just long enough to shoot pangs of longing straight to her heart. "You need to be careful who you say these things to, Em." She dumped the dishes in the old utility sink and filled it with water, watching the suds expand over the surface.

"I can help," Henry offered.

"Don't be silly, you're our guest," Ma said, struggling to get out of her chair.

"No, I insist," Henry said, rolling up the sleeves of her charcoal grey dress. "After all, you fed me a delicious meal when I invited myself to your home, it's the least I can do."

"We'll leave you two to it, then. Luce, Em, go work on your studies. As for me," she said, heaving herself out of the chair, bracing on the rickety table, "I think I need to lie down a while."

"You alright, Ma?" Georgie asked, supporting her mother's elbow. She hated to see her mother like this, a woman who was once strong as an ox and ten times as fast reduced to a feeble husk of who she once was, courtesy of the Coalition factories.

"I'm fine, Georgie," she replied, waving her off. "Just need to rest."

"So tell me more about this new governor," Henry said, submerging her soft hands into the harsh detergent.

"I've only met her once. She looked me right in the eyes and poured ink all over the table. My opinion of her, as you can probably imagine, is not very high."

Henry's face fell. "Oh."

"Were you hoping for someone with a better reputation?"

"I suppose so."

"Fat chance of that happening here, I'm afraid." Georgie dried a dish with a threadbare towel before stacking them in the open cupboard. "You'd be best off if you never had to speak to her at all, in fact."

"I'd hoped for someone a bit more reasonable than Lawrence Tripp, in fact. The man is the bane of my existence. Refuses to listen to my findings, disregards scientific advice, and is quite possibly the most petulant person I've ever met."

"Not the first time I've heard that about him, I'm sorry to say."

"He cut off our access to the wire terminal! All I wanted was to contact someone back home, to request an extension of my assignment—"

Georgie's heart leapt. "An extension? For how long?"

"We were asking for at least a few more weeks, but I've not heard anything yet, unfortunately. I had to send the communication from the tower outside the city when we left on an observation expedition, hacked into the channels, but there was someone interfering with messages coming and going. Some kind of monitor."

"You hacked into the communications tower?" Georgie asked, equally impressed and incensed that Henry would put herself directly into harm's way like that. "That's so reckless! What if you'd been caught?"

"That's so cool!" Emeline shouted from the other side of the room.

"Don't listen to us!" Georgie yelled back. "And don't get any ideas, either!"

"Well, if I'd been caught, I suppose they'd have yanked our grant money and sent us home. And I didn't get caught, but I'm not sure the message got out, either." She drained the sink and wiped her hands on her dress, the pads of her fingers wrinkly. "I asked whoever was monitoring the channel to pass along a message to a friend in the security sciences department, but if it was a Coalition monitor, they may have been instructed by whoever the previous governor was—"

"Ralph Baker."

"Yes, Baker, to stop any unauthorized transmissions. It would make sense to do that, I guess."

"And what's the other possibility?"

"That it's rebels intercepting messages for information, for codes, anything they could possibly use to help their cause."

Georgie saw Emeline lean forward off the bed with interest at that, so she guided Henry to the door. "Let's talk outside."

CHAPTER NINE

"Outside? But surely that's—"

"It will be fine. Just keep your voice down." The door latched close behind them, the warped wooden stairs creaking with every step until they were standing under them, shielded from the light of the street lamp. "Why would the rebels be intercepting communications? To what end?" The last thing they all needed was another rebellion, another war to claim thousands of lives just for things to end up the same as they'd always been.

"Georgie, I don't know. I'm not part of those circles, this is just conjecture."

She sighed, resting a hand on Henry's hip. "I just worry about my mother and the girls."

Henry nodded. "I know." She reached up and brushed a stray hair from Georgie's face, tucking it neatly behind her ear. "They're good people, your family."

"Some of the best."

"I meant what I said about Lucy, you know."

"Don't fill her head with those kinds of ideas. We'll be lucky if she gets to be a janitor like me, instead of down in the factories. If we had the money to send the girls off-world, we'd have done it years ago. There's no future for them here, regardless of their grades."

"I'm sure I could help, maybe I could scrape up some scholarship money, or talk to some of my superiors in the Coalition Science Association, or—"

"We'll see." Georgie wanted all of that to be true, but she'd seen enough dreams die slow, painful deaths to know that it was impossible. No one from Skelm ever amounted to anything. It was an achievement just to live past forty. "I just don't want to get their hopes up."

"I should go," Henry said, lingering. "I just wish you could come with me."

Georgie wished she could go anywhere and everywhere with Henry. She wished that things were different. "I know." She kissed Henry, savoring the sweet taste of her lips, and climbed the stairs back to her apartment.

CHAPTER TEN

"*You're dismissed from your position.*"

Governor Allemande's words still rang in her ears, even hours later, as Henry wandered aimlessly through the streets of Skelm. Mr. Tripp had apparently reported her covert wire transmission to their new head of command, the ass-kissing bastard. According to her, disrupting the chain of command regardless of the reason was unforgivable, the telltale sign of a troublemaker, and she wasn't interested in having any troublemakers in her settlement. Roger, while not the one who had sent the wire, was also implicated, and fired unceremoniously just minutes later. He'd taken off straight back to the hotel to clear his apartment and try to secure them a transport back home.

There'd be no more grant money after this, no funding to research the storms here or anywhere else. They'd both be pariahs in the science community, with no careers, no access to equipment, and nothing more than whatever clout her family name still held. She'd have to move back in with them, now that her housing stipend had been stripped bare. It was a waking nightmare, and she couldn't even tell Georgie until later. Not that it would matter. She'd be on the first transport out of Skelm in the morning.

The governor didn't care about Henry's findings about the storms, either. She said she'd already been informed of the heightened storms, and they'd be dealt with by Henry's successors. The immediacy of the danger was lost on her, or so it seemed, almost as though she knew something that Henry and Roger didn't. As governor, perhaps she did, and all of this was nothing more than a colossal waste of time, and a self-destructive plan from the start.

She had nothing now - no career, no research, no prospects for a better future, and by this time tomorrow she'll have said goodbye to Georgie, too. With no more funding money, she'd have to pay her own way back to Gamma-3, and that would all but bankrupt her. She couldn't pay for Georgie and her family, too. The thought of leaving her behind made her feel like her heart was being squeezed in an industrial strength vise. She hadn't eaten anything all day, but her appetite was nowhere to be found.

With her lab key yanked away by the military police officer who escorted her from the Administration building, she couldn't return to perform further analysis. To do so would be trespassing, a risky move that would almost certainly land her in a work camp filing paperwork for six months or more. She was glad that she had at least thought to stash her notes and the tape readings from the balloon in her briefcase when they came to tell her that the governor was requesting an immediate audience.

"Henry!" Roger shouted from the end of the road, dragging his luggage and hers behind him, the edges of the leather scraped from the cobblestones. "Henry, thank the gods I've found you."

"What's wrong? Why are you dragging all our things through the city?"

"They've canceled our accommodation for this evening, said now that we're no longer employed by the CSA, they aren't obligated to pay for our rooms."

"Damn it!" Henry took her bags from him, trying to hold them and her briefcase at the same time. "Can't we just pay them out of pocket for tonight?"

He shook his head. "They've already been booked."

"So what now?"

"I nabbed us the last two seats on the last transport out of the city tonight, and there's a connection from the station hub back to Gamma-3 late tomorrow."

"Well, I guess that's that, isn't it?"

"I guess it is."

She sat on the crumbling brick curb and buried her head in her hands. "Rog, I'm so sorry. If it wasn't for me, you'd still have a job and some prospects."

"If it wasn't for you, I'd be a grunt in a lab processing samples all day like a droid. You know I've always needed you as my lab partner."

"I just don't understand how they can disregard our research. It's not as though they have months or even weeks to debate this, if those storms keep approaching at the current rate, everyone is going to be dead within ten days or so."

"Maybe once we get back to Gamma-3, we can release our findings, hope that a journalist picks them up and puts pressure on the government."

"That would take too long. We won't even be back on Gamma-3 in ten days." She sighed and rubbed at her temples. "Not to mention, all the journalists with jobs are no doubt employed by the same kinds of people who are trying to silence us."

"How about getting a message to Jhaveri some other way? Send some code to a family member, or a friend?"

"Our wire access has been blocked, remember? Even if I managed to convince them that I wasn't trying to contact the CSA, which I would be, they'd rip that message apart and censor anything suspicious. Besides, I don't think we can count on Allemande letting us back into the building."

"So what then, we just... give up?"

Henry shot him a look. "Of course we're not going to godsdamn give up, have you met me? No, we're going to get out beyond the barrier again and try to flesh out our research. Allemande can't ignore us forever, her life would be on the line here, too."

"And how, pray tell, are you going to achieve that, Miss Weaver?"

She stood and dusted off her skirts with a smirk. "We're going to steal us a monorail."

* * *

CHAPTER TEN

Henry hesitated at the Paynes' door, her fist poised to knock on the rotting wood, covered over with layers of peeling white paint. To her surprise, the door opened.

"Henrietta!" Georgie's mother said, leaning against the door frame. "What are you doing here? What's wrong? Is Georgina alright?"

"Mrs. Payne, I'm so sorry for the intrusion. Georgie is just fine, I caught a glimpse of her in the halls before her shift started this morning. I'm afraid I need to ask for quite a substantial favor." With nowhere else to go, or stash their luggage, Henry was out of options. If they were going to try to repeat their experiment, she was going to need some help.

"Anything, darlin', why don't you come in?"

"Actually, I have my lab partner with me, Roger, he's a nice fellow, and—"

"Why didn't you say so? Come on now, pile in, I'll put on a pot of coffee. Cream? Sugar?"

"Black for me, thanks," Henry replied, waving at Roger, who was waiting near the street with their things. "Rog! Come on!"

"So what's got you all in a tizzy? What happened?"

Henry was wary of telling her the whole story for fear of implicating her in what she was about to do. "We had a small mix up with our accommodations, they booked the rooms right out from under us, would you believe that?"

"That's just terrible. Where will you stay?"

"Oh, don't worry about us, Mrs. Payne, we'll manage. But if we could just have somewhere to go over our notes before our expedition, we'd be incredibly grateful."

"Y'all can just spread out over the table here," Mrs. Payne said, setting down a chipped enamel mug brimming with piping hot weak coffee just as Roger dragged the last piece of luggage through the door. "Though - don't y'all have a lab you can work in?"

"Would you believe they gave our lab to the new team who rotated in from Gamma-3 last night?"

"Almost like they forgot you were even here! You're welcome to stay here as long as you need." Mrs. Payne looked over her shoulder at Roger. "Coffee?"

"None for me, thanks," he said, wheezing from the effort of dragging their things up the stairs. "But I'd love a glass of water."

"I'll have to boil some for you first, but that's no problem."

Henry and Roger exchanged a concerned look. "Mrs. Payne, why do you have to boil your water first?" Henry asked. "Surely everywhere in the city is all piped in together?"

"Oh, no, not for years," she replied, shaking her head. "The Administration building and a few other locations get water piped in from the big reservoir tank down by the docks. The apartment blocks here and the tenements rely on recycled factory runoff. Boiling is safer, you never know what they're doing down there."

"Gods," Roger breathed.

"We do alright. I'll just put some on for you, and if y'all don't mind, I might need to rest a spell on the sofa."

"Please do, we'll be alright here," Henry assured her. "Thank you so much for opening your home to us."

Mrs. Payne waved them off. "It's no trouble. Take your time. Don't mind me, I'm hard of hearing, anyway."

"Henry, you know this idea is crazy, right?" Roger asked in a hushed voice, spreading his notes over the table. "Even if we manage to break into the building, the odds of us hijacking the monorail without detection are zilch."

"We just need to get out there and launch the balloon. Once we confirm our hypothesis about the storm strikes, Allemande will have to listen to us. She'd be risking her own life too if she continued to ignore us, and I have the feeling that woman has a very keen sense of self-preservation."

"And what if she's a step ahead of us? What then? We'll have committed treason by way of trespass, and we're already in hot water. We can't hide out in this city for long, it's too small, and we'd stand out too much."

"I want to try getting a message to Jhanvi Jhaveri again. If nothing else she can let our superiors know what happened, tell them that Tripp blocked our wire privileges, that Allemande gave our lab away, ask for some mercy. The governor won't have much authority off-world."

Roger sighed and wrung his hands. "This all seems crazy."

"You can go home if you want, Rog. I wouldn't blame you one bit if you wanted to opt out of this plan. Take your things, get on that transport, and get as far away from here as you can. If we're right about the storms, Skelm might not be here much longer, anyway."

"What and miss all the fun?" He smirked. "No chance, Weaver."

"Besides, if we can get word back to the CSA about what's happening here, maybe they could influence some kind of decision to get Allemande to stand down. Maybe we could even get our jobs back."

"Somehow I doubt the governor would want us in her city if we go over her head on this."

"I'm not afraid of her, are you?"

"I am, yes. From what I've heard about her, she's not to be trifled with."

Henry ignored his warning, shuffling through her notes and settling on the pages with the transcription from the weather balloon. "If our calculations are correct, the next storm movement should occur near sunset."

"Is it smart to be out there that close to dark, that far away from the city?"

"Probably not, no."

"Never a dull moment with you, is it?"

"You know what you signed up for, Beauregard," Henry laughed.

The door burst open to reveal Georgie, distraught and frantic, stray hairs stuck to her tear-stained cheeks. "Ma! Ma, I don't know what to do, I can't find Henry and her lab is empty, I'm afraid something terrible happened to her!"

Henry ran to her and threw her arms around her, burying her face in the worn orange coveralls. "I'm so sorry, Georgie, they escorted me from the building, and—"

"They *what?*"

"Allemande dismissed me, fired us rather, and we had nowhere else to go, and I couldn't risk not seeing you again, couldn't risk our research being buried, I'm so sorry I came here, I didn't know where else to turn!"

"It's alright," Georgie said, tightening her embrace. "I was worried you'd left without saying goodbye."

Henry relaxed into her arms. "I would never."

"Weaver, the storm," Roger reminded her. "We don't have time to spare."

"Right," she said, succumbing to the pull of the emergency at hand. "Georgie, there's something wrong. The storms beyond the barrier, they're moving, getting closer and closer to the terraformers. If one gets struck—"

"Then we're all dead," Georgie finished. "Did you tell anyone?"

"Of course I told someone! I told Tripp, but he blocked our wire access and cut our funding. The next thing I know, Roger and I are being fired by Allemande and thrown out of our apartments."

"So what are you going to do?"

As much as she loathed the idea of putting Georgie in danger, Henry knew that she desperately needed her help. She had keys for every room in the building, access to the janitorial shafts and the monorail maintenance station. "We have to get out beyond the barrier to fly the balloon again, and we need to try to send another message to the CSA."

"And how do you intend on doing that? Without access to the Administration building, it's going to be a challenge to get out there, and it would take you days. There must be another way."

Henry and Roger exchanged a look. "Well, actually, we were thinking we could steal the monorail. Borrow, actually, just for a few hours to confirm our findings, and—"

"Have you lost your marbles?" Georgie asked, laughing. "There's no way you wouldn't be detected, and they'll throw you straight into a work camp."

"We were hoping you could help us with that," Roger said, sipping his boiled water, still steaming. "If we could get access to the areas we need without forcing our way in, we might have a better chance of pulling this off."

"No. Absolutely not," Georgie said, turning to bolt the door. "And keep your voice down, will you? The people around here will turn you in for a crust of bread."

"Georgie please, we don't have any other options!" Henry pleaded. "Trust me, if there was any other option, any at all, I would take it in a heartbeat."

She took Georgie's hands and pulled her close. "We have to get a message out. Allemande won't listen."

"What makes you think that the CSA isn't in on this?" Georgie challenged. "For all you know, this Jhaveri woman did get your message and didn't respond because they already know the storms are moving closer. Maybe that's the whole point."

Henry pulled back. "That doesn't make any sense. Why would they do that?"

"You Gammas don't know what it's like out here," Mrs. Payne piped in. "They work us like dogs until we're dead, and the ones lucky enough to live to old age get put into mandatory studies, given experimental drugs. We're no more than guinea pigs to them. There's no hope, no opportunity for people like us in Skelm. We've seen them allow workers to become poisoned by the materials they're forced to work with and hide the evidence behind locked doors. We're all just waiting to die."

"Ma—"

"No, Georgina. Your pop died doing what he thought was right for our family. Now I'm sorry what it's done to you, and to the girls, and how things have ended up for us, but he wasn't the kind of man to take things lying down." She stared and pushed herself into a standing position. "I know you aren't either, Sugar."

"Ma, this is crazy. It could get us all killed."

"Georgina, if you don't help them, there's a chance we all wind up dead. You know as well as I do that they could evacuate the Administration building onto transports in less than an hour once the terraformers go down, and they wouldn't be coming back for the rest of us."

Georgie sighed and pulled away. "And what are you going to do if you can't get a message through to the CSA?"

"We learn as much as we can, and we show our findings to anyone who will listen," Henry said, peering at her notes. "Tripp and Allemande won't listen, but maybe others in the science department might."

"And get thrown in prison for trespassing, or worse, treason. It's not like the Coalition even sees a clear delineation between the two nowadays."

"So what then, we just do nothing? We wait and hope nothing bad happens? I leave on that transport tonight and hope I can claw my job back by grovelling at the Coalition Science Association?" Henry felt the anger and indignation spark in her chest.

Georgie sighed angrily, adding a frustrated growl for good measure. "If we're going, we need to go now. We don't want to end up out there after dark, we'd never find our way back to the monorail." She pulled the heavy ring of keys from her pocket, giving them a gentle jangle. "Aren't you lucky you met a janitor?"

CHAPTER ELEVEN

The large brass key slid into the lock, and all three of them held their breath as the deadbolt clicked open. It had been easy to get into the building, given no one else knew Henry and Roger had been dismissed, and so were expected, welcomed faces in the atrium and the halls. Georgie knew that she was faceless as always, one of the working masses in orange that most never paid attention to. It was the next best thing to being invisible.

Light flooded from the green cast hallway into the monorail maintenance station, illuminating the bright silver of the vehicle and the purple and yellow Coalition logo emblazoned on its side. She closed the door behind them and flipped the lock into position. At this time of day, they should be left alone, at least until they fired it up.

"Rog, have you got the balloon?"

"Yes, of course I have it, not much point to all this if I didn't," he grumbled, pulling it from its box that he'd been carrying. "What will we do if the military police comes to arrest us before it descends?"

"Surrender," Georgie interjected, still angry that she'd agreed to this at all. Her life and the life of her family were gravely in danger, and for what? Some kind of fancy futuristic weather controlling device? It was foolish, and reckless, and yet the thought of sending Henry off without her help was even more terrifying. So she stood, staring at the crown of Skelm's engineering achievement, preparing to commandeer it so they could study some kind of storm. "You'd never make it back to the city without the monorail, it's over two hundred kilometers of uneven rocks. You'd be better off in a work camp than starving to death in the cold outside the barrier."

"Cheery," Roger griped. "I love a bit of optimism, me."

"Not much optimism on this hellscape of a rock," Georgie replied. "Hope will get you killed out here."

The monorail eased forward towards the hangar entrance, smooth and silky on the track. A technical marvel, and easily operable by anyone who could push a lever forward or backward. "Hang on to your seats," Georgie warned as they approached the exit. "Once we're out of here, the alarm will sound. Our advantage is in the sheer speed of this thing, we'll have some time before they can catch up to us."

"What about getting back?" Roger asked, clutching the balloon. "Won't they apprehend us at the hangar?"

Georgie smirked, even as fear flooded into her shoulders. "Let's hope not. If we're lucky they'll assume we're just a bunch of kids joyriding, and not, you know, two scientists and a janitor bent on undermining the authority of the new governor, who we've heard is a bit of a sadist."

"Right then," Henry said, grasping the pole for balance as they picked up speed.

Roger nodded. "Right," he echoed.

Georgie hadn't been on the monorail in years, in fact, not since its completion. They'd taken a team of janitors out to the building site to pack up the engineers' things and clean up before all their makeshift buildings were demolished. It had taken Skelm thirty years, but they completed their monorail, which spanned from the city all the way out to the barrier. Someday, it would be used as mass transit when the city expanded - at least, that's what they'd said. Even as the city grew in population, there had been no sign of additional housing being built, or public schools for the children to attend. Any education here was paid out of pocket at a high price.

The landscape whipped by the long, blue tinted windows, so fast that the mountain ranges were no more than a blur as they passed. No one had radioed in to ask who they were or why the monorail was in use, which she could only assume was a good sign. Maybe this risky mission would

CHAPTER ELEVEN

go better than she'd hoped. Perhaps even the engineering staff were too busy with their tracking cards to make their usual rounds in the building, checking transport points for malfunctions as they normally would.

The vehicle was whisper smooth, shooting them out towards the barrier faster than any steamcar ever could. Powered by the large substations along the track, it zipped along without a hitch, and Georgie tried to convince herself to relax, despite her restless hands. Without a word, Henry laced her fingers with Georgie's, giving her a little squeeze.

"Well, we're here," Henry said, snapping her helmet into the suit. "Let's get started."

Georgie nodded and snapped her own helmet on, clicking into her orange atmospheric gear. Even out here at the barrier, janitors had to be identified as such. "What can I do to help?"

"I'm fine to set off the balloon myself," Roger said, dragging them off the monorail. "Head to the communications tower with Henry, see if you can get through whatever blockade they've got intercepting transmissions. If we're lucky, we can get a message to Jhanvi Jhaveri in security sciences, give the CSA a heads up on our situation here." He bent to tighten his boot laces, tucking the balloon under his arm. "She's a good egg. She'll know what to do."

"Don't be late," Georgie cautioned, gesturing at the dwindling light from the far off mirrors above the city. "Make sure we're all back here before dark. Assuming we haven't all been arrested by then, that is." She said the last part with a hint of a smirk, painted on over worry and the building panic in her chest. As far as they knew, no alarm had sounded, but the military police could be on their steam bikes right now, on their way to take them all in for treason.

*　*　*

"So, this communication tower," Georgie said, passing Henry a pair of small pliers. "The engineers know you were messing with it last time?"

Henry shrugged. "They told me not to."

Georgie shook her head in amazement. Things were different for those higher on the Coalition ladder, even scientists who had to fight for their research to be funded. Breaking a law for her would mean immediate expulsion from any Coalition funded work, and would land her and her family on the street. No charity in Skelm, only back-breaking, body-destroying work. "Get a move on, we won't have light much longer and it's a twenty-minute hike back to the monorail."

"Alright alright, just give me a few more seconds. I've almost got it."

"How'd you learn all this, anyway? I thought you were a meteorologist."

"This is very rudimentary, to be honest, I'm only clipping into the main array. If anyone wanted to tap into the frequency, they'd hear me."

"And you're not worried you'll be found out?"

"The safety of the city is more important than my career. Besides, if I'm right about what's going on, the CSA will back us up, and reinstate our jobs here."

"And if they don't?"

Henry leaned against the structure, the glass of her helmet tapping against the metal. "Then we have bigger problems here than my job." She returned to the panel, twisting wires around each other until the radio in their helmets began to emit loud static. "Almost there."

The sound cleared, leaving what Georgie was hoping was an open line for Henry to send a message with. The absence of any alarm on the monorail lodged tension between her shoulder blades, wondering what it could mean.

"Testing, testing," Henry said, squinting at the panel. "This is lab technician Henrietta Weaver looking for an open line to the CSA on Gamma-3. Does anyone read me? Over."

The silence was suffocating.

"Radial satellite, do you read me?" Henry gave the wires another twist. "Radial satellite, this is an emergency, repeat, an emergency. We are requesting an SOS to be sent to the CSA on Gamma-3, immediate action needed, over."

"Go ahead, Skelm technician Weaver," a familiar voice said. "We are standing by for your SOS."

CHAPTER ELEVEN

"Please confirm, is this the radial satellite array?"

The line crackled with static. "Cannot confirm. Skelm technician, please relay your SOS."

"Identify your position; SOS is of utmost confidentiality."

"Cannot confirm," the voice repeated. "We are here to help. Relay your message, Skelm technician Weaver."

Henry looked at Georgie, uncertainty on her face. "What should I do?" she mouthed.

Georgie shrugged. "Ask again?" she mouthed back.

"This is Skelm technician Weaver requesting ID from contact, please identify. Emergency SOS direct to CSA transfer desk, over."

"Cannot confirm identity," the voice said. "Please relay SOS and we will pass it on."

"Oh, for fuck's sake," Georgie said, loud enough for Henry's microphone to pick it up. "We don't have any time to waste here!"

"...Payne? Georgie Payne?"

Her breath caught in her throat. There was a reason the voice was familiar, even encased in waves of static on the makeshift line. "Evie? Anderson?"

"Oh my gods, we've spent weeks trying to reach you! We've been monitoring every communication that comes and goes from Skelm trying to get into contact!"

"I'm sorry, do you know each other?" Henry asked, wires trailing from her pressurized suit to the panel.

Georgie laughed, tears springing to her eyes. Maybe they were saved after all. "I helped them, I—" she stopped short, remembering what Henry said about the open line. Anyone could be hearing this, and if they were, she'd be executed on the public broadcast for treason. "Unidentified contact, be advised this is an open line, over."

A moment of silence passed, and the line buzzed. "We understand. Please relay your SOS."

"Please contact Jhanvi Jhaveri at the security services desk, we are requesting immediate action. The city is in danger of total destruction, I repeat, a total loss of life if action is not taken."

"Shit," Evie Anderson said. "We will relay. Be advised your previous message went unanswered, over."

"Godsdamnit," Henry shouted. "Unidentified contact, we repeat, total loss of life. Can you help us?"

"Stand by for confirmation."

"Gods, Georgie, who the hell are these people?" Henry asked, muting her microphone with the button on her suit control panel. "Rebels? Insurgents? Coalition spies?"

Georgie shook her head. "Pirates."

"Pirates don't get involved with political affairs."

"These ones do."

"Are you sure about them?"

"I smuggled one out in a trash bin a couple months ago, the same day as the boiler explosion at the Administration building, the same day Ralph Baker died in his office."

"Aren't you the dark horse?" Henry asked, raising an eyebrow. "You're all responsibility and distancing yourself from active rebel cells, all the while you're blowing up buildings and assisting pirate escapes."

"I didn't blow up the building." Georgie craned her neck to check the light. "It was just a boiler. I didn't think it would blast every single window in the place, that was just an added bonus." She'd never felt more alive than when she was helping the janitorial crew to replace each and every window in the Administration building. A rousing success. "Henry, we don't have long, the light is fading fast."

Henry removed the mute, gently lifting the wires. "Unidentified contact, please respond. We are losing the light beyond the barrier, over."

"We hear you loud and clear, Skelm technician, please stand by for confirmation."

"How long does it take to decide if they'll help us or not?" Georgie muttered. "If we get stuck out here, we're dead anyway." At this rate, they'd barely have enough time to replace the wiring and run back to the monorail, and running in these pressurized suits was near impossible.

"Standing by," Henry confirmed, shifting her weight from foot to foot.

CHAPTER ELEVEN

"Skelm technician Weaver, you are confirmed for assistance. We have identified multiple recipients for your SOS, which has been received. Be advised that this line cannot be used again, as precautions are highly recommended. Stay safe. Keep alert. Over and out."

As soon as the line disconnected, Henry ripped the wires from her suit and began splicing them back into the panel. "I hope you're ready to run, Payne," she said, slamming the panel door shut. "If we aren't back at that monorail, we'll never find it in this darkness." Thunder cracked overhead, and she winced. "And that storm is going to be gunning for us."

Georgie nodded. "I'm ready."

They ran as fast as their pressurized suits would allow, their boots heavy and clunky against the uneven, rocky ground. What little light they'd had was fading fast, disappearing into the darkness as the mirrors over the city rotated inward.

"Almost there," Georgie wheezed, the monorail in sight. The bright silver metal had already begun to disappear into the black. Still, they'd made it back in time, and even though the lack of military police on their tails was troubling, she couldn't help but feel relieved as she stepped through the atmospheric barrier and unclipped her helmet.

"Rog, we're back!" Henry shouted into the monorail carriage. When there was no response, she stepped inside and shouted his name again. "Come on, Beauregard, this isn't funny!"

"Shit," Georgie muttered under her breath. She should have known it was much too early to be celebrating their success. Roger was out there somewhere, and every last ray of light had been swallowed up.

"Georgie, he's not here!" Henry shouted, panic lacing her voice. "He's not here, we have to get him back! What if we turn on the tunnel beams?" She reached for the control panel, but Georgie stopped her.

"Those beams aren't strong enough to penetrate the dark, and if they were, you'd risk us getting found out. No monorails are supposed to be out this far at night." She put her helmet back on and stepped backwards out of the carriage. "Stay here. I'm going out to look for him. How far do the in-suit radios transmit?"

"A couple miles at best, in this terrain."

"Good. I'll be back."

"Georgie, no, let me come with you!"

"No." She squinted into the darkness, a certainty that this could be what killed her. "One of us has to stay behind, to keep the monorail engine warm for us. And it's been a while, but I've been out here before, more than you, remember? I know the terrain." This, too, was a lie - she'd only experienced being out past the monorail for the cleanup efforts, and that had been once, and in broad daylight.

"Please be careful," Henry said, tears welling in her eyes. "I don't know what I'd do if I lost both of you."

"You'd better get back to the city in that case," Georgie scolded gently. "I mean it. If I'm not back in an hour, you need to leave. Someone will notice the monorail is missing, if they haven't already."

"And what if they have?"

"Lie. Say you were abducted, forced onto the monorail by rebels. You'll come up with something."

"Georgie, I—"

"I have to go. I'll be back. Keep the channel free in case he tries to get in touch."

She stepped away from the monorail, and already the minimal light from inside the carriage was all but invisible. She inched forward toward the barrier, and though the lights on her suit were on full beams, they did nothing to penetrate the darkness. She wished she'd thought to bring rope, though in the quickly approaching storm she doubted it would do much, anyway. The winds beyond the barrier were deadly strong.

Straight out and straight back, she thought to herself. As long as she didn't turn or adjust her position, she should be able to find her way back. She stepped over the terraformed threshold and static buzzed over her radio.

"Roger? Are you there?" she called.

"Oh gods, please help me," he replied, his voice choked with panic. "The balloon got stuck on a ledge, and I climbed up to get it. By the time I got down, I couldn't see a damn thing."

CHAPTER ELEVEN

"Are you still at the launch site?"

Static buzzed through her helmet. "...yes."

She breathed a sigh of relief. The launch site was a straight shot from the terminal monorail station, directly through the boundary. "Stay there, I'm coming to get you."

"...No. The storm... stronger. Can't..." the static swallowed his voice, and the radio channel went dead.

Lightning flashed overhead, and struck about half a mile away. Despite the lack of military police, luck was not on their side. She could only hope that he would follow her instructions and stay put for her to retrieve him. Her pace was painstakingly slow, the unexpected rocks causing her to stumble every other step. Acid rain began to fall, sizzling into the surrounding ground into the permanently parched earth, despite the frequent storms.

"Roger, if you can hear me," she said, her voice calm and smooth, even as her own heart pounded in her chest, "don't go anywhere. I'm coming to get you. We have a plan, but you have to stay put." She tripped over another rock and sprawled out, careful to fall in a forward direction. Losing her sense of where the monorail was would get them both killed, and leave Henry to get picked up by the authorities. "I'm almost there, just stay calm."

In fact, she didn't know where she was in relation to the launch site. All she knew was that she'd been walking for approximately fifteen minutes, the normal amount of time to get from the station to the cliffs, but her pace was slowed and clumsy. Lightning stuck off to her left, a blinding flash of light that was gone in an instant. Still, it was enough to know that her estimates weren't too far off. She pressed on, saying encouraging things to the static in her helmet that was just as much for her own peace of mind as Roger's.

"Almost there."

The storm was behind her now, moving closer to the monorail. If lightning struck the tracks, Henry would be trapped, if not dead. The thought gave Georgie a surge of energy that dulled the ache in her tired legs, and she pressed on, her arms held out in front of her like a child playing a dangerous game.

"Roger, are you there? I'm close now, but I need you to help me."

Static.

Her eyes were wide, searching for any faint gasp of light to help her find her way. Each time the lightning flashed, it lit up the cliffs for the briefest of moments. She was almost there, but still no sign of Roger. What if the silly fool had tried to find his own way back to the monorail in the dark? He could be anywhere, his body hidden in a shallow ravine, or behind a rock formation, or splayed out flat across the earth somewhere in the hundreds of miles of terrain out here. They'd never find him before he froze to death.

Though the light had only been gone for a short while, Georgie could already feel the cold biting through her pressure suit. It wouldn't be long before the temperature was well below freezing, and even she would have to turn back or risk frostbite and losing the feeling in her extremities. She flexed her fingers out, and then curled them into a fist, willing the circulation to keep her warm.

"Roger, you've gotta help me out here, where are you?"

No response.

Now at the cliffs, she felt her way around the jagged rocks, terrified that any pivot in her position would cause her to lose her way. Her gloved hands snagged on something metal, and she grasped and pulled. Part of the weather balloon, the data box from the inside. She strapped it to her waist and kept moving. "Henry, I found the data. How is that storm looking?"

Nothing but static filled her helmet. The electrical storm was interfering with their radios, and now she had no way of talking to either of them. Careful to keep her back to where she'd come from, she picked her way over sharp rocks that jutted up out of the ground like razor blades lying in wait to puncture a pressure suit. She wouldn't die immediately, but she would definitely die. There wasn't enough breathable air out here past the barrier. Her foot caught on something soft.

"Roger? Roger!" she shouted, pressing gently on his sternum to bring him around. It was something she'd seen her mother do when the worker across from her collapsed at the factory. If they could be brought back to consciousness, they could go back to work. The only other option was to be fired - or end up incinerated, their long-dead corpses without a grave.

"Roger, wake up! We have to get back to the monorail, I need you to help me."

The man wouldn't come to. Lightning flashed and the brief glare on his helmet was interrupted by the deep cracks looking like a spiderweb across the glass. His suit had been compromised, and she didn't know for how long. It was likely he wouldn't regain consciousness until she could get him some oxygen, and that's if he didn't sustain a head injury, too.

"Henry, I've found him!" she shouted into the thick static. "If you can hear me, I'm going to bring him back! Wait for me please!" She was unlikely to make it back to the monorail in time, before she'd told Henry to leave without her. The storm was speeding towards the track, and she had to drag Roger back with her. She knew they'd never make it.

Roger was heavy and limp, and she struggled to clasp his hands around her shoulders, securing them with some copper wiring she'd brought along in case the communications panel needed it. She'd need her hands free to grope through the darkness if they were ever going to make it back alive. With every flash of lightning, she took another step, her eyes fixed on the horizon, praying to all the dead gods that she'd see the silhouette of the monorail in the distance.

"Henry," she said, breathless with the effort of carrying Roger, "I'm coming. Don't give up on me. I'm almost there." She said it more to reassure herself than assume she'd be heard through the impenetrable wall of static that pounded through the speakers inside her helmet. Her thighs burned with every step, the muscles in her back stiff. Roger was a tall man, at least a head taller than Georgie, and so his feet dragged behind him. If he ever woke up, he was going to be mighty sore.

The storm had slowed, lingering at the barrier. She wiped the rivulets of acid rain from her helmet, but only succeeded in smearing the water and further obstructing her vision. The constant, rolling thunder seemed to vibrate up from the ground, a deep, low growl of protest. She'd have to get through the storm to get to the monorail and weather the downpour of rain that was making the rocky earth slippery beneath her boots. Lightning flashed again, striking near the boundary, and forking out into the sky before sending down a dozen more bolts of electricity.

They'd never make it.

Roger's lifeless weight dragged on her, making her slow and cumbersome. She wouldn't be able to run, or dart through the rain, or dodge. If she fell, she'd never be able to get them both to safety. The storm grew in intensity, and the wind pushed against her as she approached.

"Henry," she said, her voice cracking from fear, "we're not gonna make it. Go. Go back to the city. Tell my mama that I tried. Make sure they're taken care of, please, I—"

"Don't be so dramatic, tell them yourself," said Henry's voice through the static, and Georgie felt a hand on her arm. "I'd never leave you alone, you daft woman. Come on, I'll get his legs. It's not so far to the monorail now."

"I told you to stay on the monorail!"

"Yes, and where would we be if I had listened? I'd be without a lab partner *and* the love of my life."

Georgie's breath caught in her throat, but there was no time to dwell on what Henry had just said. Any hesitation would likely get them killed. "Yeah, get his legs. This storm looks like it's hovering right near the barrier."

"If we're lucky, it will stay there. They've never come this close before, it's less than a kilometer from the terraformers. If it breaks through that barrier, the city is in real danger."

"His helmet is cracked through. Dunno how long he's been on low oxygen, and I can't see if he has a head injury."

"Let's go."

Georgie immediately felt the weight lessen as Henry hoisted up Roger's legs, and they stumbled across the terrain together like a drunk pony, slipping and sliding across the rocks but somehow, miraculously, staying upright. Lightning cracked, and the monorail appeared against the blackness of the horizon, like a lighthouse amid waves, guiding them to safety.

"We're almost there!" Henry screamed, barely heard over the din of the

CHAPTER ELEVEN

storm and static in their helmets.

Rain pelted down on them so thick and fast that they could barely see more than vague shapes in every flash of light. They were so close now, almost to safety, they'd get Roger medical attention and everything would be okay. The storm would die down and Henry would get Tripp and Allemande to reconsider, saving the city from the encroaching storms that threatened the terraforming machines.

She lunged forward in determination to reach the monorail and watched as it exploded into flames when the lightning hit.

CHAPTER TWELVE

They both stumbled backward away from the blaze, tripping over Roger's unconscious body. The light from the flames danced off the glass of their helmets and illuminated Roger's face. A threatening purple bruise spread across his head from his temple down across his cheekbone, his head lolling in the helmet.

"Fuck," Henry whispered. "What now?"

"We have to get back to the city," Georgie said. "If we follow the tracks—"

"It's fifty miles back to the city! It would take days to get back, we'll never make it!" Their pressure suits were quickly losing their moderate insulating properties to the soaking rain and icy wind. If thirst didn't kill them, the cold would, and Georgie knew it.

"We have to try!"

"Shouldn't we just wait for the maintenance crews here? Surely they'll send someone at first light, if we can just survive the night we can hitch a ride back with them!"

"And what, get thrown into a work camp for treason?"

"Don't be ridiculous, Georgie, it's a minor work offense, and if I can just get word back to the CSA—"

"And what do you think they'll do with me? I'm not a fancy pants scientist like you, I'm just a fucking janitor!"

Henry stared, the fire reflected in her deep brown eyes. "A work camp isn't so bad, it's probably better than..." she trailed off.

"Better than what?" Georgie pressed. "Better than my job now? Do you seriously believe that?"

"Now isn't the time for this—"

"If we stay, they're going to throw me into an interrogation cell. I've seen it happen, and those folks never come back. They're burned, beaten, tormented for weeks by the sick, twisted interrogators, and then they're shipped off to a work camp where they'll cart around toxic crap for the rest of their short lives. Is that what you want for me?"

"No, of course not, I—"

"People like you get a desk job as punishment. People like me wind up fucking dead." She shifted Roger's weight to her other shoulder and stared down the track through the flames that engulfed the charred monorail. There was nothing anyone would be able to salvage from that mess, nothing more than scrap metal to be melted down and sent back to the factories.

"Alright, let's go then," Henry said quietly. "If we keep our pace up, we might not feel the cold so much."

Georgie just nodded. No matter how this ended, it was a death sentence for her. Being caught by the military police and dragged back to the city to be thrown into a cell, or ending up dead in a rocky ditch in the middle of nowhere, there was no way out that didn't end with her mother and sisters homeless. The thought seared into her gut and leached a poisonous fear into her blood that sank into every vein. "Once he wakes up, we might be able to make better time," she said, knowing full well there was a strong possibility that he would never wake up.

"Is following the tracks the best option?"

"I guess." They were going to die anyway, it was just making the choice of following the tracks and being discovered at first light, or laying down on the rocky ground to die when the thirst became too much. Her mouth already felt dry, and it had only been a couple of hours.

They skirted around the monorail, narrowly dodging debris that floated down from the track. The heat from the blast felt good, and the light was comforting, and Georgie wished they could just stay, and wait for morning, enjoying the last hours of freedom before her inevitable death sentence. As the warmth faded on her back, and they headed into the velvet black, she wished everything could be different. With each step, she imagined what life would have been like if her family had stayed on Gamma-3. Her father would still be alive. Her mother wouldn't have been ravaged by the factories. Her sisters wouldn't be worried about how much food they were eating, or wearing too-small shoes as long as they could, or getting top marks in their classes just to be a fucking janitor. Maybe she would have met Henry under different circumstances, maybe they'd have gotten married and had a few kids, maybe she was just living her own worst nightmare but couldn't wake up.

"Georgie?"

"Yeah?"

"We're not going to make it out of this, are we?"

"No." Georgie stopped, wiping the last droplets of rain from her helmet. Mercifully, the storm wasn't following them. The monorail was its only casualty, for now. "You should go back to the monorail. Take Roger. Like you said, if that message gets through to the CSA, you'll both be off the hook."

"And leave you out here alone? Absolutely not. Off the hook or no, they'll still put me on the first transport back to Gamma-3 and I won't be able to come back for you."

"It's stupid for all of us to die on my account."

"We might make it. We could still make it. Come on, the faster we get moving, the faster we get back to the city."

They must have walked for hours in silence, their boots scraping softly against the rock. There was nothing but darkness in front of them, and they were guided only by grasping the track's pillars every few steps. She was weak, hungry and thirsty, her muscles aching with Roger's weight. He still hadn't even stirred, though they knew he was still breathing. It was too dangerous to remove his helmet without knowing the extent of his head injury, and so long as he was breathing, he was still alive.

"How far do you think we've gone?" Henry asked, her voice hoarse and ragged from the clouds of dust kicked up from their boots.

CHAPTER TWELVE

"Hard to say. The track hasn't curved yet, so we're still closer to the terminal station than the halfway point." Georgie stopped and felt Henry stumble as a result. "I think we should go back. I'll turn myself in, this is crazy, I'm sorry."

Henry sat down, and leaned against one of the steel pillars that held up the track. "I don't think I'd make it. Roger definitely wouldn't. Maybe... maybe this is as far as we go."

Georgie unwound the wire around Roger's wrists and guided him gently to the ground. "We might have made it, if things were different." Now that they'd stopped moving, her teeth began to chatter with the pressing cold that sank into her bones.

"We tried," Henry said, reaching up for Georgie's hands. "At least now someone will see our bodies from the track, they'll find the data we collected. They can't ignore that."

"Mm," Georgie agreed, not having the heart to tell her that the newly minted Governor Allemande most certainly would not be allowing a scandal during her first week in office. Rather, she'd send their bodies to the incinerator, wipe their names from history. She'd claim that Henry and Roger had boarded that transport, and run away for the shame of their dismissal. She wouldn't even have to explain Georgie's disappearance. Janitors were a dime a dozen, and no one other than her family would care. Her heart ached a slow throb in her chest at the thought of what would happen to her mother and sisters now that she wouldn't be there to protect them.

"Georgina?"

"Yeah?"

"I'm glad I met you."

"Me too." She felt the cold settle beneath her skin, and she sat next to Henry to wrap her arms around her. She felt tired. She knew they wouldn't last much longer. The temperature was dropping by the minute.

"Georgie?"

"Yeah?"

"I love you."

The steel creaked in the wind, an eerie, ghostly sound. "Yeah. I love you too."

She pulled Henry in closer, their bodies sharing what little heat there was left. Georgie kissed her, their lips chapped and dry from dehydration, accelerated by the arid climate this far from the city. She closed her eyes, no longer desperate to see, resigned to what fate had planned for them. Wind bit at her ears and nose, and she let herself feel the pain. She knew there wouldn't be much to feel for much longer. The wind picked up and seemed to grow warmer, a glow leaching through her eyelids. It was the end.

"Hey, Georgie Payne," a voice said, "I heard you needed a pick up."

CHAPTER THIRTEEN

Georgie's eyes flew open, and she stared, open-mouthed. An entire ship had landed just a short distance away. A hallucination.

"Well come on, we don't have all night!"

"Who are you?" Henry asked, shielding her eyes against the bright light flooding from the ship's loading bay.

If Henry saw it, too, then it wasn't a dream. "Oh my gods," Georgie breathed. "Evie Anderson." She never expected that she would come back as she had promised, but there she was, stood on the ship's ramp, the shock of blue hair on her head almost luminescent with the light from the ship.

"In the flesh. Now let's get going, you look a little rough." Evie reached for a radio on her belt. "Hyun, looks like we've got an unconscious male with a head injury, can you send Jasper with the stretcher?"

"On it," the radio crackled, and in seconds a muscled man with close cropped hair and a tall woman with long silver braids appeared in the doorway. *The Cricket* was emblazoned on the side of the ship, illuminated by the woman's kinetic flashlight as she swung it around to secure it to her belt. They jogged to the pillar, rolled Roger onto the stretcher, and carried him inside.

"Are you alright?" Evie asked, her brow furrowed.

Georgie threw her arms around the woman. "You came back for me," she sobbed.

"I'm not one to welch on a deal, Ms. Payne," Evie said with a wide grin.

"I told you we'd send help, you're lucky we were in the area, you could have died out there! We've got to go, though; our cloaking device is drawing too much power to stick around."

Henry cleared her throat.

"Oh, Evie, this is Ms. Henrietta Weaver, she's a scientist."

"Henry."

"Nice to put a face to a name, Henry, but we have to go. *Now*."

Georgie felt her limbs start to defrost the moment she stepped foot on the Cricket, and she squeezed Henry in a tight embrace as the loading bay doors sealed. "We made it," she whispered. "We actually made it."

"And who is this?" a short woman with the air of ultimate authority asked, gesturing at Henry. "You said we were picking up one, not three, Anderson."

"I couldn't just leave them there to die," Evie argued as Roger and the stretcher disappeared through the crew's airlock onto the ship. "This is the scientist who hacked into that comms tower. Without her, we'd never have found Georgie."

The woman massaged the bridge of her nose in frustration. "We don't have time to waste, we're burning too hot as it is with those cloaking shields on full. We'll drop them off at the nearest beacon."

"Captain Violet, please, maybe they could be of use? After all, this one's a scientist!"

"We have plenty of scientists on this damned ship already," a woman in a black cloak grumbled, pulling a small gun with a snub nose from her deep pockets. "Hold out your arms," she instructed, and grabbed at Henry's wrist, pressing the little gun into her arm with a pop.

"Uh—" Henry started, but the woman snatched at Georgie's arm next.

"It's to deactivate your Coalition tracking chips. We can't have them realizing you're escaping onto a pirate vessel now, can we?"

Georgie snatched her arm back. "Wait!"

"We don't have time for that, give me your arm!"

"How will I get back into the Administration building for my shift without a functioning chip? It's not as though I can pretend it was deactivated on accident, I've been nowhere near a recorded electromagnetic pulse."

CHAPTER THIRTEEN

"Why in all the gods' names would you want to go back?" Evie laughed. "We just rescued you! You're free!"

"The deal was to get my family out of here, not just me!"

"Of course," the captain muttered. "Anderson, what the hell?"

Evie gave the captain a sheepish smile. "She's not wrong, I did promise that."

"The hell am I supposed to do, just casually set down in the godsdamn Skelm port and wait until we can get her whole family on board?"

"Wouldn't be the first time you were in the Skelm port," Georgie challenged.

"Yeah, and if you remember correctly, we nearly got blasted out of the sky last time. That's why I agreed to stay in the area after Evie intercepted Ms. Weaver's initial distress call, because you saved two of my crew, and we owed you one." The captain sighed with resignation. "You saved two of my crew. I owe you one."

"If I may?" Henry interjected, wobbling slightly on her feet. "We may have uncovered a significant meteorological anomaly occurring here at the edges of the settlement, something none of our predictive analysis has indicated. If Georgie can get back into that building, maybe she can get the data to Allemande, or—"

"Allemande?" Evie uttered, recoiling. "No. She isn't dead?"

"Governor Allemande now," Georgie said. "Seems no one else wanted that shit job, and she was just the kind of power-hungry manager to take it on."

"Gods," Evie breathed, rubbing her arms. "Governor. Funny how the power always ends up with the ones who will abuse it the most."

Captain Violet nodded. "Indeed. Given your... history... with Allemande, Evie, it's best you aren't seen in the city." She turned to Georgie. "How soon can your family make it to the docks? Maybe if we get in and out before daybreak, we'll have less risk."

"Hang on a second," Henry said, shaking her head. "Are you seriously just going to damn this whole place to destruction? Didn't you hear me? People could die if they don't get a team in here right away to find out why those storms keep encroaching. They passed through the godsdamned barrier tonight, that's why the monorail exploded!"

"Listen here, whatever your name is," Captain Violet said, leaning in close to Henry's face. "I'm not going to risk my whole crew for this place. We barely made it out last time, and Anderson here had to give me one hell of a bribe to convince me to come back this soon."

"One day. That's all I ask. Let Georgie get information to Allemande, or Tripp, and maybe they'll do the right thing."

"I fucking doubt that," Evie muttered.

"We've already sent your message to the Coalition Science Academy," the cloaked woman said, still waiting for Georgie's arm with an outstretched hand. "I'm sure they'll take it under advisement and send a team."

"No!" Henry shouted. "There needs to be an immediate evacuation of all citizens until those storms are under control, or they reinforce the terraforming machines. There's no time to waste waiting for a team, it will be weeks before they get here."

"And you expect Allemande to evacuate them? Don't be a fool. She embodies every bit of rot present in the Coalition. She'll save her own ass and let everyone else burn." Evie's eyes were squeezed shut, her fingers tugging at the loose threads on her starched white shirt.

Georgie pulled her fingers through her half-matted ponytail. "Regardless, my mother will need time to get to the docks. The factory ravaged her lungs. She can't walk far before she's out of breath. She can't run, and the docks are far from where we live." She intertwined her fingers with Henry's, and felt the warmth of her hands send a sense of calm to her heart, slowing the pounding in her chest that mirrored the roar of the engines as they lifted off the ground. "If I miss a shift, they'll suspect something, especially with that busted up monorail. I can't risk them showing up at our apartment while they're trying to gather the few things they have."

Captain Violet sighed. "And if Allemande doesn't issue the evacuation order, which I suspect she won't, given her less-than-stellar humanitarian reputation, then what? We can't stick around waiting for the CSA to make a decision, nor are they an organization we want to tangle with, regardless of

CHAPTER THIRTEEN

their supposed neutrality."

"We could ask Captain Tansy to reallocate some of her refugee task force," Evie suggested.

"They're stretched thin as it is with the current unidentified threat. I doubt they'd be able to get enough ships here in time."

"It's better than nothing."

"Yes, well, let's call that a last resort then, shall we? Scientist, does that plan work? It better, because it's the only one you're going to get."

Henry nodded slowly. "We'll make it work."

"Ned, change of plans, set us down at the docks, and wake up Ivy, tell her we're going to need her for an extraction."

"Aye, Boss," came the gruff reply. "Touch down in twenty."

"You'd better get in an out as fast as you can," the captain said, looking at Georgie. "We won't have much time."

CHAPTER FOURTEEN

"Please, Mrs. Payne, you have to open the door, it's important!" Henry hissed through the wooden door, nose to nose with the layers of peeling paint. The city was still dark, but the mirrors above the buildings had begun to shift into place, casting weak beams of light into the thick smog, where they dissipated into the dust and smoke that still churned from the factories. There was no downtime in Skelm, no matter the risk.

"Henry?" The door creaked open, and Georgie's mother looked from Henry to Ivy, the young Cricket apprentice that had accompanied her. "Where's Roger?" she asked, her face paling. "Where's my Georgie?" she added in a small voice.

"She's fine, please, you have to let us in."

The door widened, and Mrs. Payne ushered them in. "What's going on?" She whispered, and nodded her head towards the wall they shared with a neighbor. "Be quiet, it's still early."

Henry nodded, understanding that it wasn't just the time of day that required hushed tones, but the interested ears of those that might report them to the management in order to get half a day off, as well. "This is Ivy, she's here to help."

"Hiya," Ivy said, sticking out her hand. "Pleased to meet ya." Her green hair was braided into two short pigtails that poked out from under the grey flat cap she was wearing. "Just point me at whatever you want packed up, and I'll heft it on over to the Cricket. Though I'd appreciate it if we didn't

CHAPTER FOURTEEN

take any furniture, if that's okay. If you need something bigger than I can carry, we'll have to call Jasper to come help."

"The Cricket? Packed? Henry, what's going on?"

"Evie Anderson came back for you! You're to be evacuated to a refugee camp with the girls."

"Who in the hell is Evie Anderson?" Mrs. Payne asked, leaning on the back of a chair. "Where's Georgie?"

"She came back?" Emeline said, stood at the foot of the bed she shared with her sister, holding her school dress in one hand and a clean pair of stockings in the other. "Mama, Georgie helped someone a few months back. When that boiler exploded up at the Administration building. She didn't think they'd keep up their end of the bargain, but..." she looked at Ivy. "I guess y'all did?"

Ivy nodded. "We keep our word. But we don't have much time - our ship is likely to get recognized if we stick around too long."

"*Where's Georgie?*" Mrs. Payne asked for a third time.

"She's at work, or heading there, with a copy of some data we retrieved. She's going to try to talk to Tripp or Allemande, show them what we discovered, see if they'll listen to reason. If those storms aren't pushed back to the cliffs, the entire city will be in danger."

"You sent her back there? Have you all lost your minds?"

"Mama, shh," Emeline said, rushing to her mother's side and wrapping an arm around her waist. "Georgie's tough, she'll be alright. We can't let the whole city die, she has to try to get them to listen."

"Emmy, they're not gonna listen to her, and she knows that. She went back to avoid raising any suspicion, so we can get on this ship of theirs." She glared at Henry, who felt her stomach knot uncomfortably.

"Mrs. Payne, you know she'd never have had it any other way. She'll keep her head down, keep out of trouble, and once you and the girls are on the ship, she'll come meet us. The quicker we get started, the sooner she'll be back."

"We don't have much," Georgie's mother admitted. "Just the girls' clothes, a few busted up pots and pans." She limped to the counter and reached underneath the lip, tugging at a loose chunk of roughly hewn wood, until it came loose in her hand. "And this." It was a piece of pine, with *Sandrine + Lucas* carved into one side, with a tiny hinge holding the sides together.

"Oh, Mama," Emeline breathed, wiping a tear from her eye. "You didn't tell us you still had that old box Pop made."

"It's the only thing I have left from him. Well, and what's inside," she said, opening the box. "He always said we could use it if we had the opportunity for a fresh start." She pulled out a small, sparkling jewel, set into a white gold pendant, suspended from a delicate chain. "I guess that might mean now." She tucked it into the pocket of her apron and squared her shoulders. "Emmy, wake up your sister. Do it quietly. Pack your things as quick as you can, whatever you can fit into your school bags. We can't look like we're going anywhere unusual. The sooner we leave, the sooner Georgina is safe." She turned back to Henry and Ivy. "Too many snitches around here desperate to give up their neighbors for a scrap of bread. We can't risk anyone saying anything that might get Georgie into trouble before she can get on the ship."

"I'm sorry this is so sudden Mrs. Payne, I—" Henry started.

"No," Georgie's mother interrupted, holding up a hand. "Thank you for coming. A lesser woman would have stayed safe on that ship instead of risking her face in a city she's not supposed to be in. Now. Where's Roger?"

"We'll have to talk on the ship," Ivy said, looking around, shifting her weight from foot to foot. "It's for the best."

"I see. Henrietta, did you get my Georgie into trouble?"

"Um…" Henry said, searching for the right words.

Mrs. Payne chewed at her lip. "Let's hope it's not too much trouble, then."

"Henry!" Lucy shouted, springing out of bed to throw her arms around her waist in a tight hug. "I have lots of questions for you. I was reading about tornadoes, and—"

"I'll answer every single question you have, but right now you should do as your sister said," Henry said hurriedly, picking up her own bags as well as Roger's.

CHAPTER FOURTEEN

"She'll be heading into work now," Emeline said, squinting through the dirt on the broken window above their bed. "How long does she have to stay?"

"As long as it takes to be sure we don't attract any undue attention, Emmy. Now both of you, hurry up!" Mrs. Payne smoothed the fabric of her worn, threadbare apron. "I have to warn you both, I don't move too quick. All those chemicals in the factories all those years, well, my lungs ain't what they used to be."

"Don't worry, uh, ma'am, we came prepared. I have a specially made chair waiting at the bottom of the stairs for you. It can easily handle the uneven brick roads here in the city. It's built for speed!" Ivy said, her excitement dancing at the edges of her voice. "Alice and I worked on it just in case. Seems like everyone ends up needing some help sooner or later."

"Well, that's very thoughtful of y'all. I do worry that it will attract attention. Not many folks have decent medical care, especially not us affected by the fumes and the factories."

"If anyone asks, we'll just tell them that it's part of a new study up at the Administration building from a team that's rotated in from Gamma-3. By the time anyone figures out that it's a lie, we'll be long gone."

Mrs. Payne looked at the chair through the window and sighed. "If only everyone here could get something like that. I've seen too many old friends end up prisoners in their own homes, unable to get out even for a short trip down the street to play a game of cards. Not much to see here in Skelm, but being trapped in the house all the time isn't a good feeling, either." She smiled bravely. "Emeline, Lucy, come on girls, we've got to go."

The girls clambered to the door with their book bags, their lumpy cardigans tied around their shoulders to ward off the morning chill. A few blond ringlets peeked out of Lucy's bag, the only doll she was taking with her.

"Honey Bee, you okay? I know it's hard to leave things behind."

"It's alright, Mama. I'm getting older now anyway." She stood as tall as she could and grinned at Henry, her lopsided braids tumbling over her shoulders. "We gotta do what's right for Georgie."

"We do," Mrs. Payne said, nodding. "We're good to go here, friends. Let's go on and start a new adventure."

CHAPTER FIFTEEN

Georgie stood outside Governor Allemande's new office, the gilded doors ornately carved with the skyline of the cliffs, and then the mountains outside the city. She turned the small box over in her hands, her heart pounding in her chest as she tried to figure out what she would say that might change the woman's mind. They hadn't had much time to come up with a plausible story that wouldn't implicate her with the missing monorail, landing her in a work camp or worse, an interrogation center.

She took a deep breath, and cleared her throat, raising her closed fist to knock on the door, when it opened in front of her.

"What do you want?" Governor Allemande demanded. "You're not supposed to be here. I could have you punished for this, you know. Where is your supervisor?"

"I, uh—" Georgie stammered, shoving the small box deep into her jumpsuit pocket. It was clear that she was in a dangerous mood.

The governor narrowed her eyes and then gave an almost imperceptible smirk. "Never mind. Get in here, my fireplace needs cleaning. None of you cretins seem capable of clearing out ashes and leave it looking filthy. It's a disgrace to the Coalition to be working amid such filth, wouldn't you agree?"

"Yes?"

"What are you waiting for? Get to work!" Allemande stepped aside, her long black coat tails sweeping around her.

Georgie slid into the office and knelt by the fireplace, which by anyone else's standards would be considered pristine. There were no chunks of coal left, no sooty residue clinging to the gold bricks at the back. She wasn't sure what she was meant to be cleaning, but pulled the rag from her belt loop anyway, scrubbing away at nonexistent dirt, wishing she could escape through the chimney. Something about Governor Allemande felt very threatening, her presence a fatal undercurrent that grabbed Georgie by the hairs at the back of her neck. She scrubbed harder, feeling her fingernails shred from the friction.

The governor stared at her, an unsettling smile spreading across her face. "Hurry it up," Governor Allemande said, unblinking. "You shouldn't even be in here. I thought I made it very clear to Mr. Jackson what his responsibilities are, they're very simple, and yet you people continue to disappoint me."

Georgie looked at the floor and nodded, afraid to say anything. She wiped away imaginary grease, and stayed silent, wishing she could be anywhere else. Allemande seemed even angrier and more dangerous now that her jaw was unwired.

"You're late, Mr. Tripp," Allemande said as a small man closed the door behind him. "That doesn't bode well for your perilous position in the employment of the Glorious Coalition."

He looked at his watch, confused. "You said—"

"I said be here promptly at nine. It is now nine and forty-five seconds."

"Apologies, Inspector Allemande." He sat in the chair opposite and took out a folder, spreading the contents across the table.

"Governor Allemande."

"Yes, yes, of course. My apologies," he said through gritted teeth. "Now if I can just present my findings—"

"There will be no need for that, Mr. Tripp."

"Pardon me?"

"I already know what you've been up to."

Georgie's heart pounded in her throat, and her hands shook with every push of the rag against the smooth metal. She could feel the danger in the air, thick and manipulative, and bile rested painfully at the back of her throat.

CHAPTER FIFTEEN

"I'm - I'm sorry?" he stammered. "Governor Allemande, I can assure you, I just have the qualitative findings to present with some recommendations—"

"How long have you been working on this weapon, Mr. Tripp?"

"Weapon?" he asked, his face draining of all color.

"Don't play coy with me, I've seen the historical data. I'm now privy to every underhanded, deceitful project the late Governor Baker ever had his hands on. Assassinations, illegal medical procedures, it's all just very distasteful fanfare, wouldn't you agree?"

Tripp swallowed hard. "Sure."

"After all, the Glorious Coalition is built for efficiency, not power hungry operatives who dabble in political intrigue. I've reported my findings up the chain of command to the regional senators, except for this." She slid a file across the desk and raised an eyebrow. "Go on, open it."

Tripp spread pages across the table, his chest rising and falling rapidly with every shallow breath. "This is a project the late Governor Baker had me consult on."

"Yes, fascinating stuff, isn't it? It made for some very compelling bedtime reading. Who'd have thought that he was working on some kind of weapon that could generate super storms? Quite honestly, I didn't think he was intelligent enough for such a clever solution."

"I did the work of prototyping it, but the project ceased when he sadly passed."

"Mr. Tripp, if that's the case, then can you kindly explain to me why this technology has been spliced into our very own terraforming devices?"

"A-Are they?" he stammered, scooting his chair away from the desk. "If that's the case then it certainly wasn't with my authorization, and—"

"Don't lie to me, Lawrence," Allemande growled hoarsely. Her voice was still weak from months of not speaking. "I'm going to give you one more chance to tell me the truth about what you've done."

He tilted his chin upwards in defiance. "I don't know what you think you've found, Amaranth, but you have a reputation for drawing some wild assumptions. Not everyone is a rebel informant."

"Rebel informant?" she laughed, sliding her fingers over a silver pen that shone in the verdant light of the algae. "I didn't say anything about a rebel informant." She leaned across the desk and carved a deep notch into the table with a hidden blade on the underside of the pen's sharp nib. "You, however, did."

Tripp looked at Georgie, who turned back to the fireplace, her heart pounding.

"Don't look at her, she's not going to help you," Allemande said, standing up and bolting the door, locking it from the inside with a wide bronze key.

Georgie's heart leaped into her throat. There was no escape now.

"Mr. Tripp, I asked the lovely girl at the wire transfer desk to give me a comprehensive list of everyone you have contacted off-world since the start of the little project Ralph Baker assigned you to."

He smirked.

"As you well know, there was no record of any unauthorized communications from you or anyone else in your department, though it did seem interesting that you routinely block their access from sending reports back to the CSA, or even sending messages home to Gamma-3. Why is that?"

"One thing you and I have in common is that I believe employees should be focused on their work, not becoming overly involved with sentimentalities back home, or superseding the established line of command with their research."

"Well, that I can agree with," Allemande said, advancing on Tripp slowly, the pen sliding between her fingers one at a time. "However, when I accessed the raw data from the communications array, I discovered that someone very naughty had been sending communiques to known rebel settlements on Delta-4 and throughout the Near Systems. Who do you think that could have been?"

Tripp stood, stumbling over his chair in a desperate bid to put more distance between himself and the governor. "It could have been anyone who's had access to the tower, anyone who's been out beyond the barrier. You know as well as I do that monorail was taken last night and the gods only know what they were out there doing."

CHAPTER FIFTEEN

Georgie's stomach lurched with the realization that the Coalition management knew that the monorail had been taken. Of course they would know, even if the alarms were broken, which seemed likely given their escape the night before, the engineer team would have known the second they saw the empty hangar. They'd have driven all night to the terminal station and found the smoldering remains.

"Ah, but it wasn't just anyone, was it, Lawrence? It was you."

"Amaranth please, I—"

"It's Governor Allemande now, actually," she said, and leapt forward, the pen flashing in the light. Bright red blood erupted from his cheek, spurting across the white wall.

"Have you lost your fucking mind, woman?" he screamed, holding a palm against the wound. "Help! Someone!"

"I think you'll find that your colleagues won't be rushing to aid a rebel sympathizer," she said in a low voice, a strange grin spreading across her face. "Especially not one who endangered their livelihood, and their bank accounts, by attempting to destroy this entire settlement, and destroying the monorail, the crown jewel of Skelm. I do have to ask, though, did the rebels know you intended on letting everyone here die in order to disable the factories?"

"We had a plan for evacuating all *worthy* human life," he sneered, bright red blood covering his face, dripping lazily into the rug. "But The Scattered know that occasional sacrifices must be made in order to reclaim peace. You'll never stamp us all out."

"Oh, believe me, I will do exactly that," Allemande said, and slashed the blade across his throat. "Disgusting cretin."

Lawrence Tripp died on the carpet, bleeding out onto the rug, gasping and spluttering as he clutched at the gaping wound in his throat.

"Well, well, aren't you the little murderer?" the governor asked, her head tilted as she stared at Georgie.

"Wh- What?"

"You killed that man, your superior! A travesty and a stain on this settlement's history. If I was you, I would clean up this disgusting corpse immediately." She looked at the tracker around Georgie's neck, which had begun to start flashing a warning. "And you'd better make it quick, or Mr. Jackson will have no choice other than to write you up for inefficiency." She stepped over Tripp's lifeless body and unlocked the door, stepping over the threshold and disappearing down the hallway.

* * *

Sobbing, Georgie dragged Tripp's body off the cart and dumped it into a large utility vat. She was no stranger to dead bodies, but she'd never been responsible for disposing of one before. Even the late Governor Ralph Baker's body had been collected before she was sent in to scrub the blood out of the carpet, and it wasn't lost on her that this was the second dead body in that office in just a few short months. Tripp's corpse splashed into the murky water and disappeared beneath the surface, still clothed in his finely tailored jacket and new leather boots. She had to finish her shift, or risk her family's one chance to get the hell out of Skelm. If she left, the military police would go looking for her, and the first place they'd go was her home, where her mother and sisters were conspicuously packing their things. She couldn't risk raising that alarm. She had to act as though everything was normal.

She lit the pilot light beneath the vat, wiping snot and tears from her face with the sleeve of her orange jumpsuit. An entire package of caustic powder under her arm, she climbed the ladder attached to the vat and dumped it in, watching it dissolve into the water and begin to bubble. These vats had likely once been used for distillation before they banned alcohol, and now they were in storage, some used for boiling hazardous laundry from the medical research unit. Now, it was being used to turn the head of the science department into soup.

Tripp had apparently been a rebel, part of a new group called The Scattered. She'd heard whispers about them, of course, but as far as anyone knew, they weren't active in Skelm. No, the rebel cell here was known to be impotent and ineffective, no more than a group of desperate people with no resources.

CHAPTER FIFTEEN

They hadn't accomplished anything since her father and the others died. They didn't even help two months ago, when the pirates were in Skelm to break into the Administration building. That was all up to her.

"Georgie!" Erin yelled, skidding into the storage room. "What the hell are you doing in here? Your next assignment is the conference wing toilets, not down here – this is my assignment."

"Swap with me," Georgie said, tossing her lanyard across the room, where it landed at Erin's feet. "I have to finish this."

"What are you doing?"

"Special assignment for our new governor."

"What kind of assignment?"

Georgie looked over at her and weighed her options. "She killed someone. The science head. Mr. Tripp."

Erin laughed. "Stop messing with me, Georgie. What are you really doing, trying to make some gin?"

"You wouldn't want to drink this gin."

"You're not serious."

"She just left him there, bleeding out onto the carpet. I had to drag him down here to... dispose of him."

"Oh, gods."

"Someone will have to go back and scrub the blood out of the rug. I probably shouldn't leave him unattended," she said, gesturing at the vat. Her limbs were still shaking after witnessing Tripp's murder. It was clear that Allemande blamed him for the monorail, but it was only a matter of time before she rounded up security footage and saw Tripp in his office while the monorail was being stolen. Georgie could only hope that happened after she was long gone.

"Okay, don't worry," Erin said, sliding her lanyard across the floor. "I'll go do the toilets. Mine should be fine, I was allotted thirty minutes in here." She looked at the vat. "How long will that take?"

"As long as it takes, I guess."

"Turn the fire up higher and put the cap back on, it should speed up the process."

Georgie raised an eyebrow. "And how would you know that?"

"Oh, you know," Erin shrugged. "Common knowledge. I'll be back in thirty to swap back." She picked up Georgie's lanyard from the floor and scurried out of the room, dragging her cart with her.

As soon as the squeaks from the worn soles of her cheap work boots faded down the corridor, Georgie burst into tears. It was all too much, and now her family was caught up in it, too. She could only hope that they were already on their way to the Cricket. Even if she was apprehended, Captain Violet would know to get them as far away from here as possible, as soon as possible. At least then, they'd be safe, and nothing the Coalition could do to her would matter. She thought of Henry, and her heart ached. She'd been so close to knowing love, but unless a miracle happened and Allemande didn't figure her out, she'd die without being able to live out that life.

"Georgina Payne, would you mind explaining this?" Mr. Jackson stood at the base of the stairs, holding her tracking card in his hand, dangling it by its long orange lanyard. "And why precisely are you using one of the old distillation vats?"

"Mr. Jackson, I—"

"You've been slacking lately, Ms. Payne, and I don't think I have to tell you that. But *this*? This is inexcusable, to use Coalition property to produce illegal liquor."

"It's not liquor, sir, it's—"

"And to traipse around the Administration building without your tracker is an immediate firing. Not to mention swapping with another member of the janitorial staff to cover your little gin ring here. How long has this been going on, exactly? Does Erin know that you're doing this, is she an accomplice?"

"Mr. Jackson, please! If you'll just look inside, you'll see it's not gin."

He furrowed his brow. "What is it, then?"

"Something terrible." Georgie took a deep breath. "Governor Allemande asked me to clean her fireplace this morning, and while I was in there, she killed the head of the science department. I guess he was a rebel spy, he said something about The Scattered, and she told me to dispose of the body, and

I... well, I thought this would be the best way. She tried to say that I killed him, but I didn't, I promise! It was that pen she always has in her breast pocket, and you won't find my fingerprints anywhere near it."

"What?" He rubbed his temples. "If he was a rebel spy, why not have him arrested and interrogated? She doesn't have the authority to unilaterally pass capital punishment on a Coalition employee, or anyone for that matter." He climbed the steps and lifted the lid of the vat, the strange stench of lye seeping out. He recoiled, nearly falling backwards off the stairs. "Gods."

"I told you sir, I'm telling the truth."

"How do I know this isn't all some elaborate lie, and that you didn't kill him?"

"Why would I kill a man and try to dispose of his body in the same building we both worked? I know I'm no genius, Mr. Jackson, but I'm not a fool."

"I'll have to report this up the chain of command, go over her head."

"She's monitoring wire transmissions from the courtyard and from the communications tower beyond the barrier."

He swore under his breath. "I'll have to figure something out, then. This can't go unchallenged, no matter what Tripp was accused of."

"So what now?"

"Go swap back with Erin and finish the bathrooms. Tell her to report back to my office, I don't need another employee mixed up in all this. I'll alter the records so this never happened." When Georgie hesitated, he thrust his arms out at her. "Go!"

* * *

Georgie flung Erin's tracking badge into the bathroom, her boots skidding against the smooth marble. "Go!" she shouted, panting. "Mr. Jackson's office. He's covering it up."

"Covering it up? What do you mean, covering it up?"

"All of it. Just go!"

Erin squeezed past her in the doorway and took off at a full sprint towards the janitorial area of the building, down several flights of stairs into the basement. Georgie stood there, rag in her hand, looking from the half-cleaned bathroom to the cart that Erin had left in the hallway. If she left now, she might make it to the docks early, and they could leave quietly. The longer she stayed, the more her empty stomach roiled, anxiety building a feast of acid in her gut. It would take her mother a long time to walk from their apartment down to the docks in her condition, so she couldn't risk leaving too early, or someone might follow her right to the ship, and they'd take off without her family safe inside.

Yet the longer she risked staying in the Administration building, the more likely it was that Allemande would discover it had actually been her who stole the monorail out from under their noses and lead it to its own destruction from the storm. All it would take was one glance at the security footage for the new governor to send her to an early grave, too.

The memory of Lawrence Tripp grabbing at his own throat, desperate to stop his lifeblood from spurting out over the floor in erratic, darkly artistic splashes pulled at Georgie. In one instant a powerful, healthy man was cut down, left to gasp and splutter into the fancy, hand woven rug. His death would be recorded as a cardiac event, they'd tell his family, if he had any, that his body had been immediately cremated for maximum efficiency. That's what they had told her family after their father went missing. No need to radicalize a family, or provide a growing movement of rebels with a martyr.

Georgie was poised in the doorway, one hand on the bathroom knob, one in her pocket, running her fingers over the smooth metal of the data casing. At least now they knew why the storms had been getting worse, and in all likelihood Allemande had already disabled whatever was wired into the terraformers, but that technology was already with the Coalition. They could do whatever they liked to wherever they wanted and blame it all on a freak storm. It was genius. It was also elegantly monstrous. It was strange how often genius and monstrosity coexisted peacefully, a symbiotic relationship; almost as if they needed each other to survive.

The sharp click of new boot heels on marble was all it took to jerk her out

CHAPTER FIFTEEN

of her thought paralysis, and she'd made her decision. It was time to go. The danger in the building was growing with every moment, and the sooner all of them were out of Skelm, the better. She hung her tracking card on a peg behind the bathroom door and walked calmly down the corridor with her cleaning cart. She'd have about ten minutes before the tracking card began to give warning flashes, and then a few moments after that it would trigger a spot check by one of the many armed guards in the building, who marched around in their sharp grey uniforms emblazoned with the purple and yellow Coalition crest, imposing weapons at their sides.

No one would notice her until then, just another faceless janitor in a sea of orange jumpsuits. She'd leave right through the front doors of the building, as if she was merely going outside to scrub a week's worth of grime off the alabaster fountain in the courtyard. Her heart pounded in her chest, and part of her expected to be yanked up by her collar and dragged to Governor Allemande's office for her own death sentence. The memory of that bladed pen stuck in her mind's eye, glinting with threat.

The green cast of the light from the algae lamps flooded the main hall and swept over the pale marble staircases that led to each wing. Janitors were only allowed here after hours, unless they were on a specifically requested assignment. Gods forbid if visiting Gamma-3 management happened to see one of the ugly orange jumpsuits in their sight line, the entire empire might then fall. With shoulders squared, she marched her cart straight through the open doors and into the courtyard.

There was a pathway behind one of the tall moss-covered stones, hidden amid a tangle of ivy that had to be misted every day in this arid climate, done painstakingly so by one of the many gardeners on staff. A gardener was no more than a janitor, at least, that's how management saw it. Georgie had tried for years to get a gardener position to no avail - once someone was hired into that role, they toed the line until death released them from duty. There were still plenty of toxic pesticides, and the gardeners were still expected to work in a janitorial capacity when necessary, but at least they got to feel the distant sun's rays on their skin a few hours a day.

Luckily, there were no gardeners there at that moment. Janitors didn't perform gardening duties, which were jealously guarded. She glanced over her shoulder, and when the courtyard was empty, she swept aside the tangle of ivy and pulled her cart through into the hidden alleyway. She pulled down some strands of ivy and draped them over the cart in a futile attempt to cover its loud yellow presence.

The alleyway led to the back streets of Skelm, where it would be a short jaunt through winding roads and through unlocked gates to the docks, the same route she'd taken just a few months prior to smuggle Evie and the unconscious woman in the bin to the Cricket. She wondered what happened to that woman, but had always suspected she'd had something to do with the death of the late Governor Ralph Baker, given how much blood she'd had to scrub from the saturated fibers of the rug. It was amazing she'd been able to clean it at all.

She reached the end of the alley where it forked into two cobblestone paths, one that looped back up toward the Administration building, and the other which led into the back streets of the city.

The alarm began to sound. The high-pitched wail ricocheted off the brick walls surrounding the narrow street, echoing down into the small storage areas where the Coalition steamcars were kept. Georgie's heart leapt into her throat, and she began to run, dodging abandoned boxes of parts long since rusted and jumping over fences instead of pausing to unlatch the gate. The guard stations at the edges of the city picked up the alarm, adding their own to the cacophony. Someone had discovered her hidden tracking card earlier than she had anticipated, and they knew that she was on the run.

The military police would be on high alert now, and preparing to check every ship in the port for stowaways or signs of rebel behavior, and the Cricket had both. Georgie flung herself over a low wall made of stacked stone and stumbled into the next alley. If she could just make it to the docks in time, everything would be alright. The alarms screamed across the city, sending anyone who'd ever done anything wrong into a flurry of bodies running through the streets, panicked they'd been found out. She pushed her way through a throng of people that clogged a back street. There weren't many rebels here in Skelm, but everyone had a past. Everyone had stolen a crust of bread from a dumpster, or showed up late to work, at least once, both crimes in Coalition settlements.

"Please remain calm," the loudspeakers screeched from the tops of the street lamps, "or we will be authorized to use force." The voice repeated on a loop, and the crowd began to thin. Everyone remembered how the last riots ended, with bodies left in the streets for weeks to teach the agitators a lesson. It felt like a lifetime ago, but it had only happened a few years back, as a result of increased military police patrols. The riots only led to more policing, more dead bodies in the streets. People had given up, they couldn't risk their family's safety. She understood. She hadn't participated in the riots, either.

The docks were in sight now, the ships glinting in the sun with their names shining in metallic paint. She ran, despite her lungs aching in protest. She was almost there. She'd be safe soon.

Military police were approaching the docks, closing ranks around each ship one by one. Georgie ran faster, willing her legs to carry her faster towards the Cricket. She could still make it, if she was lucky. Her boots pounded on the worn wood of the docks, pushing her way through lazy looking officers.

"Hey asshole, watch it!" one shouted after her. "I could have you thrown into lockup for that!"

She ignored him. Henry was standing in the loading bay of the Cricket, tears streaming down her face as she mouthed, "I'm so sorry."

The loading bay closed when Georgie was less than twenty meters away, and the Cricket lifted off into the atmosphere, and along with it, her last chance at survival.

CHAPTER SIXTEEN

"How could we leave without her?" Henry sobbed, kneeling on the floor of the loading bay, feeling the vibrations of the ship shudder up into her bones. "She was right there! She would have made it!"

"We couldn't wait," Kady said, perched on a nearby overturned crate. "Those military police were closing in. If they so much as got wind of us, we'd all be on a one-way ticket to a work camp, or getting interrogated by some asshole like Allemande. Maybe someday Evie will tell you all about it, if you stick around long enough."

"But she could die!"

Kady jumped down from the crate, landing soundlessly on the metal flooring. "She seems tough. Hell, you all do. Not many could make it in that desert at night without any extra weight, much less dragging along your unconscious pal." She clapped a hand on Henry's shoulder and offered what was probably supposed to be an encouraging smile. "She'll be alright. I bet she finds another way off that rock in no time."

Henry shrugged off Kady's hand and got to her feet, smoothing the soft wool of her skirts. "I want to go back for her."

"Don't be ridiculous, we can't go back, not now. They'll have that whole dock closed off and anyone left will have to acquiesce to thorough searches." Kady gestured around at the stacks of crates teeming with all manner of things: produce, medical supplies, scrap, parts. "Do you think we have the proper paperwork for all this? We're *pirates*."

CHAPTER SIXTEEN

"Then I'll go back alone. Drop me at the nearest trading beacon and I'll find my own way back."

"And then what? Then you're both stuck in that godsforsaken city under the watchful eye of the newly minted Governor Allemande."

"Then I'll book us passage."

"With what credit? I've seen those salaries, I know you're not paid particularly well. The Coalition might pay for decent travel when on assignment, but outside of that, I'd be surprised if your pay as a meteorologist could pay for two nights at the local speakeasy."

Henry bristled. "I have some credits set aside for emergencies."

"Of course you do. Let me guess, rich parents?"

"We weren't rich, we just—"

"You were rich. The high quality dresses, access to top schools, I bet you never wanted for anything, right? Well, let me tell you, most parents are wildly uninterested in supporting their rogue child who willingly boarded a pirate vessel. Ask me how I know."

"I don't need your family history, I need to get back to Georgie, and I'll do so if it takes every last credit I have. She's worth it."

Kady rolled her eyes. "Listen, Ms. Weaver, we have bigger fish to fry here, alright? You need to talk to the captain before you make any big decisions."

"Give her a few minutes to process, I think," the medic said from the doorway, her dark hair piled high in braids atop her head. "Henry, did you want to come see Roger?"

Henry glanced from the loading bay door to the airlock that led to the ship, feeling something inside of her tear into pieces. She'd have to tell Georgie's mother she hadn't made it. The poor woman had already lost so much, and now she was going to lose another member of her family. "Yes, I'll come see him," she finally answered.

The corridors of the ship were long and narrow, a far cry from the slick newer models that had spent years mapping the average walking route to place high-traffic areas close to each other for maximum efficiency. The heels of her boots clicked and scraped against the rusted metal grate, echoing off the walls, covered in yellowed maps from decades prior. She recognized the names of famous rebel settlements, the same ones her parents had sneered at over their supper.

"He's not awake yet, but he's stable," the medic said. "My name is Hyun. Radio me if anything changes. My assistant, Jasper, will be along shortly to check on him." She pushed the door open to the small med bay and gestured for Henry to go in. "We won't know if there is any brain damage or lasting effects until he comes to."

Henry sat down heavy into the chair at Roger's bedside and started to cry again, as soon as the door clicked shut. "Oh Rog, I can't do this alone." She took his hand and squeezed gently, watching a teardrop fall onto the stark white sheet and darken it. "You've gotta wake up or I'm going to ruin everything. They left without her, Roger, they left her there on the docks. The only woman I've ever felt that strong a connection to, and now I might never see her again."

She leaned down and buried her face in the crook of Roger's elbow, and cried. Proximity to her oldest and closest friend was the only thing keeping her from suiting up and trying to thrash her way back to Skelm, back to Georgie, to make sure she was safe. "She told me she loved me, Rog."

The sound of a rasping breath made her jump, and she yanked at the curtain next to the bed. "Mrs. Payne! I didn't know you were in here, I—" she stopped short, remembering the woman was hard of hearing, and likely hadn't heard her confession. "How are you?"

"Where's my Georgina?" the woman wheezed through the contraption strapped to her face. "Tell me she's alright, Henry."

Henry swallowed hard. "She didn't make it onto the ship. We left without her."

Mrs. Payne squeezed her eyes shut, her forehead creased with worry, and Henry could see the tears gathering on her lashes. "She's a strong woman. She'll be alright."

"She is strong, yes."

Georgie's mother wiped away the fat tears and forced a smile, one that didn't reach her eyes. "How are you doing?"

"Me? I haven't really thought about it." Henry reached over and patted

CHAPTER SIXTEEN

the woman on the arm. "I'm sorry, I didn't know you were in here at first, it was very rude of me."

"Don't be silly," she said, waving her away. "They've got me on this strange thing, that lovely doctor, Hyun, says that it should help my lungs. It can't repair what I've lost, but it should make me feel better, get more air."

Henry nodded. "And where's Lucy?"

"If you think she isn't already poking around that lab they've got on this ship, you've got another thing coming. Girl's eyes were big as moons when she saw it. Lucy is the most adaptable child I've ever met, she'll be just fine."

"Did they tell you where we'd be heading next?" Henry had been glued to the spot on the loading bay deck waiting for Georgie and had missed anything that had happened elsewhere on the ship.

"We're going to a pirate settlement!" Mrs. Payne said excitedly, wiping away the tears left on her cheeks. "Evie said there's some kind of refugee camp there where we can stay while we get back on our feet, and there's a school, and a place to stay, and enough food to go around."

"That sounds wonderful." Henry knew that Georgie would love knowing that her family was going to be cared for, safe, away from the Coalition where they could rebuild their lives. "Do you know how long we'll be there?"

"Sounds like long enough to drop us off and refuel, trade. Not long. I saw the captain say earlier something about a storm in a rebel encampment, wiped out every structure they'd built and destroyed most of their supplies, killed some people. Seems to me they'll be heading back out that way to help out."

"Not back to Skelm?" Henry asked, her heart sinking lower in her chest. "I'd hoped we could go back for Georgie when things had cooled off."

Mrs. Payne turned away to face the black darkness outside the small porthole window. "The captain seems mighty hesitant to ever return to that place, not that I blame her. I certainly don't have any intention of returning, either."

"I'll get her back, don't you worry," Henry said with what she hoped was a reassuring smile. "I'll get her back."

CHAPTER SEVENTEEN

Georgie unlocked the door to her family's small apartment and squinted through the dust particles that sparkled in the mid-afternoon light. Her mother's favorite cast iron pan was missing, as was Lucy's most treasured doll. She heaved a sigh of relief, and collapsed against the wall to cry, kicking the door shut. At least her family had made it out. They must have been on the Cricket when it took off. They were safe and secure, headed off to a new life somewhere, while Georgie was trapped in Skelm, probably a wanted woman at this point. She shouldn't even be here, really, but she had to know if her family made it out alive.

There weren't many places in Skelm to hide, not with this heightened number of military police wandering the streets. No one was allowed in or out of Skelm without paperwork, though the traders on the docks sometimes ran a dangerous scheme of smuggling Skelmians out with their shipments, in which many had died, suffocated in the crates as they waited for inspection and clearance to take off. Georgie refused to risk that for her family, especially with her mother's health.

Her legs carried her to the one hiding place she knew of: the Twisted Lantern speakeasy. She pushed open the door and whispered "Tarantula juice" to the open slot. The wall opened, and she walked in and sat at the bar, her head in her hands.

"Hard day?" the usually snarky bartender asked, his dark hair set in a fashionable coif.

CHAPTER SEVENTEEN

"The worst."

"Sounds like a double to me," he laughed, pouring a healthy dose of cloudy liquid into a smudged glass. "Your bad day have anything to do with the security alarm from earlier?"

She didn't want to admit she was a fugitive on the run from the law, endangering their place of business, so she necked the gin and shuddered as she felt it scrape down her esophagus. Illegal swill was less than smooth, and better when mixed with something else. "What security alarm?" she asked innocently, holding out her glass for another shot.

"What alarm?" the bartender laughed. "Gods, you could probably hear that thing all the way at the Outer Rim. What, did you sleep through it?"

Georgie closed her eyes and remembered bolting down back alleys before watching the Cricket ascend into the sky without her, taking her family and the woman she loved with it. "Something like that, I guess."

"You know they're going to have a public execution tomorrow," he said, mixing a drink for another patron. "By decree of our new governor."

"Execution? Who?"

"You really haven't heard?" He poured the drink and slid it across the worn bar top, scratched from decades of use.

"No!"

"That must have been some nap to miss all of that, it's been all over the public broadcasts for hours."

"Are you going to tell me, or not?"

He rolled his eyes dramatically. "Some low level up at the Admin building tried to pull a fast one on Allemande."

Georgie swallowed hard and downed the second glass of gin. "Oh?"

"Yeah, word on the street is that he tried to report her to her superiors, said she was taking the law into her own hands. He used the wire transfer desk, tried to send it in code. She was too quick for him though."

"Mr. Jackson?" she sputtered, sending a spray of gin over the bar. "He's the one they sounded the alarm for?"

"Try and keep your mouth closed, will you?" the bartender said with disdain, wiping gingerly at the splatter of droplets with an old rag. "I don't know his name, though it seems you sure as hell do."

"I don't know for sure."

He stared at her with suspicion. "Seems you know more than you're letting on, despite being apparently unaware of that alarm earlier."

"He's the head of the janitorial department."

"What would the head of the janitorial department have to report to Coalition management? I mean, if that's even true. Could be the rebels are stirring up stories to swell their ranks. Could be he was just the traitor the management says he is."

"What are they saying?"

"Honestly, don't you listen to the news?"

"Not usually."

"Well, you should. They're saying that he helped some rebels escape a few months back, that they've been monitoring him for activity to uncover the cell he was working with."

Georgie's breath caught in her throat. They were blaming Mr. Jackson for what she'd done, using that as a cover to kill him. She was sure that he had tried to squeal on Allemande. He was a man of law and order with a dead body in his storage closet, murdered by the governor. "Gods..." she uttered.

"Hey, tell that new girl we need more bottles brought up from the basement. Seems we have a thirsty crowd tonight," the bartender shouted behind a curtain.

"Yeah, yeah," came the disgruntled reply.

"So they're just going to execute him tomorrow? No investigation, no work camp?" Georgie asked.

"By order of the governor," the bartender muttered. "She can make executive orders here now, apparently. Seems no one else cares enough about this shit hole to come in and take her down a few pegs. I tell you, if this is what she's like after ten seconds in office, we're in for one hell of a bumpy ride."

"But she can't just... kill someone," Georgie said. "That's absurd. It goes against the rule of law. It's not even Coalition doctrine to do so."

"*Au contraire,* unfortunately. When martial law is in force, the highest

CHAPTER SEVENTEEN

position in the settlement can act as judge, jury, and executioner."

"Martial law. So that's what the alarm was about, and the crowds." She couldn't bring herself to breathe a sigh of relief, not when poor Mr. Jackson was awaiting his public execution, but at least she knew now that hoards of military police officers weren't pounding the pavement searching for her. Maybe she'd have a reprieve, maybe she could just keep her head down and hope that the Cricket would come back for her someday. It was unlikely, but what else did she have to hope for? Her family was gone, and it would be years before she got to hug the girls again, if ever. She stared down at the deep scratches in the wood, tracing her fingers along the paths they created.

"Hey, Cole, here's those bottles you asked for."

"Thanks, New Girl, you can put them under the bar."

"You know my name, Cole," a familiar voice said.

Georgie snapped to attention, craning her neck to see the girl crouched behind the bar, her face hidden from the dim light. "*Emeline?*"

"Georgie!" her sister shouted, and all but leapt over the bar to throw her arms around Georgie's neck. "I thought you'd gone!"

"Why aren't you on the ship?" Georgie shouted, so loud that the other speakeasy patrons stopped their chatter to look. "You're supposed to be safe on the godsdamned ship!"

"I told Mama I wanted to stay, I wanted to fight to make Skelm better! I'm sixteen, Georgie, I—"

"You're *sixteen*!" Georgie bellowed. "You should be studying, not gallivanting around with rebel cells!"

"Hey!" the bartender interjected. "Would you mind keeping your *fucking* voice down with that kind of talk?"

"She's my sister, I—"

"I don't give one fresh fuck who she is to you, keep that bullshit outside of my godsdamned speakeasy or neither of you will ever set foot in here again, *yeah*?"

"Yeah, we got it, Cole," Emeline said quietly. "She's just worried."

"You're damn right I'm worried," Georgie said, but rogue tears spilled out over her cheeks, dampening the collar of the orange jumpsuit she was still wearing from earlier. "But I'm so glad to see you, Em. I was feeling so lonely." She returned her sister's hug and squeezed tight. "I can't believe Mama let you stay."

"She didn't really... let me stay. I boarded with everyone else, but I sneaked out when they were waiting for you at the docks. I slipped out behind Henry, she was sitting there just waiting for you, crying. I think she really loves you, George."

"Don't change the subject. You left and didn't tell anyone? Mama is going to go berserk when she finds out."

"Too late now," Emeline grinned.

"That's too reckless. Where were you going to stay? How were you going to keep paying for school? What exactly is the plan here?"

Cole gave them a warning look, and Emeline nodded at him sagely. "I can't keep going to school, not without Lucy. It would raise too many questions. If we both go missing, people will just assume we couldn't afford it anymore."

"I don't like this, Em."

"And I got a job here with Cole and Judy, she's the one working the door. I'm helping out but they said I can stay in the basement, there's a bed roll down there."

"Absolutely not," Georgie said, shooting Cole a dirty look. "I'm not having you sleep in the basement of some old speakeasy where you'll catch your death. No, we'll stay in the apartment as long as we can, until someone figures out Ma and Lucy are gone. We've got until the next census, a few months. Then we'll... I don't know. I hope we can be out of here by then."

Emeline pulled her arms back. "Georgie, I still want to stay, even if you go. I want to make this place better, it can be so much more than what it is. Skelm has so much power if we all just stand together, we could collectively bargain—" she was interrupted by a loud cough from Cole. "Anyway, we can talk about that later."

"We need to get word to Ma that you're alright."

"Georgie..." her sister shifted her weight from foot to foot and stared at the floor. "Do I have to? Surely she'd just assume that I stayed here..."

"Yes. You have to. She's probably halfway to wherever the hell they're

CHAPTER SEVENTEEN

headed, thinking you're lying dead in an alleyway or something. It's not fair to make her worry like that. Not after what happened to Pop."

"*You* stayed."

"Not by choice, and besides, I'm grown."

Emeline rolled her eyes. "I'm as good as."

"I'm not going to baby you, Em. We've got a hard road ahead of us. I'm going to need you to help hide some money away, just in case this plan of yours doesn't quite work out the way you're hoping. For contingency."

"If you can't keep your traps shut, maybe you should take your conversation outside," Cole hissed, angrily pouring a drink. "You two forget that we serve all citizens of Skelm in this speakeasy, it's not safe to be talking openly about whatever you're talking about." He glared at Emeline. "And you should know better, after what happened to your father."

"Hey there, *pal*, take it easy," Georgie warned. "She was only a child when that happened, she barely remembers."

Cole waved her off. "I'm not trying to say anything untoward here, alright? Just try to keep quiet about all that until we're closed. You never know who's listening, here." He turned back to Emeline and shook an empty frosted glass bottle at her. "And if I'm paying you in credits, then you need to do your job. We need another crate of the imported stuff from the basement. People are spending freely tonight, and we don't want to keep them waiting, yeah?"

"Alright, alright," Emeline relented, stepping back behind the curtain. "Georgie, wait for me. We can walk home together. It's safer that way, I don't want you to get hurt."

Georgie smiled and shook her head, but felt warmed by her sister's concern for her well-being. Emeline was young, but she was smart, and brave, and would conquer the whole of the New Systems if given half a chance. She was charismatic and could talk her way into anything, including, apparently, a job working for a speakeasy. Still, she'd rather have Emeline working at the Twisted Lantern than down at the factories by far. She'd seen what those fumes did to young lungs, and it was irreversible.

Sitting back into a plush blue chair, she spied the book she'd been reading before she met Henry just a week or so ago. The cover now had a water mark on the cover, stained into the pale fabric of the binding. She frowned, thinking how irritated Henry would be at the state of it, and turned it over in her hands, feeling the rough texture of the embossed spine under her fingertips. The page marking her place was still folded down, an invitation to jump in right where she'd left off, to lose herself for a few hours in the story, forget everything terrible that had happened, forget for a moment that tomorrow she'd have to watch Mr. Jackson be killed. Public executions were mandatory viewing, after all.

Cole set a drink down on the table and gave her an apologetic look. "Don't be mad at Em. She just wants to do the right thing."

"I know."

"Enjoy your book."

Georgie nodded, already turning the page, her mind on the high seas of Gamma-3, far away from Skelm and its politics, far away from everything. The story twisted and turned, page after page, dastardly crooks getting their fair comeuppance and being thrown into prison while the pirates sailed free, off to right another wrong. She'd forgotten how enjoyable a story would be without the Coalition's fist punching through anything meaningful. Where once there were bright, vibrant stories of bravery and challenge, now the shelves were stuffed full with false narratives praising the government and its enforcers.

Hour by hour, the thick crowd in the Twisted Lantern thinned to a few drunks desperate to forget the horror their lives had become. Cole stuffed fat sandwiches in their pockets, wished them a pleasant evening, and showed them the door. It was clear that they were regulars, known to Cole and Judy by their first names, their life stories spilled out over the bar night after night, the sad ramblings of old folks with nothing left to live for.

"That was nice, to give them food," Georgie said as Judy latched the door closed.

"They don't have anywhere else to go," she replied. "Most of them are too sick to work anymore, they live on the streets, sleep in doorways, always trying to stay one step ahead of the military police. At least here, they can rest for a few hours, have some food, feel like a real person."

Georgie didn't want to think about how likely it was she would become one of those lost people, unable to work and left to rot by the same government that lured them here under false pretenses. The gin, although watered down, had made her feel sleepy, and all she wanted was to go home and sleep on the floor, the same way she had every night since they left Gamma-3.

"Alright, Em, you can tell her the plan now," Cole called down the stairs into the basement. "We're clear."

"Listen, we need to know you're solid before we tell you anything," Judy said, an eyebrow raised with suspicion. "We don't need any rats."

"I'd never do anything to put my sister in danger."

"She said you're a square. Are you a square, Georgie? Are you gonna squeal on us?"

"No."

"Actually," Emeline said, bouncing through the curtain that separated the bar from the back room and kitchen area, "she's not a square. My big sister blew up the Administration building a few months back."

"That's being a bit generous," Georgie said quickly. "I was helping some friends, they needed a diversion."

"The same friends that smuggled your mother and sister out today?"

"Yes."

"They rebels? Part of The Scattered?"

"Pirates."

Cole snorted. "Pirates don't help people like us."

Georgie shrugged. "These do."

"So they're not Scattered, then?" Judy pressed.

"Listen, I'm new to all this, I don't know what they are or aren't a part of. I helped smuggle them out, they helped smuggle us out. Or at least, my mother and other sister. Our interaction has been fairly minimal, aside from them saving our asses out by the monorail tracks last night." She'd barely slept since then, and thinking about it made her eyelids feel heavy.

"What happened with the monorail?" Cole asked. "There's been nothing about it on the underground stations, and nothing about maintenance or repairs on the official broadcasts."

"It blew up. Struck by lightning, I saw it myself. Something about some weird storm technology tied in with the terraformers, yadda yadda, positive charge or something. I don't know, I'm no scientist. I just know that monorail isn't going anywhere other than the scrap yard."

"Storm technology?" Emeline shook her head, as if trying to clear her thoughts. "Well, what happened to it?"

"Disabled, probably. From what I can tell, Allemande found out about some unauthorized transmissions sent out there. Lawrence Tripp, head of the science department, she killed him."

"Fuck," Cole said. "Fuck!"

"You knew him?"

"He was one of us, of course I knew him."

"I'm sorry."

"We were going to wait until the terraformers were out of commission and send an S.O.S for humanitarian aid. We've spent years planning for this, years of work wasted. Ever since Tripp came to us saying that Baker had him working on some kind of superweapon, we'd planned to use it against them." He rounded on Georgie, his face red with rage. "This is your fault! If you and that fucking scientist hadn't gone out there looking for trouble—"

"How the hell were we supposed to know what was going on? As far as most people here know, the rebel cell collapsed in on itself years ago. Henry saw anomalies and wanted to make sure everyone here didn't fucking die!"

"What the hell are we supposed to do now? Our plan to get people relocated out of here, take the manufacturing power away from Skelm, is ruined. They'll all die here regardless, it will just be longer and more painful."

"They'd just have rebuilt, gotten new people to join up," Emeline said. "It would have stopped them only for a little while. They have so much more power than us, but if we work together, if we can get everyone together to make our demands, then—"

"Then they'll gun us down in broad daylight and shoot our corpses into the atmosphere. You sound just like your old man, Emeline, full of hope and idealism, and it's going to get you killed if you're not careful."

CHAPTER SEVENTEEN

"What, and planning to hijack one of their new weapons won't get *you* killed?" she snorted. "I'm not afraid of fighting for a cause in broad daylight. Why are you?"

Cole frowned, but closed his mouth, his brows knitted together in thought. Georgie knew that even progressive minded men didn't like being shown up by a woman, much less by a teenage girl, and Emeline was certainly a challenge to the old schools of thought. Though she was still furious with her for sneaking off the Cricket to stay in Skelm, she was also, secretly, so proud of her that she could burst.

"She's right, you know," Judy soothed, wrapping an arm around Cole's shoulders. "They don't see us as people. We're replaceable, nothing more than a means to an end, something that affects their bottom line. They'd sooner let us all die to bring in new recruits with healthier lungs than shut this place down." She turned to Emeline. "What would your idea be, then? It better be a good one if we're going to get everyone onside."

"We need to present the workers as a unified force," Emeline began. "Collectively bargain. Go on strike, disable the machines. We'll need to get reporters in here, otherwise they'll just kill us all and be done with it."

Cole barked a laugh. "You're naïve if you think the Coalition will allow that kind of reporting. That's completely absurd."

"Excuse me," Emeline said, staring him down, her head cocked to one side, "but are you telling me that the underground radio you listen to doesn't have satellites peppered all throughout the Near Systems, all the way to the Outer Rim? And here I thought The Scattered were better organized than that."

"Of course we have radio, but how the hell are you going to get a reporter in here? No one is going to be allowed in or out."

"We'll just have to come up with a solution, then," Emeline said. "But we need word to get out to other settlements, get people to put pressure on the government if anything is going to change."

"And if it doesn't?" Cole asked.

"Then we burn the factories to the ground and make sure everyone sees it," Emeline replied casually. "But first, we do our best to change things from within the existing system."

"What if we found a way to hack into that comms tower?" Georgie asked. "We know now that Allemande is monitoring it, but what if we, I don't know, find some way to… hide it?"

"I'll talk to my engineer on the inside, a big fellow named Bale," Judy said. "That's a good idea, if we can make it happen."

"I know him! He worked on the monorail."

"Yes, I'm sure he'll be thrilled to discover what you and that scientist pair did to it. But if there's a way to get communications out without alerting good old Allemande, then that's going to save us a lot of trouble in the long run."

All Georgie could think about was that she would be able to send a message to Henry, letting her know they were alright, and to wait for her. Her heart ached knowing it may be a very long time before she saw her again, before she could run her fingers through Henry's long dark hair and feel her arms around her.

"Alright, we'd better lock up before dawn hits," Judy said, sliding the wall panel open for them to leave. "Stay sharp. Georgie, please, get some sleep. I don't want to see you in here again tomorrow night. We need you to keep your job up at the Administration building, be our eyes and ears, yeah?"

"I don't know if I'll still have a job tomorrow."

"You'd better, or this isn't going to work." Judy sighed. "We've got a hell of a fight on our hands, Payne. You'll need sleep if you don't want to fuck it all up."

Georgie nodded. "I'll let Emeline know as soon as I find out, I imagine right after the… execution."

"See you tomorrow, New Girl," Cole smirked.

* * *

Their apartment was eerily quiet without their mother and Lucy, and despite still being too small for both of them, felt empty. Emeline curled up on her side of the bed she had shared with her sister, and Georgie laid blankets out on the floor, the same way she'd done every night.

"Georgie, you should sleep on the sofa. Mama's not here."

"I guess you're right." She spread the blankets out over the couch and kicked off her work boots, shimmying out of her dirty orange jumpsuit, leaving her in just an undershirt and some tight-fitting shorts. She turned out the lights, dim already from the rationed electricity, and snuggled under the quilt.

"Sounds like that communication tower idea might work," Emeline said, her voice muffled by the pillows.

"We could get a message to Ma."

"Alright, alright," Emeline relented. "If we manage to get communications set up, untraceable, then I'll try to send her a message."

"She'll be worried sick, Em."

"I know."

As they both drifted off to sleep, Georgie was glad she had missed the ship. Now she could be there to protect her sister, and after all, she didn't want to go through this alone.

CHAPTER EIGHTEEN

"What do you mean, she's not here?"

"Mrs. Payne, I'm so sorry, we've searched the entire ship," Captain Violet said.

"But I saw her board! You *all* saw her board!"

"We were in port for hours after you boarded, waiting on Georgina. It's possible she slipped out."

"I knew she would want to stay, but I thought I'd convinced her it was for the best! Oh, gods, what's going to happen to her? She's only sixteen, not even through school yet, she's just like her father, trouble always finds her."

"I'm very sorry, Mrs. Payne," the captain repeated. "We're scanning all frequencies in case they try to get in touch, but given what we've just learned about Skelm's new governor, I wouldn't get your hopes up."

"What did you hear?" Henry asked. "About Allemande?"

"She's been monitoring all calls in and out of the registered wire station and the communications tower you and Georgina hacked into. Luckily she's not able to trace our messages, or we'd be in real trouble, but she'll know it was us. She'll know you're the one who did it."

"So I'm a fugitive now?"

"Nothing has been confirmed over the public broadcasts yet, no, but you'll need to be very careful with who you contact and how you do so. If you have any questions, you can talk to Kady. She has all of our security

CHAPTER EIGHTEEN

issues handled. It's possible that she accessed the panel before you, and so has no record of that currently, but we won't know for a while."

"My girls are down there all alone," Mrs. Payne said, a tear escaping from beneath her eyelids and skirting around the breathing apparatus strapped over her mouth and nose. "I can't help them."

"You can help them by making sure Lucy is safe and fed," the captain said, her voice kind and reassuring. "And when we get to Bradach, if you're feeling better, I'm sure Evie and Larkin would appreciate any assistance you can offer in getting the refugee sites set up. The more people we can smuggle out of places like Skelm and relocate them somewhere safe, the better off we'll all be, and the stronger the resistance against the Coalition will become."

"This Bradach place, what's it like?" Henry asked.

"It's a safe place, away from the prying eyes of the Coalition. People can be free from that oppression there. Evie and Larkin run one of the taverns in town, the only one worth visiting if you ask me, and we have contacts throughout the city that can help Mrs. Payne and Lucy get settled in, and make sure Lucy gets into an accelerated science program. From what we've already seen in the lab, she's on a path to accomplish great things."

"What about me?"

"We are hoping that you will stay on the Cricket with the rest of the crew and help us figure out what's causing these storms. They seem to be cropping up all over the Near Systems, but especially in close proximity to rebel settlements and campsites. We can't force you to stay, of course, but to leave would be a waste of your research. Roger will also be allowed to leave if he wants, but Hyun's current recommendation is that he will likely need to remain under the care of a trained medic to assess him on a daily basis."

"When can we go back for Georgie and Emeline?"

Captain Violet shifted her weight from foot to foot like a boxer preparing for a fight as she stared at Henry. "We won't be returning for the foreseeable future."

"We can't just leave them there! That's barbaric! It's basically a death sentence!"

"It's too dangerous right now, and unless tensions cool off, it's going to continue to be risky. We're damned lucky we got out with you four. They've since implemented martial law and are executing stringent searches on every ship, even ones that only have dry goods. It's going to be next to impossible even to try smuggling them out at this point."

Henry brushed the angry tears from her eyes, but she couldn't stem the flow. "Then I'm not staying. Drop me at the nearest beacon, I'm going back for Georgie."

"Ms. Weaver, I'm asking you to listen to what the bigger picture—"

"I don't give one single fuck what the bigger picture looks like if she's not in it."

Captain Violet's radio crackled at her hip. "Boss, another one hit. It looks worse than the other, might be dozens dead."

"Shit! Which one, Ned?"

"Hjarta. It's bad. The lightning took out their comms tower. Looks like their terraformers, maybe a generator. If you come up to the bridge, you can see the damage on the radar. I only happened to see it doing some preliminary scans looking for alternate trade routes, the Coalition traffic in this area is thicker than usual."

"You. Come with me," the captain said to Henry, gesturing for her to follow. "You know storms, right? Now's your chance to see the aftermath."

Henry resented the interruption, but followed her nonetheless, her boots tapping rhythmically on the flooring behind the captain's as she wiped her sweaty palms against the smooth wool of her blue dress. The Cricket's bridge was old and dated, the carpet threadbare and worn through in places where the scuffed wood showed through, indicating where the captain had probably paced for decades during stressful times.

"It's bad, Boss. I don't know how much longer they'll last without assistance," said the chief navigator, a large, burly man with a thick ginger beard and a ponytail gathered at the base of his neck.

"Can you reach anyone down there? Anyone we know?"

"Not without a working comms tower we can't."

CHAPTER EIGHTEEN

"Shit." Captain Violet squeezed the bridge of her nose, her eyes shut tight. "What do you think would happen if we stopped to drop some supplies, maybe lend Alice and Ivy to their repairs?"

"Might be okay. Might not. Hard to know if the Coalition is going to use this as an opportunity to swoop in and take them out for good."

"If we didn't have refugees on board, there'd be no question."

"I know, Boss."

Henry narrowed her eyes at the blurry radar, then looked out towards the settlement, a tiny dot amid swirling storm clouds on the small moon they were orbiting. "Ned, can you get me a copy of whatever data you have? Something down there is definitely strange. That's not a normal storm pattern, it doesn't make any sense. It's like what we saw back outside Skelm, near the cliffs, completely unpredictable paths, one anomaly after another. I'd hesitate to say the same thing is happening here, but…"

"Sure thing, I'll get you that straightaway." He looked at the captain, his eyebrows raised in question. "So what's it gonna be? Are we stopping, or do we slingshot past and stay on course for Bradach?"

"If their terraformers were damaged, they won't survive long enough for us to circle back. Set a course, I'll tell Alice and Ivy to be ready with a team. Henry, monitor the path of this storm, it looks to be dissipating but we can't risk getting caught in it if it builds again."

"I can help with the relief efforts."

"I didn't think you'd want to get your hands dirty, but if you insist, you can go with Kady to offer assistance to whoever might need it. Hyun and Jasper will be on the ground distributing first aid. We don't have room for many refugees, so it's of utmost importance to get their comms tower and terraformers up and running as soon as possible."

Henry rankled at the captain's comment, but didn't want to miss the opportunity to observe the storm's path from the ground, see if there was anything that might help determine what was causing the anomalies. "Sure thing."

***

    Hjarta had been all but leveled by the storm, the devastation a wide path of rubble that stretched from one end of the settlement to the other, extending out past their own atmospheric barrier, with huge native trees torn out by their roots and left on their sides to rot. Alice, the tall woman with the silver braids, and Ivy, who'd helped the Paynes get to the ship back in Skelm, went straight to work on the terraformers, piecing back together what had been destroyed, cobbling together replacement parts for the metal that was melted from the super-heated electricity that struck it. The comms tower was offline too, the electrics inside the panel one solid brick of melted copper and wiring casing all mixed up together.

    Hyun and Jasper had already set up a first aid tent, but were fast running out of supplies. The people caught in the storm were badly injured, some with the telltale fractal patterns of being struck by lightning burned into their skin, others needing limbs amputated from being crushed, several who had been blinded from the swirling debris, nearly all of them now homeless with nothing to their names.

    The lump in Henry's throat burned, and she tried to swallow down her tears. They wouldn't help anyone here, but maybe if she could figure out what was causing these huge storms, she could keep one from happening again, or at least be able to better predict them to evacuate people in the storm's path.

    "It's not easy seeing this kind of destruction, is it?" Kady asked, kicking the dust from a buried toy box with the toe of her boot.

    "No, it's not. It makes you feel helpless, like there's nothing you can do to stop it. These storms are like nothing I've ever seen before, they don't make any sense. You shouldn't be having electrical storms alongside tornadoes without clear indications of a weather pattern." She shook her head and bent to pull someone's pink plush rabbit from the rubble. "It's going to take them weeks to find and bury all their dead without better equipment."

    "These small settlements aren't equipped for major infrastructure. They were built as stopovers for the Coalition before ships had the technology

CHAPTER EIGHTEEN

to fly for weeks like they do now, then abandoned. Not financially viable, they said. Put thousands of people out of work, the businesses all closed, these places were like ghost towns until some rebels started to reclaim them, restarted the terraformers, began to build up a community. The people here are trying to escape their lives from before, lives that probably looked a lot like they do in Skelm. Some are fugitives from the law."

"What will they do?"

"We'll give them what they need to survive a while longer, maybe we can take some of the worst off with us, though our med bay is already full. If they're lucky, Captain Tansy might be nearby, or one of her fleet with a transport they can load everyone onto. Let them rest, recover, and maybe when things have settled down, the strongest will return to start the process of building it up again. But don't be mistaken, this is a devastating loss."

Henry felt pain sear across her heart as she brushed the dust from the toy, not daring to wonder what had happened to its owner. "We can't let this keep happening," she whispered. "We—I have to do something about it. Have to figure it out. There must be an answer."

"So you've given up on that idea to ditch us at the first opportunity and go running back to Skelm?"

"I will go back for her, I promise that. I won't abandon her. But Georgie would want me to help these families, since she cares so much about her own. She'd see Emeline, Lucy, and her mother in each of these faces."

"You're probably right." Kady stepped over the remains of a home's foundation and cupped her hands around her mouth. "Hey Alice. Any luck with that terraformer?"

"Yeah, it'll hold for a few weeks. It won't last through another one of those storms, though, there'd be nothing left!" Alice called back, holding a charred hunk of metal aloft for them to see across the torn up field, once planted thick with corn and other crops, now razed to the ground. "I reckon we need communications up as soon as possible, so we can send Tansy the coordinates?"

"Right you are," Kady shouted back, and gestured for Henry to follow her. "You have any experience with comms panels?"

Henry shrugged. "Some. I rewired the one outside Skelm that you all intercepted. I'm no expert, though."

"Today you're going to become one. The more of us who know how to repair these, the better. Even before these freak storms, the Coalition ships were targeting them from outside the atmosphere, sometimes remotely, in a bid to reduce the spread of rebel settlements and make things as hard as possible for them. Some have reinforced their towers, but it's only a matter of time before the military ships get wind of that and up the ante."

"Lucky for you, I'm a quick learner."

"Yeah, well, that better be true, because we don't have a lot of time to spare. We need to get to Bradach and drop off Mrs. Payne, Lucy, and Roger, stock up, and head back out, try to predict where the next storm might land."

"I would imagine Roger would prefer to stay on the Cricket, if he's well enough."

Kady grimaced. "We'll see about that."

"What's that supposed to mean?"

"It means we'll see." She waved at Alice and Ivy, and picked up a bundle of copper wiring from the ground. "We ready to knock this out?"

"Quicker we get reinstated, the quicker we can get to Bradach," Alice agreed, pulling a large wrench from her toolbelt that hung at her ample hips. "I just hope Tansy isn't too far away, there's a lot of people here that need more medical assistance than we can give them right now. Hyun and Jasper are flat out trying to keep up."

"Shit. There's not much more we can do, other than leave them with whatever supplies we have, and try to cram a few of the most injured on the ship, get them to Bradach a few days earlier."

"Would it be a good idea for someone to stay behind here, in case there's a second storm?" Ivy asked. "To be on hand to repair the terraformers again?"

"Are you volunteering?" Alice laughed.

"I might be, if it was for the best."

Kady rolled her eyes. "She's only offering because of that cute girl in the first aid tent. What was her name?"

"I didn't catch her name," Ivy mumbled, a blush creeping across her pale cheeks.

"Whoever it is, it's clear you've got a crush," Alice teased. "And yes, it is a good idea for someone to stay here for a couple of weeks until everyone can get evacuated. We'll swing back for you when Tansy gives us the all-clear. Grab your stuff from your room, okay? At least we can fit a couple more people on the ship this way, too."

"I'm on it!" Ivy shouted, already sprinting back towards the Cricket.

"Ivy! Make sure you also take a spare box of droids from the storage room, you can use their fuses!"

"Ugh, I know!" the girl laughed over her shoulder.

"She better not get herself into any trouble here," Kady grumbled. "Last time she had a breakup, she was a mess for weeks."

"To be fair, I was also sitting in the brig at the time," Alice said cheerfully. "It was a lot for anyone, much less an eighteen-year-old. Don't you remember being that young, Kady? It was much more recent for you than it was for me."

"I was already blowing up labs at that age, and besides, my mentors were never stupid enough to end up in the brig," Kady grinned. "You have to admit that was your own fault, Al."

"Maybe." Alice wrenched open the twisted metal covering the communications panel and examined the inside. "Gonna need a whole new panel. What do you think, Henry?"

"I, uh, it doesn't look salvageable to me, but I've only done hacky rewiring jobs before, not a full replacement."

"If you can rewire, you can replace a panel," Kady said, thrusting a new panel into her hands, fresh from a box sitting beneath the tower. "We've been trading for these non-stop with all the attacks, it's the quickest and easiest way of restoring communications without spending days soldering damaged metal to frayed cables. It's just not worth the effort, not with everything else going on."

Henry turned the heavy panel over in her hands, examining each port and connection. "Yeah, I think I've got it. Alice, pliers?" The old wiring was damaged, but easily stripped back and spliced with the new panel, twelve ports in all. Not nearly as many as a city like Skelm, and a quick job with the right tools. "How does that look?"

"I'd say that looks passable," Kady said, examining the new shiny panel. "You'll want to keep those splices tidier, in case you need to replace it again in the future, you don't want to run out of connection wire, that's a much bigger job."

"Sure."

"You've passed the test, cadet. Alice and I are going to head back to the ship, you're welcome to join us; I can show you your room, let you get settled."

"Maybe later," Henry said, looking out over the now barren landscape. "I want to examine these patterns from the ground, follow the path of that storm, and see if it sparks any new information."

"Suit yourself," Alice said, tightening her tool belt. "You know where to find us."

Henry nodded and began to walk through the small settlement, following the path of the storm. It seemed indiscriminate in what it destroyed, which wasn't unusual, but the way it had begun at one end of the settlement, and dissipated just past the other side seemed strangely targeted, more so than they had witnessed outside Skelm.

The problem with storms was that the more established, wealthier cities would always recover in time. Fewer people died thanks to the improved infrastructure: stable bridges, strong buildings, well-equipped medical facilities. The more rural and impoverished areas could be flattened, literally and figuratively, by one unlucky storm, and Hjarta was proof of that. This community might never recover from the damage that had been done, and they'd lost dozens of their people.

Everything else Henry had ever done seemed unimportant in comparison, no amount of casual rainfall statistics or observation of storm patterns to protect Coalition buildings on Gamma-3 could come close to knowing that if she and Roger didn't figure these storms out, more people would die. The weight was crushing, and yet, it felt like what she had been studying and training her whole life for.

When she pulled back the loose flap, the first aid tent was crowded with people, some holding their dirty, crying children, some leaning on one another for support. Hyun and Jasper, the tall, muscular man with the square jaw, were sitting behind a small table doling out bandages and medications, triaging those who needed more immediate and expansive care. The two exchanged a concerned look over a gangly boy with an obviously broken leg, who clutched onto his mother's arm and buried his face in her sleeve.

"Psst. Henry. Move on out of the way so I can get inside," Mrs. Payne whispered.

"Oh! Sorry," Henry said, shifting into the corner. "Did you need something, or—"

"Direct me, Hyun. How can I help? I'm no fancypants doctor-medic like you, but I did train a little in first aid," Mrs. Payne declared, bursting through the tent flaps.

"Ma'am, you can stay in the med bay, your lungs could use additional treatments—"

"Hogwash. I already feel better than I have in years, and this nifty chair Ivy and Alice put together is the bee's knees. It makes me feel like a new godsdamned woman." She glanced at the boy and grimaced. "Sorry for my language," she apologized to the mother.

"If you're comfortable looking after minor wounds, you can take these supplies and patch some folks up," Jasper said, pushing a pile of bandages and bottles of antiseptic towards her.

"Jasper, no! She needs rest!" Hyun protested.

"She seems fine, and wants to help, and you can't say we don't need it," he shrugged. "She doesn't seem like the sort of person who will listen once she's got her mind made up."

"You're damn - er, darn straight," Mrs. Payne grinned. "Now hand it over and give my space in the med bay to someone who really needs it. I'll bunk in with my Lucy, and we can continue my treatments when there aren't people sicker than me in need of help." She scraped the pile into her lap, using her apron to gather it together.

"Alright, little man, I'm going to carry you to the ship, is that okay?" Jasper asked, rolling up his sleeves.

Ezekiel nodded. "Yes."

"Hey, Weaver," Hyun called. "Take his place, I need you to take notes for me and Mrs. Payne. He might be gone for a while, he'll need to get the kid settled in the med bay." She tossed a clipboard, and Henry snatched it out of the air.

"Happy to help," she said, winding through the crowd of patients and sitting in Jasper's chair. She picked up the pen, drew up a makeshift table to fill in with information, and tried to push the guilt of leaving Georgie in Skelm out of her mind. She would be okay. Probably.

CHAPTER NINETEEN

Three months had passed since the Cricket left her behind. Three months since she last saw her mother, or Henry, or Lucy. The loneliness was palpable, even with Emeline snoring softly in the bed across the room. If she didn't have her, she wasn't sure she'd even be able to carry on. She missed Henry with every cell in her body, a permanent ache that wilted her soul with longing.

Mr. Jackson's execution had been terrible, a firing squad set up to murder the man who had committed the highest of treasons, they'd said. He was charged with a number of offenses, including aiding and abetting pirates and stealing the monorail with intent to destroy, both of which Georgie had done. The guilt ate at her daily, despite knowing that the real reason he'd been killed was to protect Governor Allemande's murder of Lawrence Tripp. Despite his sedition, the Coalition officially frowned on extrajudicial punishment. Unofficially, however, they had no problem with taking out rebels and pirates as quickly and quietly as possible.

Georgie rolled off the couch and yawned, stretching her arms over her head. She still had the early shift up at the Administration building, having somehow managed to escape punishment for leaving early the day she tried to leave Skelm altogether. It hadn't even been noted in the logs; the tracking badge was hanging right where she'd left it the next morning. As much as she wanted to be alongside her sister at the Twisted Lantern, working to overhear any useful information, and planning strikes in the hours after closing, the growing rebel cell had determined it necessary for her to continue in her role as a janitor.

She pulled on her orange coveralls and slid into her work boots, snatching a day old muffin from the counter. With Emeline working now too, and two fewer mouths to feed, there was a little more food to go around. For the first time since they'd left Gamma-3 when Georgie was young, her bones didn't sharply protrude from her body. It was a small mercy, given the escalating tensions in the city. Mr. Jackson's execution led to angry whispers in the janitorial division, which spread easily to the gardeners. He had been their manager, too.

"I'm leaving, Em," she whispered to her sister. "I'll see you tonight."

Emeline grumbled a garbled reply and rolled across the bed, pulling the thin pillow over her head to block the light from the broken window. She'd been working later and later, with longer meetings after the speakeasy closed. With Georgie's early shifts, they rarely saw much of each other.

The calendar on the wall next to the door announced a new month, and Georgie grimaced. The census would be soon, and they'd have to figure out how to account for their mother and Lucy missing. The ports were completely locked down, no one in or out without special dispensations from Governor Allemande herself. After a smuggler was executed for trying to hide a family in crates to get them off-world, there were no more smugglers willing to risk their lives to save others, no matter how many credits were involved.

If she lied and said that her mother and sister were dead, they would want paperwork, official notices proving as such, which obviously, they didn't have.

The city's streets were cleaner than ever, the result of Allemande's new guidelines on expectations. Janitorial staff was expected to do twice the work in half the time and be fired if they couldn't keep up. Georgie's bones ached at the end of every day, and she was so tired that she barely remembered what it was like to have the energy to sit up and laugh with her sisters like she once did.

The factories belched more and more black smoke into the fragile at-

CHAPTER NINETEEN

mosphere, with workers being forced to work double shifts to increase productivity. Governor Allemande impressed visiting dignitaries with hugely profitable margins, the best they'd ever been, while workers dropped dead during shifts at an alarming rate. It didn't matter to them - it was all for the glory of the Coalition, and victory through profits at any cost.

Georgie trudged up the hill to the Administration building, feeling every cobblestone through the soles of her boots. Despite having a little extra food, they certainly couldn't afford new boots, not with paying for Emeline's private tutoring. She hated the idea of her sister missing out on the rest of her education, so they were paying a young man to teach her what she would have learned in school; they paid a premium to keep him quiet about the circumstances.

A guard scanned her arm to detect the Coalition chip beneath her skin before she was allowed to enter the building. The advanced security protocols were another one of Governor Allemande's brilliant ideas, and an excellent excuse for her to request more budget for the military police operations within the settlement. Georgie overheard the meeting where Allemande dumped a heap of charred scrap from the monorail on the conference room table in front of the budgetary committee and said, "This is what happens when you don't police your people."

Their lockers weren't allowed to have padlocks anymore, not that Georgie had ever bothered in the first place. She didn't have much to her name anyway, and she doubted anyone would want to steal her old, worn-out coat that she'd had since she was fifteen. The elbows were worn through in patches, and on cold mornings the draft snaked up her arms and settled in her bones.

Georgie sat heavily into one of the half broken chairs in the janitorial department, waiting for her day's assignments. They'd cut the staff by half, sending the unlucky others back to the factories to work themselves into an early grave. The remaining few had to do more with less, Allemande's rallying cry to the Coalition investors that praised her so highly.

"Good morning, staff," Erin said, swooping into view with what looked like a brand new dress. "I've set your daily tasks on the rota, which you can see behind me. Unless anyone has any further news, I think it's best we all get started."

"Uh, Erin?" Georgie asked, half raising her hand. "I was just wondering—"

"You should address me as Mrs. Talbot now, Georgina. We've been through this time and again since I settled into the previous manager's office."

"Er, right. Mrs. Talbot," Georgie corrected, swallowing back her pride. "I was just wondering if it was possible for us to get slightly larger rations of caustic soda, the increased smog from the factories is leading to more build-up on the windows, and we—"

"You will do with what you have," Erin said with a fake smile plastered across her face. "You know as well as I do that we can't allow for that, not when you all have yet to earn my trust."

"For fuck's sake, Erin, we've worked together for years," an old man shouted from the back of the room. "We can't clean the godsdamned windows without the proper materials, and you know it."

Erin turned and blinked slowly at the man. "How can you expect me to put my own livelihood in jeopardy for you? What do you think would happen if that cleaning product went missing? If somehow it was used in a chemical blast, like the one the late janitorial manager executed just five months ago? Do you think they would let me off with a warning?"

Georgie had done that, too. Guilt burned in her stomach. She hated how Erin wouldn't even say Mr. Jackson's name. It was as if even uttering it would taint her, make her unworthy to the management she was now so desperate to impress.

"How can you expect us to work twice as fast with half the supplies we need? It's ludicrous!" the man shouted, exasperated.

"You should feel lucky to be here, sir," Erin said evenly, her hands clasped in front of her. She had taken to management like a duck to water, completely comfortable in the environment where productivity and efficiency were law, even though just six months ago Georgie had caught her smoking back behind the gardening sheds. "You could be down in the

CHAPTER NINETEEN

factories."

The man clenched his jaw, a vein pulsing in his forehead. "*Mrs. Talbot*, if you would just listen—"

"In fact, I think it would be an excellent learning opportunity for you to spend the next several months down there. Maybe when you come back to us, you'll be a little more grateful for the leniency you get in this department."

The man stared at her.

"Go on, off you go," Erin said with a smile. "I hear there's an opening in the chemical refinery sector."

He hesitated, sitting at the edge of his seat. "Mrs. Talbot, I'm sorry, I spoke out of turn."

"My decision is final. We'll see you in three months. Please remove yourself from the Administration building voluntarily, or I will be left with no other choice than to call the military police to escort you, and I can promise you that they aren't as kind and understanding as I am."

"Please!" he shouted, tears welling in his eyes. "My lungs can't take the factories, you're sending me to die!"

"Don't be dramatic, it's only for a few months. Now please, remove yourself." She reached for the radio sitting atop the table next to her. "Or I can assure you that you will be permanently unemployed."

He looked around the room, silently pleading for someone to support his cause. Georgie stared at the floor in shame, unable to meet his gaze. "Right then," he said, squaring his shoulders. "I'll see all you cowards in a few months." He spat on the floor as he left through the open doors and marched out into the street.

"You're all dismissed, see me if you have questions about your assignments," Erin said, the smooth calm of her voice a thin veneer over her frustrated, fragile ego.

Georgie dawdled just long enough for the others to shuffle out of the room, slowly tying the lace of her boot until she was left alone with the woman who was once her friend. "Erin, you can't just do that. You heard the man, three months in the factories could kill him."

"Then he should have thought about that before he took a tone with me,"

Erin replied. "What am I supposed to do, overlook his insolence? Where would that leave me as your leader? It would be total anarchy."

"Maybe you could advocate to the higher-ups for us, get us a little more leeway. We're breaking our backs out here, there's only so far you can push people before they snap."

"They chose me for this position to keep order, to make sure that what Governor Allemande wants is achieved. It's my job to make sure that our department doesn't falter or slip up, not after what happened with the previous manager."

"You can say his name, you know. He was a good man."

"He was a fucking traitor, Georgina, and he got what he deserved," Erin hissed. "If you so much as reference him in my presence again, you'll be written up for insubordination if you're lucky. If anyone else had heard that, you'd already be on your way to an interrogation cell."

"You've changed, Erin."

"People have to change with the times, otherwise progress is impossible. Some of us want better things in life than to be scrubbing shit out of toilets until we're old and grey. I'm just sorry that you're apparently content to be mediocre, and die without having achieved anything. I'm working towards a better future, Georgina, what the hell are you doing?"

All Georgie could say was, "Yeah," before turning and pushing her cart into the corridor. Anything else and she would have been in danger of calling Erin a two-faced sellout. Law and order, her ass. Erin was still in the speakeasy three nights a week, getting drunk and disorderly. Rules didn't apply to Coalition management.

***

"How long until it's operational?" Georgie whispered, slowly sweeping nonexistent dust into a pile in the monorail hangar.

Jess tied her unruly ginger hair into a messy topknot. "A week, maybe two tops."

CHAPTER NINETEEN

"Gods, it feels like it's taken ages for this thing to get completed."

"And yet, twice as fast as the first time. Still, they're going to be monitoring the hell out of it once it's done. Allemande can't risk the same thing happening again, it would be an embarrassment, especially with all these new military police walking around. I heard one of them say a new transport would be arriving in a few days, and most of them are going to be tasked with guarding the monorail specifically."

"Shit."

"Yeah. And we'll have at least five of them on every trip out, whether we have a scientist team or not, even just for standard repairs. I don't know how you're going to make this work."

"We have to. If we don't get contact established, we can't move forward."

"You're risking a lot for this."

Georgie sighed and tipped the empty dustpan into the trash bag of her cart. "Risking everything."

"I'll get word when it's finished. I can't promise anything more than that."

"We understand. Thanks." She pushed her cart back out the door just as the tracking card around her neck began to flash and brought rage to a simmer just beneath her skin. They had made it nearly impossible to talk to anyone on the job, or take a piss, or do anything on Coalition time that wasn't working themselves to the bone. It was the most demoralized and unappreciated she'd ever felt.

There was no way they could get to the communications tower beyond the barrier without the monorail. Georgie had been hoping to get assigned to the cleanup efforts like before, so she could sneak off and rewire the panel, install the chip Judy had procured from some black market trader that would allow them remote access. If they couldn't make contact with other rebel settlements, or the Cricket, then things in Skelm were only going to get worse.

Three months since she'd spoken to Henry. One of the last things she'd said to her was, "I love you too," as they sat, ready to die, at the base of a pylon between the city and the terminal station near the boundary. Nothing since then, not when the wire transfer desk was off-limits for janitorial and factory workers. No messages in or out, not that she could risk giving away the Cricket's position, anyway. Even if they managed to secure the comms tower, she couldn't send Henry a heartfelt message about how much she missed her, and missed holding her in her arms, or that at night, she dreamed about the night they shared together.

Weight settled between Georgie's shoulder blades, a little more every day. She felt the heaviness of what they were doing, and the pressing guilt of Mr. Jackson's death, and the gravity of Henry's absence pulling her into the ground. She might not have bothered trying to survive, if it hadn't been for Emeline. Her sister's safety was still her top priority, especially now that she was mixing with known rebels after hours in the speakeasy. It was dangerous, and important.

Emeline said that sometimes, to recenter a government's moral compass, rules had to be broken. She was wise beyond her years, and an inspiration to many who had joined the cause, sneaking around in back alleys at night, trading information under the cover of darkness and beyond the watchful eyes of the military police. Georgie didn't know how Emeline did it day after day, and night after night, propping up flimsy hope and pulling people together to unite under one cause. She was just like their father, and Georgie was proud.

*　*　*

Georgie always waited up for her sister, even when the day's work was heavy on her eyelids, tempting her to sleep for just a few moments. She wanted to know that Emeline was home safe, that she hadn't been thrown into the back of a military police van and carried off to an interrogation cell for questioning. Every night when she heard her sister's key in the lock, she breathed a sigh of relief.

"Heya Georgie," her sister said, hanging her key on the hook beside the

CHAPTER NINETEEN

door. "How was work?"

"Gonna be a week or two before it's finished."

"Not long, then."

"Mm."

"We got a few new ones at the meeting tonight. We missed you."

"I'm sorry, Em, I'm just... tired."

"I know." Emeline sat next to her on the couch and leaned her head on Georgie's shoulder. "It will be nice when they ease up on you a little and you can come back."

Georgie produced a single cupcake with one candle, slightly smushed from being left in the bag. "Happy birthday, Emeline." She struck a match on the sole of her boot and lit the candle. "Make a wish."

"You shouldn't have!" her sister said, squeezing her eyes shut and blowing it out. She removed the candle and took an enormous bite. "Here, share it with me."

"Nah, it's yours."

"It's crazy to think it's been a year since Lucy tried to make that cake."

Georgie snorted. "I don't think I'll ever forget what a cake without sugar tastes like."

"I wonder what she's doing now. And Mama, too."

"With any luck, they're safe somewhere, and Lucy is in school, and Mama is able to rest sometimes."

"And Henry?" Emeline probed.

"I hope she's safe, too." She sighed, her heart aching with loss. "I miss her."

"I know."

"I hope I see her again."

"That's what I wished for, Georgie. That you'll see her again soon."

CHAPTER TWENTY

Even after several trips to Bradach, the infamous pirate settlement, Henry still managed to get lost amid the winding cobblestone streets. Tiny pop up markets lined the roads, selling hot food, cold drinks, and a bevy of black market items from droid parts to weapons small enough to conceal beneath a corset. She herself had purchased a silver revolver that sat comfortably at her hip, the holster nestled amongst her skirts. She had no need to conceal it, not here, but it was a possibility if she ever wound up in a Coalition settlement again.

Storms continued to rip through rebel settlements at an alarming pace, and the targeted nature proved it was no coincidence. Somehow, they were directing storms at specific locations, and causing the storms to increase in volatility. She'd spent three months now working on a solution, but with Roger's short-term memory loss from his head injury, it had been fruitless. Kady was an accomplished scientist in her own right, but bringing her up to speed on the latest meteorological advances was taking too long.

Henry wandered through the streets, allowing her mind to wander; sometimes she found that it sparked a new idea. Wandering was as productive as spending an all-nighter in the Cricket lab, poring over what little data they had. She was tired of rescue and supply missions, and had a growing desperation to find the root of the problem. The longer she took to figure it out, the more people were dying, the more homes were being ripped apart by high-speed winds and unprecedented levels of electrical storms.

A used book stall sat at the end of the dead end road, piles of worn out tomes with creased covers hiding the seller. "Hello?" Henry said, peering over the stacks. "Anyone there?"

"Aye, I'm here," someone said, emerging from beneath the table with a red hardcover book. "Just shifting some things around. How can I help ye?"

"Just browsing."

"Take your time, then, I'm in no hurry. Got all the time in the world and plenty of books to read." They sat back in a rickety looking chair and cracked open the book to the first page. "If you're looking for a bargain, I've got some slow movers there toward the bottom. Credit or trade, I don't mind."

Henry nodded, and bent to look through the pile, holding each book in her hand, flipping through the yellowed pages. They were all banned books, each and every one of them, removed by the Coalition for encouraging sedition and rebellion. "Where did you get all of these?"

"Used to be a librarian," the bookseller answered sadly. "Long time ago. Before the book burnings."

"You stole them?"

"I took what the Coalition considered trash," they answered in an irritated voice. "Once they decided what was and wasn't allowed, any of us in disagreement were hunted down and thrown into work camps for reeducation. I am personally not fond of manual labor, so I hitched a ride on the first transport I could get that would also bring my books."

"I'm sorry, I didn't mean it like that," Henry conceded. She still had a long way to go when it came to dismantling old ideas, the kind that she was raised with - not that her parents would speak to her anymore, now that she was running with pirates and not slowly ascending the career ladder at the CSA. "It's wonderful you rescued all these old stories."

"You'd be surprised how many people value a story," they said, softening. "We all need to be able to escape sometimes. The universe is a harsh and unforgiving place."

"Mm." Henry sifted through a stack of old novels about the pioneers of space exploration, brave souls who risked everything to ride on primitive shuttles, long before the Coalition took hold of the Near Systems.

"Here, have a look at this one. Just got it in a trade today. You might like it, if you like adventure." They tossed a paperback over the tall stacks and laughed. "You seem the type."

Henry caught the book in midair and gasped. It was the same book as the one she and Georgie had read in the speakeasy. It gave her an idea, a dangerous, brilliant idea. "I'll give you whatever you want for this book."

"Aha! Something told me that you'd enjoy it." They smiled, and the light sparkled in their hazel eyes. "Go on, take it. No charge."

"You can't just give me a book, how would your business survive?"

"Old librarian habits die hard, I guess. But I can read people as well as a book, and I know you'll be back."

* * *

Henry clutched the book to her chest as she pushed open the heavy door of the Purple Pig tavern. Feeling the smooth cover beneath her fingers made her feel closer to Georgie, even though they were an impossible number of kilometers apart, and they hadn't even spoken in months.

"Hey Henry, what will it be?" a slight woman with a long dark braid and a wide hooded cloak asked.

"Just water, if you don't mind, Larkin."

"Everything alright?"

"Just wondering if you and Evie have managed to establish contact with Skelm yet."

Larkin filled a tall glass with clear water from the barrel in the corner. "Nothing yet, I'm afraid."

"It's been months, how come it's taking so long?"

"We can't risk them tracking those messages, you know that. Besides, with all these godsdamned storms, we're all barely keeping our heads above water with spreading rations around. Hell, with Eves out on the ship half the time, I'm run ragged keeping this place open."

CHAPTER TWENTY

Henry sat heavily on one of the plush covered stools at the bar. "I know. I just..."

"Yeah. Tough times." Larkin set the glass on the bar and slid it over. "I don't know how you're not losing it, not even being able to talk to her. I don't know what I'd do if I was away from Evie that long."

"You know, I was wondering, what if we could get some kind of coded message sent? Maybe through one of our contacts in the Coalition. Just so I can tell her that we're okay, that her family is doing well."

"It's risky. Allemande is going to be monitoring everything that goes in and out."

"What about an interdepartmental memo? She might not be looking at those."

Larkin raised an eyebrow. "Well, that's an idea. But who do you know in the janitorial division?"

"I don't, but Roger might. He knows everyone."

"You'd have to come up with a code they're unlikely to break, but wouldn't look too suspicious." She shook her head. "I just don't know if that's possible anymore."

Henry frowned, insulted. "I'm one of the best code breakers in the CSA. At least, I was, before I got fired and ended up here."

"You must be joking."

"Why would I joke about that?"

"Evie!" Larkin shouted into the kitchen. "Eves, come here!"

"Gods, what the hell are you shouting about?" Evie asked, emerging from the doorway with a plate of freshly baked cinnamon rolls, which filled the room with a deliciously sweet, spicy aroma. "You'd think the building was on fire, the way you're screaming the place down."

"Eves, she's a *code breaker*."

"What? No." Evie slammed the plate of pastries down on the bar and grabbed Henry by the shoulders, grinning widely. "Why didn't you tell us? Henry, this is amazing!"

"I have to admit I don't understand what's going on here," Henry said, snatching one of the pastries that had slid off the plate. "None of you seem to operate with codes, rather you're using encoded frequencies and algorithmic automated sequencing. What good is a code breaker when you've got that kind of advanced technology?"

"Follow me upstairs," Evie said with a mischievous smirk. "If you're as good as you say you are, this could be huge."

"Alright, but I'm bringing this cinnamon roll," Henry laughed, smoothing her skirts after sliding off the bar stool. She climbed the creaking wooden stairs behind Evie, who practically leapt up the steps in excitement. She unlocked the cherry wood door to their lofted living space above the tavern and pushed it open.

Before Henry entered, she didn't expect to see a chalkboard wall covered with photographs and papers, with lines drawn between them in a complicated web of information, but there it was anyway, behind their sofa, strewn with cushions. "What's all this?"

"Research!" Evie answered excitedly. "I've been working on it for months, ever since Georgie got us out of Skelm. I managed to get my hands on some coded files we think might have something to do with the storms. We were tipped off by Barnaby—do you know Barnaby? Long story. We were tipped off that the Coalition was planning some kind of large scale attack on the rebel settlements. We didn't realize at first what that attack would look like, though now it's safe to assume that it's the storms."

"Right."

"I'm a decent researcher, I can find information on just about anything - bit of a nerd, you know - but unfortunately, my code breaking skills are woefully underdeveloped. None of us have managed to crack it, and it might be the key to some really useful intel."

"Have you tried a shift—"

"Yes, yes, of course we've tried shift codes," Evie said, waving her away. "I've even created concentric circular devices to try to discern some sort of pattern, but no luck. It uses some kind of encryption I've never seen before and don't recognize from any of my research."

"How come you never mentioned this to me?"

Evie shrugged. "We'd all pretty much written it off as an impossibility.

CHAPTER TWENTY

Plus, once the storms started, well, there wasn't much of a mystery left as to what that large scale attack was going to look like." She shoved a stack of files across the tea table. "Have a look."

"I'm due back on the ship in a little while."

"All I'm asking is that you take a look."

Henry sighed. "Alright then."

* * *

Day turned to night when the mirrors above Bradach shifted away for the evening cycle. Henry was sitting on the floor, surrounded by files, papers scattered across the table and tacked up on the walls as she worked with Evie, who was a much better code breaker than she'd given herself credit for. Some lower level classified files were one step away from decryption, with just one tiny piece missing from the impressive research she had done.

"One more here, Evie. Another one of these characters decoded."

"Excellent. Are we getting closer to piecing any of this together?"

"We are. Hand me that file over there, the one with the photos of Skelm from outside the atmosphere."

She took the file from Evie and flipped it open, copying down notes from the margins of the pages into her notebook, squinting at each letter and character, trying to will them into forming some kind of readable pattern. They were almost there, she could feel it. Common words like "it" and "the" seemed to leap off the page, but left the more important information in the dark. She'd forgotten how much she enjoyed code breaking, the way it sizzled in her brain, igniting every neuron. At least she felt useful, for once.

"Have you got it?" Captain Violet shouted, bursting through the door. "Larkin said you could break it, is it done? Do we have the information?"

Evie shot a dirty look at Larkin, who was lurking behind the captain with a guilty face. "Not yet."

"Sorry, Weaver, the captain came looking for you and I mentioned you two were up here with the files," Larkin said apologetically.

Captain Violet looked at Evie with questioning eyes. "I thought this wasn't possible?"

"It wasn't, but Henry has knowledge of Coalition codes."

"That's a slight overstatement on Evie's part there, Captain, I just have a knack for it. Comes from years of staring at binary data from the weather balloons, trains you to look for patterns in unlikely places."

Larkin set a huge dish of paella on the counter in their small, personal kitchen. "I brought some food over from José and Mrs. Payne, they had a little extra after dishing out meals to the refugees."

"Oh gods, I'm starving," Evie said, piling a bowl high with the steaming rice and vegetables. "Henry, you want some?"

"I'm due back on the ship—"

"Oh no, Ms. Weaver, you're cleared to stay right damn here until you get through those codes. It could be incredibly valuable to know what they're up to. We can't lose any more settlements, any more people." The captain draped her legs over the arm of a chair and poked at the food with a fork. "I'll delay setting off until morning. Do you think you'll have it by then?"

"I'll do my best—"

"Good. I'll reallocate whatever teams you need to get this done."

"Can someone please be reallocated to scanning frequencies?" Henry asked. "It's just that Evie is in here with me, and they might try to get into contact."

Captain Violet sighed and laid a hand on Henry's shoulder. "Of course, but I wouldn't get your hopes up. If we haven't heard from them by now, months after we left, it's possible that the situation in Skelm has deteriorated more than we had initially feared."

Henry felt her heart throb, the pain oozing out over her lungs and making it hard to breathe. "Please don't say we're giving up on them," she pleaded, tears welling in her eyes. "You can't. She's the only reason why I didn't die that night after the monorail exploded. She helped Evie and Larkin escape! Please, Captain, promise me you're not just going to leave Georgie and Emeline to the wolves."

CHAPTER TWENTY

"Just get that code done, alright? Every little bit helps."

"Fine."

"All due respect, Captain, but what lengths would you go to if it was Alice?" Larkin asked, leaning against the doorway with her hood pulled up over her head.

"I'm doing everything I godsdamn can!" the captain retorted. "Until they get into contact, or that governor stops monitoring all incoming and outgoing transmissions, we don't have a lot of options, here. Not without endangering the entirety of Bradach, or the crew if sent from the ship. I've spoken with Captain Tansy and she's on full alert waiting on them, waiting for any sign of rebellion or refugees. Allemande is making our lives very difficult."

"I said, fine. I'll do it. But I need peace and quiet if you don't mind," Henry said sternly, staring at the wall and trying to blink back tears. She couldn't bear the idea of leaving Georgie to fend for herself in Skelm, not when she spent every night imagining their reunion, the feeling of her strong arms and rough hands, the peace of falling asleep in her arms. "I want to finish working through the code from my quarters." She gathered up the piles of papers and the stacks of files and marched out of the room, sniffling as she went.

Back on the ship, she sat at the small desk and pored over the papers, willing herself to focus on the task at hand, staring at letters and symbols until they swam in front of her eyes. It was the most difficult code she'd ever come across, and the frustration of being almost correct, but not quite, was starting to wear on her.

"Hey," said Roger from the doorway. "Need some help?"

"Hey yourself. How are you holding up?"

"Ah, you know, got lost about half a dozen times on my way here, but getting better all the time. Just hoping I continue to improve, maybe be of some real use to this here pirate crew."

"I think you have surprised them with how adaptable you are. Seems Kady thought you'd be ready to disembark at the earliest opportunity, medical care or no."

Roger shrugged. "It's about the science, you know? And you're my best friend, I'm not leaving you behind. I've been gone too long to beg the CSA for my job back, anyhow. Despite what they reported in the press, I think it's likely that we're fugitives, at least internally."

"You could always claim kidnap."

"What, and besmirch my bravado? Never."

Henry snorted and leaned back from the desk. "Rog, this code, I swear. It's impossible. They're all thinking I can decrypt these files, but the more I stare at it, the more I'm convinced that all the work I've done is incorrect."

"You'll get it. You're the best godsdamned code breaker I've ever known."

"I'm also the *only* code breaker you know."

Roger shrugged. "Irrelevant."

"I worry that even if I do manage to decode it, the information will be useless, tell us everything we already know. Storms being used as a weapon, early tests, which settlements to be targeted first, things that are outdated and meaningless now."

"Might have information on how they're using those storms, though." He crossed to her desk and picked up one of the torn pieces of paper and squinted at it. "Honestly, Hen, I don't know how you make any sense of this shit at all. Even before my head injury, this all just looked like incomprehensible gibberish to me."

"It's just finding patterns, the same way we do when working on storm algorithms. They're just... better hidden."

"I'm sorry I can't be of more assistance," he said, laying the piece of paper back on the desk sideways. "I can offer a cup of coffee, though I can't promise that it won't be cold by the time I find my way back here. This ship is like a labyrinth of corridors, honestly."

Henry stared at the piece of paper, and turned her head sideways and back again. "Roger, you absolute genius," she said, snatching her notebook from the drawer. "We've goddamn cracked it."

CHAPTER TWENTY-ONE

"Message for you from off-world," Erin said in a bored voice, sliding a slip of paper across the table. "You should feel lucky. Not many of us get those anymore with the new restrictions." She narrowed her eyes, suspicion cast over her face. "Who is it from?"

Georgie's heart leapt in her chest, hoping against hope that it would be from Henry. "Probably my aunt back on Gamma-3," she lied. Both her parents were only children. A dangerous fabrication, if Erin ever followed it up. "Last we heard, her husband - er, my uncle - wasn't doing well."

"You know everything gets opened and read, right Georgina?" Erin's hand darted across the table and snatched the slip of paper back. "*Pirates and Queens*? What is that supposed to mean?"

Involuntary tears sprang to Georgie's eyes. "It's, uh," she sniffed, trying to pass off her elated crying as sorrow, "a book my uncle used to read us as kids. It's her way of saying he's passed."

"Oh."

"I'll have to tell my mother and sisters."

"I'm sorry for your loss, then." Erin tossed the paper back onto the desk. "Strange way to tell family that someone died, and there's a load of numbers at the bottom."

"She's old and confused. Her messages don't usually make sense."

Erin leaned back in her chair. "Don't get used to getting these messages. I'm not here to be your personal secretary, I just agreed to pass it on as a favor to the mail room."

"I appreciate it."

"Make sure your aunt knows that communications in or out of Skelm are for emergencies and necessity only. You're here to work, not write leisurely letters home to senile family members."

Georgie gritted her teeth. "Yes, I understand."

It was no surprise that Erin changed the moment she put on the new managerial uniform, but it was still jarring that someone she'd worked with for years would go from being a kind, compassionate person to a Coalition lackey that never questioned the grand empire. A tiny modicum of power would corrupt anyone desperate to escape their bleak, directionless life in Skelm, and Erin was no different. Georgie wondered if she herself would do anything different, given the chance. In a place where stability was rare as gold dust, people could be tempted into anything just for the chance to feel normal.

She slid the slip of paper into the breast pocket of her orange coveralls and dragged her janitorial cart into the corridor to start her shift. Another day, another impossible efficiency target to meet, but this time, she knew that Henry was out there somewhere, thinking of her. She hoped Henry was safe, far away from the unrest that continued to build just under Skelm's surface, angry, disenfranchised people like a powder keg ready to explode.

Emeline, Cole, and Judy were doing their best to keep people calm and open to listening, but it grew more difficult with every passing day. She knew that establishing contact off-world was the cornerstone of the movement. People outside Skelm needed to know what was going on, and what was going to happen, if they were to effect any actual change. Otherwise, the Coalition would divide and conquer, scare people back into their homes to cower for another decade.

Her shift passed quickly, a rare temporal mercy given how desperate she was to get home and examine the note. Erin had mentioned numbers, but what could those numbers be? Some kind of coded message? She pushed past the stragglers on the street, people reluctant to return home to nothing more than hunger and crowded, cramped spaces. As imports got hung up

CHAPTER TWENTY-ONE

due to the new mandatory searches, the flow of illegal spirits slowed to a dribble, and those who only just managed to cope with their hopeless lives before, were now even more despondent than ever.

"Georgie," her sister said when she opened the door, "I heard the monorail went out for testing today."

"It did, as far as I know it went smoothly. Should be sending a task force out to clean up the construction mess any day now."

"Are you still okay to do that?"

She kicked off her boots and slumped on the couch. "Not like we have much choice. That thing is going to be under armed guard from here on out, and this is our only option."

"What if you don't get assigned to that team?"

"It's a big job, Em. All hands on deck. I bet they have us all out there at one point or another. I just hope I get assigned a night shift, easier to sneak around that way, plus by then some of the guards will have started drinking."

"I'm worried you'll get caught."

Georgie laughed. "Yeah, I'm worried I'll get caught, too. But don't worry, even if I do, I'd never tell them anything."

"You have to promise me to be careful," Emeline scolded, flopping on the couch next to her. "I don't think I can do this without my big sister." She leaned her head on Georgie's shoulder and heard the crinkle of the paper in her pocket. "What's that?"

"Note from off-world. It's from Henry."

Emeline sat up straight. "That's dangerous, doesn't she know that? She could get you killed, or interrogated, or—"

"Relax. It's a code, I think." She took the slip out of her pocket and smoothed it out on the table. "This is a book we both read at the Twisted Lantern. It's her way of telling me that she's thinking about me."

"What are the numbers for?"

"I don't know yet."

"Hmm," Emeline mumbled, inspecting the note closely, her nose nearly touching the paper. "It can't be any kind of recognizable code or cipher, or they'd have thrown you into an interrogation cell, or at least censored it."

"That was my thought too."

"Georgie! What if it's page numbers, or something?"

"What?" she asked, snatching the note from her sister. The numbers were in an odd format. The list read:

12-3-17
  12-3-36
  12-3-54

"Page numbers, but then what?"

Emeline was already tying the laces on her boots. "What are you waiting for? Let's go get the book!"

* * *

The Twisted Lantern was busier than it had ever been, with a line gathering near the front of the store. "Come on," Emeline whispered, "we can use the back entrance." She grabbed Georgie by the arm and pulled her past a pile of garbage bags into an alley so narrow, they could barely fit without rubbing against the mysterious green slime on the worn brick.

"That line is going to draw attention," Georgie hissed. "They need to either let those people in, or tell them to disperse."

"It gets worse every night. The smugglers aren't able to bring booze in, so people are forced to get it here."

"And how in the hell is Cole getting a hold of it?"

"Brews it himself using some old abandoned distillation vats they stole from storage. He does it in the basement."

"That's one way to make some credits in a crisis."

"Georgie, please, you know as well as I do that they plow almost every credit they get from this place back into the rebellion. How else are we going to pay for food and supplies? Someone has to finance it." She yanked open an old rusted door and gestured for Georgie to enter. "It's just the back

CHAPTER TWENTY-ONE

room, where I usually work."

"That better be the case. I don't want to hear about you drinking."

"As if Cole would let me drink his profits," Emeline snorted. She turned on a flickering light and shouted through the curtain that led out into the main room. "Cole, you've got a line out front. Oh, and don't worry, it's just us."

"Who the hell is us?"

"Me and Georgie."

"Right. You're early!"

"And a damn good thing, too, given those people gathering in the street! You can thank me later!"

"What now?" Georgie asked.

"Go get the book, you can sit back here if you want to, or just head home. I'm sure Cole and Judy won't mind if you borrow it."

"Stay safe, please, Em. That line makes me nervous."

Emeline hugged her around the neck. "Me too. I'll be careful."

Georgie swept past the curtain and Cole, who was running from patron to patron taking orders, jacking up the prices due to scarcity. The book was right where she'd left it, the worn blue cover like a beacon amid the dozens and hundreds of other forbidden books on the shelves. She tucked it under her arm, slipped out the back door and made her way home, anxiously awaiting what message could possibly be hidden within the note, her footsteps quick on the pavement, illuminated by the yellow glow of the street lamps. When she arrived home, she opened the book to page twelve, paragraph three.

"I'll bet you never thought we'd succeed in pilfering that hidden treasure," Mara said. "In fact, **I** will bet you never foresaw an attack at all. No, you're much too foolhardy, and you're certain to **miss** the point of all this entirely. It's almost a shame that no one is coming to rescue **you** and your crew."

The message was clear: "I miss you."

She almost missed the last two codes, printed tiny in the corner. 12-3-24, 12-3-51.

Be careful.

* * *

She awoke with a start at the heavy pounding on the door. "Open up! Census!"

"Fuck," she hissed under her breath. "Em! Wake up!" She threw a cushion across the room at her sister and stuffed the note and book inside her coveralls. "Uh, just a second," she yelled to the door, struggling to shove her feet into her work boots. What the hell were they doing here so early, anyway? The mirrors hadn't even begun to shift for the day cycle yet.

"We have reports that you are harboring fugitives. Open the door, or we'll break it down!"

"I said I'm coming!" She yanked the door open to discover five military police in armor, far too many for a standard census. Georgie swallowed hard and plastered a smile across her face. "How can I help, officers?"

"We're going to need to search the premises," one of them grunted, shoving a piece of paper with a smeared signature on the dotted line and a coffee stain at the edges. "Anyone else here?"

"It's just us," Georgie said, and then caught the look that her sister shot her. "Er, I mean, my mother and other sister live here too, but they're… out."

"Out? It's not even dawn yet."

"They like to take early walks. My mother says it clears her lungs."

"Hmm." The second guard was rifling through the cupboards, knocking on the base to look for false doors or hidden compartments.

"There's another apartment below us, we would be hard pressed to hide anyone here!" Georgie spouted in a voice too chipper for that time of the morning.

"You'd be fuckin' surprised what cockroaches will try to hide from us," the third guard laughed, the sound strangled by the wood and metal of their full face coverings.

"I assure you, we're not hiding anyone," Emeline chimed in, perched at the edge of her bed in her worn plaid pajamas. They'd been their father's. "May I ask where this accusation originated from?"

"None of your business," the first guard said, yanking open the closet door and running his hands over Emeline's school dresses. It made Georgie want to vomit. "If you're hiding anyone or anything, it will go better for you if you say so now, instead of making us rip through everything." He pulled at an old shawl of their mother's, drawing a long tear down the center.

"You won't find anything here, sir," Emeline repeated, now gripping the edge of the bed with white knuckles. "You could turn this home into rubble, but there're no fugitives or contraband."

Georgie flattened herself against the wall, trying to stay out of their way. She knew they shouldn't have pushed their luck in staying here, that they should have moved back to the tenements where people we much harder to keep track of due to all the deaths from poor sanitation, or squat in one of the few abandoned buildings around the city, most bought up as investment before the factories were announced. Landlords weren't interested in housing poor people.

"Tell us where they are!" the second guard shouted.

"Where who are?" Georgie yelled back. "There's no one here except us!"

The third guard grabbed Emeline by the arm and wrenched her up off the bed. "Tell us now!"

"Don't touch her!" Georgie screamed, yanking the guard away from her sister. "Don't fucking touch her!"

"Piss off," the guard said, shoving Georgie to the ground. "It's our job to find these fugitives, and you're interfering with justice!"

"There's clearly no one here," Emeline repeated for the third time, her voice clear, hiding the terror that made her hands shake. "My sister works up at the Administration building, perhaps she should have a word with Governor Allemande about your conduct."

The guards all exchanged a look. "There's no need for that, we're just on patrol," the first one said. "Got reports of rebel activity, said you had ten people coming and going from this residence."

"I can assure you, once again, that those reports are unsubstantiated. There's just the four of us here."

"We'll be making random spot checks to make sure that's the case," the second guard said in a gruff voice. "And next time, we'll want to see your sister and mother for questioning, so tell them no more early morning walks until we close this case." He looked around at the overturned chairs and the broken mug that had fallen when Georgie moved to defend her sister. "I know the stench of an uprising. It stinks of shit, and it smells like this place does."

The guard carefully considered the shelf he was standing near, which held a couple of family photos and trinkets they'd collected over the years, and scraped his arm over the shelf, sending the porcelain crashing to the ground. "Next time, we won't be so nice if you don't comply." He gestured for the others to follow him back out the door. "Come on, boys, let them clean up. No surprise that factory animals would live in a pigsty."

After the door closed, Emeline began shoving clothes into her school bag, leaving her uniforms hanging in the closet untouched. "We need to leave, Georgie."

"Yeah. It's going to be harder from here on out."

"Won't your job require proof of address?"

"Not if I tell them we moved back into the tenements. There's so many people crammed in there, it's almost impossible for them to keep track. Either way, the next time they show up here, it will be empty or occupied by new people. We can't harbor fugitives in a tenement."

"Who do you think it is?"

Georgie picked the photos up from the floor and dusted off the shards of glass, feeling them wedge painfully beneath her skin. "I don't know. It's clear someone tipped them off, no matter how untrue the accusation. Who do you know that might do something like that?"

"I barely even talk to anyone who isn't you, Cole, or Judy."

"Shit."

"What else do you want to take before you hand in the keys?"

"Nothing." She looked down at the photographs in her hand, a rarity for families as poor as hers, taken just before they left Gamma-3. She looked like a sullen teenager, angry that her parents were choosing to uproot their family to chase opportunity across the Near Systems. Her mother and father looked proud, one holding a small Emeline's hand, and the other cradling the newborn Lucy. It felt like a different life, now. Georgie slid them into the book to keep them safe until the day she could return them to her mother. "I have to go to work, Em."

"Meet me at the speakeasy after. I'm sure we can stay there a few days while we figure things out."

"Yeah, alright." She set the book gently into her sister's bag. "Take care of that, will you? And make sure you pick up an extra blanket or two, I don't want you getting sick down in that basement." Georgie took one last look at the home she'd shared with her mother and sisters before closing the door behind her.

CHAPTER TWENTY-TWO

"Hurry it up, Weaver, what else?" Kady demanded from the doorway, the toe of her boot tapping impatiently against the metal grate flooring.

"Give me a minute, it takes time to decode this shit, alright? It would be much faster with the kind of high powered computing the Coalition has access to, but this is just me working through it, and I'm working as fast as I can. It's not like I have Roger to help me, I'm doing it all by myself."

Kady rolled her eyes. "Alright alright, don't get upset!"

"I'm not upset, I'm just tired." Henry rubbed her eyes and stared back at the stacks of paper strewn across her improvised desk, now several tables pushed together in the mess hall. She had more space, and besides, she was closer to the coffee this way. "So far I know the next planned attack is in a few days, but I don't know where yet."

"That's not much time to chart a course."

"I know, which is why I'm in here every spare second I get. Poor Roger can't even remember what he had for breakfast or how to get back to his room, I'm not going to ask him to do this, too."

"He's improving every day, you know."

"I don't want to frustrate him, Kady. He's a brilliant scientific mind, but this code breaking stuff uses a lot of short term memory, which is precisely the thing he's struggling with."

"Alright, so teach me instead."

"I didn't think you'd have the time, not with the constant upgrades to the

CHAPTER TWENTY-TWO

ship you and Alice are working on."

"I have more time than you right now. Now come on, show me how this complex pile of crap works. They need you up on the bridge soon to go over landing plans. Ned doesn't want to get caught up in residual electricity in the atmosphere like last time. Our hull just can't take that kind of sustained damage, not without the kind of repairs that would take months to complete."

"Now you're sounding like Alice," Henry laughed.

Kady shrugged. "She knows her stuff. I follow her lead when it comes to ship repairs, no one knows old vessels like she does. They don't even teach how to fix these old rigs anymore, it's probably the last one left in the Near Systems if I had to guess."

"So the code is up on the wall here, with the step by step process of decrypting these files. Follow it exactly, and each sequence should take about an hour if you're careful. They've padded the files with nonsense, so if it looks like unintelligible garbage, there's a good chance that's what it is."

"Oh perfect. Leave it to the Coalition to make things as difficult as possible."

"Mm," Henry agreed, laying out a new string of words for Kady to practice on. "Try with this. Only work forward, never backward. It's entirely too easy to lose your place with this one, it's a real bastard of a code."

"I'm about to make it bend to my will," Kady replied, notebook in hand and a fresh well of ink at the ready.

She worked through the code. Henry sighed again, frustrated. It was difficult to stay focused on teaching decryption without any of the usual entry level puzzles, and not on Georgie, stuck in Skelm with her sister while the Coalition plotted an attack. What kind of attack, she wasn't sure, but she knew it wouldn't look like the storms the rebels were buried beneath. They would never damage their own factories in such a short-sighted way, not when Skelm held a large slice of the manufacturing pie.

She wasn't even sure that Georgie had received her message. It could have been censored, arriving in Georgie's hands covered in illegible black boxes, obscuring the code she'd created. It was rudimentary, but unless there were extra copies of that book hanging around in Skelm, it would be safe enough. The message might have been lost, or maybe not delivered at all, the new workplace culture Governor Allemande had created being so punishing and sterile. No news in or out except for Coalition sanctioned business. If Henry hadn't sent the note through Jhanvi Jhaveri, she doubted it would have been delivered at all. With Skelm's communications tower under Allemande's watchful eye, there was no way of knowing if Georgie received the warning at all.

She'd heard that the smugglers weren't operating at all anymore, not for refugees, but Henry was still desperate to find a way out for Georgie and her sister, rebellion or no. It had been months since they'd last spoken even a word, and the thought made her feel sick with worry. Sometimes, at night, she'd dream that Georgie was dead, killed in the quiet of the night by military police, or lying next to a monorail pylon in the middle of that rocky desert, pleading for help from cracked, parched lips. The thought made her stomach churn, her lungs fiery in her chest.

"Weaver!" Kady shouted, her brows knitted in concern. "You okay?"

"Sure, I'm fine, why?"

"Because I've been calling your name and you just kept staring off into space."

Henry sighed. "Just distracted, I guess."

"If half the stuff Mrs. Payne says about Emeline and Georgie is true, they're going to be just fine."

"I wish I could believe that. The Coalition is just so powerful, and—"

"How's she doing?" Alice asked, a smug look on her face as she wandered into the room. "Can the scientist hack the code?"

"I haven't checked it yet," Henry said, her attention returned to the notebook that Kady was holding out for her to inspect. "Hmm." The code had been applied only half correctly, leading to a string of garbled words.

"It was one of the nonsense ones, right?" Kady said proudly. "This code breaking stuff is easy."

"Er, no. It was one I've already worked out, it definitely should have made

CHAPTER TWENTY-TWO

sense."

Alice burst out laughing. "Not so smug now, are you?"

"Yeah, well I'd like to see you do better," Kady grumbled.

"Alright," Alice said, sitting backwards on a chair. "Let me at it. I'm ready."

Henry looked from one to the other, and sighed in resignation. Maybe their strange competitive friendship would be helpful. "I'll tell you exactly what I told Kady," she said, preparing the training code again, rearranging the scraps of paper on the table. "I'll be back in an hour. I hear they need me on the bridge."

* * *

Henry trudged up to the bridge of the ship, the weight of her own exhaustion pulling at her limbs and making her feel fuzzy, like she was viewing everything from underwater. She needed sleep, and a hot meal, and above all else, she needed Georgie. Without Roger to rely on for his comfortable companionship, she felt isolated and alone, more than she ever had in her life. She smoothed her skirts and asked the same thing she did every day. "Any word from Skelm?"

"Not yet," Ned replied, the same way he did every time she asked, each day a little sadder and less hopeful. "But I'm sure they're working on it."

"The next shipment is being re-routed to one of the hardest-hit colonies," Captain Violet said from her chair, her elbows perched on her knees, chin in her hands. "A second storm just ripped through there, took out anything they'd been trying to rebuild."

"Are you sure it wasn't a naturally occurring one?"

Captain Violet nodded. "Very sure. It looks to have all the same paths and markers as the others." She handed Henry a piece of paper that showed the storm's characteristics, its beginning and ending points marked in red. "Perhaps the code isn't complete?"

"Of course the code is complete, this doesn't make any sense. Why would they hit the same settlement twice, instead of wiping out another? To what end?"

"To ruin relief efforts. To maximize pain and suffering. It's psychological warfare, and they're good at it."

Henry examined the paper. "Fuck."

"We need you to see if there's a third storm on the way in that colony before we chart a course," Ned said, tapping his fingers on the console.

"Yes, that's what Kady said." She stared at the paper, looking for any kind of discernible pattern. "Is there a possibility that there's some kind of device triggering this?"

"You're the meteorologist, you tell us," Captain Violet replied.

"Trouble is, none of it makes any sense. These storms, they're not following established patterns, they seem totally unpredictable, like there's something else causing an interference. I could look at the current readings, assure you that everything is clear, only to have the ship mired in another electrical storm upon landing." She shook her head. "No, I don't like it. It's too dangerous. I can't in good faith tell you what is or isn't going to be safe."

"These people need those supplies. We can't just leave them to die."

"No, I know that, Captain, but I'm telling you these weather patterns are too unstable for me to give you any kind of assurances. There's no telling if that site will get another blast or not, none of the existing methods would work to predict that."

The captain sighed and leaned back in her chair. "What would your best guess be?"

Henry leaned against Ned's desk, wiping her sweaty palms on the smooth wool of her dress. "Captain, all due respect, but I'm not comfortable guessing at something that could lead to a loss of life for anyone on this crew or down in the settlement."

"More will die if you *don't* give your expertise, Henry."

She fiddled with the buttons at the cuff of her sleeves, an old, nervous habit that had recently reared its head. "I need some time to go over the data."

CHAPTER TWENTY-TWO

"Fine. You have three hours."

* * *

Henry walked the long corridors back to her cramped quarters, tiny in comparison to what she had in Skelm before she was unceremoniously fired by Governor Allemande, probably tipped off to her insubordination by that rat Lawrence Tripp. She kept glancing down at the data, scribbled into the margins of the paper in her hands. None of it made any sense, there were no models to follow or base predictions off of. She might as well be throwing darts at a board while blindfolded for all the good her useless education was doing her.

The captain wanted answers she couldn't give, not confidently or with any modicum of scientific accuracy. She'd spent her whole life studying storms, and these had her stumped. If only Roger was recovered, she could ask for his help. They worked so well as a team, professionally and in their friendship, but she was hesitant to burden him with her personal problems, much less the fate of thousands of innocents and the lives of the crew who had saved them both from certain death. It was a heavy burden even for someone not in recovery from a significant injury.

She could hear Alice and Kady bantering over the code, their muffled voices echoing through the halls as she approached the kitchen. She was unsure whether to interrupt them, or return to her own room for some solitude. Pausing just outside the door, she stopped and listened, unwilling to interrupt their competitive game about the code. At least someone was having fun with the damned thing.

"So how come you never gave Henry the third degree when she arrived?" Alice asked. "Or Georgie, or her family, for that matter. Gods, when I showed up, you were all but convinced I was a deep cover spy for the Coalition for months."

"She's a scientist."

"So?"

"We're all about the science. The facts, the cold meat of a situation. I knew she'd help us with the storms, because studying anomalies has been her entire life's work, her whole career. No scientist could resist it, regardless of who they work for."

Henry smiled to herself, proud that Kady had known she wouldn't betray them even from the start. It made her feel the tiniest bit less alone on the ship, away from Georgie, with Roger still healing in the med bay.

"Well I hope you know now that I'm legitimate," Alice grumbled. "All I had to do was marry the captain for you to take me seriously and stop monitoring my every move."

Kady laughed. "Oh, I still monitor your every move. The captain's wife or no, there's still that slim chance you could be a plant. When we found you sending those messages to Coalition domains a while back, I thought for sure that was it. I was ready to throw you out an airlock for endangering the rest of the crew, and for breaking the captain's heart in the process. It wasn't until later we figured out it was only Jhanvi and Barnaby you were talking to, and sending a mixture of real and false information, at that."

"Mm." The sound of papers being shuffled around made Henry tense; she worried they would mess up her established decryption system.

"Alice, how come you never told me what you were doing, then? Why did you leave us all in the dark?"

A moment of silence passed, the only sound the creaking of the old wooden chairs in the mess area. Henry held her breath, not wanting to be discovered eavesdropping on their conversation. She should have kept walking, but now it was too late, and too obvious in the vacuum of sound.

"I thought your fears about me would make you think you'd always been right, that I *was* a spy. And I was right, you did."

"Only because you never said anything! Gods, Alice, you should have trusted me!"

"How could I, when you never trusted *me*?"

Henry knew she shouldn't be listening to this. It was a personal conversation between two friends, or two peers, at least, and it was none of her business. She didn't even know what they were talking about, other than the other vague comment Kady made about Alice spending some time in the ship's brig. She'd just assumed that had been when they first took Alice on board a year previous.

"I know you've never trusted that I'm not a spy, Kady, but I've always seen you as one of the most capable members of a crew I've ever seen. All I ever wanted was for you to see me as an equal, as someone who cares about this ship and this crew as much as you do."

"Alice, I—"

"I'd lay down my life for anyone on this ship, and if you don't know that by now, then I don't know what to tell you. I lost a godsdamn eye for this crew, because I took the hit from that blast instead of Hyun, and I'd do it again without a breath of hesitation." The sound of a chair scraping against the metal floor implied that Alice had stood up. "I'm tired of trying to prove myself to you and everyone else here, while new folks can wander onto the ship almost by accident and immediately be given a welcoming embrace."

"Alice!"

"What?"

"Sit down, for all the gods' sakes," Kady huffed. "I know you're loyal to this crew. I know it, and everyone else knows it, too, even before you lost an eye to save Hyun. I just never understood why you didn't tell me about those messages." She sighed. "I'm sorry I made it so that you didn't think you could come to me."

"You suck at codes, you know," Alice said, sitting back down. "I would have thought a genius scientist like you would be able to figure this stuff out in a snap."

"Yeah, well, for the best mechanic in the Near Systems, you suck at codes, too."

Henry used the sound of approaching crew members to cover her move away from the door and back to her chambers. If she was going to give the captain and Ned an answer about these storms, she had to get some peace and quiet, without any distractions. She needed to dig deep into her mind and think about the implications of a wrong answer, what it would mean not only for the crew of the Cricket but the people waiting for aid in the ruined settlement below.

She pushed open her door to find Roger sitting on her bed, notebook in his hand. "What's wrong?" she asked. "Do you need me to show you back to the med bay?"

"I've been released," he said proudly, wiggling his eyebrows. "I'm to reintegrate with my normal life and duties, under Hyun's supervision, of course."

"Is that a good idea? I don't want to upset you, or—"

"Oh come on Weaver, enough already," he said, rolling his eyes and tossing his notebook on the bed. "I've been injured, I'm not a child."

"Hyun said that—"

"What she said is that I'm to return to normal duties, and for me, normal is working on problems with you, analyzing data, getting to the crux of the anomaly. There's no need to keep treating me like a fragile egg, I'm a grown man, I know my own limits."

She sat on the bed, running her fingers over the worn leather cover of his notebook. "If I lost you too, I don't know what I'd do."

"Well it's a good damn thing I'm not going anywhere then, isn't it?" He reached over and squeezed her hand gently. "Now come on, let's work this out. What's the problem?"

"These storms, Rog, they don't make any sense. No patterns to predict or follow, they seem to ignore everything we've ever learned. They're asking me to give them a definite answer of if another one is going to hit that settlement down there, and I don't even know where to begin."

"Alright," he said, flipping to the first blank page of the notebook. "Let's start at the first storm. Landed just outside, cut a path right through the main utilities of the settlement, took out the terraformers and the comms tower."

"How did you find that out? You were supposed to be on bed rest!"

He shrugged. "Eavesdropping."

"Of course," she snorted, worried for him but so grateful to have him back. "The second one did the same, similar trajectory, and it hovered around the same utilities, though they'd protected them after we repaired it the first time, rubberized coatings all across the exposed metal."

CHAPTER TWENTY-TWO

"Strange then, that the storm would do the same thing."

"It doesn't make any sense. There was no change in pressure or cloud cover that would indicate a second storm. I can't speak to the first, because we arrived after it touched down. Now they're asking about a third and there's no way I can say for sure."

"Then the only thing to do is get down there and have a look," Roger said grimly. "These storms can't continue unabated. It would wipe out half the existing colonies."

CHAPTER TWENTY-THREE

The last thing Georgie wanted to be doing that day was drugging the military police supervisors, and yet, there she was, dumping illicitly gained sedatives into a line of lukewarm mugs of coffee. It was the only way if she was going to get out to the communications tower and back without being seen and dragged back to the city to be thrown into an interrogation cell. Her heart pounded as she stirred the white powder into the drink, grateful that her years of unquestioning obedience on the job earned her their trust.

She willed her hands to stop shaking as she carried the mugs back to their owners posted outside the small tent with a grin. "Here you are, officers," she chirped, hoping that she sounded more neutral out loud than she did in her own head. "I'm going to head back to my post now unless y'all need anything else?"

"Get back to work," one of them laughed, pointing out at the barrier. "Wouldn't want to leave a job unfinished, now would we?"

"No, sir," she said, looking at the ground, swallowing back the rage and bile that bit at the back of her throat. Ever since Allemande's increased patrols and policing, these officers had become even more brash and ugly.

The barrier wasn't far, only a few minutes' walk from the tent in the heavy pressurized suits they all wore in case of a boundary breach. Of course, the janitors were given the old orange models, the ones with patches covering the elbows and thighs, whereas their new overlords were granted the newly developed suits, which came complete with their own radar and

CHAPTER TWENTY-THREE

communications in case they got stranded out here. Their lives were worth more to the Coalition, and especially to the governor.

The mess they were out there to clean up was mostly industrial waste, though not as toxic as the materials found at a work camp. Barrels of dirty oil, tarps covered in rocks and dust, empty cans of paint they'd used to make the monorail tracks reflective, in case of a low flying craft too far from the docks. A day's work, but Georgie would have to work fast if she was going to spend part of that day wiring the tiny chip in her breast pocket into the communications tower.

Two of the five officers were beginning to doze, their heads hung in drowsiness. She almost hadn't expected the drugs Judy gave her to work, and certainly not that fast. Part of her worried she had overdosed them, and no one wanted to be explaining away a dead officer with a mountain of sedatives in his bloodstream, even if many of them were known for drug use.

She took a deep breath and paused to gather some of the trash scattered at the barrier, blown in all directions from the ever-present wind that swooped low over the cliffs in the distance where Henry and Roger had almost lost their balloon. The boundary almost shimmered in the dull afternoon light, the differing atmospheres swirling around each other but not quite mixing. Terraforming science seemed like magic, if you didn't know any better.

One eye on the guards, she carefully piled the garbage atop a tarp, with a mind she would drag the entire thing back to the tent when the day was done. No sense in making multiple trips back and making herself more of a suspect if anything went wrong, even though she'd already be the prime target as the last remaining janitor who had served under poor Mr. Jackson. Erin had made short work of that, firing and relocating anyone who questioned her newfound authority.

When the last guard slumped against the monorail track support beam, she moved as fast as she could for the barrier. After telling the others that she had been given a special assignment by Erin, it was unlikely any of them would question her or mention it to their manager for fear of reprimand. It was a lie that would almost certainly come back to bite her in the ass someday, but for now, it was a necessary fabrication to get the job done and secure an open line of communication for The Scattered, a rebellion she was apparently now an important part of, despite her protests.

The suit seemed heavier and clumsier than she remembered, even without the weight of Roger's unconscious body hanging at her shoulders. Her heart pounded in her chest with every laden step she took towards the tower, and every second the light from the city dimmed. The tower was bolted into the rocky ground with thick metal plates, drilled into the earth to keep it stable and secure, safe from any attempt to knock it from its post. She gasped when she saw the panel door, locked up tight with a thick padlock. The plan hadn't accounted for this, and every moment was crucial.

They should have guessed that Governor Allemande would do something like this after she discovered that Lawrence Tripp was using it to communicate with far-flung members of The Scattered. Yet there Georgie was, standing and staring at the lock, willing it to disappear. She patted down her pockets, hoping to find a lock pick she'd never placed there, or a key that fell in there accidentally when she was last cleaning the governor's office. There was nothing, not even a hair pin to give a clumsy attempt at picking it.

"Fuck!" Georgie yelled, being sure to cover the microphone on her suit. It was unlikely that anyone was listening, but you couldn't be too careful in Allemande's Skelm. "Fucking godsdamned shit!" It was their one and only chance to get the chip installed, now that the monorail was under constant surveillance. She bit down on her tongue, willing the fog of panic rolling through her mind to dissipate. She'd have to get the lock off, that's all there was to it.

There was a hacksaw in the tent back at the base of the monorail that she'd seen when they arrived. It had likely been left behind by one of the engineers, or maybe a builder working to repair the ruined transit vehicle. Without any other options, that seemed like the only way forward. She swore again, under her breath this time, and began the trudge back towards the tent, praying to old, dead gods that the guards would sleep through her entry and exit, and that she'd be able to make it back before dark.

CHAPTER TWENTY-THREE

Holding her palm to the light, she estimated that it would be a very close call, and there was a strong probability that the rest of the team would leave without her. No one cared about janitors. In the eyes of the Coalition, she was expendable. She wondered if the crew of the Cricket thought that, too. Now that they had Henry and Roger to uncover the mystery surrounding the storms, and Evie had fulfilled her promise of getting her family out of Skelm, she couldn't help but think that they'd never come back for her and risk the ship again.

She pushed the thoughts from her mind as she stepped over the unconscious bodies of the military police officers in their pressure suits, one of them emitted a muffled snore. If another one of the janitorial staff saw them, all piled in a heap, they might report it up the chain. If it got reported, the higher-ups would investigate. Georgie was banking on everyone's mutual fear of being written up to protect what she was about to do. The hacksaw was hefty, made for cutting through the thick iron pipes that criss-crossed the under section of the track. She exhaled slowly, lifting it off the hook.

"Hey, what are you doing in here?" one of the guards asked, flipping open the helmet's visor to rub his eyes. "And how come you have that saw?"

Her heart pounded in her throat. "I, uh... there's some trash out yonder, some big chunks of discarded metal that the builders left," she began, and squeezed her eyes shut to concentrate on what she was saying. There was no room for stumbling, now. "I can't bring it back all in one piece, it's too heavy, and it would tear the tarp. You see, sir, I thought if I could just slice it into pieces I'd be able to make sure it all gets packed out of here when we leave. We both know that Governor Allemande isn't interested in inefficiency, and I was hoping that—"

She opened her eyes at the sound of a loud snore and saw that the guard was slumped against the tent beam again. A close call, and one that might come back to bite her later. The Scattered were asking more and more of her, to copy notes found in the trash, to monitor conversations being had in the conference room, and now drugging military police and hacking into communications equipment. Dangerous didn't even begin to cover it.

The guard snored again as she leapt over the pile of bodies and hustled back out to the communications tower. There was no time to waste, not when the sun was already starting to set, the mirrors above Skelm already beginning their tilt to face their solar panels to the sky. The padlock changed everything. If Allemande *was* monitoring the tower, she'd know someone had tampered with it. Tripp was dead and dissolved, and the Governor would be hunting down whoever he'd been working with. Their signal might only be good for one night, two if they were lucky. A lot of risk without substantial reward. Emeline would be devastated to hear that their ingenious plan had been kneecapped by their new governor.

Light glinted off something in the corner, buried beneath a pile of old rags her janitorial comrades had dumped there, crusted with the fine sandy dust that blew everywhere out here, far from the city. She bent and pulled at it gently, freeing it from the rags, and stifled a gasp. Somehow, somewhere, from shrines long toppled, a force greater than her had smiled on her. It was another padlock. She could replace it after hacking away the old one, and hope that the key not fitting would be chalked up to the incompetence of whatever poor administrator whose job it was to check the comms tower.

Hacksaws designed for iron pipes moved through softer metal like butter, a cut as clean and surgical as the sutures Georgie had once seen her mother sew on a fellow factory worker's when their fingers had been lopped off by a piece of machinery. The lock fell to the ground with a soft thud, and she yanked open the panel, fumbling at her pocket for the small chip Judy had given her, so tiny that they hoped it wouldn't be noticed, even with regular surveillance.

Light faded over the track beneath the monorail, and Georgie squinted in the dark as she slotted the chip into place. It made a quiet chirp and then silenced itself, and she heaved a sigh of relief as she snapped the replacement lock closed. Now all she had to do was get back to the tent, dragging the tarp the last distance to the track where the trash would be loaded into carts and shuffled back to the city to be incinerated or melted down.

Darkness fell quickly out here, but Georgie had come prepared this time, with a small little lamp that Emeline had sewn into the front of her pressure suit, illuminating the rocky ground as the blackness closed in. Even at this

CHAPTER TWENTY-THREE

distance, Georgie could hear the trash being dumped into carts, and hurried herself along, tying the edges of the tarp as she went. If they left her out here, she wouldn't survive the night. After her last experience, she wasn't keen on the idea of repeating it.

"Hurry the fuck up!" one of the guards shouted, visibly disoriented, waving at another janitor. "We could be home already if it wasn't for you assholes!"

Perhaps they all felt embarrassed for having fallen asleep, and if she was lucky, they wouldn't question it or ever mention it again. After all, she was the obvious choice to pin it on if they decided to, and the thought of being dragged into an interrogation room made her shiver, even as prickles of sweat covered her brow. There was nothing she feared more than those rooms, the ones that were now set at the back of the Administration building so you couldn't hear the screams from within. She'd die before giving up her sister, or the rest of The Scattered, or the crew of the Cricket, but that didn't mean she wasn't terrified of the idea.

"You there," the guard who had earlier accosted her in the tent shouted.

Georgie felt her blood run cold, and her mouth felt drier than a fistful of sand. He remembered her.

* * *

The flickering yellow light of the interrogation room made her feel queasy. She'd been waiting for what felt like hours, but with no clock, and no windows, strapped to a rickety wooden chair, Georgie had long since given up the idea of rescue or escape. As much as she hated to admit it, that would cast her as guilty without a shadow of a doubt. At least this way, there was a tiny, infinitesimal chance she might be cleared and set free.

"Ms. Georgina Payne," an investigator said, closing the door behind her. "I am Inspector Klein." She sat across the table, stained dark and blotchy with what Georgie hoped wasn't blood. "Do you know why you are here today?"

"No."

"Are you sure about that?"

"Yes." The Scattered taught that if interrogated, short, one-word answers were best, even if under duress. The more you rambled, the more they could extract. Even lies sometimes held a nugget of truth, a truth that could get your fellow rebel killed.

"You've been accused of tampering with military police rations. Did you do it?"

"No."

The inspector stared, unblinking. "I assure you this will go far more smoothly if you cooperate, Georgina."

"Georgie."

"Ms. Payne, the entire guard force reported falling unconscious after drinking coffee that you served them. I cannot believe that is a coincidence."

"Could be."

Silence filled the room so thickly, Georgie thought she might drown in it. The inspector was leaving room for her to talk, to cut through the uncertainty with explanations and plausible deniability. She stayed quiet, willing her face to remain neutral even as panic wracked at her insides.

"Ms. Payne, I don't think I have to remind you what's at stake here. If you refuse to confess to your crimes, I will have no other choice than to bring in your mother for questioning." Inspector Klein examined her file and smiled. "Given her health complications, I think we can agree that wouldn't be best for her. Yet, without a confession, or an explanation, we will have no other options left on the table." She gave a strange, toothy grin, and Georgie had to resist recoiling in her chair, as much as the restraints would allow.

It was reassuring to know that the Coalition still thought that her mother and Lucy were in Skelm, within reach of their manipulation, instead of hundreds of thousands of kilometers away, she hoped, safe and happy in a refugee settlement. It was imaginary leverage, and had they still been there, Georgie would have buckled right then and there. The knowledge that Emeline was safe in the basement of the Twisted Lantern gave her the strength she needed to stay silent.

CHAPTER TWENTY-THREE

The inspector began to grow flustered. "Ms. Payne, did I make myself clear? I will drag your mother into this room, strap her to that chair, and interrogate her, find out why she raised such a rebellious, loathsome slug. Don't test me, Georgina."

Georgie stared straight ahead, her shoulders relaxed despite the sound of blood pounding in her ears and the sharp spike of adrenaline in her veins. They wouldn't break her. She was stronger than that.

"Ms. Payne!" Inspector Klein shouted, leaning over the table, spittle flying. "Why did you drug those officers? Tell me now, or I'll—I'll—"

The doors burst open to reveal one Governor Allemande, strikingly dressed in her trademark tailored black tail jacket and matching silk top hat. "Get out of my sight," she hissed at the inspector. "You disgust me."

"But Governor, I—"

Allemande stared the inspector down, her eyes cold and unfeeling. "I said, get out."

One of the military police stationed at the door of the room grabbed Inspector Klein's elbow and yanked her from the room, latching the door behind them and leaving Georgie alone with the governor.

"Ms. Payne," Allemande said quietly, sitting down across the table. "I do apologize for such an embarrassing display from one of my very own inspectors. I assure you, we do not condone that sort of behavior here." She opened the file and spread out the pages, peering at them through a silver monocle. "I trust your mother is well?"

"She is well enough, thank you," Georgie responded, every muscle clenched. Things had just become far more dangerous for her, and she knew it. She'd heard stories about the governor's tactics, and she had seen Evie's arms for herself, albeit briefly. It didn't take longer than a glance to see the damage, both physical and emotional, that Allemande had wreaked on Evie.

"And your sisters? I see a note here they were taken out of school?"

Georgie shrugged. "Times are hard."

"Mm, they are indeed, there's no helping that, I'm afraid." The governor looked up from the file and smiled, more warmly and charming than Georgie had anticipated. It was almost amiable, a disarming visage. Lawrence Tripp's face as he gasped for air through dark red bubbles of blood hung heavy on her mind.

"Tell me, Ms. Payne, do you believe that the Coalition wants the best for its people?"

"Yes."

"And you've worked hard for us over the years, yes?"

"I have always tried to do my best."

"You're the only one left of the crew that worked under Mr. Jackson, that's credibility enough for me. Our new manager down there, what's her name?"

"Erin Talbot."

"Ah, yes, Mrs. Talbot. She runs a tight ship, so I'm told. An excellent choice for that role."

"Yes."

"Well, between you and me, Mrs. Talbot seems to be over-compensating for something."

Georgie twisted her wrists in the restraints. "Ma'am?"

"Oh come now, Georgina, you and I both know you had nothing to do with those officers getting drugged."

Her mind raced. What the hell was going on? "No, ma'am, I didn't."

"There are no sedatives that work that fast, none available in Skelm anyway. I've made sure of that with the increase in shipment inspections. Those officers would have had to ingest them at least ninety minutes before they took effect, maybe even more."

"Oh?"

"You see, Ms. Payne, not everyone believes in the Coalition as you do. Some would work to undermine it, destroy it, send all the Near Systems into chaos. Mrs. Talbot, your manager, provided the officers with home-baked muffins before they boarded the monorail as a thanks for their work on the project."

"She does enjoy baking."

"So it would seem! And thus, Ms. Payne, given your loyalty to the cause and in fact, to me in the past, clearing up some rather unfortunate messes,

CHAPTER TWENTY-THREE

leads me to believe that Mrs. Talbot is to blame for the drugging, not you."

Georgie remained silent, afraid that one wrong move would ruin whatever strange miracle this was. She wasn't even sure she was still breathing, afraid to upset the precarious balance that held her between freedom and prison, life and death. When she closed her eyes, she saw Tripp's body disappearing beneath the placid surface of the vat.

"Unfortunately," Allemande continued, "I do not have any such proof. A cursory search of her person and her home did not uncover any evidence of my suspicions, and although a test has proved all the officers were dosed with some sort of sedative, there are no concrete clues as to where it came from."

"I see," Georgie said carefully.

"I need your help, Ms. Payne. I need you to be my eyes on the inside of that department. Keep watch over Mrs. Talbot and report back to me if she seems to be falling prey to any ridiculous rebel fantasies of anarchy. Would you do that for me?"

"I, uh—yes," Georgie mumbled. This felt equally like a victory and a trap.

"Excellent," the governor said, leaning across the table to unhook the restraints. "I know that I can count on your discretion."

Georgie rubbed at the raw spot on her wrists under the cuffs. "Absolutely."

"Don't let me down, Ms. Payne. The Coalition is counting on you to help dismantle the pockets of rot that would see us all burn." She flipped the file closed and smiled again. "It would seem your shift is over! Be here bright and early tomorrow. We wouldn't want you to miss anything important, now would we?"

"No, ma'am."

An officer burst through the door. "Governor Allemande, I do apologize for the interruption, but we need to escort you to a safe premises immediately."

"Excuse me? What's going on?"

"Ma'am, we have credible intel that suggests an explosive device is ready to detonate."

CHAPTER TWENTY-FOUR

"Gods, Weaver, what the hell do you have in this thing, bricks?" Kady huffed, heaving the large sack onto her back.

"Yes, I asked you to bring bricks down to the settlement."

"I said I'd help, I didn't volunteer to be your pack mule."

"This is the best way to monitor the weather patterns. It's clear I can't predict the storms, but these might be able to work as an early warning system for the people here if you can help me boost their signal."

Kady shifted the weight of the bag to her other shoulder. "Fine, I guess if it's for the greater good," she grumbled. "I still think that the better option would just be for Captain Tansy to get the lead out and get these people the hell out of here."

"Obviously, but with all the evacs her fleet has been doing, it can't be easy."

"No one said it was easy, I just said it would be better than dragging around whatever the hell you have in this bag."

Henry smiled at her sweetly and gave her a mock curtsy in her blue pressure suit. "Weather balloons, my lady."

"Cut the crap, Weaver," Kady said with a snort. "Grab the ass end of this bag or I'm leaving you here with it to drag your balloons across the settlement yourself."

"Alright, alright," Henry relented, hefting part of the bag onto her own shoulder. "Let's go. If we want to get these set up before nightfall, we'd

CHAPTER TWENTY-FOUR

better get a move on."

"I didn't think you'd tell the captain to set down here, you know."

"Why?"

"Scientists tend to be risk averse. Other than me, anyway. And my friend Livia who blew up a lab once."

"I'm a storm chaser, you goon," Henry laughed, tripping over a rock that jutted from the surface. "That's the opposite of risk-averse."

"Yeah, well, I thought you'd want to get Roger back to Bradach as soon as possible now that he's showing signs of complications."

Henry nearly dropped her end of the bag. "What?"

"Oh gods, you didn't know."

"What complications?"

"If Hyun didn't tell you, maybe she wanted to wait until after the mission—"

"What complications, Kady?" Henry pressed.

"They're not sure, they can't tell without proper imaging equipment, but that won't fit in the med bay."

"Why didn't anyone tell me? I'm basically his next of kin, for the gods' sakes!"

"I imagine that they were worried you'd want to prioritize him above the settlement."

"That's unfair," Henry said, tears springing to her eyes. "I've done nothing but help this crew, and put my career, whatever was left of it, aside to help people."

Kady balanced the bag on a large felled tree as she climbed over it and squelched into the sodden marsh on the other side. "I know, Weaver, and I told them that. They just worry. There have been others who have endangered the crew for personal reasons. It happens. We're all human, emotions can get the better of us. Hell, even I've done it from time to time."

"It's a double standard, is what it is," Henry snapped. "Alice and Violet can make wild decisions that endanger everyone and the mission for each other, but they won't trust me to make a responsible decision where my best and oldest friend is concerned?" She dropped the bag, and it landed heavily on the ground with a squelch, yanking Kady down to her knees. "This is too damn heavy!"

"You want to warn me before you try that?" Kady retorted. "You need to calm down before you lose your focus or land me in the med bay with a torn rotator cuff," she continued, rubbing her shoulder. "We're almost there, just suck it up, Weaver."

Henry picked up the back end of the bag again. "This was always much easier with Roger, you know. He didn't mind carrying the equipment."

"Roger is twice my size, of course he didn't mind."

"I appreciate the help. I'm sorry I dropped the bag." She stepped over a puddle and felt a fragile twig snap beneath her boot. "This shit isn't easy, you know. A few months ago I was working my way up the ladder, I was falling in love with Georgie, Roger and I were on the cusp of a major discovery. Now I'm hefting equipment through a torn up marsh in some desperate attempt to figure out why the hell these storms keep happening."

"Look, I get it. It's a tough transition, and truth be told, you're handling it better than most, and better than I thought you would. A spoiled rich girl whose parents probably bought her way into the CSA Academy? I thought there was no chance you'd be able to hack it with us."

"My parents didn't buy my way into the academy," Henry replied, insulted, the shame of the accusation burning red in her cheeks. "I worked just as hard as anyone else there, I—"

"Yeah? You think that Lucy would get a place in that school without some kind of financial assistance, or an inside helping hand?"

"I would have helped her, I might still be able to!"

"Weaver, come on. How many people in your classes came from factory or farm families?"

Henry clammed up, fighting the indignant rage that was starting to boil in her stomach. Her instinct was to lash out, to defend herself and her academics, but Kady was right. Lower class workers rarely, if ever, had the opportunity to climb the ranks of the Coalition. She didn't know anyone from her program that didn't grow up in the same social circles that she had.

CHAPTER TWENTY-FOUR

"I guess you're right," she admitted through gritted teeth. It felt like Kady was trying to undermine her achievements, that she was saying Henry didn't deserve the education she received. She took a deep breath to try to calm her temper, the anger settling just below her skin.

"Relax, Henry. No one is saying you're not smart, or that you didn't achieve some impressive feats of meteorology. I'm just saying that the CSA isn't exactly a meritocracy." Kady balanced the bag on one shoulder and held a hand to her eyes to peer into the distance. "Almost there. Few more minutes."

In the distance, storm clouds began to gather.

* * *

"At least we got those balloons up before the storm hit," Henry said, wringing water from her pressure suit. The thin fabric wasn't built for the kind of torrential downpour that was outside. Rain pelted down on the roof of the thin tent, sending a steady stream of water through the gap at the peak, and Henry shivered with the cold wind that blew the flap open.

Kady peeked out of the tent and scowled at the darkened sky. "Yeah, but now we have to ride it out. Can't have the Cricket setting down in this mess."

"Hopefully it will skirt around the settlement this time. Not everyone has pressure suits and helmets in case those terraformers get taken down again, and Alice said she's not sure how many more repairs they can take."

"She's damn right about that," a woman in a dark grey set of coveralls said, squeezing water from her long auburn braid. "You can only solder those things so many times before the main components get fried." She stuck out her hand and grinned. "Hi. Name's Bailey Stockton. And you're Henry Weaver."

"Sorry, have we met?" Henry asked, shaking the woman's hand.

"Not officially, no. You may know me as 'that strange woman helping Alice with the repairs,' or 'who is that devilishly handsome woman staring at me?'"

Henry coughed. "I'm sorry?"

"I'm just teasing, Weaver, relax," Bailey said with a wink. "Everyone left in this settlement knows who you are, you're the fearless scientist trying to solve all our problems."

"So you're a local, then."

"Born and raised. Not many can say that off Gamma-3, now can they?"

"Certainly no one older than a toddler," Kady said, maybe a little jealous. "So Bailey, what can we do for you?"

"Not much you can do until this storm burns itself out, I reckon. I did bring a campstove, if either of you are interested in a cup of tea. It's old and a little stale, but definitely not the worst I've ever had." She pulled a damp paper sack of tea leaves from her pocket, crumpled and leaking on one side, and set it on the rickety table. "Would pass the time, trying to get this damn thing lit, anyway."

"Oh gods, I'd kill someone for a cup of tea," Henry said, reaching for the bag. "I'm no stranger to storms or leaky tents, but a hot cup always makes you feel better."

"Consider it done!" Bailey crowed, setting the ancient looking camp stove on the table. "Anything for the prettiest girl in the settlement."

Kady coughed and elbowed Henry in the ribs. "We shouldn't stay long, what was it? Bailey? We'll have to catch those balloons when they descend."

"Oh, come on, Kady, we can spare a few minutes, the storm is still raging anyway," Henry protested. She knew that Bailey was flirting, but it was harmless, really - and it felt nice to be flirted with after months of pining after Georgie, who was hundreds of thousands of kilometers away in Skelm.

Kady raised an eyebrow, but sat back in her chair without further comment.

"So, Henry, how does a top notch scientist like you find herself all the way out here in the middle of nowhere with a bunch of dirty rebels?"

"She's not the only scientist here," Kady grumbled under her breath.

"Oh come now Kady, no need for hostility. I already know about that lab you blew up. Impressive."

Kady smirked and leaned forward to block the weak pilot flame from the wind. "Hell yeah, it was."

CHAPTER TWENTY-FOUR

"I don't know, it all happened so fast," Henry explained. "One minute I was on a routine rotation into Skelm to observe those storms they have outside the city, try to examine any kind of pattern we could use to predict things better back on Gamma-3. Next thing I know, I'm stealing a monorail with Georgie—" she stopped short, guilt swirling in her chest. She cleared her throat and continued. "With Georgie and Roger, and being rescued by the Cricket, and now I'm here, I suppose."

Bailey twirled a loose strand of damp hair around her finger. "So who is Georgie to you, then? Someone I should be jealous of?"

"She's—" Henry started. She didn't really know what they were.

"Complicated?" Bailey finished for her.

"Yes, I suppose you could say that." Henry held her hands over the tiny kettle, letting her hands warm through the clumsy gloves of the pressure suit. "In any case, I think the tea is probably ready to be brewed, don't you?"

"Aye. This is the fastest this damned thing has ever started up for me." She smacked it on the side, and something rattled within. "Of course it would do that the very moment I have some interesting conversation." She poured the hot water from the kettle over the leaves, sending them swirling in circles in the cups. "I wonder how long this storm will last."

As if in response, thunder rumbled in the distance, and Henry frowned. "I don't like the sound of that. Strange, I used to love watching storms build, but now, knowing so many lives are at risk here, I resent them."

"Doesn't sound as bad as last time," Kady said hopefully, taking a mug from the table and drawing her knees into her chest on the chair. "Gods, it's cold."

Bailey shook her head. "They always start like this, far away and non-threatening, and then, bam!" she punched the table, making Henry and Kady jerk back in surprise. "The fucker rolls into the settlement and just sits here, sending dozens of strikes down on all our equipment. If I didn't know better, I'd say someone was controlling the whole damn thing." She laughed and sipped her tea.

"Problem is, they are. We don't know how, but—" Henry was interrupted by a thundering crack, and she nearly choked on her tea, the leaves catching in her throat. "That sounded like a tree."

"Yep, it sure did," Bailey agreed, leaning back in her chair to squint through the gap in the tent flaps whenever the wind blew them apart. "A big one."

"If the storm is that close, then it's likely it will go for the terraformers again, they're like a godsdamn lightning rod with all of that—Kady, we need a lightning rod."

"Where the hell am I supposed to get that? It's not like I have one stashed up my sleeve, Weaver."

"It just needs to be taller than the equipment, nothing fancy!" She stood and looked around the tent. "Bailey, what do you have around here that conducts electricity? Tall, or could be piled high."

"Scrap? It's all the way down in the—"

Another flash of lightning streaked across the sky, and Henry braced for the roar that followed. The noise was an ear-splitting crack, followed by the sound of metal bending under its own weight, and the smell of burning electronics.

"That will have been the comms tower," Kady shouted over the cacophony of the rain, now pelting down hard and fast, sending rivulets of water into the tent. "If this keeps up, those terraformers are next."

"Get everyone you can, start piling that scrap about two hundred meters from the terraformer generator," Henry said, pushing Bailey towards the open tent flap. "That thing can't take another hit, and who knows when the Cricket will be able to land. We can't risk it." She turned to Kady and shook her head. "It's like it came out of nowhere. The skies were clear when we touched down."

"Well, it's here now, no time to be messing around. I'll go with Bailey, you get to the cliffs and pull those balloons back before the storm tears them apart."

Henry nodded. "Deal. I'll meet you at your improvised lightning rod, hopefully with balloons that haven't dumped their data boxes." She watched the two women scurry out into the storm, shielding their faces against the blowing rain. Henry followed, taking a deep breath before she trudged through the wind towards the nearby cliffs, where they had launched the balloons not long before.

The sky was dark and growing more ominous by the moment, with tinges of green scattered at the edges of the thick cloud cover that hung low enough to obscure the tops of the cliffs where the balloons were gathering information, being tossed around by the storm. Despite the adjustments she and Roger had made back in Skelm to make them stronger and less susceptible to storms, nothing would be able to escape these kinds of winds without damage. In fact, she hadn't seen winds like these since she was stationed back on Gamma-3 in one of the plains stations, where tornadoes regularly ripped across the land.

Her boot caught against a sapling, her vision obscured by the smear of rain across her helmet. She dare not take it off now, not when the terraformers were in danger - not that it would do anything to improve her eyesight right now, anyway. This place was nothing like the land outside Skelm, which was rocky and barren, more like a desert than anything else. Here, it was verdant and lush, a marshy landscape with stunted trees thick with leaves and the ever-present scent of algae, even through her pressure suit.

When she reached the cliffs, she hauled back on the cord for the first balloon, willing it to return to the ground without incident. Her stomach turned when she heard the telltale snap of the battered rope, knowing the balloon would end up dashed against the cliffs, unreachable. Hjarta no longer had access to the kind of equipment needed for expeditions, either. She held the second rope in her hand, and pulled hard, her eyes squeezed shut. There were only three balloons they could use, being difficult to manufacture on a small, outdated ship whose lab was a converted set of sleeping quarters.

The balloon descended with erratic, jerking movements as the wind pulled it one way, and then another. Henry shielded her visor from the rain to watch, her heart in her throat. If it dumped its data box from that height, there was no way she would be able to recover anything useful, and her presence here would amount to nothing more than a hindrance to the relief efforts. Hell, without her and Roger, the Cricket would have two more rooms for refugees.

Twenty feet from the ground, Henry watched in horror as the punishing wind shot something straight through the balloon, sending it plummeting to the ground, where it landed with a sickening crunch, nearly clipping her helmet on its way down. She didn't have time to examine it now, and snatched at the third balloon's tether, feeling it respond to her tugs. It began its descent, emerging from the heavy clouds dripping with rain and the corners covered in frost.

She reached up for it and clutched it to her chest, the only one that was likely to have any usable data. Another flash of lightning streaked across the sky, and she marveled at its smoothness and lack of forks or inter-cloud connections. Almost as if an old god, sleeping for thousands of years, had awoken to discover the people had forgotten about them, and sent it as punishment.

Henry hooked the punctured balloon to her belt and squinted into the horizon. In theory, the plan should work, and it was lucky that Hjarta had spent years mining the resources. All that scrap and raw ore might just save them.

The clouds swirled, menacing with the threat of more destruction than this place could handle. The strongest would survive the wait to be evacuated. The old, the young, and the sick, however, would not. Henry felt guilt burn in her gut. She, at least, had a pressure suit, but such luxuries were rare in settlements anyway, much less ones that had already been razed by these godsdamned storms.

Even through the blinding rain, and despite the wind and the flashes of lightning in her periphery, Henry could see that two huge copper rods were being lifted by steam powered cranes and leaned against each other. They weren't stable, but far from any other structures, it didn't matter. They only needed to deflect the electricity from the terraformers for the duration of this storm, and then they could keep evacuating the settlers still there. And through the storm, she saw the bolt of lightning streak past the copper, and slam straight into the terraformer.

CHAPTER TWENTY-FIVE

The military police whisked Governor Allemande away, encircling her like a precious, fragile thing. Georgie scrambled from her chair and ran for the door, escaping into a corridor rife with chaos. People were scrambling, shoving each other in desperate bids to reach the front entrance of the Administration building. Clearly, someone had leaked news of this threat, and now panic reigned, turning calm, reasoned scientists, lawyers, and translators into terrified wild animals. There was no way she'd be able to get out in time if a detonation was imminent.

Georgie tore a cover from the ventilation shaft low on the wall and clambered in, using her elbows to drag herself through the walls. She knew that it led to the back courtyard, where the hidden alleyway was, and ignored the pain in her arms as the protruding screws shredded her skin. The steel ducts bowed noisily with every frantic move she made, trying her best to ignore the thought that she'd be dead for sure if she got trapped in there.

She was sure she could smell gunpowder, a surefire sign that an explosion was coming. The Scattered hadn't planned any attacks, their numbers were still much too fragile after so many were picked up in the last raid. So who the hell was trying to blow up the building?

The grate to the outside was just a short distance away, and she kicked and spluttered her way to it, reaching for the screwdriver she always kept in her belt in case of emergency maintenance repairs. She felt her shoulder pop out of place when she wedged it to the side to unscrew the grate and nearly screamed from the pain. She bit her tongue and tasted blood, but it was better than alerting anyone to her presence. Whoever these saboteurs were, she didn't know their intentions.

The grate gave way, dumping her unceremoniously into the courtyard where several gardeners stared in confusion. "Are you alright?" one of them asked, holding a spade in her hand like a weapon. "Should we call the guards?"

"Didn't you hear?" Georgie replied, breathless. "There's a bomb somewhere in the building."

"A bomb!" another one yelled, stumbling backwards over their boots. "Gods, no one tells us anything out here!"

"Get away from the building, as far as you can!" Georgie insisted. "There's an alleyway over here, follow me!" She beckoned for the gardeners to follow her, pushing away the ivy and revealing the escape avenue she'd now used twice. "Come on, hurry up!"

The three gardeners ran after her, following into the alley. "Where does this go?" the one with the spade asked.

"It dumps out into the back streets, you can get all the way down to the docks if you need to."

"I want to get home to my family, they'll be worried sick if they hear about the bomb and I'm not home."

"Where do you live?"

"The tenements."

"Take the next fork and go left, keep going until you reach the alley that runs behind the factories. You'll know when you see them."

"What about the high rise?"

"Three rights and a left at the fourth fork," Georgie gasped, still running. One by one the three gardeners peeled off, leaving her to rest, her hands on her knees, in the alley behind the Twisted Lantern. After all, it was home now. She shielded her eyes against the mid-afternoon light and looked up at the Administration building on the hill, waiting for an explosion.

Nothing came. No fireball, no shattered glass, not even the low rumble of a punctured boiler.

CHAPTER TWENTY-FIVE

"What the hell?" she said under her breath.

"Cole, have you lost your godsdamned mind?" Emeline screamed from inside. "My sister is in there!"

"I thought we agreed that what we do should be for the many, not the few? What happened to that, Em?" he shouted back.

"I didn't think you were going to condemn dozens, maybe even hundreds of innocent people to death!"

Georgie yanked open the door, the rusted handle catching against the calluses on her hands. "What the hell is going on?" she demanded.

"Georgie, Georgie!" Emeline sobbed, rushing to her side and throwing her arms around her neck. "You're all right! I thought I'd never see you again, I was so worried!"

"Ouch! My shoulder, Em, watch it. Here, help me pop it back in." Grimacing, she pushed against her sister's hands and grunted through the pain of resetting the joint. "Yes, I'm alright," she said.

"Jess told us you got thrown into an interrogation cell, she saw you get dragged off the monorail in iron cuffs!"

"Does someone want to tell me what happened?" she pressed after a moment.

"I planted an incendiary device in one of the outward facing ventilation shafts of the Administration building," he said defiantly. "We all decided that the needs of The Scattered were to come before our own."

"I knew you were a firebrand, Cole, but I never realized you'd do something so reckless," Georgie said, her arm around her sister's shoulders. "Do you have any idea how many janitors and gardeners work in those areas? Gods, I just crawled through one to get out!"

"You could show a little appreciation, you know. After all, part of the reason I set that bomb was to give you an opportunity to escape." He gestured at Georgie with an eye roll. "Lo and behold, it worked."

Georgie shook her head. "I didn't need to escape. Allemande took off my cuffs herself."

"What? Why would she do that?" Emeline asked, still gripping Georgie's arm with a fierce protective grasp.

"She thinks it was Erin that drugged all those officers," she whispered. "She wants me to be her eyes and ears in the janitorial department, report back to her about any suspicious behavior."

"And you said yes? Gods, so much for that oath of loyalty, eh? The second you were offered a leg up, you snatched that opportunity. What next, Georgina? You going to rat us out, too?"

"Don't call me that. Only my family calls me that," Georgie hissed, a pang of ache for her mother and Lucy throbbing in her chest.

"Shut up Cole, it's not like she had a choice," Emeline snapped. "Allemande is hardly the kind of person that accepts no for an answer."

"Why would she trust you anyway?" he asked, his voice growing in volume. "What have you done for her that made you all friendly with our most dangerous opponent? How much did you tell her about us?"

"Hush, Cole," Georgie said, glancing around. "Someone might hear."

"Who's going to hear? The military police you led to our doorstep?"

"No, the people who are still running home to their families after that bomb threat, you cretin!"

"It's not as if it went off anyway, so I don't understand what you're both so upset about." He pushed past them to the door and looked out expectantly, as though he really did think that Georgie had betrayed them and all of The Scattered.

"Where did you get that pipe bomb from?" Emeline asked. "Does Judy know what you did?"

"On the docks in a black market deal, obviously. And yes, of course she knows." He turned back inside, locking the door behind them. "I don't know why you're angry with *me*, Emeline. You said we needed a diversion to give your sister a chance to escape, which I dutifully provided. She's here, alive, and you're both thanking me with this inquisition, when *she's* the one who agreed to work for Allemande!"

"Maybe it's because I got rid of Tripp's corpse for her," Georgie shrugged, trying still to forget the image of the man's body disappearing beneath the frothing liquid of the vat. "She had Mr. Jackson executed when he questioned her on it, and now Erin is the only one left who saw it. She wants

CHAPTER TWENTY-FIVE

to make sure Erin isn't preparing to make any moves against her."

"I think at this point you need to assume she might have told Erin the same thing about you. Keep you both on your toes, walking the straight and narrow to keep your friends and family safe." Cole peered out the dirty window at the gap in the thin curtains. "How do you know you weren't followed?"

"She was whisked away by security. No way would she have seen where I went."

"Maybe so, but did anyone else see you?"

"Some confused gardeners around the back of the building, near the courtyard with the fountains. I helped them get away from the building, when we still thought it was going to explode." She nudged Cole out of the way and looked out at the back streets, empty now, and still no sign of an explosion. "Any ideas why that building is still intact, then, and not a smoldering pile of rubble?"

"It was reckless," Emeline reiterated, and Georgie found herself marveling again at her little sister's aptitude for leadership. "Bombs are too easily traced, you know that."

"You're blaming me for our proximity to danger? When your own sister is probably going to bring Allemande directly to our doorstep?" He spat. "Honestly, you've got to be kidding me. It's the last time I do something to help you, that's for sure."

"Oh please, as if you weren't itching for the opportunity to blow something up. Seems like every meeting you're agitating for immediate action, when you know full well we don't have the numbers yet, and won't until we get access to the comms tower." Emeline leaned back against a rickety stool, covered in peeling pale blue paint, a remnant of the bookshop the speakeasy had been before the book burnings. "Which won't happen for a long time now. That was our last real chance."

"Oh, I got the chip installed," Georgie piped up, a mischievous grin spreading across her face.

"Why didn't you say so?" Emeline shouted, nearly rocketing up off the stool. "And no one knows that you broke in? I thought you got caught!"

"Not with that part. They thought I drugged the officers to get out of my work duties, or to make them look bad. Imagine the promotion I'd get if I showed evidence of a whole team of passed out guards on duty? It would look like intoxication."

"Gods..." Cole breathed. "You really did it."

Georgie cocked an eyebrow at him. "Oh, so you're done accusing me of being a traitor now that you know I got the job done, is that how it is?"

"I didn't think it was going to work," he mumbled. "When Jess came flying in here earlier saying you'd gotten arrested and were in an interrogation cell, I went straight down to the docks to get a little something to cause a diversion." He glanced toward the window again. "Though it seems my efforts were in vain. You managed to get it done and get out unscathed. Well done, Payne."

"I'll accept your appreciation in the form of lavish gifts," Georgie snorted. "And let me be clear, I am not doing that again, so you'd all better hope that chip Judy gave us was legitimate."

"Only one way to find out," Emeline said, running down into the basement, taking the steps two at a time. Georgie and Cole clambered after her, both of them clumsier on the steps, holding the rail-less walls for balance. The small, dented radio sat on a table in the corner, cobwebs hanging at the edges. It hummed gently when it was turned on, the low static enveloping any discernible language.

"Well?" Cole prompted.

"Hold your horses, I'm working on it," Emeline said, waving him off with one hand and adjusting the knobs with the other. "Possible the frequencies were jammed."

"And that's the news at seven. I'm Delia Dodson, signing off," the radio crackled.

"Georgie! You damn well did it!" Emeline shrieked, grinning from ear to ear.

"We missed the broadcast," she replied, disappointed.

"There will be another one in an hour, and besides, that's just the Coalition bulletin. Nothing but lies," Cole piped in. "But it means the chip worked.

CHAPTER TWENTY-FIVE

It means we can get word out about what's going on here. It means we're ready to blow the lid off this thing."

"Where's the transmitter?" Emeline asked, bending down to search a grimy shelf.

"To the right of that box."

Emeline hooked the transmitter to the radio, which emitted a screech so loud they all couldn't help but cover their ears.

"Em! Turn it off first!" Georgie yelled over the din.

"Sorry!" her sister shouted back cheerily, unplugging the radio from the tiny generator that hummed softly above the boiler. She inserted a metal rod from the transmitter to the radio and plugged it in again, tapping gently on the rusted microphone that sat on the table. "Testing, one two, one two," she said.

Static.

"Adjust the frequency and try again," Cole said urgently. "Just turn the knob, and—"

"I know how to work this, in fact I know more than you, so sit down while I work," Emeline replied firmly. "You don't have to manage me."

"I am your manager!" he protested. "I own this place, and I'm letting the two of you stay here free of charge—"

"Cole," Georgie interrupted. "Don't."

Emeline adjusted the many different knobs, one at a time, all the while holding down the transmission button and repeating "testing, one, two" over and over. Still, there was nothing but static.

"Are you sure that thing is strong enough to catch a signal from down here?" Georgie asked, looking sideways at Cole. "Maybe because we're underground—"

"Well, we can hardly broadcast from the top of the Administration building, now can we, Georgie?" he snarked. "Even upstairs here we'd run the risk that someone would hear us."

"Shut up, both of you," Emeline said, still twisting the knobs.

"Excuse me? Who is this?" the radio crackled. "It's hardly customary to radio someone just to tell them to shut up."

Georgie and Cole tripped over each other trying to get to the table where the radio was, and Georgie fell against the rough wood, a splinter driving its way into her index finger.

"Who is this?" Emeline asked.

"This is Captain Tansy of the R.S Dry Barrel, unidentified transmitter."

"Dry Barrel?"

"Yep. Always looking for ways to fill 'er up." Static crackled. "What can I do for you fine folks?"

"We were testing our equipment."

"Sounds like it works to me. Now I'll ask again who I'm speaking to? After all, gotta be careful these days."

"Emeline."

"Em—well gods be damned, your mama has been worried sick. Where's your sister?"

"Me! I'm here!" Georgie shouted, swallowing back the lump in her throat. Her mother was okay, and if she made it safely, then Lucy had, too. "How do you know our mother?"

"Let's just say our paths have crossed. Can't be too cavalier on the radio waves, you know."

"What about Henry?" Georgie blurted out, tears threatening to spill down her cheeks. "Have you heard from Henry? Tell her we're okay!" She leaned in closer. "Tell her I love her."

"Not in the past few weeks. Last I heard she was still running around with the crew of the Cricket. They've not been reachable for some time, too far out of range for this old equipment. Shall I pass on your message when next I hear from them?"

"Yes, ma'am, Captain Tansy," Emeline cut in. "Is there any news we should know? We've been in the dark for months."

"Storms running wild all across the Near Systems, no sign they'll abate any time soon. We've got our hands full with that, no resources for anything else, if you catch my drift."

Emeline wilted in her chair. "Oh. Yes. I catch your drift. Thank you, Captain."

CHAPTER TWENTY-FIVE

"I'll pass on that message. Keep strong down there! R.S. Dry Barrel, over and out."

"Shit." Emeline sat back in her chair, drumming her fingertips against the table. "No resources means we won't be getting any help from anyone."

"That was just one ship, there's bound to be other sympathizers who want to help our cause," Cole argued. "Just because one shitty captain says so doesn't mean it's the honest truth."

"She's got a whole damn fleet, Cole. She's not one shitty captain, she's the head of a whole group of folks working to evacuate refugees." Georgie sucked on her finger, trying to staunch the drops of blood from the splinter. "I still think we need to start getting word to the off-world underground, though. Maybe if people hear what goes on here, they'll change their minds about the Coalition."

"Sure," Emeline said, defeated. "I just thought—" She shook her head. "I don't know what I thought."

Georgie draped an arm over her sister's shoulders. "It takes time, Em. This is only the first step." She leaned over and flipped the main switch back to the Coalition frequencies just in time to hear the proud chimes of the Coalition anthem come to a close. "Let's listen."

"Good evening, I'm Delia Dodson with the nightly news. The Administration building was evacuated today as part of a routine drill to practice and prepare for a systems malfunction or a chemical spill from the laboratory wing of the compound. No one was harmed in this exercise, and our very own Governor Allemande would like to commend everyone involved on a job well done."

"See? Nothing but lies," Cole muttered.

"Skelm exports are up and imports are down, in a breathtaking resurgence of economic activity that will continue to allow this colony to truly thrive. When profits are up, we show the rest of the Near Systems just how important we are."

"Funny how the people breaking their bodies apart in the factories don't feel like that."

"Cole, hush."

"Job retention is at an all-time high in the factories this quarter, something for all of us to feel proud of. When we all work together, we all win."

"Nothing to do with the fact no one can even get smuggled off this fucking rock anymore, I suppose," Cole grumbled.

"If you're just going to talk through the entire broadcast—"

"Alright, alright."

"Military service enrollment has increased for the thirtieth straight month and counting. Let's all take a moment of silence to show our appreciation for the brave souls who risk life and limb every day across the Near Systems to protect us and keep us all safe. Without them, we would all be living in chaos."

Georgie snorted.

"In a new law passed today, able-bodied workers aged twelve and up are now eligible to take on paid employment, in a move hailed by workforce experts as 'brave' and 'the best way to keep progressing and achieving.' Those who do not wish to work will have to show notarized proof that they are enrolled in an upper-tier academic program in the top ten percent of their class, and pay a stipend to remain exempt. This new legislation will allow families to earn more, keep their children off the streets, and contribute to the glory of the Coalition."

"Gods, that would mean Lucy," Emeline breathed. "What are they thinking?"

Georgie could only shake her head, and allowed herself the tiniest bit of happiness that she'd gotten Lucy out in time.

"That's all for this evening. Stay tuned in for the anthem sing along to follow, and come back tomorrow morning for all the freshest news. And remember, if you can hear us, we can hear you." She paused, and the static buzzed. "Remember. We can always hear you." The opening bars of the anthem drifted onto the waves and began to swell. "I'm Delia Dodson, signing off for the evening awash in the Coalition's continued success. Good night."

Emeline turned to Georgie, her eyes wide with fear. "What if they heard us, Georgie?"

CHAPTER TWENTY-SIX

Burning wreckage drifted through the air in the devastating aftermath of the storm in Hjarta, falling to the ground and igniting whatever laid in its path, like a thousand tiny wildfires. Henry bent double, desperate to catch her breath despite the limited oxygen flow in her pressurized suit. The weather balloons dragged through the dirt behind her, a smooth, uneven track showing where she had been.

"Weaver? Hey! Are you alright?" Kady asked, wiping smudges of ash from her helmet's visor.

"Oh, thank the gods you're alright," Henry gasped, wishing she could take off her helmet for some fresh air. "What about the others?"

"Bailey got everyone else evacuated to the tents near the landing site, I don't think we have any casualties." She looked up at the sky, at the dissipating clouds, and sighed. "Not yet, anyway. Atmosphere won't hold long without those terraformers."

"Any word from the Cricket?"

Kady shook her head. "Storm took out the comms tower, too."

"Shit. Unless we can get those terraformers back up and running, or get these people boarded on a rescue transport, it's going to get ugly, and fast."

"I'm no mechanic, but we could give it a shot. Might be able to get them to at least struggle along until help arrives."

"If help arrives," Henry corrected her. "No, I think getting to that communications tower is more important right now. If we can get word to the ship, maybe Alice..."

"Yeah." Kady ducked into their supplies tent and returned a second later with a tool belt secured around her waist. "Come on, then."

"Gods, I'm sick to death of fixing comms towers," Henry muttered under her breath. "Sick of these storms that don't make any sense. What I wouldn't give for a hurricane with a predictive pattern right now, honestly."

"You and me both," Kady laughed with a bitter tinge. "Science was more fun when the problems had answers."

"How long do you think we have?"

"Few hours, maybe."

"We can only hope that the Cricket saw the storms on the radar and know we need assistance. Now that it's clearing, they'd be able to land, even if just to drop Alice and some supplies, take some folks up to wait for a refugee transport."

"It's a mess, Weaver."

"You can say that again," Henry said, approaching the smoking communications tower. "Just look at this. Seared from top to bottom, I bet half the wiring in there is all melted together."

"More than half, if I had to guess."

"Know any workarounds?"

"For an entire tower full of fused copper? No. Shockingly, Henry, I don't think a few new nuts and bolts are going to fix it this time."

Henry looked at her sideways and frowned. "What about the terraformers, then? If we buy a little time—"

"If the comms tower is this burnt up, I doubt the generators fared any better."

"So what, then, we're sitting ducks? Just waiting for rescue, nothing we can do?"

"Looks like it," Kady said, sitting down on the ground, leaning against the tower. Blue paint flaked off against her pressure suit, and she brushed it away with a shaky hand. "Might as well conserve oxygen."

"This settlement won't ever recover from this. One storm, maybe even two. But three? Their equipment isn't even salvageable anymore, their

CHAPTER TWENTY-SIX

homes, nearly every structure demolished." Henry sat on the ground next to Kady and hugged her knees, the thin fabric of the pressure suit pulled taut. "At this rate, we'll be lucky if we even get out of here alive."

* * *

An hour passed, and then two. Clouds rolled by in clusters, calm as a stagnant pond, as though they hadn't ripped through the town just that morning. Even after a predictable storm, the gentleness of the ensuing clouds always intrigued her. They seemed to mock, to ask why anyone was worried to begin with, and where did all the destruction come from, anyway?

"Hey, any news?" Bailey called, her voice carrying freely over the grassy hill that crested beneath the mangled tower. "They sent me to see if you'd managed to fix anything yet. People are getting worried."

Kady held a fistful of melted copper in her gloved fist. "There's nothing in existence that can fix this."

"Shit."

"Yeah, and the terraformers aren't looking any better. The electrical current fused almost all the wiring." She shook her head. "Not much you can do when that kind of heat is involved. Sometimes the internal structure can ground around the wiring, but not when there's been this much damage."

"So what's the plan?"

"We wait," Henry said, staring up at the sky, watching a cloud shaped like a duck float by. Bastard things. "And hope that the Cricket was watching the radar, and that they come down and get us."

"There's over a hundred people left in that encampment!" Bailey shouted. "Are you telling me that they're all going to fit on that tiny, outdated ship?"

"Listen, it's not like we have a choice, unless you have miles of copper wiring stashed somewhere," Kady said defensively. "I'm sure they're already liaising with Captain Tansy to—what the hell is that?"

Henry squinted into the distance at what looked like some kind of transport. "One of Captain Tansy's, it must be," she said, pulling herself to her feet. "See, Bailey? We told you they'd—" she stopped short. The vessel began to descend out of the atmosphere, the yellow and purple insignia emblazoned onto its side.

"It's Coalition," Kady breathed, her voice almost inaudible through her helmet.

Bailey turned back and started down the hill. "We've gotta get back there and warn them!"

"No, wait!" Henry said, grabbing her arm and yanking her backward.

"What do you expect me to do, let them all get captured?"

"If you run in there, they'll scoop you up, too! Some of those people have got to be struggling with the lack of oxygen already, this might be their best chance at survival."

"They're not going to be given rest and relaxation, Weaver, they'll be thrown into work camps!"

"There's nothing we can do, Bailey! Not unless you have several dozen high-powered weapons hidden in that jumpsuit somewhere."

Bailey sat down, slumped against the tower. "So now what? We wait to die?"

"We hope the Cricket comes back for us after that transport leaves," Kady said sullenly. "We cross our fingers the oxygen holds out until then." She turned and looked at Bailey. "You do have a pressure suit back in the tent, right?"

Bailey's face paled. "No. I gave mine to an elderly woman who wouldn't have lasted much longer without it."

"Don't worry," Henry said, patting her arm. "I'll share my oxygen, if it comes to that."

The trio watched from a distance in silence, the remaining settlers being lined up and marched onto the transport. From this far away, they couldn't see the terror on their faces. Maybe that was for the best. It's not as though they could do anything for them, anyway. Not without weapons, and an army, or at least a defensive plan.

"They must have been watching," Bailey said, staring down the hill as her people were unceremoniously loaded onto the transport by military police officers in state-of-the-art pressure suits. "They must have known about the storms and waited until they knew people wouldn't be able to resist. No guns, nowhere to hide, and staring death in the face," she wheezed. "And then they just swoop in and scoop them all up as though we wouldn't have destroyed them just a few weeks ago." She looked down at the bare patch of dirt beneath the tower and dragged her fingers through it. "It's cowardly."

"The Coalition isn't known for their bravery," Kady agreed after a moment. "They'll pull whatever tricks they can to crush the slightest whiff of dissent."

"We used to feel safe out here, you know," Bailey whispered. "So far out, we rarely saw or heard anyone. Most comms signals from Gamma-3 can't even reach here, and we were so insignificant that even the closest Coalition base didn't bother us, so long as we supplied their merchants with copper from the mines now and then." She squeezed her eyes shut. "It's ironic that we have mountains full of the stuff, but not in a way that can be used to fix the equipment. Not in the way we'd have been able to save them."

"At least the others got out," Henry offered. "I guess that's something."

The transport's large loading bay door raised up and latched closed, locking the settlers inside as the engines fired up and blasted hot air against the ground below, waves of heat distorting its crisp edges while it pushed off and raised into the atmosphere.

"Here," Henry said, hearing Bailey's labored breathing. "Put my helmet on a while." She rested a hand on her back to comfort her. To her surprise, Bailey didn't object or resist the offer of help; she set the helmet on her shoulders and breathed deep as tears slid down her cheeks, the white trail of the transport streaking across the sky.

* * *

When the Cricket finally landed, long after the Coalition transport had left, they were down to the dregs of their oxygen, wheezing and gasping for breath as the three of them tumbled into the loading bay. Henry knelt on all fours, trying to convince her lungs not to hyperventilate at the sudden influx of air, listening to Bailey and Kady cough alongside her. The door began to close with a long creak, and when she laid on her back, she found herself looking up at a grim-faced Captain Violet.

"Captain?"

"You three are lucky we were able to skirt past the blockade and make it back past the gunships."

"Blockade?" Kady asked, sitting up and taking off her helmet. "What happened?"

"Storms touched down in settlements all across the Near Systems, all at the same time. We could barely tell one S.O.S call apart from another."

Henry propped herself up on her elbows, scrambling to get her feet under her. "Gods. What now?"

"I honestly don't know," the captain said, shaking her head, the solemnity of the gesture weighing in Henry's chest. "It sounds as though they had transports standing by, waiting for the storms to clear." She sighed and rubbed at the bridge of her nose. "It certainly was no coincidence."

"Where are they taking them? My people? All those people?" Bailey asked, already upright, the helmet she'd shared with Henry tucked under her arm. "Wherever they're going, we need to follow, we need to get them back."

"We don't have that kind of firepower, or the numbers to have a fighting chance in hell," Kady said. "Those transports are heavily armed at all times, especially when there are prisoners involved."

"Then we need to gather our resources, mount an offensive. There's gotta be enough rebels and pirates around to make it happen."

"Captain Tansy is already organizing relief efforts, and once she and the rest of her fleet have dropped off the latest group of refugees, we will meet in Bradach to compare notes." Captain Violet clasped her hands behind her back, her posture rod straight, and stress knots in her shoulders Henry could see from across the room. "We've been in and out of communications for weeks, between broken satellites the Coalition is sabotaging, and running under deep stealth to avoid detection. If not for the emergency distress calls, we wouldn't even know what was going on. Nothing else breaks through."

"Boss," the overhead radio buzzed with Ned's voice, "we'll have to be careful getting through this blockade. They're using energy signatures to

CHAPTER TWENTY-SIX

track ships."

"Again?"

"Looks to be more and more common technology every day. Alice is down in the boiler room preparing to take us down for a quiet coast. Stand by."

"Copy. Over and out."

The lights dimmed to almost nothing, leaving Henry to squint in the darkness, unable to make out anything more than vague silhouettes. She'd become accustomed to it, but still resented the loss of productive lab time during the blackout. No power, no tests, no research. So much time wasted sneaking past Coalition gunships.

"How do you work like this?" Bailey asked, fumbling in the dark.

"We don't," Kady sighed, and rescued one of the weather balloons from the floor. "It's one of the reasons why we're so behind in figuring these storms out. There's only so much you can do by lamplight."

"I'm going to my room," Henry announced, suddenly desperate to get out of her pressure suit. "I'll start the manual analysis of the data I collected down there."

"Manual? Weaver, that's going to take forever."

"It's better than sitting around waiting for something else bad to happen," she snapped, and immediately regretted it. "I'm sorry."

Kady didn't respond and instead held the balloon at arm's length for Henry to take, which she did, before feeling her way to the crew airlock and stepping into the ship proper, feeling her way along the long corridors, dragging her palm against a protruding screw that bit into her skin. Only she would manage to escape the clutches of the Coalition by a hair's breadth, just to contract tetanus from a busted up old ship.

Her room was just as she'd left it early that morning, though that seemed like a lifetime ago now. Her bed was sloppily made, the covers half piled on the floor, a pillow lopsided against the faded leather headboard. Henry sloughed off her pressure suit like it was superfluous skin, and shivered as she stepped out into the chilly air. No power meant no temperature control, either. There was barely enough to keep the air filtration running. The bathroom was pitch black, not having a window, and so she lit an old gas lamp that hung on the wall, casting long, unsettling shadows over her body.

The mirror held her reflection in an odd yellow glow that made her look pallid and unwell; she supposed the lack of sleep wasn't helping her much, either. Goose pimples spread over her pale skin as she dripped icy water over it in a clumsy bid to freshen up. Dirty water washed down the drain, black in the dim light. The shadows danced on the wall, menacing with an unintelligible premonition that almost seemed to whisper in her ear.

Henry had always hated the dark, but she especially hated shadows, and the way a tired mind could make a monster of anything given the opportunity. She didn't want to be alone, she was tired of waking up clutching the pillow as if it was a lover, and despised retiring to her empty room night after night. At least when they were in Bradach, she could stay up in the Purple Pig with Evie and Larkin, laughing and trading stories as though they'd all known each other their whole lives. But here on the ship, the nights were cold, and lonely.

She stepped into her soft wool dress and sighed, her fingers almost too worn and sore to button it up. She was once again grateful to Roger for packing up her rented room back in Skelm, at least she had several changes of clothes. Evie told her that when she was first on the Cricket, all she had was a prison jumpsuit and some borrowed coveralls from Alice. The blue fabric of her dress felt comfortable against her skin, familiar and pleasing in a way that the pressure suits were not.

"Hey, you in there?" came a knock at the door. "It's alright if you're busy, I just—"

Henry opened the door, expecting to see Kady, but found Bailey instead. "Oh, it's you."

"I can go if you want."

"No, don't be silly. Come in." She closed the door behind them and sat on the bed, the mattress a little lumpy. Her cheeks burned when she realized the state of her quarters. "Sorry about the mess, I—"

Bailey waved her away. "Don't. I don't care about things like that." She sat on the bed, gripping her knees where the coveralls were almost worn through. "I just wanted to say thank you."

CHAPTER TWENTY-SIX

"For what?"

"Saving my life, I guess. If you hadn't stopped me from running back to the encampment, I'd be on my way to a work camp with everyone else." She sighed and picked at the ends of her braid. "At least now I might have a chance of getting them out."

"I'm so sorry we couldn't do more for them," Henry said gently. "I'm sure we'll be able to get them out soon."

"And thank you for sharing your oxygen, too. Not everyone would have done that."

"Anyone who wouldn't has a faulty moral compass, in my opinion."

"Even so."

Henry smoothed a corner of the covers, still embarrassed at the mess. She really should get into the habit of tidying up in the mornings, but she also knew she'd never do that. Time was too precious to waste on such trivial matters. In the moment, however, she wished that she had taken just a moment to clean up before rinsing the grime off her skin. At least the relative darkness hid most of her domestic sins. "I imagine we'll be headed for Bradach now. Once we're past the blockade, we'll be able to be back in communication with the other ships, and maybe Captain Tansy has some ideas on how to get your people back."

"I hope so. Some of those people won't survive a week in a work camp."

"That will be difficult news to pass on."

"If the captain heard all those distress calls, chances are they did, too. Still, I should tell them myself, just to confirm what happened in Hjarta. No doubt some of them are holding onto the thread of hope that we weren't one of the ones affected. That we managed to get everyone out, or that the Coalition didn't come to us. I'll have to cut that thread, break the news."

"I'm sure some may not take that well."

"No. It's not easy knowing someone you care about is in trouble, and there's nothing you can do about it." Bailey tugged at her long, auburn braid. "My friend Yannick got taken. He's a fool, but a friend, and he's likely to get himself killed because he can't keep his damned mouth shut."

Henry looked at the floor, her stockinged feet peeking out from under her

237

skirts. She thought of Georgie, but pushed the memory down, unwilling to allow herself the gratuitous anxiety it always brought. There was more at stake, now. "Not now, anyway."

"Do you have someone you're worried about?" Bailey asked.

Unwilling to delve into the details, Henry settled on "We all do, these days."

"True enough. Well, I didn't mean to barge in, I just felt..."

"Lonely?"

"Yeah."

"Me too," Henry admitted. "Even with all these people around, I still wind up feeling like I'm adrift out here. It's not how things used to be. It's not how I thought being a renegade would turn out."

"How so?"

"The equipment sucks. These blackouts that protect us from detection slow down research and development of new ideas and tech for Kady, they stall my own analysis. It's like being in a fist fight with one arm behind your back, you end up using all your ability to avoid hits, yet you keep taking punches."

Bailey laughed. "You don't strike me as the kind of woman who spends a lot of time brawling."

"I've had my fair share," Henry replied, squaring her shoulders. "You'd be surprised what we get up to in academy preparatory schools."

"I can't imagine a reason you'd need a punch up in a preparatory school, to be honest, Ms. Weaver."

"My lab partner passed off my research as his own and dared me to teach him a lesson. So, I punched him."

"That has to be the nerdiest, most badass thing I've ever heard," Bailey snorted. "What happened then?"

Henry shrugged. "Well, I'll tell you one thing, he never stole my notes again."

"Did you get into trouble?"

"Nah. He didn't want to admit being beaten up by a girl. Told everyone he got into a fight with a guy three times his size in a tavern. I never corrected

CHAPTER TWENTY-SIX

him, I was happy to just let him stew in his own failure." She surreptitiously fluffed a pillow. "He's one of the higher ups in Coalition management now, though. Last I heard, he has the weapons development laboratory under his purview."

"Figures. The worst ones always get promoted."

"Exactly," Henry said. "Plus the fact they have all kinds of funding for the military police, and weapons research, but when it comes to biodiversity or meteorology, they couldn't care less. We get laughed out of the budget every year."

"How come you never got poached, then? You seem very poachable to me."

"No interest in weapons research, probably to my detriment, given what we're seeing now. The Coalition has all this technology we know nothing about, and I feel useless." She nudged a stray sock under the bed with her foot. "Did you just say I seem poachable? What am I, an egg?"

"Well, if you are, you're the best looking egg I've ever seen, and I grew up eating farm fresh."

"Farm fresh? In Hjarta?"

"You don't think we imported all of our fresh food in, did you? Sure, our biggest trade was in copper, but we still had farmers, Henry. Even I did some farm work now and then."

"I guess there's a lot I still don't know about life outside of Coalition control. To think, I used to believe that they were mostly good, just corrupted by leadership. The more I see, the more I realize the whole thing is rotten from the inside out."

"I wish you could have seen Hjarta in its glory. I would have taken you for long walks in the marsh, alongside the rare plants that grow there, one of the only places in the Near Systems that the soil pH was just right for them to be propagated by the first settlers. We'd have gone to the shopping district to pick out fancy clothes for one of the parties during the festival, stopped at the fountain to marvel at the sculptures. It's all gone now, though. By the time you got there, it was all rubble, destroyed by the fires and the wind."

"I'm sorry, Bailey."

"Nothing I can do about it now, is there? Best thing I can do for that place will be to rescue its people and then forget it. It won't ever get rebuilt to its former glory. It's one more chapter in the never ending book of settlements that don't make it. We did, though. We did for a long time, before this." She stood up and forced a smile that didn't reach her eyes. "Anyway, I didn't mean to take up so much of your time like this, I just wanted to drop by and say thank you for everything you did today."

"Of course," Henry said, and gave her a hug that lasted an instant more than it should have, finding comfort wrapped in Bailey's strong arms. "You should get some rest. It's going to be a long few days until we get to Bradach."

Bailey lingered in the doorway, her eyes sparkling in the lamplight. "Yeah. I'll see you at breakfast, Weaver."

CHAPTER TWENTY-SEVEN

"My friends, we are gathered here tonight to celebrate our liberation from our fascist chains," Emeline said, her calm, collected voice reverberating off the walls of the empty factory. They had lookouts stationed along the docks and at every entrance, but Georgie couldn't help but fidget, stealing glances out the window at every opportunity. "With collective bargaining, we can force the Coalition's hand, and make them provide us with adequate shelter and rations!"

One man whooped from the back of the small crowd, the others shifting nervously. What they were doing was tantamount to treason, if caught, and they'd struggled to get even this paltry amount of people to show up.

"We will have schools for our children!"

A few perked up at this, and Emeline saw, drawing into their enthusiasm.

"The youth of our people will be educated, and given equal opportunity to climb the ranks of the Coalition, to choose a career and a life for themselves, and—"

"Why not just burn the whole city down?" an old woman in the front shouted. "We've been their pawns long enough, it's time to make them feel the pain they've inflicted upon us. We want revenge, not a continuation of grievances!"

"Shut up Fiona, talk like that will get us all killed!" the man in the back retorted. "It's bad enough we're even here talking about a strike, and here you want to talk about property damage and threatening lives? Have you lost your mind?"

"I've spent nearly half my life in this sorry excuse for a settlement," Fiona said. "I'm tired. I'm old, and I want to die in peace or as I burn this place to the ground, not crushed under some machinery!"

"Some of us have children to think of!"

"How dare you say that to me, you—"

Emeline cleared her throat and put her hands up to quiet them. "Alright, let's get back to the matter at hand, shall we? Before we can resort to anything else, we have to start with actions that look reasonable to an outside eye. Yes, they've had their boots on our necks for decades, almost a century in Skelm, using our bodies as fodder for their factories, and to line their pockets with credits. But people who have never set foot on our shores don't know our story, they haven't heard our tragic losses and heartbreak."

"Using the communication system, we have been able to send coded messages to resistance bases across the Near Systems, at least five in range of our signal. We've told them to watch what's coming, to leak any and all information concerning our fight for freedom. What I need from you is to talk to your fellow workers, to show them the value of our demands and what could be possible if we retake our power and our independence from Coalition rule. They may have the weapons, but we hold the factories that make them."

"And what if they drag us all into the street and have us executed for treason? Where will this rebellion be then?"

"They don't have enough bullets to kill us all," Emeline said with a solemn tone. "Especially if we refuse to make them more. Where would they get a new workforce from, that could step over our still-warm bodies to take our places at our stations? They need us, and they need to be reminded of that." She took a breath and waited a beat before she continued. "We need justice!"

"Yeah!" the man replied, elbowing the woman next to him.

"We need schools for our children!"

"Education for all!" the woman shouted back. "We want our kids safe!"

Emeline nodded. "We need clean, fair housing, not rat-infested tene-

CHAPTER TWENTY-SEVEN

ments. Skelm is plenty big enough for us all to have a space of our own to raise our families!"

"We want a place to cook our own meals!" another man yelled.

"We deserve fair pay for fair work. We want safety and equality for our families. These are not radical demands, they are what should be afforded to us as humans, they are what was promised when we came here to help the Coalition build itself." Emeline punched her fists in the air. "Justice for workers!"

The crowd echoed her, timid at first, and then louder and more fervent until one of the lookouts popped her head into the room. "Do y'all want to keep it down? Half of Skelm can probably hear you right now!"

Emeline nodded and shushed the crowd with her hands, motioning for them to disperse as she stepped down off the overturned crate. "I'll see you all next week. Bring a friend, hell, bring two! Once we fill this factory, pack it to the rafters, we can organize a strike." She turned, and came face to face with a large man, a finger pointed in her face.

"You think you know everything, little girl, but you've never worked a real day in your life. You'll never be able to lead anyone to overcome this shit pile we all live in."

Georgie leapt between them with a protective snarl. "Hey, back off!"

"It's alright," Emeline said, smoothing her worn, threadbare skirt. "Sir, you're correct that I am young, and you are right that I don't work in a factory. But my father died for this cause, and for his sake, I have to see it through."

"What makes you think you have what it takes?" he spat.

"What makes you think we don't? As an individual, no, I can't affect any lasting or meaningful change. I can only achieve that with the help of the other workers in Skelm, of the other people who long for a better life, for more opportunity, for some semblance of hope. You're right that I can't do this alone. That's why this movement needs people like you to stand alongside and fight for what's right."

The man softened and stepped back. "Well, I still think someone else would be a better leader than you."

Emeline nodded. "Maybe so. If you find anyone willing to take on the mantle, send them my way. But until someone else appears from the mist on the docks, ready to risk life and limb to lead a ragtag group of workers into treason, I'm going to carry on." She reached up and clapped a hand on the man's shoulder and smiled. "Thank you for being here. We need you."

He replied with a grumble before slinking off into the shadows towards the rear exit, the one that led to the large tenement buildings where most of the factory workers lived.

"I don't know how you do it, Em," Georgie said, "not the meeting, or dealing with men like him, or any of it."

Emeline shrugged. "I don't really know either. I just know that no one else has stepped up to make this revolution happen, they're all too scared." She picked up the crate and set it back on the stack. "Rightfully so. People have been killed for less. Pop was."

"I'm proud of you." Even though Georgie said it all the time, she meant it from the depths of her soul. Her sister was only seventeen, and already a leader, already inspiring people to believe that they could have better lives. "You're doing more for this place and these people than I ever could."

"I wouldn't even be here if it weren't for you," Emeline said, linking her arm with Georgie's. "Lucy and I might have starved once Mama couldn't work anymore. You kept a roof over our heads, kept us fed. Not every member of the resistance has to be the face they put on the posters, you know. Change needs people keeping everyone healthy and fed, too."

"So what's next?"

"We hope to hell we start increasing in number, or all the information leaked to rebel frequencies won't matter in the slightest. If we want this to work, people need to have faith."

"I still think you should wear a mask or something. Once this picks up steam, you'll be the most recognizable face, and the easiest to pick out in a crowd."

Emeline shook her head. "No. That will only show people that they should be scared, and I don't want that. They should feel like they can be brave." She flipped the circuit breaker, turning out all the lights in the factory, leaving

CHAPTER TWENTY-SEVEN

them with only the light from the street lamps that struggled to penetrate the thick grime on the windows. "I think you should, though. Especially if Allemande is keeping an eye on you."

"It's hard to know. I don't notice anyone following me, but then I don't think Erin realizes when I note down her whereabouts, either."

"You have to be careful, George. I can't do this without you."

"Sure you can," she replied, playfully shoving her sister. "You're a big shot now."

"No, Georgina, I'm serious. I wouldn't have the courage to stand up there and make speeches if I didn't know you were behind me. I don't have anyone else now."

"You have Cole, and Judy, and—"

"Hush. You know what I mean."

Georgie wrapped an arm around her sister's shoulders. "Yeah. I know what you mean."

"Heard from Mama?"

"No." Georgie had taken to sitting up with the radio at every spare moment, hovering around the desk like a hungry, wild animal pacing the edges of a campfire. She hadn't slept in days, not since they first made contact with Captain Tansy. She was desperate to get word from the crew of the Cricket to hear for certain that Lucy and their mother were alright, that Henry was alright, and that Roger had managed to survive that injury.

"You should sleep tonight, Georgie."

"Someone needs to watch the radio, in case—"

"I'll keep watch. You sleep. I doubt they'd be trying to get in contact in the middle of the night, anyway. Now come on, or we're going to miss the evening broadcast."

* * *

"Good evening, I'm Delia Dodson. In today's news, we can report that the storms seen raging through derelict, abandoned colonies have finally ceased. We still don't know the cause of this phenomenon, but we can at least be grateful that there were no fatalities of Coalition citizens, or damage to Coalition property. As those colonies had been long-abandoned for being inefficient and unsustainable, *we* have suffered no losses."

"How long do you think she'll keep passing us crumbs of information?" Georgie asked, leaning back on her thin bed roll.

"Don't know. Can only hope as long as possible," Cole replied. "It's the one good thing about these broadcasts, if you know how to read through the lines, you can at least get *some* accurate information."

"In other news, the High Council has announced a new public holiday on Gamma-3 to celebrate the sacrifices of the military police, the brave souls who defend the very fabric of our glorious society. It will take place fortnightly and include a big celebratory parade with all the might and weaponry we have to display."

"Great," Georgie muttered. "Just what we need, more displays of force and bravado."

"The racing championships have begun, with this year's course set at the edge of the asteroid belt. Participants include people from all over the Near Systems, ready to race to prove their speed and agility, and their corporate sponsors are very excited to see if they survive the event. Tune into this frequency tomorrow night to hear more about the racers, and get ready for them to start their engines!"

"What a crock," Judy said, rolling her eyes. "Everyone knows those racers are nothing more than cannon fodder for free advertising."

"Coalition Citizens are reminded that alcoholic beverages are strictly off-limits. Anyone found to be illegally importing or brewing spirits or ales will be prosecuted to the full extent of the law, in accordance with existing regulations. Remember, you can always engage in safe fun without unlawful substances!"

"Gods, I hate it here," Cole grumbled.

"Our brave military police has engaged in conflict with a fleet of pirate vessels near the Outer Rim, which sadly ended in bloodshed."

Georgie sat up, her eyes glued to the radio.

"General Wilhemina Fineglass has reported that at least a dozen of our brave soldiers lost their lives in this clash with the despicable, law-flouting pirates who sought to scrap and steal Coalition property. However, we are pleased to announce that the pirates in question have been imprisoned indefinitely, pending an investigation and sentencing."

"That can't have been them, right?" Georgie asked, her voice quivering with all the worry she'd been suppressing, now lodged in her throat. "We'd have heard if it was the Cricket, or Captain Tansy's fleet, right?"

"I don't think they'd have been all the way out there, would they?" Judy said. "That's a long way to go for an evacuation. More likely it was some scrappers."

"When was the last time you heard scrappers take out over a dozen military police?" Cole asked, knocking back a shot of bourbon they'd imported inside a barrel of oil.

"Shush!" Emeline hissed.

"And finally, the local news. In response to recent claims, a message from Amaranthe Allemande, governor of Skelm. 'My dear citizens, it has come to my attention that some rebel agitators are calling for work reforms, threatening to burn down our beautiful city if they are not handed riches on a gilded platter. I would caution those easily taken in by this kind of rabble-rousing to think twice before joining a cause that would jeopardize your employment and your housing as provided by our fine empire. If you have concerns about your work environment, you are always welcome to bring them up with your immediate supervisor, who will of course accommodate any needs you might have. Please remember that we all have an at-will employment partnership, which means you are free to leave the moment your work is no longer a suitable fit for you and your family. The Coalition cares about you and wants us all to prosper as one.'"

"So who thinks we have a mole?" Judy asked. "That bit about burning the city down seemed particularly on the nose."

"It's likely we'll always have moles. That's why we need to make sure we only ever advocate for better working conditions," Emeline said with a sigh. "The rest of that is garbage. We've been politely asking for better conditions for years, and nothing's been done about it."

The radio crackled and popped as the broadcaster shuffled her papers. "That's all for tonight's broadcast, folks. My advice to any agitators out there would certainly be to take heart in our governor's words, and go through the proper channels if they are dissatisfied with their work environment - but remember, we are all parts of one whole. Without each and every cog working hard to advance our society, we will likely fail. I'm Delia Dodson, goodnight."

"That was clear as mud," Cole said, switching the radio back to the scanning frequency. "If she's going to drop us hints, she may as well make them clearer."

"We don't even know if that's what she's doing," Judy argued. "For all we know, she's a Coalition lackey through and through, and we're just reading into nothing."

Georgie shook her head. "No, I don't think so. Seems to me our friend Delia is trying to tell us that we need to disrupt the supply lines, shut down the factories. 'Without each and every one of you, we will likely fail.' Seems clear to me."

"We could sabotage the factories, or slow down supplies at the docks," Emeline said, scribbling notes on a scrap of paper. "If the factories can't get the raw materials, they won't run. If they don't run, there's no finished goods, not weapons, or chemicals, or vehicles. None of it."

"What happened to the importance of collective bargaining?" Cole sneered. "Last I checked, you two nearly had my head on a pike for placing a small pipe bomb into a ventilation duct."

"You endangered innocent lives," Georgie said, stretching her legs out in front of her. "We're not going to endanger anything other than efficiency. And you know as well as I do that they're not going to give one single shit about a general worker's strike. It's for optics."

"At least I know where Em gets it from," he muttered, rolling his eyes. He stood and stretched, the soft black knitted sweater grazing the top of his waistband. "But for whatever it's worth, I'm glad you're here. People listen to you."

Emeline smirked. "Yeah, aren't you glad you offered me a job here?"

CHAPTER TWENTY-SEVEN

"If I'd have known I'd get saddled with the both of you, I'd have closed up shop a long time ago," Cole snorted. "A force to be reckoned with, you are." He straightened the pens on the table. "You monitoring again tonight, Georgie? If there was a big attack, they might be trying to get in touch."

"Nope, I'm on duty tonight," Emeline said proudly, sitting cross-legged on the rickety wooden folding chair. "Georgina needs to get some sleep, or she'll never stay on top of things at work. And we need her in there as our eyes and ears. She's indispensable."

"Alright, alright, I hear you," Georgie said, kicking off her boots and laying back on her bed roll. Before her head even hit the pillow, she was almost asleep, dreaming of Henry's touch and the last kiss they shared so long ago.

* * *

"What people really crave, at the core of their being, is rules," Governor Allemande recited from a card, a monocle perched over her eye. She looked up from her desk. "Wouldn't you agree, Ms. Payne?"

"Sure," Georgie said, emptying the wastebasket. She hated that the governor insisted on being present for her office cleaning. Even being around her made the tiny hairs at the back of Georgie's neck stand on end in warning.

"We need order and structure, a stability granted from the framework of society," Allemande continued. "Without this framework, we fall into chaos, careening out of control until all progress has halted." She set the cards down on her pristine desk and folded her hands. "This speech is for the gala banquet being planned, you know. The first one of its kind here in Skelm, a real achievement. We'll finally be able to show people why this is such an important cornerstone in the Coalition's development of backwater settlements."

"Mm," Georgie mumbled, wishing the governor would either say something interesting, or shut up. The Scattered had known about the gala for weeks already, having sourced the information through a whisper network at the docks. There had to be some reason they were importing expensive new furniture, after all.

"Ms. Payne, may I remind you that you serve here in the Administration building at my pleasure? A little more enthusiasm would be customary for such an announcement, I should think."

"Sorry, Governor, just distracted today. The gala sounds wonderful, as does your speech."

Allemande tucked the monocle into her pocket. "Pray tell, why are you distracted today? That doesn't sound like the kind of efficiency I've come to expect from you, Georgina."

"Didn't sleep well," Georgie said through gritted teeth, hoping that her sneer looked more like a polite smile than she suspected. They were close in age, and yet the woman spoke to her as though she was a child. "Nothing more than that."

"My dear Ms. Payne, surely you know that we as humans sleep entirely too much? After all, I only sleep three and a half hours a night! Anything more than that is self-indulgent and a detriment to your own potential." She stood and straightened her black velvet skirts, tucking the silk top hat under her arm. "Time to finish up now, Georgina, I have a meeting which I must attend to. Have you any information about our dear Mrs. Talbot I should know about?"

"Not today, Governor. I've seen neither hide nor hair of her for three days, I'm afraid."

"How very strange. Who is checking you in, who is assigning the cleaning rotas?"

"It's been automated."

"How efficient of her! I must commend her on her efforts." She swept to the door and gestured for Georgie to leave. "On your way now, Ms. Payne, there's no shortage of things to clean here, as you're well aware."

"Governor Allemande, I have to ask something of you, and I'm afraid it won't be well-received."

The governor paused, her gloved hand resting on the golden doorknob. "Go on."

CHAPTER TWENTY-SEVEN

"I was hoping - er, rather, I was wondering if—"

"Spit it out, Ms. Payne."

"It would be a real honor to attend the gala, even as part of the support staff, and I was hoping you might consider me to be part of the event. Ma'am."

"Well, now, that's more the reaction I had hoped for from you! I would be honored to put you on the list of janitorial workers for the night. You are right that it's an honor, and as such there will be no extra pay for the event, in line with the new regulations put forth for employment contracts. Please let the others on this list know," she said, handing over a crisp leaf of parchment with several names written in a florid script, with Georgie's at the top.

"Thank you, Governor."

"I think you could go far, Ms. Payne. The sky is the limit for someone like you, who values the structure of our society, and works to maintain the rule of law even in the face of adversity. I wouldn't even be surprised if you sat in Mrs. Talbot's chair one day." Allemande gave a smile that didn't reach her eyes. "Especially if you glean some useful information for me, yes?"

"I'll continue to do my best."

"Are you... quite sure you have nothing else you wanted to tell me?"

Georgie hated these odd mind games that the governor liked to play, fishing for more information in the hopes that you'd slip up, that you'd say more than you meant to and implicate yourself. Her act of being a magnanimous employer was just that - an act.

Governor Allemande stepped back from the door. "You can tell me, you know. Your honesty would immunize you against all manner of prosecution, if you'd witnessed treason, or heard whispers of, well I don't know, plans to smuggle in rebels through the docks."

"What?" Georgie croaked, caught off-guard. Even she hadn't heard of any such plans, and in fact, there were no plans like those, at least not within The Scattered. What had Allemande heard, and from who?

"Rebels. In the docks. You've not heard our own Mrs. Talbot speaking on these matters?"

"No!" Georgie shouted, louder than she meant to. "No, I would have told you, ma'am. I've heard nothing of the sort."

The governor tilted her head and stared for a moment. "Very well. I trust you would inform me if you heard whispers of sedition. That is our agreement, isn't it, Ms. Payne?"

"Yes."

"I do hope you wouldn't forget our accord, if presented with the no doubt difficult choice of protecting friends in opposition to protecting our glorious empire."

"Governor Allemande, I don't have friends, certainly none that would engage in behavior like that."

"I'm glad to hear it!" the governor said, brightening. "After all, with our efficient, law-abiding searches of every ship that lands in our docks, rebels wouldn't get very far, now would they?"

"No, ma'am."

"Absolutely not, you're correct, Ms. Payne. They'd be thrown into an interrogation cell and likely executed, to set an example for the other citizens of this fine city on how to behave in a way that will allow us to advance, and show the Coalition how important we are, despite our distance from Gamma-3."

"Have... have *you* heard that rebels are coming in through the docks?" Georgie asked, almost bracing for the answer.

Allemande threw her head back and laughed, an empty, joyless laugh that sent shivers down Georgie's spine. "Of course not, Ms. Payne," she chuckled, "why would you think that?"

Great, more mind games, Georgie thought, and forced a smile across her face. "I'm very glad to hear that, ma'am. I can't wait for the gala, it's going to be the most exciting event in Skelm I've ever seen, and I've lived here half my life."

"That's one of the things that makes you so valuable to me, Georgina. You know this place like the back of your hand, and you are doubtless dedicated to its continued success, in part due to concern for your family." She tucked an additional silver pen into her breast pocket. "It's just a shame what

CHAPTER TWENTY-SEVEN

happened to your father, all those years ago."

Georgie froze and felt a cold sweat prickle under her arms. "He went missing."

"Yes, some say he boarded a ship at the docks as a stowaway, and left you all here to fend for yourselves."

She swallowed hard. "Yes, that's what they say." His official file read that he'd gone missing, that he had either left the settlement or been involved in some kind of industrial accident, though his body was never recovered.

"It must have been hard for you, taking care of your sisters and your mother."

Georgie noticed the use of past tense, a tiny, insignificant thing, but all a part of the governor's games. "It's still hard, ma'am."

"Yes, of course, that's not the sort of thing that gets any easier. I for one will never understand why a man would leave his family, leave his wife and children. It's cowardly, wouldn't you agree?"

"Yes."

"Cowardly, and the opposite of what we want to encourage in the Coalition. Has he ever contacted you?"

"What? No."

"You could tell me, Georgina."

"Governor Allemande, if my father did escape as a stowaway, he forgot all about us the second that ship got through the atmosphere. It's likely he died in a ditch somewhere, his belly full of bathtub gin and his head full of nothing." Georgie stuffed her hands into her pockets to hide their shaking. What was she getting out of all this, anyway?

"It's a terrible shame what alcohol does to a person," the governor said in a solemn tone. "Even with the blanket ban across the Near Systems, some small-minded citizens still find themselves addicted to the drink, throwing all caution and mindfulness to the wind. I didn't know your father was one of those souls, Georgina, I'm sorry."

"You couldn't know, ma'am."

"I'll expect to see you at the gala, then, in your best work uniform," Allemande said, opening the door and ushering Georgie out. "It will be a pleasure to have you in attendance."

"I look forward to it, Governor."

As Allemande turned down the hallway, Georgie pushed her cart into the alcove, buried her face in her sleeves, and cried. Never in her life had she been more exhausted.

CHAPTER TWENTY-EIGHT

Bradach was fast becoming one of Henry's favorite places in the near systems, with its laid back, casual way of life mingled with incredible technological advances from their brand new, up and coming research facility, staffed mainly by refugees brought there by Captain Tansy. She stepped into the huge tent, with lamps hung from a heavy cord strung across near the apex, her arms burning with the weight of boxes of data she was bringing from the Cricket.

"Henry!" Lucy shouted, running over from one of the lab stations, her hair in two golden messy braids, her cheeks pink from the pressure of the safety goggles. "You're back!" She took one of the boxes from the stack and peered inside. "What have you brought us?"

"Storm data, most of it already translated in that box there. We're looking for patterns, so we can try to predict where they'll strike next."

"What about those?"

"Code. Some of it translated, but there are boxes and boxes of this stuff. Some of it is nonsense, I suspect padded into the files to discourage people from decoding them."

Lucy abandoned the box of the storm data on the table next to her and reached for another box. "So it's like a puzzle? I like puzzles."

"I'll bet you do," Henry laughed, and set the rest of the boxes down, rubbing her arms. "This is a very difficult code, though, I wouldn't want you to get discouraged."

"Henry," Lucy said, giving her a withering look, "you haven't even let me try yet."

"Alright, well, try, then! The formulas are in there... somewhere. I lost track of which box they ended up in. There are still at least a dozen on the ship, I have to go back and get them." She examined her hands, red and chafed from carrying the heavy weight all the way across the small city. "I wish we had a steamcar, or something."

"No steamcars allowed here, ma'am, but I'm happy to help," Bailey said, as she appeared from beneath a table.

"Where did you come from?"

"I was moving some medical equipment for Hyun. Some of the refugees are still having problems with their lungs and such, you know. It's all she can do to keep everyone supplied with the medicines they need."

"Are y'all running out of my mama's medicine?" Lucy asked, suddenly much more childlike than Henry had ever seen her, with worry clouding her eyes.

Henry shot Bailey a warning look. "Don't worry, Hyun is doing a great job of making sure everyone gets what they need. Besides, from what I hear, your ma is doing very well indeed."

"Er—did you need some help with those boxes?"

"Yes, if you have time. I'm supposed to be meeting with the captain and some other officers at the tavern soon to talk about some plans. We've been in and out of communication so long, I feel like we barely know what's going on outside the ship."

"For a woman like you, I have all the time in the world."

Henry blushed, and cleared her throat, looking askance at just the right moment to see the dirty look Lucy was giving Bailey. Damn. "Yes, well, they're in the kitchen area, by the long table."

"Maybe you should come show me, I don't want to move anything you need."

"Uh, sure. Best make it quick though, I'm already likely to be late."

Bailey gave a mock salute to Lucy. "I'll be back soon, Boss."

Lucy glared from Bailey to Henry, and back again. "You'd better be."

CHAPTER TWENTY-EIGHT

Henry exited the tent, gratefully breathing in the fresher air of the settlement.

"Tough crowd, eh?" Bailey said, nodding back at the tent. "She looked like she was ready to hand me over to the Coalition herself."

"That's Lucy."

"And Lucy is...?" she prompted. When Henry remained silent, she blew out a puff of air. "Oh. Complicated."

"Her little sister."

"I gathered that much. I don't mean to pry, but—"

"Then don't." The guilt Henry had been swallowing back for weeks prickled at the back of her throat and tasted of bile. She enjoyed Bailey's company, but she still missed Georgie more than anything, so much that sometimes, it physically hurt.

Bailey held her hands up in surrender. "Alright, I hear you, Weaver. We've all got broken hearts down the line. Love isn't as easy as they say it is in the books."

"It's not—you know what, forget it." She sighed heavily. "Thank you for the help. I'll be glad when they get some wagons down here."

"Sure," Bailey said with a nod, before continuing, "No one would blame you for feeling lonely, you know."

Henry sighed and wiped her sweaty palms against her skirts. "Seems this job is lonelier than I had anticipated."

"What about your friend? Roger?"

"Back on bed rest until they're sure he's okay. Hyun was worried about him, healing can take so much longer in space, especially with all the blackouts we've been having to get past blockades." She kicked a small pebble and watched as it bounced up the copper colored brick path. "I imagine he'll stay here now, anyway. Injury or not, he's needed in the research tent, his knowledge and experience is second to none."

"Second to you, maybe, from what I've heard."

Henry blushed again. "We each have our strong suits. I prefer to observe weather at the source."

"I knew you were a badass," Bailey laughed, raising an eyebrow in

257

appreciation. "A legitimate storm chaser. No wonder you wanted a steamcar, I've heard your types go tearing off in search of storms, driving into tornadoes and hurricanes like you've been possessed."

"Something like that, I guess." She pointed at the ship, safe in its dock, the loading bay door raised up to the ceiling. "Easier to go through there than the side door. Might as well, if it's still open."

"So why storms?"

Henry shrugged, passing through the open airlock. "They're interesting. Dangerous."

"So you like dangerous things, then?"

"I guess you could say that."

"How long do you think you'll stay with the Cricket?"

"Until we figure these storms out, until people stop dying because their terraformers get destroyed."

"It's a hell of a life mission. Most people would have run back to their home comforts the second things got hard. You're a real woman of integrity, Weaver."

"I sure as hell hope it doesn't take me the rest of my life to figure this thing out."

Bailey held the door to the kitchen open for her. "Ah, you know what I mean. It's admirable. Rare for someone to sacrifice themselves and their wants and their needs for those of others. It's not something you see much, especially from Coalition lackeys."

"And how would you know, Ms. Hjarta? I thought that was the only place you'd ever been, born and raised, you said."

"I've been around. I've seen some things."

Henry snorted. "Oh yeah? Like what things?"

"New tech, when the settlement needed it most. People climbing over each other for a scrap of power or food. Jealousy. Pride." She turned to face Henry, her eyes searching for something. "But I've seen beauty, too. Selflessness in places you wouldn't expect, generosity in dire circumstances." She smirked. "And pretty women."

"The boxes are under that table, and also those stacked in the corner,"

CHAPTER TWENTY-EIGHT

Henry said, ignoring her.

"That's loads!"

"You said you wanted to help!"

"I didn't realize I'd be here all night," Bailey grumbled.

Henry hefted a box and balanced it on her hip. "So much for all that selflessness and generosity, then?"

"I never said it came from *me*."

"Let's go, the quicker we get these boxes back to the tent, the sooner I can get to the tavern for the meeting, and the sooner you can go find yourself a new conquest."

"Is that who you think I am?" Bailey asked, carrying more boxes than Henry could ever take in one trip. "You think I run around seducing women, taking them to bed and then forgetting them?"

"I, uh—no?"

"I'll have you know, Weaver, my tastes are a little more refined than that. I'm picky. If I like a woman, it's because she's cream of the crop, the best of the best."

Henry looked at the floor, willing the burn in her cheeks to subside. "Alright, I'm sorry, I—"

"Just leave the boxes, I'll take them."

"But there are so many!"

Bailey turned away and sniffled. "I said leave them, Weaver."

"Okay, well... thanks." Henry backed out of the room, berating herself for pushing away one of the few people she could still talk to. Georgie's absence weighed heavily on her mind.

* * *

"So you finally decided to show up, Weaver?" Kady snarked, her legs draped over the side of one of the plush armchairs that dotted the main room of the Purple Pig tavern. "Took you long enough."

"I was taking the unfinished boxes of code to the research facility, thank you very much."

"It's amazing how far they've come in such a short while," Alice said, after swallowing several mouthfuls of ale. "To think, there was nothing there but some gravel just a few months ago, and now it's a real hub of innovation, a place for refugees to get back to what they do best."

Evie slid platters heaped with food across the long oval table. "Mm, and that's saying nothing of that community garden some people have built up. All this is freshly picked this morning."

"What, you're not going to give me any credit for my efforts?" Larkin protested, sliding her arms around Evie's waist.

"Sorry, dear, you're right, you chopped at least one and a half carrots."

Captain Violet snorted. "I don't envy you, Larkin. Always in Evie's shadow in the kitchen."

"Who cares, let's eat," Ned laughed, piling his plate high with crisp leaves of lettuce, fresh goat's cheese, and a handful of pomegranate seeds over the top.

"You have to try the fried tofu," Evie said, passing Ned the plate. "I used that tip you gave me and it's much crispier this time."

"Don't worry, there's plenty of room in here for a little bit of everything," Ned said, slapping his belly.

Henry slid into one of the seats and grabbed a piece of steaming bread from the center of the table, slathering it in recently churned butter, which melted in slow drips down the side with every pass of the knife. "So what's the plan?" she asked.

"Still waiting on Captain Tansy," Alice grumbled. "Though it's not like her to be late."

"The blockades are wreaking some serious havoc on transit routes even for vessels that have the correct paperwork," Larkin said, passing the captain a tall, frosty mug of ale. "Hell, you lot were supposed to be back two days ago. All that running in blackout takes time, and you can bet she's being as careful as possible to get those folks here safe."

"We barely have any idea what's been going on, other than a few broadcasts here and there," the captain sighed, taking two helpings of

CHAPTER TWENTY-EIGHT

the tofu before passing it along the table. "For all we know, we've missed absolute tons of information. Godsdamned blockades and their new radar, our existing cloaking tech was basically useless."

"It wasn't *basically useless*," Kady pouted, "it just wasn't made to deflect this new tech. Without it, no amount of blackouts would have kept us invisible."

"Check this out," Evie said proudly, setting a small sphere on the table next to the bowl of salad. "Newly developed at the research facility."

"What the hell is it?"

"It's an advanced cloaking mechanism, it wraps into your radar console. Bounces signals back, makes it as though you were never there." She grinned and flopped back into her chair, pulling Larkin into her lap.

"Did you make this?" Alice asked, examining it.

Evie shook her head. "No. It was my idea, but an engineer down in the tent made it."

"It's ingenious, uses materials we wouldn't normally have access to." She passed it to Kady with a nod of appreciation.

"Yeah, so be careful with it," Evie said with a laugh. "I doubt we'd be able to get another one of these made, but I thought it might be useful for skirting around those military outposts that keep giving you trouble between settlements."

"The gods be damned, Anderson, this is fucking brilliant," Captain Violet said, before stuffing a forkful of tofu into her mouth. "This thing is going to save lives. How can we get more? You know Tansy is going to want—"

"Tansy's gonna want what?" the figure in the doorway said in a smooth, honeyed voice.

"Finally decided to show up, eh?"

"Look who's talking, it's not as though you arrived on time either, Vi," Captain Tansy said.

"At least I arrived in time for the food."

"Move your ass, I'm hungry."

"You can sit here, Tansy," Alice said through gritted teeth.

"You don't have to give up your seat for me, I was just teasing this old goat."

"I insist."

Captain Tansy rolled her eyes and sat, lazily, in Alice's chair, putting her boots up on the table, her cybernetic leg sparkling in the mid-afternoon light. "You don't need to be like that, Alice, I know she's your wife."

"Ahem," Ned said, eyeing Captain Tansy's boots. "Did you want something to eat?"

She caught his glance and arched a perfectly shaped eyebrow. "You forget, Ned, I'm still the owner of this place."

"Partial owner," Evie chimed in with a grin, setting another plate of food on the table.

"Alright, alright," she laughed, taking her boots off the table and loading up a plate with food. "One thing is for damn sure, the eating is a hell of a lot better here since I left this place to those two. How come you never volunteered to be the main cook when I was the boss, huh Evie?"

"I got better when José taught me a few tricks. It's just too bad Larkin is basically hopeless in the kitchen." She grinned. "I think I'll keep her around, though."

"Yeah, well, those dishes will have hell to pay in that sink of soapy water when we're done here," Larkin laughed. "And I've been working on something new that's keeping me busy. Bar tending, with a twist. It's no high-profile job, but it's the perfect one for me."

"How are you doing, anyway?" Ned probed, his voice gentle. "We worry about you, Larks."

Larkin waved him away. "Stop. I'm fine. Well, not fine, fine, but I manage. Besides, I feel like I can contribute more here in Bradach than I ever was out there, hunting down marks for a hot meal and a tankard of ale." She rubbed her arm and looked away, her jaw set firm.

"So, those plans?" Henry interrupted, her mouth half full of food. It was clear Larkin didn't like talking about what she used to do, and Henry couldn't help but shoot a glare at Ned for bringing it up. True to form, though, he didn't notice.

"Right," Captain Tansy said, taking a bite of bread, "what was it you said

CHAPTER TWENTY-EIGHT

I was going to want?"

"And here we thought we could distract you with food," Captain Violet said with a smirk. "It's a bit of tech that the research team here cooked up, something that will make it possible for us to stealth with comms."

"Well you're damned right I want it. Do you have any idea what a nightmare those blockades have been with all these refugees? Gods alive, the storms are hitting everyone faster than we can evacuate, trying to establish lines with the rest of the fleet has been a thorn in my side for weeks."

"We only have the one right now," Evie said apologetically. "But we can make more, if you can get us the materials."

"Whatever you need, I'll make it happen. Having functional communication is going to be the backbone of this whole mess, and the only way we're going to make it out alive and thriving."

Kady turned over the sphere in her hand. "Rhodium."

"Fuck," Alice said under her breath. "Are you sure nothing else would work? Platinum, Palladium?"

"It needs to be rhodium, at least, that's what the researchers said down at the tent," Evie said, taking the sphere and setting it back in a fabric lined box on the bar. "Something about reflective properties, and emissions, and..."

"And resistance to natural elements," Kady finished. "Of course rhodium, why didn't I think of that?"

"It's not like we have the stuff hanging around, why would you?"

"Alright, so this rhodium stuff. Where do we get it?" Captain Tansy asked, laying a single leaf of lettuce on her plate.

"Well, unless you can get some from a trader on Gamma-3—"

"I'll tell you right now, that's not going to happen. Restrictions on movements are too precise there, too much surveillance for us to be moving around unseen. The black market coming from there is all but erased with the new legislation that's come down from the Coalition."

"Then the other option is to mine it yourself from an asteroid, maybe."

Captain Tansy choked on her mouthful of food. "Have you lost your mind?"

Kady shrugged. "It's rare stuff. If it was easy to get hold of, then we wouldn't have a problem of sourcing it."

"Yes, thank you, I'm aware of what *rare* means, but you're casually suggesting we set up a strip mining operation on some unknown asteroid without a base, in the hopes we find one of the rarest metals in the Near Systems."

"What if we knew someone who could get their hands on some?" Ned mumbled. "For a price."

"And who the hell would have those kinds of connections?" Captain Tansy asked. "Every black market trader I know is long out of business, at least when it comes to something other than booze or scrap."

Alice sighed heavily and braced herself against the back of Ned's chair. "Barnaby."

"No way," Captain Violet said, pushing away her empty plate. "I said before, we can't trust him. He was selling our own stock out from under us, don't you remember that? What kind of hold does that man have over you two?" She stood and pointed at Ned, her face cloudy with anger. "I know the hold he has on you, and that's no surprise, but why my wife continues to trust him, I'll never know."

"You have to admit, Vi, he's the only one we know that might be able to get hold of this stuff. These stealth capacitors, they could change the tide for us." Alice brushed a stray silver hair from her face, her fingers grazing the black patch that sat over one eye. "And he did fulfill his end of the bargain with passing us information."

Violet squeezed her eyes shut and rubbed at her temples. "Gods be damned."

"I'll drop a line," Ned said, a little too eagerly. "I'm sure he'll be in touch soon—"

"No. Not you. You're weak around that man," she said, laying a hand on his shoulder. "I don't want you to get hurt again."

Ned looked down at his plate, and Henry nearly missed the look that Captain Violet and Alice exchanged over his head. Whatever had happened with this Barnaby, it can't have been good.

"Kady," Captain Violet said, snatching the last piece of fried tofu from

CHAPTER TWENTY-EIGHT

the platter, "get in touch with Barnaby. Tell him it's urgent. Tell him we'll match whatever price he could get elsewhere."

* * *

Henry sat in the tavern long after the rest of the crew had gone back to the ship, their bellies stuffed full of food, ready for a good night's sleep before tomorrow's job of unloading supplies and scrap. Captain Tansy had disappeared upstairs with Evie and Larkin, no doubt to settle the month's accounts. The door was locked, and she sat alone at the bar with her lukewarm cup of tea, stirring it absentmindedly as she tried to distract herself from thoughts of Georgie or Bailey. When had life become such a mess?

She didn't mourn the loss of her family, never having been close with them even from childhood. She was always the black sheep, so to speak, shunning the family profession of politics and campaign management to chase storms across the sky.

She tipped a swig of whiskey into her tea and stirred, the tiny tornado swirling in the porcelain cup. This whole fucking thing was a godsdamn mess. The storms she couldn't figure out or stop, the continued radio silence from Georgie, it was all just too much. The tea slid easily down her throat, despite the whiskey and the tepid temperature, and she filled the teacup again, watching the amber liquid slosh in the crisp white cup.

Why had Georgie been quiet, anyway? Surely they had reestablished comms by now in Skelm, and yet there had been no response to her message, not even a vague acknowledgment, and certainly no reciprocation. Yes, the Cricket had been in and out of contact for weeks, but she could have left word with someone here in Bradach if she wanted to. Maybe she'd decided that Henry wasn't right for her, after all. Perhaps they were just too different, or Georgie had met someone back in Skelm, an attractive rebel who ran the underground distillation vats, or a military police officer who abandoned her post to join The Scattered, or…

Her thoughts trailed off with the dregs of the whiskey. Enough. Nothing good would come of this spiral staircase in her mind, going round and round but never getting anywhere. Georgie hadn't responded, and that was that. Henry slid off her stool, rinsed her teacup, smoothed her skirts, and headed back to the Cricket for a hot bath and another crack at the data from the balloons back on Hjarta. It wasn't going to solve itself, that was for damn sure.

The street lamps were lit, casting an eerie yellow glow over the uneven cobblestones in the streets. Steamcars weren't allowed here for a reason - they'd never be able to handle the roads in Bradach. It was nice, being able to wander through the city without looking both ways before crossing an intersection, though she was beginning to take it for granted. If she ever did end up back on Gamma-3 or in Skelm, she'd end up flattened.

The Cricket was quiet, with only the odd chuckle from the kitchen drifting down the long corridors that wound through the ship. Henry found herself lingering in the hall, not wanting to be alone, but unwilling to make company with the rest of the crew, either.

"Hey," Bailey said, rounding the corner, a note of surprise in her voice.

"Hey yourself."

"I guess I shouldn't be surprised to see you on the ship we both inhabit, and yet…"

"Bailey, I—"

"It's alright. You didn't mean to hurt me, I know."

Henry shifted her weight from foot to foot, her hand resting on the knob to her room. "Do you want to talk?"

"We don't have to talk about that, I—"

"No, I just mean… about anything. It's just an odd night."

"Sure."

"Sorry for the mess," Henry declared, opening the door, even though she'd made a concerted effort to keep her quarters neat and tidy after the last unexpected visit. This time, her bed was neatly made, everything put away in its place, despite the distinct lack of space. She'd never realized

CHAPTER TWENTY-EIGHT

before how most people lived.

Bailey made a show of looking around, squinting at all the corners. "Mess? I don't see a mess here, Weaver. You don't have to show off for me, you know."

"I'm not showing off!"

"If you say so." Bailey lingered at the door, cracking her knuckles nervously. "We can go to the kitchen if you want, or—"

"I don't want to be anywhere near that code right now. I feel exhausted by the damn thing."

"What about that code on your desk?"

Henry shuffled some papers and closed them in a drawer. "Binary. It's different. I know that one. Just can't figure out the pattern I must be missing." She sighed and sat on the bed. "I feel like a fool for not being able to do my job here, you know."

"You're no fool, Henrietta. You're one of the smartest people I know."

"Just feels like too many people are depending on me to do something I'm not sure I'm able to accomplish, not under these circumstances."

Bailey joined her, perching at the edge of the bed, her boots firmly planted against the thin carpet that covered the metal grate floor. "You'll get it, I have faith in you. I bet you wake up tomorrow, fresh as a daisy, with all the information nearly sorted in that head of yours."

"If only it was that easy."

"Maybe it will be."

"Or maybe I'll let everyone down again." Henry smoothed her skirts and sighed again. "I'm sorry, I don't mean for this to become some kind of pity party. I'm just feeling discouraged, is all."

"Tell me about when you knew you wanted to be a storm chaser."

"Oh, I don't know, I was young. A child, really. I've always been fascinated with them, watching them gather on the horizon where I grew up on Gamma-3 near the Capital, observing the cloud formations as they changed, trying to predict what would happen next."

"They didn't scare you?"

Henry shook her head. "No. They can be devastating, of course, but it feels like such a force of nature that being in it almost feels powerful, caught up in something so much bigger than yourself and being able to know what will happen next. Not like now, not these storms. They're unpredictable, they don't behave in a way that makes any sense. It's like running after something you'll never catch up to."

"You're not like anyone I've ever met, you know."

The admission caught Henry off guard and jarred her from her meteorological thoughts. "What do you mean?"

"You gave up everything you've ever known to chase storms all across the Near Systems, you don't even think twice about putting yourself in harm's way to learn more about them, you sacrifice your own oxygen for some random settler... you just amaze me."

"It's nothing anyone else wouldn't do."

"You're wrong."

"I don't know about that."

Bailey bit her lip and leaned closer. "I do."

Henry froze, not sure if it was the whiskey or something else keeping her from saying anything. And when Bailey kissed her, she let it happen.

CHAPTER TWENTY-NINE

"Have you figured out how to bypass the monitors yet?" Georgie asked, rubbing the sleep from her eyes.

Emeline sighed. "No. From what we can tell, anything we send would be intercepted by whoever is listening in on all frequencies. Cole was hoping we would be able to get underground broadcasts, but they're being blocked, overcast with static."

"Why did we even bother with that stupid chip? It's not done us one bit of good, bastard thing. We don't even know if Captain Tansy passed on our message."

"At least it's there, Georgie. We can try to create workarounds."

"It's been weeks."

"I know, but we have to be careful."

Georgie tugged on her boots, the basement floor being far too cold and damp to walk around in her socks, and no extra money for slippers since the new Coalition budget had cut everyone's salaries by a third. "I'm tired of being careful. I'm just tired, Em."

"We'll get it soon, I know we will. Judy said that Jess and Bale are working on an idea that will allow us to covertly hijack the signals for short periods at a time, by remotely activating the chip you planted and creating a loop for the monitors to avoid suspicion."

"Maybe they could hurry the hell up, then. I'm sick of this place. If I have to keep going into that building every day and dealing with our not-so-benevolent dictator, I might lose it."

"They're working as fast as they can."

"This revolution is going to die if we can't get started soon, and you know it. What about the strike? How will we keep people motivated down at the factories if we keep telling them to wait another week, another month?"

"The strike is going ahead today, we decided while you were sleeping. It's a start, at least.

"When were you going to tell me about it? Or should I just be sure to leave a message with your secretary?"

"What's going on with you, Georgie? I swear, lately you seem poised to snap at anyone who says a damn thing to you, and we're all tired of it."

"Oh, you're all tired of it, are you?" Georgie growled, buttoning up a clean set of orange coveralls, the only thing she seemed to wear lately. "Maybe one of you can take my place up at the Administration building then, and work at being Allemande's little spy! Do you have any idea what I'm risking, staying there so that you can get your inside intel?"

Emeline shrank back, wounded. "Of course I know, I worry about you every time you leave, and worry all day until you come home!"

"Home," Georgie scoffed. "It's a basement death trap just waiting to give us pneumonia. If we'd just left with the others on the Cricket—"

"Then we'd be leaving thousands here to suffer at the hands of the Coalition, with only a handful of people willing to fight against these conditions."

"Maybe I'm tired of fighting."

"We're all tired of fighting, Georgie." Emeline turned back to the radio and continued to turn the dials slowly, scanning for any hint of a transmission. "But we're at a tipping point, I can feel it. The salary reductions hit everyone hard, and people are angry. They're ready to demand change."

"How many have you got for the strike today?"

"At least half from each factory, maybe more. Hard to tell without keeping a roster, but we can't risk that. Not now, anyway."

"We'd better get going, then. It's going to be a mess out there once the military police hear about this." She stood and stretched, lamenting the

CHAPTER TWENTY-NINE

tired weight that still lingered in her muscles. "I'm honestly surprised no one ratted us out yet."

"Mm," Emeline agreed, making a note on the crumpled piece of paper on the desk. "I think even those who aren't convinced enough to participate in the strike don't want to put their fellow workers in danger. There's a real community spirit down there, you'd love to see it."

"Would be a nice change from the Administration building, anyway. Feels like everyone up there is just waiting to put a knife in your back."

"I know it's been hard on you. I'm sorry we've had to ask this of you."

Georgie sighed. "I don't mean to snap at you, Em. I'm just... I've never been this tired. It feels hopeless. I fall into a dead sleep as soon as I get home, and I wake up feeling like I've not had a single wink."

"Did you hear back about the gala?"

"Yeah. I'm in."

"That's great! A real opportunity to get some deep intel, and it will keep you safe and out of suspicion during the strike."

"Ugh, gods, the gala is tonight, isn't it?" Georgie wanted to climb back under her thin covers and wait for the military police to come drag her from bed to throw her in a cell. At least then she'd get some rest. "Double shift for me it is, then."

"Coffee?" Emeline offered, sliding a steaming mug she just poured across the table.

"Coffee."

* * *

The Administration building was decked out for the gala, with strings of sparkling lights draped between each pillar that glistened in the reflection of the courtyard fountain. Georgie puffed out her cheeks, already exhausted from a full day's work, about to start another. In reality, the cleanup wouldn't even begin until all the dignitaries had dispersed, and it would be nearly dawn before she'd be able to stumble into bed for a few hours. Her muscles ached, her mind foggy.

Guests arrived in pairs or trios from a stream of steamcars that drove them up from the hotel where they were staying. No doubt some of the latecomers had seen the start of the strike gathering, and whispers questioning the governor's power drifted through the air. They were dressed in their finery, dripping in silk and lace, accented with jewels larger than any Georgie had ever seen. These people were the decision makers in the Coalition, and it was a wonder Allemande had convinced them to come to Skelm at all.

Georgie hovered in the shadows, trying to ignore the fierce rumbling in her stomach that came with every wafted scent of the extravagant food being served. They'd only had expired tinned food for weeks, with barely any fresh food coming through the docks at all. The increased shipment searches meant that produce rotted in loading bays, and so traders had begun to avoid delivering to Skelm. At least, that's what their sources down on the docks said.

"Friends of the Coalition, I am thrilled to welcome you to Skelm, jewel of the sector," Allemande announced.

Georgie stifled a snort, turning it into a cough instead, muffled by the sleeve of her jumpsuit.

"Here, in this city, we manufacture much of the Near Systems' raw materials into products we need to grow our cosmic empire, and increase our prosperity beyond all projections. Our factories produce weapons for the brave officers of our military police units, mechanical parts for ships, steamcars, and more, chemical refineries that keep our colonies ticking, working toward a brighter, richer future."

There was a polite smattering of applause from people who had been to hundreds of these galas, people who would rather be left alone to enjoy their food and make deals under the table with other merchants and managers of the Near Systems, rather than listen to another self-congratulatory speech from one more backwater governor. The boredom was palpable, the sound of forks scraping against porcelain the proof.

"Some of you may have witnessed a disturbance in our workforce on your way here this evening," the governor continued, "and I for one would like to address those concerns."

CHAPTER TWENTY-NINE

Chatter ceased, ears pricked up at the mention of a potential failure. Public shame of others was practically currency to those who had enough credits to last them twenty lifetimes, the possibilities to gossip and whisper a tantalizing temptation.

"It's true that a number of our factory workers have made the grievous error to lay down their tools and organize collective action to try to force our hands into giving them what doesn't belong to them. They ask for handouts and special privileges, instead of focusing on improving their lot in life through honest hard work."

A knot began to form in Georgie's stomach, a churning anxiety that something was very, very wrong. From the corner of her eye, the twinkle of landing gear from at least a dozen transport ships descending at the docks. Adrenaline pumped into her veins, and she wanted to run, to find her sister and hide.

"At this very moment, fresh, able-bodied workers are disembarking at the docks, ready to start their new lives in Skelm, ready to work and fight for our glorious empire. One thing is for certain, and that is the fact that there is no shortage of willing people, ready to innovate, to improve, to increase efficiency. We do not need to tolerate the childish demands of this so-called union, like toddlers crying for another sweet before supper."

A smattering of applause, and nods of approval. *Fuck*, Georgie thought.

"Those who decided that refusal to work was more important than the collective efforts of the city have been immediately terminated from employment and barred from holding any other position within the Coalition. They are exemplary of a rot within humanity, one that wants something for nothing, that thinks themselves deserving of everything we have all worked our whole lives for, delivered to them free of charge and allowing them to laze their lives away, a burden on society."

There was nowhere for those people to go. With no money to get off-world, and no ability to work, they'd become destitute and homeless, desperate people trying to provide for themselves and for their families. It was a disaster.

"Furthermore, they are being rounded up by military police on site, and escorted onto ships to be relocated to work camps, where they will undergo reeducation and learn the importance of hard work within the Coalition. When they have served their sentences, they will be released into a newly created job matching service, where their skills will determine where they may go to work for their shelter and food. What people really crave, at the core of their being, is rules..."

Georgie couldn't hear the rest through the blood pounding in her ears. They were going to take everyone. All the workers, their families. Cole and Judy. Emeline. Without thinking, she began to run, her worn boots squeaking with every step on the shining, spotless marble. The door to the back courtyard was locked, but she jammed her key in and ripped off the padlock, throwing it to the ground. There were no gardeners, not at this time of day, and this area was off-limits to the gala guests, being less presentable and manicured than the front of the building.

Her foot caught on a hidden root in the darkness, and she yanked it free with a painful pop of her ankle. It didn't matter. She kept running, heading for the hidden alley that would get her down to the docks to save her sister. The mossy fountain sprayed water into the air, the sound of the droplets inaudible against the soundscape of raucous cheers from the gala, signaling the end of Allemande's speech.

She felt her way behind the fountain, grasping for the vines that covered the opening to the alley. Her fingertips ran across fresh brick and mortar, and she sucked in a breath. The alley had been closed. Georgie stumbled backwards, fumbling for something to grab hold of, the rough cement finish of the fountain tearing at her palms.

"You thought you were so clever, didn't you?"

Georgie whipped around and came face to face with Erin, who, even in the dim lighting, looked like she hadn't slept in weeks, her cheeks gaunt, and her skin sallow. "Erin—"

"You're a fool, Payne. Did you really think those gardeners wouldn't tell us about the secret alleyway, or the helpful janitor that helped them escape the Administration building during that terrorist threat?"

She swore under her breath. Fucking gardeners. "It's not against the law

CHAPTER TWENTY-NINE

to help people get away from an incendiary device."

"No, but it's treason to plant one." Erin reached out for Georgie's wrist, but she yanked it back.

"I didn't do that."

"You know who did. I've been watching you, Georgie, the governor's new pet project. I know she asked you to spy on me, to report back to her any misgivings you had about my leadership."

"I never told her anything."

Erin laughed, but it was empty. "Please. I know your kind. You'd sell me out for table scraps."

"I wouldn't." Georgie was shifting her weight from foot to foot, wondering if she could shove past her and still get to the docks in time to get to Emeline. "Besides, you've not done anything worth reporting."

"You told her I baked those officers muffins before they ended up drugged."

"I didn't."

"Here I am, working hard to prove myself, all the while being undermined by Scattered scum like you." She spat on the grass, her saliva sparkling in the distant light. "I know what you've been hiding. Your mother and sisters, missing? Clearly smuggled out, and months ago, too. Your employment record says you moved back into the tenements, but no one there has seen hide nor hair of you, not after curfew."

"Erin, there are thousands of people who live in those buildings, I couldn't even begin to tell you the names of the people who sleep in the bunks next to mine, much less whether they were in before building curfew or not." Her eyes flicked to the door she'd left open, the only way out of the back courtyard.

"Don't even think about it," Erin hissed, catching her glance. "I've followed you for weeks, spent the past week hiding out, waiting for you to slip up. I knew you'd come back here if you thought your scummy friends were in danger, your little comrades at the Twisted Lantern. And here you are, just as I knew you would be." She closed her eyes and swayed on the spot, as though she could hear her own music playing inside her mind.

Georgie bolted for the door, her ankle screaming in pain. She could feel the swelling already, the tissue around the bone pushing out against her boot. Time was running out, and she had to get to her sister. Had to save her, keep her safe.

"Oh no you don't," Erin screeched, and dove for Georgie's knees, taking them both down to the freshly cut grass, the only place in Skelm with a lawn. "I'm going to drag you in front of the governor and you're going to tell her what you did."

"Get off me!"

Erin held her knees in a vise grip. "Do you have any idea what I've sacrificed? What I've given up in order to ascend the ranks and leave my old life behind?"

"I don't care!"

"Where are you going to go, Payne? You can't hide. You can't get off-world. Better for you to own up to your crimes and serve your punishment with gratefulness you won't be used as an example!"

"What, so you can show Allemande what a good little pawn you've been? Fucking goon, you're no more than a lackey!" Georgie shouted, hauling back and punching Erin right in the face. Blood spurted from her nose and she fell backwards onto the grass, clutching her hands to her mouth.

She didn't wait to see what happened. She stumbled to her feet and ran for the door, her gait a limping lilt that sure as hell wasn't going to get her to the docks in time. No, she needed something faster. Like a steamcar. She skirted around the gala hall, keeping to the shadows and taking the back hallways to get to the front gate. With a mighty yank she pulled a driver from a car, despite his shouts to the contrary, she leapt into the steamcar and floored the gas.

It had been a long time since she had driven one, but like riding a bike, the knowledge and the muscle memory was always there, even though it had been over half her life since her pop let her drive around in their neighbor's truck. She'd taken to it like a duck to water, and she was grateful, now that she was in a car screaming towards the docks, careening down the main roads with the horn blaring, a warning to stay the hell out of her way.

CHAPTER TWENTY-NINE

They'd be after her now, of course, but she'd worry about that later. She couldn't let Emeline be taken. Her sister was all that she had left, her only source of hope and light. The steamcar skidded to a halt at the docks, rammed with lost, confused looking people, some who looked like they were on death's door. There were no familiar faces, no striking workers. There should be a sea of picket signs, the air thick with chants and singing, but the only sound was the distant whine of transport ships, ascending into the atmosphere.

"Have you seen my sister?" she shouted at a man in a pair of torn coveralls. "Her name is Emeline. She organized the strike."

He shook his head. "Ma'am, we all just got here. Flown in from Fort Gelad. Others from other places. We don't know anything or anyone."

She pushed her way through the crowd, screaming her sister's name, knowing any moment a guard would snatch her up and drag her back to an interrogation cell. "Have you seen my sister?" she asked a woman who was holding a baby on her hip. "Do you know if they've taken her?"

The woman shook her head as well and turned her back.

Georgie shoved past a small group of men shouting about new opportunities and new beginnings, cursing them as she went. Fools, all of them. There was nothing new about Skelm. She ran through back streets, sprinting from one shadowy corner to the next, trying to ignore the searing pain in her ankle. When she reached the back door of the Twisted Lantern, she jerked the door open and screamed Emeline's name.

"Are you fucking crazy? Shut up!" Cole hissed, yanking her inside. "You shouldn't even be here right now."

"Where's my sister?" Georgie demanded, hot tears now spilling down her cheeks. "Where is she, Cole?"

He sighed and bolted the door. "They took her."

"No. No, that can't be right," she sobbed. "Cole, tell me it's not true, tell me it's some kind of sick joke!"

"I'm sorry Georgie, I couldn't get to her, I—"

"Liar! You didn't like that she was the one people related to more, wanted to lead, you wanted the glory for yourself! You let them take her!"

"Fuck you Payne, I'd never have let anything happen to any of you if I could help it! What the hell was I supposed to do when there were twenty military police between me and her?"

"You and Judy could have at least tried!" Georgie choked out. "Where's Judy?"

He shook his head. "They took her, too. They took everyone, even Jess and Bale. It's just us."

"No."

"You can't be here, Georgie. They're going to come looking for both of us."

"Where am I supposed to go?"

"I don't know, but you can't stay here." He shoved a canvas sack at her. "Supplies. Change of clothes, first aid if you need it."

"Where will you go?"

"I know a guy with an apartment in the Dockside District. I'll lie low there until the heat cools off. Meet me in the factory lane, behind the chemical refinery plant, in two days, at noon. We'll regroup."

Georgie took the sack and stumbled back out the door, her mind reeling with the news that Emeline had been arrested, taken to an off-world work camp, unreachable. She might never see her again, never find where they took her. The knowledge hung in her gut and the bile ate at the back of her throat until she threw up what little she'd had to eat outside someone's door. There were empty buildings at the edge of the city, meant for an expansion that had yet to happen. Most investors pulled their funds before the apartments were finished, leaving behind a strange cavernous labyrinth of half built walls.

She pushed the rusted door open tentatively and was relieved when no one jumped out to drag her to the ground and slap iron cuffs around her wrists. A moldy bed was upturned in the corner, the mattress half-rotted from damp. Georgie pulled it to the floor and sat down, the rusted springs inside creaking as they popped and poked at her from beneath the mildewed floral pattern.

Her boot wouldn't come off, the ankle was too swollen for the thin leather

CHAPTER TWENTY-NINE

to budge. She took a small pair of scissors from the sparse first aid kit Cole had given her and cut the boot off, letting it fall to the floor with a soft thud. She wrapped her ankle, curled into the fetal position on the bed, and shivered until she fell into a dreamless sleep.

CHAPTER THIRTY

Henry had spent the better part of a day and a half purposefully avoiding Bailey. She couldn't internally debate the morality of that situation, while also trying to solve the storm problem, analyzing and re-analyzing data long into the night. She was sitting on a park bench, watching sunbeams slice through the shadows, setting specs of dust alight with sparkle, and finishing her lunch of day old bread and fresh jam she bought at the small street market that morning.

She knew that she had to go back to her quarters, dive back into the data, try to find what made the storms tick, but for now, she wanted to savor the fresh air. The ship would be leaving that night, loaded up with medical supplies for settlements and encampments in dire need, with only an idea of where the storms might hit next. Trying to predict more than that was like pulling a number from a hat. The accuracy was similar.

Crumbs from the bread gathered on her skirts, and she brushed them onto the ground, for a moment forgetting that there were no birds in Bradach. Sometimes it was so civilized, so much like home, that she had woken up confused in Evie and Larkin's guest room, thinking it was Gamma-3 for just a moment. It was good of them to put her up, after she ran off the Cricket when Bailey kissed her. Something inside her had stirred, so she ran. She didn't trust herself to stay. She couldn't trust herself to be around Bailey either, not yet.

The shops that lined the side streets in Bradach were quaint, some selling

CHAPTER THIRTY

handmade soaps, which she happily indulged in, despite her dwindling credit account, some selling potent incense you could smell from four doors down, some reselling gently used boots and other clothing. Henry ran her hands over her dress and frowned at the snags in the fabric, the result of hard work both at her desk and around the ship. What she really wanted was something simple, but new, some sartorial therapy for her troubled mind.

She pushed open the door to the tailor's shop, with a polished sign hanging above reading "Mae's," and stepped inside, greeted by a pleasantly shaded room filled with all manner of clothes, from stunning finery to everyday wear, all meticulously stitched and hanging from metal hooks on the walls.

"Hello, may I help you?" a very elegant woman asked, her long, jet black hair pulled back into a shiny bun at the top of her head, the kind that dancers in theaters back on Gamma-3 would wear.

"I was looking for something new, something casual, but nice." She looked around the shop and smiled, her fingers brushing the smooth taffeta of an evening gown. "Though everything here is nice."

"I pride myself on my craftswomanship," she smiled.

"Are you Mae?"

"I am."

"Henry."

"I think you were a year or two behind me in finishing school. Interesting to see someone from there end up here."

"Oh! I'm sorry, I didn't recognize—"

"Don't worry, I spent most of my time in the sewing hall. I remember you, though. Always with a big stack of books." Mae stepped out from behind the counter, her silk skirts rustling with every step. "May I?" she asked, gesturing at Henry's dress.

"Of course."

"Mm, lovely stitching. Where was this one made? Not here, I'd imagine. The only other tailor in town is... well, let's just say his attention to detail is lacking."

"Gamma-3, in the Capital."

"Yes, that would explain it. Some wonderful places there, it's where I learned my craft."

"Oh? Why did you leave?"

Mae blinked at her and then pulled a clipboard from the counter. "What color were you thinking, my dear?"

"Blue, I guess. To replace this one when the snags become irreparable."

"Oh, no. Not this blue. It's lovely, I assure you, but we can do much better to complement your complexion and your natural features." She unhooked a set of small square swatches from the wall and held each up to Henry's face, her brow knitted in concentration. "Hmm, no, you're much more of a winter..." she trailed off.

"How long have you been here? In Bradach, I mean?"

"A long time. Years."

"You come very highly recommended." In fact, Alice couldn't stop singing Mae's praises, and practically escorted Henry to the shop herself. "That's a lot of blues," Henry remarked, nodding at the set of swatches.

Mae studied her. "Of course there are 'a lot of blues.' As many as exist in nature, and you want to limit yourself to the limited palette of contemporary design? No, not in my shop, I won't have it! Now, this particular shade of cerulean would look stunning on you." Her hands pressed gently on Henry's shoulders, she gently steered her to a full-length mirror propped against the wall. "What do you think?"

"It's lovely. You must have a huge store room to keep all these fabrics in."

"They are custom dyed for every order on blank fabric, which I do keep significant stock of. But, no, it would be foolish to keep stock of every shade and every fabric, I would need a warehouse the size Bradach would never fit, and I could never staff!"

Henry grimaced. "Sounds expensive."

"You get what you pay for," Mae said, noting down the shade number on an order sheet. "You're more than welcome to visit the other tailor in the city, I assure you he charges far less."

"It's just - I'm a little low on credit, is all. Captain Violet—"

"Violet? Alice's wife? You fly with the Cricket?"

"Yes, I've been with them several months now, tracking those storms

CHAPTER THIRTY

across the Near Systems."

"Well, you should have said so. I've been around long enough to know that crew members on that ship always come into credit and tradable goods sooner or later." She looked Henry up and down, her mouth in a gentle frown. "Unless you're a gambler. There are card sharks all up and down the main street here what will take you for all you're worth."

"No, no, nothing like that. We've just been focusing on getting supplies to the other settlements."

"Ah. More rebellion than piracy, it seems."

"I guess."

"Let's just say I have a good feeling about you, Henry. I won't take the customary deposit, but just be aware that I'll know where to come find you if you never show up for this dress," Mae said, shaking a pencil at her. "Now, what is your weaponry, and where do you prefer to carry? Under the arms, or at the waist? I can accommodate thighs or calves, but the modified pockets are an extra expense, you understand."

"Short barrel revolver."

"And the location?"

Henry squeezed her eyes shut, trying to envision where it might feel natural to pull a gun from. She imagined the feel of the cold metal against her ribs, her waist, her thighs... and when Georgie's face emerged on stage in her mind, a pang of guilt and pain flashed like lightning across her heart. "Thigh. The extra charge is fine." At least something would be caressing her skin, even if it was the deadly alloy of a firearm.

Mae raised an eyebrow. "Yes, of course."

The bells on the shop door gave a delicate jingle as it opened and shut.

"Henry! I was looking all over for you last night after my meeting with Larkin and Evie," Captain Tansy said, her trademark swagger wafting air across the delicate silks that hung on the wall.

"Me? Why?"

"Got a message from someone, thought it best to keep it between us. Not everyone's business, you know." She looked at Mae, who raised her hands in deference and swished into the back room. "From Georgie."

Henry's breath caught in her chest, and it felt like a rock had dropped into her stomach. "Is she okay? Why didn't you say anything earlier?"

"I told you, I thought it was best to keep private matters discreet."

"And?" Henry barked out, trying to swallow back the sob that was gathering at the back of her throat. "What did she say?" A million possibilities raced through her mind in the moment it took Captain Tansy to reply. Maybe Georgie said she was through with her, that she'd found someone else. That was the only logical reason for not just saying it the night before, wasn't it? Or maybe she was in terrible danger, or she decided to stay in Skelm and continue her work as a janitor, now that her family was safe, or—

"She said she loves you, and she misses you."

The sob she'd been trying to suppress escaped, along with the tears that immediately gathered and fell from her eyelashes. "Gods, it's been months, and I hadn't heard anything, and I thought—"

"Hey, it's alright," Captain Tansy said, reaching out and squeezing her arm gently. "I know it's tough to be away from the people we care about."

"It's just—" Henry hiccuped, "if you'd told me last night—oh, gods," she sobbed, the guilt settling heavily in her chest, making it hard to catch her breath.

"You should know, those lines are being monitored. Anything in or out, the Coalition there is always listening in. Whatever you try to get to her, know that someone will be taking note and knowing that someone in Skelm is sending unauthorized transmissions."

"So I can't even send her another message? I can't tell her that her mother and sister are safe, that Lucy is already an apprentice, that we're working on a way to get back to her?"

The captain shrugged. "I'm sorry, Henry."

In a daze, Henry signed her name on the order slip Mae had left on the counter and left the shop, ignoring Tansy's offers to walk her back to the ship or the Purple Pig. No, she just wanted to be alone, to stew in her own misery.

CHAPTER THIRTY

***

Henry sat hunched over the spare radio in the boiler room, scanning every open frequency, hoping she would hear something from Georgie, or from Skelm, anything to quiet the undisciplined roar of her thoughts. One hand on the tuning knobs, and the other clutching a pen as she went through the storm data another time, the notes spread across the table in the corner of the hot, humid room. She wiped sweat from her brow and watched it soak into the fabric of her dress.

"Hey," Bailey said, descending the steps two at a time, "I didn't realize you were back. Maybe we should… talk?"

"Alright."

Bailey sat on the stool opposite, perched awkwardly on the uneven seat, gently wobbling back and forth on the warped flooring. The boilers were quiet, for now, the ship stationary in the Bradach docks and running electricity from the auxiliary solar panels. "Are you upset with me? Did I… do something wrong? If I overstepped, then I'm sorry, I would never—"

Henry sighed and set the pen down on the table. "You didn't do anything wrong. It's just… complicated."

"That seems to be the running theme lately."

"What else can I say, Bailey?"

"I just don't understand what's so complicated about two people who enjoy each other's company sharing a kiss. It seems like the most uncomplicated thing in the world, to me." Bailey reached out and gently caressed Henry's arm, rubbing her thumb where the sleeve of her dress met her wrist. "Did you enjoy it? The kiss?"

"Sure, but—"

"No more buts," Bailey said, and leaned across the table to kiss her again, her soft lips parting and drawing her in.

Henry pulled away from the kiss, shaking her head. "Bailey, no. I can't."

"Don't you see I'm falling in *love* with you?"

"I'm sorry," Henry whispered, "but I think I'm already in love with someone else." She shook her head and stood, looking at her boots so she didn't have to see the tears gathering in Bailey's eyes. "She might be in trouble, and I have to go after her."

"Go after her? Who? This Georgie? Henry, if she's in Skelm, there's no way you can get to her. It's suicide! You'll get yourself thrown into a work camp, or worse, an interrogation cell, and then what? She's a grown woman, I'm sure that she can take care of herself, if all the things her mother and sister have said are true. You'd be risking your life and the lives of all the people in settlements across the Near Systems who need you to figure out these storms!"

"That's just it, don't you get it? I can't figure out the godsdamned storms, none of the data makes any sense. I've been at this for months and we're no closer to preventing them."

"You decoded those files, we were able to get supplies to settlements just after they were hit. They'd have all died otherwise!"

"Not the last time, I didn't! We had no idea storms were going to hit everywhere all at once, and look what happened as a result. People got packed up and shipped off to work camps, because I wasn't able to figure it out."

"That wasn't your fault, they—"

"Of course it's my fault! The only reason I'm here is to determine the pattern of the storms, which I can't, and discern how the Coalition is controlling them, which is impossible. I'm not an engineer, or a mechanic, I'm just a meteorologist with outdated information and half-baked ideas that haven't done one bit of good." Henry shook her head. "No, I need to try something else now. I need to save at least one person, at least her."

"You're being reckless."

"Are you telling me that you wouldn't do everything in your power to save your people? To get them back to Hjarta?"

"That's different, we're talking about dozens of people, not one fucking janitor in a locked down settlement, who, so I'm told, is there with her sister, and probably wouldn't leave without her, anyway."

"She's not any less important just because you don't know her," Henry spat.

CHAPTER THIRTY

"That's not—"

"We have no idea what's really going on in Skelm. The transmissions from rebel outposts say there's been no news from them for months, Captain Tansy says all frequencies are being heavily monitored, and the official broadcasts haven't mentioned the settlement in weeks, the only news is that production is up, exports are up, no news of its people or the storms there that nearly killed me last time."

"Then that should tell you going back is a bad idea."

"What if the storms are about to level the city?"

"I thought you said that Skelm wasn't anywhere on that decoded list?"

"It wasn't, but—"

Bailey sighed angrily, teetering on her stool. "Weaver, you're being a fool. You'd really leave the Cricket, try to get back to Skelm, and for what? To get trapped there, too? To give us one more person we have to worry about getting picked up by the Coalition? Gods, we're spread too thin as it is!"

"At least I'd be with her." Henry choked out a sob and buried her face in her hands, sweat and tears washing over her cheeks.

"This is selfish. It's foolish and to be honest, the worst idea you've ever had."

"You can either come with me, or not."

"Come with you?" Bailey scoffed. "No. I won't. I'm not about to abandon my people and all the other vulnerable settlements in the Near Systems to chase after one person who probably forgot about you the second you left her on that dock."

Henry recoiled. "Take that back."

"I won't."

"Tansy heard from her just a couple weeks ago, she sent word. She hasn't forgotten about me."

"Funny, because when you were kissing me it sure didn't seem like you were thinking about her. You were more than happy to let me chase after you like a sad puppy, keeping me on that leash until you knew for sure that she was waiting for you."

"Bailey, I—"

"You know what? Save it. Go, chase after this woman, get yourself killed. I'm done." She stood up from her seat so quick, the stool fell over, crashing metal on metal as it hit the floor and rolled toward the row of cold boilers.

When Bailey had gone, the sound of her heavy boots gone from the corridor, all Henry could do was whisper "I'm sorry."

* * *

"I want to go to Skelm," Henry said, summoning all her courage to talk to the burly, gruff pirate captain who was leaning against his ship on the docks.

"The hell you do," he laughed, spitting on the ground. "Impossible to get in or out of that place now. No smugglers have set foot there in months, not since that bitch of a governor increased shipment inspections. Can't get shit through there now."

"I will pay whatever I can, I'll work, I'll—"

"Listen, lady, we're not going to Skelm. I don't have a death wish, and neither does my crew, understand?"

"How close can you get me?"

He sighed, rolling his eyes. "Obviously you're the kind of broad that doesn't listen to reason. Bit like my ma. I've got a soft spot for my ma, so I'll tell you what I'm gonna do. We'll take you to the Salrock Beacon, but that's it. You'd be on your own from there."

"Am I likely to find passage from there?"

"Maybe," he shrugged. "It's the kind of place where deals are struck, if you catch my meaning. You'd better have credit or something worthwhile to trade or you won't get three steps off that base."

Henry nodded. "Good. I'll take it."

"You're gonna have to work for your room and board, we're not a charity, you hear?"

"Understood."

"You'll be on janitorial duty. Don't recommend bringing your finest, and if you do, it's best kept hidden. Not everyone on the Zesty Shark is as honorable as me. You'll be safe, don't you worry about that, but some of my crew can suffer from a bit of the thievin'."

"When does this ship set off?"

He pulled a silver pocket watch from his pocket and squinted at it. "An hour. You'd best be getting going, if you're collecting your things."

"I... no. It's just me. No bags."

"We'll board in a while, I need to get one last bottle of the good whiskey for my own personal stash before we head out. The stuff off-world tastes like rat piss."

Henry didn't want to know how he knew what rat piss tasted like, so she just nodded in affirmative.

"Hey. Weaver." She turned. Kady was at the end of the pier, leaning casually against one of the support beams. "Where do you think you're going?"

"I have to go back for her."

"Yeah, I thought as much. You know I have to voice my disapproval, right? To say, out loud, that I think this is a ridiculous and dangerous plan?"

"I know."

"Great, so long as you know." Kady pushed herself upright and shoved a small bag into Henry's hands. "I transferred some credit to you, should work fine with your black market chip I know you bought a few weeks back."

"How did you—"

"Larkin told me. Did you forget her job was tracking marks? Nothing gets by her."

"Thank you."

"There's some dehydrated food in the bag, it's not much, but it will keep you going if you're in a bind."

Henry felt tears welling up in her eyes for the third time that day. It was the first time she felt like part of the crew, and it was right as she was running away. "You know I have to do this, right?"

"I know. I'd do the same for any one of my crew family, as would they. The captain isn't going to be happy about this, though."

"Can you tell her I'm sorry?"

"I'll tell her, as soon as she stops yelling. I predict that will take the better part of a day, once she finds out."

"I just… Kady, I've spent too long coasting on my family's good name, and then took an easy road away from consequences in Skelm. I need to do this, I need… I need to go back for Georgie and her sister. I have to do something."

"I know." She stepped back and smiled. "Proud of you, Weaver."

"Keep scanning the frequencies for her. I'll be listening whenever I can. I'll send word when I get there, even if it's just a message."

Kady reached out and wrapped her arms around Henry's shoulders. "Please stay safe."

"I will."

"I mean it, Weaver. There's not many people that I like, and even fewer I actually enjoy working with. Don't make that list any shorter."

"I won't."

CHAPTER THIRTY-ONE

Georgie turned the tarnished bathroom tap and cold, rusted water spurted out in uneven gushes, splashing against the grime covered sink, coated in years of dust and filth from the factories. She'd been hiding in that abandoned building for two days, waiting for her ankle to heal enough to venture out. Her arm throbbed angrily where she'd cut out her Coalition chip, the edges of the wound ragged and scabby. Her stomach grumbled angrily; she swallowed back the bile that bit at the back of her throat, her body's way of letting her know that she was in desperate need of some food.

Her ankle still tender and swollen, she tied a canvas bag around her foot, knotting the straps tightly around her muscular calf. It would have to do until she got new boots, and the swelling went down. The mid morning light filtered down through the gaping holes in the ceiling, the result of rotted floorboards that had caved in after the roof gave out. Empty buildings, left empty not because there was no one to live in them, but because they had been determined to be less profitable than the investors had imagined. It made her feel sick, thinking of all those people crammed into the tenements, when there were at least seven buildings like this one, gated off and abandoned.

The city's smog was thicker than ever, and it burned her eyes, the acrid smoke settling uneasily in her nose. The factories belched smoke into the air, now running twenty-four-hour shifts with the new workers that had been brought in. *Governor Allemande must be thrilled at the efficiency*, Georgie thought bitterly, tugging her collar up over her face in a futile attempt to escape the fumes. There were military police officers everywhere, on every corner, stationed at the entrance to every shop. Getting around was going to get more and more difficult with these increased patrols, and she couldn't help but think that her capture was becoming increasingly inevitable.

"You're late," Cole hissed, beckoning her to stand alongside the huge dumpsters that sat behind the factory.

"Yeah, well, if you haven't noticed, it's a little harder to get around."

"I thought you'd been captured."

"No."

"Obviously," he said, rolling his eyes, peeling back a faded poster that led into the basement of the factory. "In here."

"This is impressive," Georgie admitted. "Why didn't you tell us about this before?" Even the word 'us' made her stomach clench, now that everyone she loved was gone.

He shoved a set of shelves aside, revealing a small crowd of people huddled inside. "We didn't need it before."

"Where did all these people come from?"

"Survivors. Some are ours, who escaped being shipped off on the transports. Some are new, from a range of places they say were hard hit by those storms. They ran away from the tenements their first night here."

"Hey y'all," Georgie said as brightly as she could muster.

"Did you bring us any food?" an old man asked, the same one who had accosted Emeline.

"I'm afraid I didn't."

"Betcha Emeline would have," he grumbled.

Georgie stared at him in disbelief. "Just a couple weeks past, you were questioning her ability to lead us, and now you're saying you miss her?"

"She was a sight better than you," he muttered. "Least we were all fed, then, even if she was a pampered little princess."

"How *dare* you," she said, advancing on the man, her hands clenched into fists. "She's on a transport headed to a work camp right now, where she'll be worked to death. Work a damn sight harder than anything *you've* ever

CHAPTER THIRTY-ONE

done."

"Alright, let's calm down," Cole said, stepping in between them. "We're all hungry and scared. We need to work together if we're going to make it out of this alive."

Georgie shot him a look. "Well, surely you're not hungry, staying in that mid city apartment."

"He kicked me out. Said he didn't want any trouble."

"Oh."

"I'm in the same boat as everyone else here," he said, plastering a weak smile across his face. "Homeless and hungry. I did get some more medical supplies before I left, though, for anyone who might need them."

"Got any antibiotics?" a woman in the back asked.

Cole shook his head. "I'm sorry, no. Mostly bandages and sutures, some inhalers, but we're going to run out fast."

"Where are we going to go?" the woman asked, pulling her young teenage child close to her. "We can't stay here, they're bound to do a sweep of this building any day now. They've already been doing exhaustive searches of other factories, I heard the workers saying so."

"What about the abandoned high rises at the edge of the city?" Georgie volunteered. "I've been there a few days, it's pretty rank but the taps run, and no one seems to be poking around over there."

"No way, it would be too hard to get around. At least here, we have closer access to the docks to steal supplies when we can," Cole said. "That's already unlikely. Taking us further away is only going to make that worse."

The lights flickered gently, and a few of the strangers huddled closer together. The woman shook her head. "Like she said, they're already doing sweeps of the factories, to make sure there isn't more information about strikes being passed around. Once they found that illegal printing press in the basement of the rubber factory, they started using official blueprints to do the searches. We're sittin' ducks here."

"What would it hurt to at least try? We all know they're looking for us, and they're not going to stop until they round us all up and send us off to work camps or worse," the old man said. "Even if we have to keep moving, it's better than sitting around and waiting for the inevitable."

"He's right," Georgie agreed. "We'd have to move under cover of darkness. There will still be plenty of guards around, but it's better than the alternative."

"And what will we do once we get there? There's nowhere there we could get food, and these people are starting to starve. They've been without food for days."

"So have I! And it's not like we have a lot of options here, Cole."

Cole sighed angrily. "Fine. But it's on your head when they all want to come back here or give themselves up rather than slowly starve in those high rises."

"Deal."

* * *

By midnight that night, all the stragglers were relocated to the high rises. Georgie, still in possession of her janitor's key ring, led the group from one empty building to the next, creeping along in the shadows like the rodents their governor was desperate to eradicate, pillaging through dumpsters as they went. They found offcuts of fabric some would use to hand sew clothing, once they got needles and thread, and vegetables that were only half-rotted, and few loaves of bread that only had mold on the ends. It was something, at least for now, though she knew it wouldn't last long with this amount of people, and not with half the police quietly looking for them.

"We need to know what's going on," Georgie said, toasting a chunk of bread over a fire someone had built in a barrel. Skelm was full of so much smoke and smog from the factories, no one would notice a campfire or two eking smoke from the half-caved-in ceiling of the abandoned building. "We need to get the radio from the Twisted Lantern."

"I don't think that's a good idea," Cole said, wrinkling his nose at some slimy cabbage. "They'll have that place locked down tighter than a drum."

"I bet I can get in and out without them noticing."

"Georgie, no. You'd be risking your life, and for what?"

CHAPTER THIRTY-ONE

She bit into the bread, the burnt edges scraping the roof of her mouth, and she resented how grateful she was for a scrap of food. "We can't stay like this. These people will be needing more food, medicine. Maybe if we hack the radio, we can—"

"Hack the radio? Who do you think you are, Jess or Bale?"

"If we can tap into additional frequencies," she continued, ignoring his interruption, "we might be able to glean information on the movements of their officers, and more importantly, those assault squads. They've got more guns than sense."

"You realize this is probably the most ridiculous thing you've ever considered, right?" he smirked, tossing another hunk of bread at her after scraping off the mold.

"Yep."

"Hey," a woman said, sitting down next to Cole with an apron full of vegetables, the pockets and neckline of her dress bulging with produce. "We can make a soup with these, it will last longer."

"Sounds great," Georgie replied, and her stomach rumbled angrily at the mere thought of hot, steaming soup. How long had it been since she'd had a nourishing meal? Since her ma and Lucy left?

The woman reached for a dented pot and tossed the vegetables in one by one, snapping off rotten bits and setting them aside. "I'm Carmen."

"Aren't you going to throw that away?" Georgie asked, gesturing at the pile of inedible produce. "We don't want rats in here."

Carmen stared at her and then laughed. "I'm not leaving it there, obviously. We can compost it. I climbed up to the roof earlier and I think we can grow some food up there."

"You climbed to the roof? In a dress?"

"It's not like it's hard," Carmen scoffed, a hand resting on her wide hips. "In Fort Gelad, every child learns how to climb. You never know when it will come in handy." She shook a stalk of celery at them before snapping it in half and tossing it in the pot. "Like now."

"Compost? Growing? We still have to stay quiet here, you know. Any evidence people were here and they'll come down hard on us." Cole flicked a crumb into the barrel. "And it would take months for any kind of harvest to come in. What do we do until then? Survive on water and air alone?"

"You're really negative, you know that?" Carmen laughed. "This is not the ideal any of us wanted, but it's better than being six feet under. While you're busy worrying about the next five minutes, let me worry about next season, alright?"

"I guess it can't hurt to prepare," Georgie conceded, "but you will have to take caution to not be seen. I'm not sure that yellow dress you're wearing is the best choice for subtlety."

"Aye, captain, I'll be sure to roll in mud before venturing to the roof, covering myself in a natural camouflage."

"That's not what I meant, I—"

"Don't worry, okay? I spent most of my life running from assholes like these officers you have running around here. They're armed, but most of them aren't very smart, and don't have much training. They're mean and stupid, and I'll bet none of them ever think to look up when searching for vigilantes like us."

Georgie looked up through the ceiling at all the other high-rise buildings in Skelm, against the backdrop of the distant stars that hung in the sky. "Look up..." she trailed off.

"I don't think we can call ourselves vigilantes if we're barely surviving," Cole muttered.

"We could be. Georgie here seems like she knows what's needed, knowing their movements and what they're up to. We could hit an armory, the docks, gather supplies, fortify this building against attack or siege."

"What if we had a way of getting around the city without them knowing?" Georgie asked, her mind already racing with possibilities. "We could send out small strike groups, steal supplies, weapons, food, and get out before they even know what's hit them."

"Tunnels? Georgie, you know those will be swarming with guards—"

She shook her head. "No, not tunnels. A sort of network of scaffolds that goes from one building to the next. People could choose where they sleep, giving everyone a little more privacy, plus if we do decide to fight back..."

CHAPTER THIRTY-ONE

"This is madness, you do know that, don't you?" Cole asked, a smile spreading over his face. "But I'm in. Like you said, it's better than the alternative, right?"

Carmen filled the vegetable pot with water. "We're going to need that radio."

"Yeah," Georgie agreed. "We need a backup plan if I get hauled in. Cole's right, that place is going to be swarming with military police, and I worry they might have taken the radio already, anyway."

"They won't have taken it," Cole said, his enthusiasm visibly growing. "They'd have no way of knowing its modifications or the connection to the chip in the comms tower. To them it would just look like another rusty piece of crap."

"How about I be the backup?" Carmen asked, dusting off her hands and setting the pot on a grate over the barrel.

"You?"

She rolled her eyes. "Don't worry, Boss, I won't wear my pretty yellow dress. I'll borrow something less flamboyant, okay?"

"We should go tonight. The sooner the better."

* * *

"This place could be pretty, without all that smoke," Carmen said, climbing out the window after Georgie. "Those cliffs, and the mountains in the distance. They almost remind me of home."

"Where's home for you?"

"Nowhere, anymore. Fort Gelad was my home for a few years, we settled there after years on the run."

Georgie edged along the side of the iron fire escape and held her hand out to help Carmen step down onto it. Though she had spent plenty of time on rickety scaffolding to clean windows and scrape grime from the high bricks of the Administration building, she couldn't expect that everyone would feel comfortable that high up, no matter how experienced they were at climbing.

"I don't need a hand, thank you," Carmen said, vaulting over the railing onto the platform. "I've climbed trees taller than this."

"Taller than this?" Georgie scoffed. Even back on Gamma-3 trees were nowhere near the height of high-rise buildings.

"You should get out more. Travel. Visit new places. I bet you'd be amazed at what you'd find."

Grabbing hold of the ladder that led to the roof, Georgie laughed. It was the first time she'd laughed in weeks, not since Emeline drew that little cartoon doodle of Governor Allemande. "I'll put 'travel the galaxy' right at the top of my list of my things to do, right after 'don't get killed or fall to my death.' How does that sound?" She hoisted herself up, rung by rung, until she was standing on the roof of the building, peering down into where parts of it had caved in from water damage.

"We should try to get that repaired, even if it's only temporary," Carmen said, perched on the short ledge. "Some wood, something to keep out the wet. It would do wonders for everyone's peace of mind."

"You sure have a lot of big ideas considering we're barely hanging on here."

"It's important to see a light at the end of the tunnel, otherwise you stop looking for a way out."

Georgie squinted through the smog at the next building, and the one after that. "This tunnel is awfully long."

"They always are. Wouldn't be a tunnel otherwise."

"If we can get across these three buildings, that will set us close to the speakeasy. I'm thinking if we can create some half-assed bridges between the fire escapes, it should work for now. Need to get some materials, though. Can't use any of the beams up here, the wood is half rotted."

"Is there a scrapyard in this city?"

"Down near the docks. I don't know how you expect to extract materials without half this city's forces raining down on us, though."

"I don't. But I know that scrappers are usually more... amenable to a bribe, shall we say?"

CHAPTER THIRTY-ONE

"We don't have anything to trade."

Carmen grinned. "Not yet."

"Are you always this annoyingly optimistic?"

"Yes."

"Good," Georgie said, detaching part of the scaffolding so that it hung off the building from one side, "it sure as hell makes a change from dealing with Cole all the time." She gestured at the rickety platform. "You okay to jump to the next one? It's not far with the extension, but—"

Before she could finish, Carmen ran and leapt from one scaffold to the next, landing in a deep squat on the other side. "Come on, slow poke!" she laughed. "Race you to the tavern!"

Georgie knew she'd never beat her to the tavern, not with those kinds of acrobatics, so she resigned herself to following close behind until they reached the street level near the Twisted Lantern's back entrance. "It's just up this alley," she whispered, peeking around the corner to look for military police. "They might have it bugged, or rigged up with a tripwire, we should be careful."

"I expected this place to be swarming from what you two said."

"It's definitely suspicious," Georgie agreed, inserting her key into the lock with an apprehensive jab, almost expecting someone to jump out, or for the door to explode, or for Governor Allemande herself to descend upon them with a host of officers. To her relief, the door swung open with a gentle creak, and the stale, stagnant air from the past week wafted out. "Come inside, I don't want us separated if anything happens."

"So this is where everyone in Skelm gets their booze?"

"Until recently."

"I'm surprised this place wasn't looted the second they found it."

Georgie stepped through the back room into the bar and groaned at the sight of all the chaos. "Looks like they did." Smashed bottles were strewn all over the floor, along with various scraps of military police uniforms, and curiously, a pair of officer's boots. "Someone had fun," she said, pulling on the boots, and discarding her one remaining shoe in the corner. They were slightly too big, but it was better than a bag tied around her foot, that was for sure.

"Lucky find."

"Yeah."

"I don't think they left anything worth taking, do you?"

"No, I'll reckon they drained this place dry. Shame, it would have been nice to have something to offer people as pain relief at least."

"So where's this radio?"

"The basement. Stairs back through there and to the left. Watch the last step, it's sorta uneven." Carmen disappeared around the corner, her soft footsteps fading down into the basement. "Can you see it?"

"Shit. Georgie!" Carmen yelled.

She descended the stairs two, sometimes three steps at a time, and nearly crashed into the officer who was wobbling on the spot, his hand clenched around Carmen's wrist. "Let her go!"

"Why should I?" he slurred. "Trespass. Thieve."

"He's drunk," Georgie said, spotting the radio, untouched, on the table.

"I know he's drunk, get him off me!"

"I'm not drunk!" he shouted. "I'll get a commendation for this, just you wait and see." He reached for his gun, and before she could think twice, Georgie headbutted him right in the face. Blood gushed from his nose. "Bitch!" he yelled, choking on his own blood. "Broke my nose! You'll hang for this!"

He reached for his gun again. Georgie gritted her teeth and shoved him with all her might, sending him flying across the room, until his head connected with the wall with a sickening crunch, leaving him slumped on the floor.

"Shit," Carmen whispered.

"I had to," Georgie said, her hands shaking. "I had to, or—"

"Shh. You had to. It's alright. Come on, let's get this radio before someone else comes."

"He might have been a deserter. Why else would he have been hiding in here?"

"Waiting for us?"

CHAPTER THIRTY-ONE

"While drunk?" Georgie asked, wrapping the radio in the blanket she used to sleep under. "Unlikely. Allemande has all her troops in an iron grip." She gestured at the officer's lifeless body. "Get his gun. We might need it."

"Right."

"Check his pockets, he might have something interesting."

"Some extra ammunition, um... hmm." She held something tiny and silver up to what little light trickled into the basement from the staircase. "Looks like a black market chip to me."

Georgie stepped over him to examine the piece of tech. "Oh, hello," she said, grinning at Carmen. "What shall we bet he was using this to hide some ill-gotten credits?"

"If he didn't piss it all away before he holed up in here, that might be of some use."

"You're damn right about that."

"We should go," Carmen said, pocketing the chip and tucking the gun into her waistband. "Grab the radio and let's get back to base."

"Hold on, how come you get the gun?"

Carmen raised an eyebrow at her, a dark curl hanging to the side of her face. "How many times have you used a firearm?"

"Uh..."

"That's what I thought. I get the gun."

"Looks like the radio was untouched, at least. Silly fool didn't realize what he had down here. He could have been contacting someone off-world if he wanted to."

"Wouldn't they hear?"

"Yes, but they'd likely have assumed it was one of us survivors, not some rogue deserter."

"The others were saying the docks are all but locked down, nothing in or out without the Coalition seal of approval."

Georgie nodded, climbing the stairs back up into the Twisted Lantern. "That much is true. Poor bastard might not have made it out regardless, unless he was able to fold himself into the size of a small meat crate. Probably why he was hiding down here, drinking whatever was left of the booze."

"He might have left us some, the bastard. What I wouldn't give right now for a drink."

"Yeah, you said it," Georgie agreed. She unbolted the back door and peeked out into the alley, releasing a breath when it was just as empty as it had been before. "Not having this place locked down tight feels weird if you ask me. They've got more officers than this city has rats, yet they've left the only speakeasy wide open."

"Given the mess in there, it's probably safe to say that they found it, emptied it, and thought there was nothing else of value in there. I told you, these military police, they aren't as smart as you'd think."

"Maybe not, but the governor is." She grasped the railing of the fire escape and began to climb the fifteen floors to the roof.

"Someone should take her out, then. Someone like you, maybe."

Georgie wheezed a laugh, her lungs burning from the climb. "Easy for you to say, you've never met the woman. She's sadistic and manipulative, and by now I'll bet she has at least twelve armed guards around her at all times."

"Where there's a will, there's a way, that's what I always say."

"Somehow that doesn't surprise me, given what I am learning about your positive sunny attitude."

"Someone has to be, you'd think I'd walked into a funeral when I found that factory hideout. Not an ounce of sunshine or hope to be found, like they'd all resigned themselves to death."

Guards shouted to one another on the street below, and Georgie froze, waiting for one of them to look up and see them, ten floors up. Neither of them did, and she released the breath she'd held. "There's not much to be had in Skelm except death if you're not even able to try to squeak some pitiful existence working in the factories."

"See?" Carmen said, gesturing towards the officers on the street level. "They never look up. Why would they? Until now, everyone in this city has more or less abided by the rules, except for a little bit of light smuggling here and there." She wiped her hands on her borrowed blue coveralls. "This place is practically a powder keg. All we need is a spark. That's what your

CHAPTER THIRTY-ONE

sister understood."

"How do you know about Emeline?"

She shrugged. "Some of the others were talking about her. You seem very proud."

"I am." Georgie squeezed her eyes shut and tried to swallow back the guilt. "I was."

"We'll get her back, don't you worry, Georgie Payne. Leaders like that don't go down without a fight. From what I hear, I'd be surprised if she wasn't already leading a breakout resistance and planning to come back and break us all out of here."

Georgie smiled, imagining her sister accomplishing those amazing things. "I can only hope you're right."

"I am. I'm right about most things."

"And modest, too."

Carmen pulled herself up onto the roof and coughed into her elbow. "The smog here is a real challenge, but we could use it to our advantage."

"Oh yeah? How so?"

"Poor visibility up here means our plan to create a network of bridges will probably work, so long as we can get those materials." She nodded at Georgie. "We have a radio now, and a gun, and a chip with some credits. That's a hell of a head start."

"No traders in town will tap that chip, they could be thrown in a work camp. Down on the docks, though..."

"Come on. We should tell the others."

CHAPTER THIRTY-TWO

Henry hugged her knees on top of the crate, huddled in the thin blanket one of the crew members had thrown at her. They were almost to the Salrock Beacon, after weeks of slow, torturous travel, stopping at every fuel beacon to fill up the huge old ship, and offload ill-gotten wares along the way. No one on the ship spoke to her, leaving her with her own thoughts, to stew in guilt and desperation for a modicum of human interaction. There wasn't even a friendly rat to toss crumbs of stale bread to. She ached with missing the friendly banter with Bailey, in spite of the complication. She wished she could be back in the tiny lab on the Cricket.

"Hey, you," one of the crew members said, a small, reedy man with a bluish cast to his face. "We're landing in an hour. Cap'n says to gather your things, he wants you off the ship as soon as we come into port. Says you're trouble, wanting to get back to Skelm or some bullshit."

"Thanks," she replied, a little too brightly, grateful for the brief conversation. "Did he say if—"

"You're crazy to go back there, you know," he said over his shoulder as he left the closet that was given to her as a room. "I heard they just shipped a whole load of 'em out to a work camp."

"What?"

"A work camp."

"No, I heard that, I just—"

"An hour. Don't dawdle."

CHAPTER THIRTY-TWO

She scrambled up off the crate, wrapping the blanket around her shoulders to ward off the omnipresent chill in the air. "No, wait!"

"Listen, lady, I don't have time to sit here and have a chat with you all damn day. I have work to do, I have duties. If the captain catches me—"

"I need you to tell me more about the people who got sent to the work camp. Do you know why?"

He shrugged, fiddling with the brass buttons on his worn jacket. "I don't know anything other than what they told me in the Bronze Bell back in Bradach. Some underlings got a bit too uppity for the management, tried to stage some kind of coup, or a strike, I don't know. They all got rounded up and shipped off, replaced with some fresh meat."

Henry's stomach felt like it was dropping through her body onto the floor. "Why didn't anyone tell me?"

"Why would we? All we knew is you wanted to get back to Skelm and were paying good money for us to get you as close as we can without getting too close to that wasp nest."

"Are you sure they didn't say anything else?"

"Cap says leave the blanket when you go, that's property of the ship." He turned to leave, but said over his shoulder, "Good luck tracking down whoever you're looking for. Sounds like you're gonna need it."

* * *

Salrock Beacon was a dark, drab place that almost made Skelm look like the Capital. When Henry disembarked, the loading bay doors still not at their full height, the icy wind that seeped through the rusted rivets of the station sank deep into her bones.

Most ships were climate controlled, but stations were larger and hungrier for energy and fuel to keep their boilers running. Solar could only provide so much out here in dark space, and it wasn't enough to keep her teeth from chattering, her arms wrapped tightly around herself. She'd have to find a coat, or a cloak, something to keep her warm until she found passage to Skelm, or she'd end up losing a finger to the cold.

"Hey lady!" a child shouted, dancing from one foot to the other. "Wanna buy some credits?"

"Why would I want to buy credits?"

The child shrugged, a shock of pink hair peeking out from under their hooded jacket. "I dunno. Surplus of scrap? Depending where you're going, trades will only get you so much."

"No thanks." Henry hurried past them, clutching her bag of supplies close to her chest.

"Hey where are you going? I could help you find a ship, or maybe a place to stay for the night—"

"I said, no thanks."

The child grabbed for Henry's bag with quick fingers, clothed in thin, torn gloves, and nearly tore it away from her. "Hey!" Henry shouted, and shoved them backwards, sending them sprawling into a shipping lane, cluttered with crates. "Piss off!"

"Fuck you!" the child yelled, scampering off into a poorly lit corner of the station. "I'll be back, you know!"

Henry dusted herself off and examined the broken strap on her bag. She'd have to be more careful, now. Fuel beacons like this one were outside Coalition control, much to their chagrin, due to an old agreement signed long before the Near Systems were as populated as they now were. The fuel barons didn't care much for law and order, only profit, and lorded over the stations in their lush penthouses while children apparently resorted to theft in the docks.

She looked around at the ships, their destinations marked on signboards next to them that flipped into place with every update. On time, delayed, early, canceled. Gamma-3, Turtawa, Nantane.

The loneliness bit into her more sharply than the cold. Here, she had no one.

She shivered and headed towards the center of the station, where some trading stalls were hocking stolen goods like scrap and tech, a few selling

CHAPTER THIRTY-TWO

weapons, which made her instinctively feel for her revolver, hidden safely beneath her dress. She hadn't needed to use it and hoped she wouldn't have to. One stall was selling hot food, a tall, dark woman with braids piled on top of her head stirring a huge pot of the best smelling soup she'd ever had the pleasure of inhaling. After weeks of stale rations, her stomach growled noisily.

"Soup?" the woman asked, holding up a ladle full of steaming liquid and what looked like roasted vegetables and stewed beans.

Henry hesitated, her hand on her bag. She should save all her credits for buying passage onto a ship and making sure she didn't freeze to death on the long journey, but the soup smelled so delicious, and she was so terribly hungry.

"What's the matter, afraid of an old lady like me?" the woman pressed, lowering the ladle back into the pot.

"No, it's just—yes, I'd like some soup, please," she said, presenting her chip to be scanned.

The woman shook her head. "Trade only. I don't deal in credits."

"Why not?"

"The Coalition, full of fascists. I don't deal in their currency, and I won't ever visit one of their pristine cities. I would trade that revolver you've got under your dress, though. That would buy you some soup."

"What—how?" Henry demanded, stepping back. Had someone been watching her?

"You pressed the fabric of your skirts against it when you walked past the table selling the electric prods and heat guns. It's clear as day you don't belong here, you don't have one ounce of sense."

"I can't trade you my gun."

"Well then, I can't give you any soup."

"You really won't take credits?"

"I really won't." Henry's stomach growled again, and the woman laughed. "Sounds like your stomach has some other plans."

"Isn't there anything else you want? I could promise to get you passage to Bradach, there's a food market there, and—"

The woman snorted. "I don't need passage to Bradach. I make much more in trades here than I ever would there. You see anyone else around here selling food that doesn't look like last week's deep fried rat? No, another few years here and I'll be retiring in peace, far away from the fools that come through this station."

Henry dug through the bag of supplies that Kady had given her, a pile of crumbs where the food had been, and some wrappers from the dehydrated food she'd long since eaten back on the ship. "I don't think I have anything else."

"How about that dress? Looks worn, but would still fetch a decent trade. Well made, and mended perfectly."

"My—but what would I wear then?"

"My advice to you is that you should get yourself some coveralls. You'd be less conspicuous then, less of a target for those urchins by the docks." The woman reached under her table and produced a pair of bright orange ones, dirty, with a stain on the collar and the left elbow.

"I'll trade you the dress for the coveralls, a *heaping* bowl of soup, and some food rations, if you have them."

The woman's eyes crinkled as she laughed, shaking her head. "Well, aren't you the little negotiator?"

"Listen, we both know you're coming out better on this deal, so that's my final offer."

"Alright, alright. But I'm doing you a favor, just so we're clear. I run into you again, we'll discuss it then."

Henry grinned and grabbed the coveralls, shimmying under the table with her bag clutched tight in her hand. "Whatever you say," she agreed, unbuttoning her dress. The table was small, and she cracked her head on the underside as she fought with the brass zip on the coveralls.

"First time changing under a table?"

"Uh, yeah."

"Amateur."

She emerged, dressed head to toe in orange, her grey boots poking out from underneath the oversized coveralls. "What do you think?" she asked.

CHAPTER THIRTY-TWO

"I think you look hungry. Here, give me that dress, I'll pour you out a bowl."

Henry carefully folded the dress and tucked in the sleeves before presenting it to the trader and taking the bowl of soup. She was damn lucky to make that trade, and she needed the warmth of the hot liquid and the tender chunks of eggplant and peppers she could feel nourishing her body. "Must be nice to have access to all the fresh produce that comes through here," she said between slurps.

"Yeah, well, they charge a premium for it. Still, I'm not going to compromise on quality. There are half a dozen places you can get watered down gruel in this trash heap, and you can only get the good stuff here."

"Thank you," Henry said, her voice earnest. The coveralls were much warmer than her dress, with light padding sewn into the lining to keep out the cold. It would be too warm in Skelm, but here, it was exactly what she needed.

"You wouldn't have lasted three days as a stowaway in that dress. These ships don't heat their loading bays, you know."

"A stowaway?"

"I don't know where you're headed, but that black market chip you've got in your arm certainly suggests you don't want anyone to know who you are."

Henry grabbed at her arm beneath the woven twill of the jumpsuit. "I don't have a black market chip."

"Please. I can spot that newly healed incision a mile off. Don't worry, I won't rat you out. But you need to know, these ships going to Coalition settlements, they shoot stowaways on sight." She shrugged and stirred the soup, adding another dash of crushed black pepper to the pot. "Do what you've gotta do, I guess."

The color drained from Henry's face, and she shoveled another spoonful of soup into her mouth. She just had to keep thinking of getting back to Georgie, so she wouldn't imagine herself getting hauled out of hiding and shoved out an airlock for the crime of hitching a ride.

"Alright, lady, hurry it up, I have more customers on the way. New ship's docking and a whole crew is going to be looking to get hold of some grub."

"Sorry." Henry drained her bowl and dropped it into the bucket of soapy water, where it disappeared below the surface little by little as it filled with suds. "Thank you again."

"Here are some rations. Should be enough to last a couple weeks, if you're careful." She handed Henry a stack of vacuum sealed bags with what looked like plain porridge inside.

Whatever happened, the next few weeks would be devoid of a hot meal, and so she closed her eyes and tried to commit the taste of the flavorful, spiced soup to memory for later. Imagination was a powerful tool, she'd found, when she was slurping at cold dehydrated potatoes from the packets Kady had given her. She put the rations into her bag and scanned the departures boards again, looking from one docking bay to the next. None said Skelm, but one was left blank. She approached the bay, keeping to the shadows, which was hard in a trading beacon covered in cheap, flickering neon signs.

"That fucking governor said she wants this stuff delivered straight to her building. We aren't allowed to leave it at the docks anymore. That's why the schedule's all messed up," A woman in a brown waistcoat said. "Gonna take us another half a day just to pack this stuff off the ship and up the hill in that shit hole."

"Why can't we just hire some bored assholes at the docks?" a man in some blue coveralls asked. "It's what we did before."

The woman shook her head. "She gave strict orders. Remember Lenny, the one who was supplying all their paper products? Well, he left his shipment at the docks and now he's banned from ever trading there again."

"For fuck's sake."

"You can say that again. Anyway, we're leaving in ten. Don't be late this time or I swear to the gods I'm leaving your ass here."

"Yeah, yeah."

The woman walked up the ramp onto the ship, and the man turned and walked back towards the flashing lights of the trading area. Henry bent and crept behind the line of crates, looking for confirmation that the ship was headed to Skelm. It certainly sounded like Allemande was behind their new regulations, but she had to be sure, otherwise she could end up hundreds of thousands of kilometers from where she needed to be. From where Georgie was, if she hadn't been swept up in getting sent off to a work camp.

Henry carefully lifted the lid off a box and peered inside, the overwhelming scent of chemical cleaner burning her nostrils. What other settlement would be using this much solvent? It had to be Skelm. Strangely, the acrid smell almost reminded her of Georgie, the way it clung to her coveralls after she'd been working. Without another thought, she climbed into the huge crate and settled between boxes of solvent, hoping that no one would notice the extra weight when the steamlift pushed it onto the ship.

CHAPTER THIRTY-THREE

"Hello, I'm Delia Dodson with this evening's news from the jewel of the sector, our proud city, heart of the Near Systems. Over the past weeks we have welcomed new workers to Skelm who have increased our productivity by a whopping two hundred percent, which shows the innate worth of prioritizing hard work over handouts."

"Bitch," Cole muttered.

"She's probably reading from a script," Carmen said, shoving a holey tarp at him. "Here, mend this. The roof is done, but some of the families are requesting additional protection from the acid rain."

"Governor Allemande has announced a new scheme to keep our children safe in this city, a monetary award for anyone with information leading to the capture of Georgie Payne and Cole Marion. They are considered armed and dangerous, and any speculation on their whereabouts should be reported to authorities as soon as possible."

"Took them long enough," Georgie laughed, sanding the edge of a ladder she'd made for one of the families upstairs.

"Probably hoped they could nab you without anyone knowing," Carmen mused. "Looks better for the governor's successes if she has a firm grip on what happens here."

The radio continued. "If you or anyone you know is thinking of abandoning their post, keep in mind that you would be ineligible for this monetary award or any promotions and pay rises within the Coalition for the duration

CHAPTER THIRTY-THREE

of your employment. Remember, a well-stocked government is a healthy government, and we're who makes what the Near Systems need!"

Cole knotted the end of the thread he was using and pulled it through the thick tarp. "They're certainly pulling out all the stops, aren't they?"

"Anything for the glory of Queen Allemande, I guess."

"We can expect rain for the next several days, so make sure you prepare for the inclement weather. Storms beyond the barrier remain controlled and predictable, with precipitation falling well within the expected range. A fabulous opportunity to curl up with one of our free Coalition sponsored pamphlets for some light reading when your shift is over. We all achieve more, when we work together."

The radio crackled and popped for a moment before the broadcast continued.

"A gentle reminder that curfew is in effect until further notice, and if you know someone breaking that rule, *there are a number of patrol teams* you can report to. Military police officers are standing by, *on every corner*, to keep our city safe and efficiency at its highest potential."

"She's laying it on thick tonight, isn't she?" Carmen laughed.

"Sounds like extra patrols have been assigned."

"Sometimes it's hard to tell if she's helping us, or trying to keep us in line."

Georgie shrugged. "She hasn't been wrong yet."

"No, but is it keeping us too cautious?"

"And as our final news piece for this evening, I would like to offer up my own personal congratulations to our very own Governor Allemande, who has been shortlisted as a contender to ascend to the rank of Sector Overseer, the youngest ever in our long history. Let us all raise a cheer for the woman who has helped put Skelm on the map, and if she is selected will bring us a profound sense of community achievement and local Skelmian pride." The radio sizzled and hissed with dead air, and they heard some half hearted whoops coming from a few blocks away. "Thank you for your continued patronage, my fellow citizens. I'm Delia Dodson, goodnight."

Cole rolled his eyes. "Of course that witch would use the displacement of hundreds of workers to further her own career."

"It was quite the stunt, I'll give her that," Georgie admitted. "Maybe it was our own fault for staging the strike on the night of the gala. We should have known she'd do something above and beyond to protect her reputation and keep things running. We shouldn't expect anything less from her."

"She's going to be on your ass now, you know. She won't want a fugitive running around organizing boycotts and strikes while she's one gasp away from the biggest promotion this sector has ever seen. It will be the first time a Sector Overseer is lifted up from within, rather than some crony brought in from somewhere else. We have to be more careful than ever."

Carmen shook her head. "I disagree. These broadcasts, while true, they're keeping us timid. If we want to upset the apple cart, then we have to strike hard, and soon. We need to hit the docks and every major factory, or we're always on the back foot."

"It's not as though we've been cowering in here, you know. We managed to get enough raw supplies to fix the roof, build rope bridges between the high rises, and people are at least fed now, even if the food is less than what they were used to back in Fort Gelad or the other places they're from."

"I don't even know how you can call this food," she said, tossing a can of unidentified meat product aside. "Where is this city's fresh produce? I've not even been able to find adequate seeds for the rooftop garden plan."

Cole picked up the can and stacked it neatly atop the pile again. "We got you as many seeds as we could, the raised beds are full. What more do you want?"

"Those beds aren't going to feed these people for even half a season! We need more, and we need to control the resources."

"We have one gun, Carmen."

She scoffed and set her tarp aside. "Then we need to get more, I've been saying it for weeks."

"Alright, alright," Georgie relented, propping the newly sanded ladder against the wall. "We'll go tonight. There should be some ships coming into port. If we time it right, we can nab a crate or two between inspections, before they take them up to the Administration building."

CHAPTER THIRTY-THREE

"It's not enough. We don't even know if what's in those shipments is useful."

"It's all I can offer you, unless you want to go and raid the city armory yourself."

"Fine. When do the ships come in?"

Georgie examined the broken pocket watch she'd stolen off an officer they'd knocked out when stealing some supplies from the scrap yard. It still kept time, but the face was spider webbed, the glass barely hanging on. "In a couple of hours. Cole, you coming?"

He shook his head. "Someone should stay here, in case there's a raid, or in case..." he trailed off.

"In case I get arrested?" Georgie laughed. "Not likely. These fools don't know what they're up against, and I'm finally getting the hang of this."

* * *

Georgie watched as a ship landed at the docks, the light from the landing gear flashing through the darkness. She furrowed her brow in confusion. "The intel said there would be two ships."

"What intel?"

"One of the dock workers. He lets us know the schedule when he can, but sometimes they make changes, and they never show anyone outside of management the manifests. It's why we never know what's on its way. Could be fresh produce for the Administration building, weapons if we're lucky, paper products if we're not."

Carmen shrugged. "We could still burn the paper, keep people warm."

"True enough, I guess."

"Hey look, there's a second ship. And a third."

"Good. You ready to zip on in after the inspection team leaves the first ship? We won't have long."

"I've been nicking crates off ships longer than you, Payne," Carmen laughed. "I should be asking you if you can even handle this."

"Shut your pie hole."

The loading bay of the first ship opened, and a trio of military police entered with clipboards and guns, kicking each crate to check for stowaways. One waved the others off and paused to get a signature from a crew member before jogging down the ramp and heading to the next ship that had just landed.

"Alright, let's go," Georgie whispered, her hands wrapped around the makeshift bat she'd fashioned from leftover plywood and razor wire. It was no gun, but it was better than nothing, and a good deterrent. "You got the gun?"

"Of course I've got the gun."

Georgie led the way, jogging from one shadow to the next, staying in the relative protection of the port buildings, empty at this time of day, their brick-framed windows dark. Management never had to work overtime. That unpaid privilege was left to the laborers in the factories, and the longer this all went on, the longer she had to run from authorities and hide, the more she knew that Emeline had always been right.

The ship's crew disembarked and gathered at the end of the dock for their personal inspection, which would be completed when the guards returned for a secondary probe of the ship's contents. They'd all be scanned in, their identities verified against the galactic Coalition database and given the same trackers Georgie had worn at her job in the Administration building, to be turned in before they disembarked with a ship full of parts from the factories, to be sent to other bases across the Near Systems.

"We're clear."

Carmen nodded, both hands on the revolver until they jumped into the loading bay, forgoing the ramp. She tucked it into the makeshift holster she'd made of discarded leather belts found in a dumpster, dyed three different colors and hung at her hip. "Do we have time to check the crates?"

"No, just pick one and let's go."

"How about this one?"

"Looks like flour, you can see the dusting at the base." Georgie had spent enough time scrubbing the Administration building kitchens to know that from twenty feet off.

CHAPTER THIRTY-THREE

"Hmm. No good."

"Come on Carmen, let's just take this one. It's closest to the door, and it's heavy. Could be scrap." She nudged the box with her boot, ignoring the pain from the constant tearing blisters from the ill-fitting shoes. Not even extra socks stuffed into the toe had helped.

"Fine. But if it turns out to be sponges or something, you're eating them for breakfast."

"In what universe are sponges this godsdamned heavy?" Georgie croaked, trying to lift one side of the box. The wood scraped at her hands and she dropped it back on the deck, grimacing at the loud echo. "Come on, we need to go." Something inside the box made a strange sound, like an engine misfiring - or a cough. Her stomach clenched.

"Did that box just say something?" Carmen asked, snatching a crowbar from a hook on the wall.

"A stowaway?"

"Could be. We can't just leave them here," she said, wrenching the box open with a loud crack.

"Shh, they'll hear!" Georgie scolded, panic rising in her chest.

"Hey, who's in there?" a guard shouted from the bottom of the ramp.

"Too late," Carmen said, throwing down the crow bar just as a woman in a set of orange coveralls tumbled out of the box.

Georgie felt time stand still when she rolled the body over. Henry's eyes were sunken, her lips cracked. "Henry! Henry, you have to get up, they're going to—"

"Stop right there!" a guard said, pointing a heat gun at Carmen, who had the revolver trained on him in response. "We're taking all three of you in on suspicion of human trafficking!"

A shot rang out in the loading bay, the ringing echo drowning out all other sounds. The guard jerked backwards and dropped the heat gun, clutching at his shoulder. Another one was right behind him, holding an electric prod, blue arcs of electricity sparking from the end. Georgie ran at her with the bat, swinging wildly. She knocked the prod to the ground and advanced on the officer, who held her hands up in surrender.

"Don't hit me with that thing," she screamed. "That's an additional offense! You'll go away for the rest of your life, think of your family!"

Georgie did think of her family, of Emeline trapped in some work camp across the Near Systems, and swung. The bat connected with the officer's knee and she crumpled, dragging herself backwards off the ramp.

"Carmen, we need to get her and go!"

"She's still unconscious!"

Georgie ran back up the ramp and bent to pick up Henry, dropping the bat. More officers would be coming, and soon. She turned to shout to Carmen, but she was gone, vanished. "Carmen!" she screamed. "Where are you?"

There was no response.

"Henry, wake up, I can't run and carry you." She shook her gently, her heart racing in her ears.

"Georgie?" her eyes were shut, her voice weak and croaking. "Georgie, I came back."

"This is your last warning!" a guard shouted.

She shoved Henry back in the crate and leaned the lid loosely against it. She approached the ramp. "I surrender!" she shouted, just before the bullets tore through her skin.

CHAPTER THIRTY-FOUR

"Hey! Get up!" A boot nudged into her side, and Henry groaned.

"Georgie?"

"No. Come on, we have to go or they'll get us, too."

Henry forced her eyes open, feeling dry and scratched. "Who are you?"

"Carmen. We'll talk later, let's go!" she hissed.

Still coated in cleaning solvent, Henry used all her effort to push herself to her feet. Her muscles were a stunningly uncomfortable combination of aching and weak, the result of weeks folded up in that crate, except the rare treat when she'd sneak out in the middle of the night to use the loading bay toilet and scarf down dehydrated food, pilfering any drops of water she could find. She knew that she was severely dehydrated, yet she couldn't manage to convince her mouth to speak the words.

"You okay?" Carmen asked, grabbing her by the elbow. "You'd better be, or you're not making it off this settlement alive. They aren't kind to sick prisoners." She pulled at her, coaxing her down the ramp, checking over her shoulder after every breath. "What's your name?"

"Henry," she slurred, her feet clumsy and stumbling. Gods, her lungs felt like they were on fire, like someone was polishing them clean with sandpaper.

"Alright Henry, I don't know why you're here, but it's clear you're important, so I'm gonna get you back to base."

"Where's Georgie?" she muttered, aware that her words were barely intelligible. "Georgie. Em'line."

Carmen tugged harder on her sleeve. "I know you're sick or something, but I need you to move a little faster so we can sleep in our own beds tonight. Just a little further, up to those buildings, and I can get someone to help carry you back."

Henry's vision swam. Everything hurt, inside and out, and she didn't like that this Carmen woman wouldn't tell her where Georgie was. She was there, and then she was gone - unless it was a hallucination, and she was actually sicker and in more trouble than she thought.

The buildings ahead seemed miles away, and for all Henry's aches and pains, and utter exhaustion, they may as well be on Delta-4. She couldn't hear much other than the blood pounding in her ears, but she did have a vague awareness that guards were running toward them. By the time she convinced her neck to turn her head, Carmen was already firing, bullets flying through the air and whizzing past Henry's face.

One officer went down, and then another. They were screaming, but Henry couldn't hear what. Carmen had one hand on her revolver, and another on Henry's collar, dragging her backward toward the cover of the buildings. Another shot, another officer felled, bright red blooms across their uniform as they clutched their side.

Adrenaline dumped into Henry's veins and cleared her thoughts, made her remember what her legs were for. A brief moment of clarity, for which she would almost certainly pay later. One officer fired a bolt from a heat gun, and she shoved Carmen out of the way and behind an empty building.

"What now?" Henry asked, panting.

"We run for it. If we're lucky, we make it back in time for breakfast."

"And if we aren't lucky?"

Carmen didn't answer, but instead gave her arm a squeeze that Henry knew meant to run, to push her limbs faster than they wanted to go, to desperately try to keep up with her punishing pace, even though she knew it might mean she died on the doorstep of wherever they were headed.

Paved cobblestones turned into roughly hewn gravel, the sound of their footsteps more muffled now than they had been on the street, and deadened by the masses of wood left to rot by contractors years earlier. Finally they arrived at a towering, derelict building, and just before Henry blacked out, she saw curious faces peek out of windows on the tenth floor.

* * *

"Her body is wrecked, Carmen. It's going to take months for her to heal from that solvent inhalation without the proper treatment."

"You better not let her die. Georgie knows— knew her. She might be important to helping us win this thing."

"I can't believe they got her. We were so sure you could get in and out without being caught."

"It's always a risk, Cole."

Henry laid on her back, finally warm, watching light lazily dance across her closed eyelids. The needle in the crook of her arm was taped down, and any movement rattled the bag it was attached to.

"I know it's a risk, but now what are we supposed to do? She was the brains of this whole operation."

She couldn't help but smile at that. Her Georgie, leading the rebellion. Of course she would. She was strong, and smart, and calm in a crisis... her thoughts drifted away from her like clouds on a windy day. She watched them go by, but couldn't grab hold of any of them.

"There are more of us than before. New ones showing up every day. We can still do this. Hell, we got two deserters yesterday, and they brought guns! This one had a small revolver, too!"

"Four guns for thirty people aren't odds I like," Cole said, and sighed. "It would have been good if you'd found some in that shipment. Instead, you only brought back another mouth to feed."

"The gardens are growing, we'll have to cut rations, but—"

"Again? Carmen, people are starving. They're concerned for their children."

"What's the alternative, then? Give ourselves up to get dumped in a work camp and be grateful for one square meal a day?" Something clattered, and Henry wondered if it was a can of food or an old pot. Could be either. Soup would be nice, like that soup Georgie's mother made her. Warm, and nourishing, and... something was nagging at her, but she couldn't place it.

"One of the families is talking about making a run for it. Back to Gamma-3."

Carmen guffawed loudly. "And how the hell are they going to manage that? Smugglers aren't taking people on, not with the current punishments. Even if they were, what would they pay with? Indentured servitude?"

"*She* managed it."

"Yes, but *she* was coming in, not going out, and as I'm sure you can divine from your rusty stethoscope, sir, she barely survived the trip in that crate. She's damned lucky we didn't discover her dessicated corpse on that ship today. Another few days in those clothes and she'd be covered in chemical burns. It's a good thing I had a spare dress to put her in."

"I didn't encourage it, Carmen. I'm just telling you what people have been saying, and that's before I told them that Georgie got shot."

Henry's eyes flew open, the echo of shots firing in her mind. Georgie. Shot. She stifled a sob and sat up, trying to yank the needle out of her arm. She had to see her body. She had to know for sure.

"Whoa, hey there, where do you think you're going?" Cole asked, grabbing her by the shoulders and pushing her back down onto the thin mattress.

"You said she's dead!" Henry sobbed, thrashing at him with her weak, solvent-singed arms. "Georgie, my Georgie, it can't be." She wished that she was dead and gone, too. If she hadn't been in that crate Georgie would have gotten away; now nothing would ever be good again.

"I didn't say she's dead! I said she got shot!"

"Keep it down, both of you," Carmen scolded, draping a thin blanket around Henry's shoulders. "We don't know what happened. She did take at least a couple hits, they dragged her off the dock—"

A sob escaped Henry's throat at the thought of Georgie's unconscious, lifeless body being thrown into the back of a truck, being sent to the incinerator.

CHAPTER THIRTY-FOUR

"Hey! Listen to me. They might have her in a cell at the Administration building, the ones down in the basement," Cole continued. "We don't know for sure."

"She might be bleeding to death in a cell and you're here having a tin of pork and beans? After all she did for all of you? You've got to be kidding me. If you won't get off your asses and save her, then I'll do it myself."

"You're in no condition to go anywhere. We can't just go barging into that place, we don't even have enough weapons for all the gods' sakes!"

"You're sentencing her to death yourselves if you leave her in there without help." She moved to take the needle from her arm again.

"Will you stop? You need fluids, or you'll die. It's a miracle your kidneys didn't give out already." Cole taped the needle to her skin again and gently held her wrist. "Do I need to restrain you?"

"No," Henry huffed.

"We're working on a plan, but it's difficult. We don't have a lot of resources here, and these people aren't soldiers. They're factory workers, merchants, farmers. If we send them into that place, they'll die. It's not a fair fight."

"Then send me."

"Have you completely lost your senses? You're barely alive right now, you need rest, you need to recover before you go off half-cocked or you won't have a shot in hell of even finding her, much less getting her out of there."

Henry pushed herself up onto her elbows again. "I know the building, I worked in there."

"We have the blueprints for the building. Lay back."

"You're sentencing her to death," Henry sobbed. She wanted to cry, but she was so dehydrated that no tears came. "Please, you have no idea what they'll do to her in there if she's even still alive." She stared at Carmen. "Georgie would go after either one of you, and you know it."

Carmen and Cole exchanged a guilty glance.

"I know I'm in no shape, but unless you strap me to this bed, I'll go myself. I'm not leaving her in there. How long has it been already? Hours?"

"You've been asleep almost a whole day," Carmen mumbled.

"A day—no, this isn't right. I demand you let me go. I'll march in their front godsdamned door if I have to, I'm not leaving Georgie to rot in a cell, and if... if she's already gone, then I'm not letting them incinerate her body, either. She's not going to burn with this city's industrial waste. You're both fucking cowards and you're not worth the shit on her boots if you don't rescue her, or at least try!"

"If you think we haven't been trying to make a plan, then you're wrong," Cole snapped. "We care about Georgie as much as you do, and—"

"I doubt that," Henry spat.

"And we're working on a way to get in there without getting everyone else here killed. Would Georgie want that blood on her conscience? The blood of little kids? No, fuck no she wouldn't. And she sure as hell wouldn't want your blood on her hands, either, so how about you sit there for five minutes while we try to figure something out, okay?"

"You've had a whole day to come up with a plan!"

"I liked her better when she was unconscious," Carmen muttered to Cole. "Of course Georgie would have the most irritating woman in the world come looking for her."

"You're damn right, and I'm not going to stop until I hear something that sounds like a credible plan."

Cole adjusted the bag of fluids. "Gods, will you shut up, woman? We're working on it, but it's a sight more challenging with you yammering in my ear." He sighed and sat back on his stool. "That place isn't easy to infiltrate at the best of times, and that raid took every single one of our people on the inside. Jess, Bale, everyone. We're working on it, okay? Now, please, lay back and rest. You'd get about half a block from here in your current state."

"I'm stronger than I look."

"Sure. Lay back."

Despite her protests, it was true that her body was fragile. She could feel it with every ragged breath that burned her lungs, every weighted gesture that pulled at her bones. She was in no condition to be storming the Administration building, especially not with the apparent increased policing measures, but even so, she couldn't leave Georgie to fend for herself. It was

CHAPTER THIRTY-FOUR

unconscionable. She'd come all this way, risked so much, only to be the reason Georgie was in trouble in the first place. It didn't matter whether the pain was from her physical condition or her heartbreak. It was there, regardless.

"What about the ventilation shafts?" Carmen offered. "The ones Georgie escaped through?"

"Too risky. They'll have locked those up by now, surely. They already bricked up the alleyway, remember?"

"It's still a better idea than storming the gates, Cole."

"She'll be under armed guard, and we have three guns. Three guns to protect people here *and* break Georgie out? It's impossible."

Carmen eyed the fire escape at the far end of the room and lifted an eyebrow. "Cole. What if we go in through the roof?"

"What?"

"The walkways get pretty close, it wouldn't take too much to extend them to more or less reach the roof of the Administration building."

"*More or less?*" he asked, incredulous.

"Well, it's not like we could build straight up to the edifice, I think they'd notice that, no matter how high up. We'd have to... jump."

"There are service stairwells you could use to get down to the basement," Henry added. "You wouldn't run into as many people there, hopefully, at least."

"And if nothing else, we can just push them all down the stairs, right?" Cole scoffed. "If you think they don't have MPOs guarding every square foot of that place—"

"That's not a bad idea, you know."

"What?"

"Stairs," Carmen said, jumping up from her chair. "We take a few extra boards, use them to push down and press back anyone we find in the stairwells. We use the boards to barricade the doors on each floor, keeping us isolated from the rest of the building." She pointed to the blueprints on the wall, held up by four small dressmaking pins. "There are only two ways into the basement, that service stairwell, and the elevator. We cut power to the elevator, block off the stairwell, and we're significantly reducing the number of guards we have to deal with."

Cole rubbed his chin thoughtfully. "That's not a bad idea."

"It's a fantastic idea! We should leave right away."

"You're going to stay put," Carmen said, pushing Henry back onto the cot again. "You're a liability. Those walkways are high and narrow, and you can barely sit up straight."

Henry shook her head. "No, it should be me. I'm the reason why she got captured."

"Those guards would have found us, regardless. In fact, if you hadn't been there, Georgie and I both might have been taken. We'd have jumped straight into the next ship and straight into a pile of MPOs." Carmen patted her on the arm. "We'll bring her back for you. This is a good plan. At least, it's the best one we've got."

"You can't just expect me to sit here and do nothing," Henry protested.

"I can, and I will. If you don't relax and get some rest, you won't be of any use to us when the time comes." Carmen stood and switched on the radio, her skirts rustling gently. "Now hush, it's time for the broadcast."

"Good evening, I'm Delia Dodson. Yesterday, our brave Military Police captured one of the main agitators that have been causing delays to the proposed updates to Skelm's infrastructure. Georgie Payne was apprehended on the docks, in the process of stealing food rations destined for the most needy of our city."

"I see the smear job continues," Cole muttered.

"That's no surprise, but didn't you hear what she said? Infrastructure. Previous reports never mentioned anything like that."

"How could that be important?"

"Now that the ringleader has been removed from the group of violent extremists, updates to infrastructure can continue. Planned improvements include repairing cobblestones near the Administration building, an upgraded inspection unit at the docks, and refurbishments on several derelict buildings. The buildings will be gutted and revitalized, ready for investment in our up and coming settlement."

CHAPTER THIRTY-FOUR

Carmen slapped the wall. "Fuck."

"You can say that again. Even if it's not this building, we'll end up with swarms of construction teams in the area. It's very unlikely we wouldn't be noticed."

"Do you think Delia is trying to warn us?"

"Maybe," Cole said, his brow furrowed in distress. "Or it might be a trap to get us out in the open. Make us flee, as a group. We'd be too obvious now with all the extra patrols, not to mention the prices on our heads. Allemande doesn't want this situation getting any more out of hand."

"Back to our top story this evening. Georgie Payne, former Coalition employee, entrusted with working in the Administration building, arrested for treason and armed insurrection. She is being held under guard in a top secret location until her trial and subsequent sentencing. Allied rebels are warned that any attempt to free her will result in a shoot-to-kill order across the city. They are strongly advised to turn themselves in at their nearest MPO watchtower in order to receive leniency for them and their families."

"That sounds like an invitation to me, what do you think?" Carmen laughed.

Cole nodded. "They may as well have sent a car for us."

A doorknob on one of the lower floors jiggled noisily, the sound of shuffling boots on pavement outside. The door exploded open, the sound like a cannon. When Henry sat up, she barely had enough time to roll off the cot before bullets began whizzing by her head.

CHAPTER THIRTY-FIVE

Georgie grimaced, her wrists chained to the table, and her ankles chained to the intentionally uncomfortable metal chair. The bandages across the back of her thigh continued to chafe against the seat, the bullet wound beneath throbbing angrily. She'd be lucky if she made it out of here at all, but at this point an infection was a foregone conclusion. They'd also gotten her through the left arm, but at least that wasn't rubbing against anything. Not yet, anyway.

The broken clock on the wall was stopped at six-thirteen. In the windowless room, there was no way of knowing if it was morning or evening, and the arm of the clock ticking, but never moving, only served to illustrate that. They'd taken the bullets out of her, no anesthesia of course, but the pain knocked her out cold. It could be hours or days after they arrested her.

With a loud creak, the imposing steel door swung open on worn hinges to reveal Governor Allemande, her black umbrella stowed under her arm. Georgie's heart seized in her chest. This was probably going to be how she died, screaming in the Administration building basement.

"Ms. Payne." It wasn't a question, it was a statement, made from behind cold, lifeless icy green eyes. Allemande sat in the chair opposite, plushly upholstered with a thick, richly dyed wool that extended over the seat all the way up the high back.

"Inspector."

Allemande's eyes narrowed. "Governor."

CHAPTER THIRTY-FIVE

"Yes, of course. How silly of me to forget."

"Ms. Payne, I'm afraid you've put me into a terribly awkward position. I thought we were allies, you and I. I was under the impression that you were a woman with aspirations, with a deep desire to provide for your family. I offered you an opportunity, and you squandered it."

"You told Erin to spy on me."

"Don't be naïve, dear girl, every ally has to be appropriately vetted. I'd hoped that you both would grow into assets for the Coalition, strong leaders to bring this city into the here and now, remind everyone in the sector that Skelm is not to be underestimated. Sadly, you both proved to be terrible disappointments."

"Both?"

"Let's not discuss the career trajectory of your peers, Ms. Payne, it's unseemly."

Georgie clamped her jaw shut, her teeth grinding in protest. Now would be a great time for a rescue, but the ten guards outside the door would keep that a fantasy.

"Now, let's discuss your collaborators, shall we?" The governor flipped open a file and dipped her pen into a well of jet-black ink. "Start at the beginning. When were you first radicalized against our great empire?"

"I don't have any collaborators."

"Don't be coy, Ms. Payne. I have been monitoring the wires and all traffic in and out for months. I know that you have people helping you in this little insurrection of yours, ill-fated though it may be. Now, as I said, let's start at the beginning. When did you first have the thought to undermine the progression of this city?"

The pen glinted even in the dim yellow light, a razor blade welded to the underside of the nib. Georgie swallowed hard. She wouldn't last through much torture in her current state. A fever from the infection was already starting to settle in, blurring her consciousness at the edges.

"Ms. Payne?"

"When my father died."

Governor Allemande raised an eyebrow. "And why is that?"

"He was killed on the docks for talk of unionizing."

"Unions are dangerous rhetoric, surely you know that. Unions halt progress! Where would the Coalition be without the constant striving for more efficiency?" She laughed, a joyless, empty laugh. "Probably stuck on Gamma-3!" She made a note in the file, her laughter gone as quickly as it had arrived. "So you've been planning to overthrow the government since childhood?"

"No."

"Ms. Payne, I'm in no mood for games."

"You asked when I first felt anger towards the city. That's when. He was taken from us. They said he went missing, that he boarded a ship and left us here."

"Maybe he did."

Georgie shook her head. "They lied. I'm in no mood for games, either, Inspector."

"Governor." She crossed out something in the file and made a note in tiny, florid writing. "Now, your collaborators."

"I told you, I don't have any collaborators. Any misdeeds that have been done were done by me alone. I have always worked alone."

"That's simply untrue, isn't it? Eyewitness accounts at the docks report two other people with you who escaped."

"I don't know who they are. Maybe one of the many starving people who live in your tenements, Governor, desperate for some food to feed their families."

Allemande dipped the pen into the ink and hesitated. "At this juncture, Ms. Payne, I would encourage honesty. Wheels are already in motion that I cannot stop, but they could be... directed, if need be."

"Wheels?"

"We know that you were staying in one of the derelict buildings. We also know that the people who were missing after the union raid are still missing, and it stands to reason that you were all inhabiting the same location."

Georgie's breath caught in her throat. "I—I don't know what you're talking about."

CHAPTER THIRTY-FIVE

"If you're willing to throw your friends to the dogs, then let's enter into a discussion about your sister."

"Emeline... where have you taken her?"

"She is being processed at a center not far from here. The judge in charge of her case has sent me a wire transmission asking for my guidance in her sentencing. They've asked if she should be allowed leniency."

"My sister never did anything wrong."

Allemande tilted her head, a small, patronizing smirk playing at the edges of her lips. "Emeline Payne stands accused of treason. As we've already agreed, it is treasonous to stand in the way of progress, to prevent others the opportunity to work hard and build a brighter future for everyone in the Coalition." She spread papers out across the desk and considered them. "Though, by my estimation, and it is mine that the judge is interested in, being the governor of this fine settlement and all, your sister might qualify for leniency if you were to cooperate."

"I don't know any collaborators," Georgie said again, but this time her voice wavered with uncertainty.

"If you don't cooperate, however, you will force my hand into guiding the judge to a harsher sentencing. After all, traitors need to be publicly punished, as a deterrent for all the other would-be rats across the Near Systems. A public execution usually does the trick."

"You can't do that!"

"*I'm* not doing anything. It's *you* who decides your sister's fate. All I'm doing is facilitating the judge's decision. Emeline's future is in your hands."

Bile burned at the back of Georgie's throat. If her stomach wasn't so empty, she would have vomited all over the table. "And what... if I do? Cooperate?"

"Well, then," Allemande said, a smile spreading across her face, "we would have a civilized discussion about her fate. If you provide me with the right kind of information, and enough names, Emeline would be placed into a Coalition-sponsored reeducation center. She'd have access to a quality education and a promising future, if she passes her exams, which I'm sure she will, she's a bright girl."

"How do I know you won't throw her into a work camp the second you have what you want?"

The governor rankled, her plastered on grin fading from her face. "Ms. Payne, I am a woman of my word. I am not in the habit of wasting the potential of any Coalition citizen. If you cooperate, she will be immediately transferred to a settlement with a top notch boarding school."

"You're not leaving me with any kind of choice."

"And yet, a choice you have. Assist the Coalition in forward movement, or send your sister to her death."

"Fine. I'll talk."

"Excellent. Now, surely you understand, if we are... interrupted... before the conclusion of our meeting, any deal will be null and void. Are we clear?"

"Crystal." Suddenly, Georgie felt herself willing her friends to stay away. Now was no time for a rescue.

* * *

"Run!" Carmen shouted.

Henry's legs wouldn't move. She was rooted to the spot, fear flooding into her muscles like a dead weight. She tried to shove her way under the cot to get away from the bullets flying in both directions. It seemed those new recruits had showed up with their guns. Everyone was screaming.

"Put the guns down!" one of the military police officers yelled. "Get on the ground!"

"Fuck you!" someone bellowed back, before tossing a smoke bomb on the ground. Black clouds billowed out, filling Henry's lungs and burning her eyes.

"Come on!" Cole hissed, and pulled on Henry's arm. "We have to get out of here!"

They stumbled through the fog, feeling their way along the wall, aiming for the fire escape. Henry's boot caught on something soft, and she could

CHAPTER THIRTY-FIVE

only hope that it wasn't a person. The old, abandoned building was a war zone, the sparks of live ammunition glinting through the dust. Henry's hands found the fire escape, and she pulled herself through the window and out onto the metal platform, gasping for air.

"Where's Carmen?" she asked, coughing.

"She'll be fine. Come on, we have to go."

"*Where?*"

"If we have one chance in hell of surviving this, we need Georgie."

"But Carmen said we'd have to build—"

"Fuck building a scaffold, there's no time now. We're gonna waltz right through the front fuckin' door."

"That's a great way to get ourselves killed."

Cole grabbed her arm and pulled her behind a solid partition just as a military steamcar screeched past. "You hear that? We don't have time for subtlety. Those smoke bombs will hold them off just long enough to get the others into the adjacent building, we can hold them off from there. There's a barricade."

"I have an idea," Henry said with a grimace, pulling herself up to her full height. "Once a respected Coalition scientist, always a respected Coalition scientist."

"Great. Let's go."

They wound their way through the narrow streets, scuttling from one shadow to the next. Patrols were everywhere, leaning against the smog coated brick buildings with half-smoked cigarettes and taking brazen swigs from flasks. Rules were rules, but only for some. The Administration building gleamed up on the hill, the only building in the city that didn't look like it had endured years of acid rain and pollution. Lights sparkled from behind the tinted windows that spanned every outer wall. Once an exciting prospective temporary assignment, she now dreaded walking through those doors.

"I can't go with you," Cole whispered.

"I thought you said—"

"Someone has to circle back and make sure any stragglers get into the other building."

Henry grimaced. "Fine. If I don't die or get arrested, I'll come back with Georgie, and hopefully some kind of plan. They know where we are now, Cole. We can't exactly go back into hiding."

"Yeah. Which is why you'd better not die or get arrested." He grabbed Henry's hands and squeezed gently. "I never thought we'd end up against the barricade with three guns and a bunch of refugees." He glanced around the corner and nodded. "Coast is clear. Good luck."

After he faded into the darkness, Henry dusted off her borrowed yellow dress, not that it did anything to make her look more presentable. It was too big, and hung off her shoulders, awkwardly cinched at the waist with a dirty ribbon. She was never much of an actor, but she was about to have the performance of a lifetime. She strode around the corner, trying to ignore the heaviness in her limbs and the desperate exhaustion that pulled at the corners of her mind.

"Hey, you. We need to see some kind of ID," an MPO barked as she approached the front gates.

"I'm a visiting scientist, I've just rotated in from Gamma-3," she replied confidently. "My chip hasn't been calibrated yet." Her Coalition chip had been deactivated months ago, when she first boarded the Cricket, and the grey market chip from the vendor at the trading beacon sure as hell wasn't going to give her access to the Administration building.

"I don't give a shit where you just rotated in from," the other MPO said, grabbing her arm and pressing a small, snub-nosed gun to her skin. The scanner chirped and blinked green, much to Henry's amazement. "Our apologies," the MPO said, gesturing for her to enter the building. "We've had some issues lately with some scum wandering the streets. Best not to be out after dark, okay? Someone will think you're up to something."

"Sure thing. Thanks." She tried not to look as weak as she was when she sidled past them with a broad smile and pushed her way into the turnstile, her stained skirts brushing against the glass with a soft whisper. The building was quiet at this time in the evening, with only a few janitors pushing their carts through the halls and a straggler scientist or two heading

CHAPTER THIRTY-FIVE

for the doors with weary, tired eyes.

Henry found herself searching every janitor's face for Georgie, despite knowing that the love of her life had left her post weeks, if not months, ago. She didn't know much other than what she'd overheard at the refugee rebel camp. She also had no idea where the service access stairwell was, even though she'd seen it on the blueprints. Somewhere near the back of the building? Sure, that made sense.

"Good evening, ma'am," the wire operator said as she passed. "Late night?"

"The work never stops!" Henry answered cheerfully.

"The governor has mandated that everyone working after hours signs in," the operator said, pushing a clipboard across the desk. "It's just for the paperwork."

Henry swallowed hard. "Paperwork?"

"Yeah, the forms—hey, weren't you here a few months back?"

"Er..."

"It's no problem, I just have to check your name against the ship manifest."

"Ship?" Henry repeated.

"Yeah, it's just to prevent folks from being where they shouldn't. Governor Allemande's orders!" she chirped. "It will just take a minute."

"I have an experiment that's about to fail if I don't get back in there—"

The operator stood, her glare steely. "Ma'am, I'm going to need you to sign in. Right now."

* * *

Governor Allemande tapped her pen lightly against the desk. *Tap, tap, tap.* "Tell me, Ms. Payne, how many other buildings are being utilized as rebel quarters in this city?"

"No others." Georgie wanted the ground to open up and swallow her whole. She'd sold out her friends, the people who had stood by her side, in order to save her sister. She was lower than low. She was less than scum. A monster, backed into a corner.

"Are you sure about that?"

Their barricade remained a secret, at least, for now. She willed them to know what was coming, to evacuate, to get everyone to safety. Her stomach turned at the thought of armed military police raiding the building, threatening the families sheltered there. How many would suffer because she was so weak, so easily manipulated? "Yes. I'm sure."

"If I discover that you have not been forthcoming—"

"I'm not lying."

Governor Allemande made a note in the file. "Good. Now, tell me, who drugged the officers the day of the boundary line cleanup?"

"I did."

"Hmm. Well, that's unfortunate."

"Erin knew it was me."

"Yes, she reported as such very early on in her investigation. Sadly, she was unable to provide me the proof or the confession that I asked her for."

Georgie shifted in her seat uncomfortably, the dull throb in her thigh rapidly becoming a sharp stab. She shivered. "Where's Erin?"

"Erin has been... reassigned."

"Did you kill her, too?"

"Don't speak to me in that tone," Allemande said, snapping the file shut. "I am the governor of this city, and I demand to be treated as such."

"Did you?"

"Erin was not suitable for management. She gave a valiant effort, but she was undisciplined. She was sloppy. If she had done what I told her to do, in the manner I suggested, you would have been apprehended weeks ago, and that silly farce of a rebellion would never have been the thorn in my side that it's become. No, Erin was put back in the factories. She is far better at manual labor than anything that requires skill and intelligence."

Georgie resisted the urge to spit at Allemande for her treachery.

"How did you drug the guards?" the governor asked.

"Sedatives."

"Why?"

CHAPTER THIRTY-FIVE

"To..." Georgie trailed off. She'd worked so hard to install the comms device, and it still hadn't allowed them to send messages to rebel settlements. "To install a chip to allow us to bypass the wire desk and send messages off-world."

"But you didn't," Allemande said, tapping her pen against the side of the desk. *Tap, tap, tap.* The sound was driving Georgie mad. "Why not?"

"We knew you were listening."

"Indeed I was. Smart girl. You see, Georgina, if you had just stayed the course, you might have escaped the doldrums of your life, created something better for your mother and your sisters. Instead, you were lazy, you took the easy way out, and now, here we are."

Georgie gritted her teeth in response. The pain was becoming more difficult to bear. She shivered again. *Tap, tap.*

"You received a message here, before you left. What did it say?"

Henry's note. "It was a message from a distant relative, saying someone had sadly passed on."

"I told you," Allemande said, still tapping the pen, "not to lie to me."

"It was nothing."

"I'll decide what's nothing. Tell me how to break the code!"

Georgie laughed. "What code?" She was starting to lose her composure, between the pain and the almost certain infection that was settling into her wounds. She was getting careless.

Silver flashed across the table and sliced into Georgie's arm. She tried to recoil but couldn't, her wrists held fast in cuffs chained to the table. Scarlet blossoms turned into rivulets that dripped down her dirty skin. She didn't scream. She didn't want to give her the satisfaction. "It was a love note."

"A—who?"

"A lover from a long time ago, when we were young. She tried to get into contact."

"Why?"

Georgie shrugged as much as she could with her wrists chained. "I don't know. I didn't respond, as you well know."

"Was it Evie Anderson?"

"Who?" Georgie asked, but hearing her friend's name in the governor's mouth was unsettling.

"How long have you had contact with the crew of the vessel called the Cricket?"

Her mouth went dry, her tongue like week-old bread. "I don't know what you're talking about."

"Ms. Payne, did you know that I am trained in the art of information extraction?"

"I assumed most inspectors were."

"Hmm, indeed, but did you also realize that I have the ability to detect lies by observing the subtleties in human expression?"

"Governor, if you tell me what information you want, instead of dancing at the edges of my love life, we might be able to help each other more effectively."

Allemande sat back in her chair. "Quite."

"I'm sure the roster of women who have been in my bed isn't of much help to the Coalition. What do you really want to know?" She'd already betrayed her friends. She didn't want to betray Henry, too. It was more than she could bear.

"Where is the Cricket? Where does it make berth?"

"I can tell you with complete honesty that I don't know. My time on their ship was brief."

The governor's face clouded with rage, a deep scarlet that spread from the small flash of neck above her high-collar buttoned shirt across her pale skin and sharp cheekbones. "They were *here*? In Skelm? How recently?"

"The night Governor Ralph Baker disappeared."

"I know that, you insolent fool, I had Evie Anderson within my grasp until she... I had her, and then she cheated the rules of engagement."

"I have not seen the crew or the ship since that night," Georgie lied.

Allemande slammed her palms against the table and leaned across, her face an inch away, so close that Georgie could smell the cloying perfume. "Did you help them escape?" the governor demanded, searching Georgie's face for the truth.

CHAPTER THIRTY-FIVE

"Yes." There was no point in lying about that, anyway. Georgie was already going to wind up in a work camp, even if she managed to earn a better life for Emeline. The more she could implicate herself, the less she'd have to shine a light on anyone else.

"I knew it," Allemande spat. "I knew that the explosion had been artificially planted. Boiler overload, pah! The engineers here are as incompetent as they are filthy."

Jess and Bale had covered it up. Where were they now? "I made the crew promise to get my family out."

"Why would you want to leave? Where would you go?"

Georgie blinked. "Governor, people here are starving. The work that's offered to them is back breaking and dangerous. People want a better life for their families, for their children."

"Rebel settlements are no more than dusty, uncivilized rat nests. Why would anyone prefer that to earning a living with the Coalition?"

"Freedom."

"Freedom!" Allemande scoffed. "Freedom to die of a preventable illness, maybe. Freedom to be shot down by the military for trespassing, freedom to suffocate once the terraformers fail—" she stopped abruptly, and smoothed an invisible hair back into her severe bun. "You have made grave errors, Ms. Payne. I'm afraid you've not given me enough information yet to secure your sister's future." She tapped the pen against the desk again, and Georgie flinched. Allemande smiled. "Let's continue."

CHAPTER THIRTY-SIX

"Ma'am?" the wire desk operator prompted again.

Anxious sweat prickled in Henry's armpits. "Uh, sure, sure," she said, approaching the desk. Maybe she could knock the operator out. Or maybe she'd just make a run for it, which would have been easier if she knew exactly where the access stairwell was. She signed her name on the sheet with a flourish.

The operator squinted at the form. "Frank Orzo?"

"It's a family name." The name of one of the ship operators, actually.

"Hmm, I see you on the manifest, but you're not slated as a visiting scientist."

Henry shrugged. "Must be an error. Now if you'll excuse me, I really do have to check on that experiment—"

"I'm afraid you'll have to wait here for confirmation. Rules are rules."

"All due respect, but this experiment comes directly from Governor Allemande. I can assure you that neither of us want to be in the firing line if it fails due to my tardiness in the lab. This research is impossibly important for the forward motion of the Coalition, and the governor said it's to continue unabated, with no undue restrictions or delays."

The wire operator wavered. "I'll have to follow that up, you realize."

"That's fine," Henry said with the biggest smile she could muster. "I look forward to signing in again." She turned on her heel and marched toward the lab wing. The access stairwell wasn't located there, but the damn operator

CHAPTER THIRTY-SIX

would definitely know something was up if she didn't at least seem like she was heading in the right direction. She was so very tired. Everything ached. Everything hurt. She had to find Georgie. She had to find some way to help the refugees and the rebels at the barricade, before they were overrun. Four guns wouldn't last long, and they'd have no chance if additional units were called in.

Her exhausted legs carried her to her old lab, the small, cramped one at the end of the corridor that she'd shared with Roger. It was empty this time of night, a small blessing. Mercifully, the door was unlocked. Whatever was being researched during this rotation wasn't a high priority, if it was assigned to a team at all. She pushed the heavy steel door open and sat on the rusted stool in the corner, her worn linen skirts snagging on the flakes of yellow and purple paint. She needed a plan. The guards would come looking for her the second the operator realized her story was a lie.

The ventilation shafts had been welded shut. That idea was out, even if she had managed to drag herself through the ducts, she would have no idea where she was headed. She couldn't make a run for it. She'd be seen, and in her condition she wouldn't be fast enough to evade the guards. She wished Roger was here. He always had good ideas, even if most of the time it involved something reckless and stupid.

A smile spread across her face. Reckless and stupid was exactly what she needed. Henry turned on the bunsen burner and began to feed the flames sheets of notes torn from the scuffed leather notebook on the table. She mentally apologized to whoever's research she was destroying, but this was an emergency. Smoke began to fill the room, and her already charred lungs burned. She dropped a few scraps of burning paper around the table and left the lab, jamming the lock from the inside before she closed the door. Fire caught on the side of a cabinet - there wasn't much time, now.

With a mighty yank, she rang the fire alarm bell. "Chemical fire!" she shouted. "In the lab!" The clanging of bells began to sound all across the west wing as other late-working scientists and night guards spread the alarm. She might have a chance, now. The wire operator had already left her desk to start evacuation of the building, and Henry headed for the back atrium as fast as she could with her worn, broken body.

The service stairwell was hidden behind a statue of the late Governor Ralph Baker, his granite form powerless to stop her subterfuge. The steps down into the basement were mercifully empty, all available guards heading towards the fire to put it out, or to escort people outside. Henry smirked. The fire would burn itself out in a while. That chemical cabinet was empty.

The basement was brightly lit, every inch bathed in sickly yellow light that emanated from the fixtures on the walls. There were no guards, but the corridors were like labyrinths. One room after another, all empty save for a table and two chairs. With every empty room, her heart sank deeper into her chest. She tried to push away the thought that her beloved might already be dead, her body sent to the waste incinerator like garbage. A sob choked in her throat, and she squeezed her eyes shut in desperate hope. It was the last room of the last corridor. She pushed open the door and gasped.

"Georgie!" she whispered, rushing to her side. Thank the gods, she was alive. "Georgie, I'm so glad I found you, I was so scared I'd find you dead!"

"Henry! You can't be here, Allemande will be back any second, and the guards—"

"They're occupied. Come on, let's get you out of here."

"No, no! You can't. You have to go!"

Henry reached out and caressed her face. "You're burning up. We have to get you some medicine, we—"

"They have Emeline."

"*What?*"

"They have her, Hen, and they'll kill her unless I cooperate."

"We'll find a way to get her out, I promise—"

"Henry, you have to listen to me. Allemande has the final say whether the judge sentences my sister to death or lets her be sent to a reeducation facility. If you spring me from this room, she'll make sure my sister is dead."

"You won't last in here! We have to go, the others—"

"I know, I betrayed them. I had to, for Em."

"Then it's your responsibility now to help them. They're at the barricade, Georgie."

CHAPTER THIRTY-SIX

"No."

"Yes. And they need you. Those people need you."

Georgie shook her head. "My sister needs me."

"*I* need you, too. We can figure out how to get Emeline out, but you can't do that if you're dead. None of us can."

"Henry, I missed you so much."

"I missed you, too. There's time for that later, come on." Henry pulled a set of keys from the wall next to the door and began trying each one in the padlocks at Georgie's wrists and ankles. One popped open, and she moved to the next.

"My mother, and Lucy—"

"Are both doing fine. Better than fine." Another lock opened.

"We tried, we tried so hard to get word out, but the signal..."

"That doesn't matter now. I'm here. We'll get help. We have to, we can't keep hiding. The city isn't big enough, and Allemande is on a rampage."

Georgie grimaced. "She's out for blood."

Finally, the last lock fell to the ground. "Come on, we have to go. That fire isn't going to burn forever."

"The governor isn't going to let us go without a fight."

"We have to get out of here first, and I don't think I can handle the stairs going back up. Neither of us are in good shape."

"We'll take the elevator, come on. It will take us to the front gate."

They hobbled, together, towards the elevator gate. Despite the danger and the pain in her body, Henry wrapped her arm around Georgie's waist and her heart thudded with happiness. Even if they died now, at least they were together. The gate slid open easily, the gilded cage sparkling in the strange warm light. Georgie pulled on the lever and the elevator began to rise. "I've always wanted to ride this thing," she said, smiling.

When they reached their floor, Henry poked her head out and looked both ways. "Coast is clear, let's go."

"I'll send the elevator up, will be harder for them to figure out where we went."

The pulleys glided the cage skyward, leaving a dark, gaping chasm of a shaft back down to the basement. "We need guns."

"The munitions depot is across the city. We'd never get there and back without a steamcar." Georgie smirked. "But I do know where we can get a hell of a lot of explosives." She limped to the wall and leaned against it to catch her breath. "That ship you came in on, it—"

"*YOU.*"

Henry whipped around and came face to face with Governor Allemande. "Oh, shit."

"The scientist, well that's very convenient, isn't it?" she hissed. "Two treasonous rats for the price of one. I suppose it's no mystery now who was sending those love notes, is it, Ms. Payne?"

"I assume this realization won't *elevate* your opinion of me, will it?" Georgie asked, looking at the governor.

"What the hell are you talking about?"

Realization washed over Henry. She grabbed the governor by the shoulders and, using all of her body weight, flung her past the open gate down the elevator shaft. She stumbled away, not wanting to wait to hear the consequences. "We need to get a message to the Cricket. It doesn't matter if they hear us now, we need help."

Georgie nodded. "We have a radio back at base—"

"It's too risky. We need something right now." She looked back into the building. "The wire desk. Let's go."

The main atrium, still empty with guards attending to the fire in the locked up lab, wouldn't be empty for long. They'd have to hurry. "Watch my back," Henry said, reaching behind the desk. "Calling all frequencies, this is an S.O.S from Henrietta Weaver, stationed in Skelm, looking for the crew of the Cricket. Captain Violet, do you read?"

"They could be planets away," Georgie said. "They might not be able to help us."

"We have to try." She took a deep breath and called again. "Calling the Cricket, this is Henry Weaver looking for immediate assistance."

"Hey, this is a restricted line," a voice shouted back.

"Fuck off!" Henry yelled. "Calling Captain Violet of the Cricket, we need

CHAPTER THIRTY-SIX

immediate assistance—"

"We have to go," Georgie warned. "The guards are coming back."

"Shit."

"Time to steal a steamcar. Again."

"Again, what do you mean *again*?"

"Come on! We have to go!"

"Stop!" a guard yelled from the entrance of the far corridor. "Stop, or we shoot!" He held up a gun, aiming with one eye shut.

"You don't have to do this!" Henry shouted back. "You can join us! The revolution is starting!"

"Fuck off with your rebellion, scum! We deal in law and order here!" A shot rang out, and Henry and Georgie ducked below the desk just as the bullet lodged in the wood behind where they'd been standing. "Come on out, and we might let you live!"

"What are we going to do now?" Henry hissed. "They've got us pinned!"

"Maybe we can make a run—" an explosion shook the walls of the Administration building. "What the hell was that?"

"It's possible that the fire I started didn't exactly burn itself out."

"You're a madwoman," Georgie said with half a smirk. "But you're a fucking genius."

Another explosion rumbled in the west wing, and dust shook from the purifying algae chandeliers that hung from the high ceilings.

"What's going on down there?" the guard shouted into his radio, the static thick and distracting. "What do you mean, it's out of control?"

"What was in that lab?" Georgie asked.

"Nothing that should cause this kind of—wait. What's that cleaning solvent made of?"

"Caustic soda."

"Georgie, we need to get out of here. *Now*. It's reacted with the metal and created hydrogen gas."

"You lit a fire with solvent in the room? Are you trying to get everyone killed? Gods, Henry, and here I thought you were some genius scientist!"

"Yeah, turns out I'm more of a pyromaniac."

The guard held firm. "You'll die if you stay there, and you'll die if you run, scum! The only way out of here alive is in cuffs!"

When the chandelier fell from the ceiling and exploded into a shower of crystal and the thick, earthy sludge of the algae, they ran as fast as their broken bodies would carry them, their hands clasped together.

* * *

Bullets whizzed past their heads as they stumbled out of the building and into the clear night. Georgie's head swam with fever, and she wouldn't have been surprised if it was all a dream, and she was still chained up in that basement, hallucinating. She'd seen people imagine all kinds of nonsense once the illnesses took over. "We have to get back to the others."

"We don't have any guns, they took my revolver! What use will we be?"

"I still have one container of solvent, that's better than nothing."

"And what, we dump it on them and hope for the best? Try to back them into a room with it, and light a match?" Henry asked, pulling them both behind a marble pillar. Another explosion rocked the building, and there were more crashes of chandeliers falling to the floor.

"Setting shit on fire seems to have worked for you tonight."

"How far is the armory from here?"

Georgie shook her head. "Too far. We'd never make it on foot. Not in our conditions." She scanned the courtyard and found it empty. "Damn. No steamcars. No steambikes either, although I doubt I'd be able to keep one upright with this leg, anyway." The bullets had stopped, at least for now. Small mercies. "We can't leave them on their own. The fire up here might draw some MPOs away, but they're not about to give up on fighting everyone else. Not when Allemande put that price on our heads." She rubbed her arms. "Bitch deserved what she got."

Henry flinched. "I guess we can assume the Cricket isn't coming. They didn't hear us."

"No, probably not."

"Then we need *guns*, Georgie. We can't win this thing with fires and pot shots."

"How about a *really big* fire?"

"And what would that accomplish, exactly?"

Georgie shrugged. "A distraction, if nothing else. We can't get everyone out with this much heat on us. Maybe if they think we're dead..." she trailed off.

"You are fucking brilliant," Henry said, and kissed her full on the mouth. "The solvent at the docks."

"Can you make it?"

"I think the bigger question here is, can *you*? Gods, you got *shot*! Twice!"

"I think I can run on adrenaline for a little while longer. No guarantees, Hen. You might have to carry me to safety."

Henry clasped her hand. "If I have to drag you from the flames myself, I will. I'm not losing you again."

"We have to get off the main streets. MPOs will be heading up this way to deal with the fire."

They stumbled through the cobblestone alleys, Georgie limping with her infected leg, which throbbed and pulsed with every step, and Henry stopping every few steps to catch her breath. Georgie was surprised that she'd survived in that crate as a stowaway at all, much less having the strength to break into the Administration building. There were fewer patrols on the streets, most being dispatched to stop the explosions at the top of the hill. As it turned out, setting shit on fire was actually a pretty solid plan.

The docks were bustling as though the crown jewel of Skelm wasn't on fire, as though there wasn't a small band of refugees and rebels gearing up to stage a revolution at the barricade. Commerce always continued. The show of credits and profits must always go on, no matter the cost. Ships landed, guards boarded to inspect their imports, other ships departed. A never-ending chorus of profits, while people starved in dusty tenements.

"Come on," Georgie whispered. "It's that one, on the end." They crept up to the ramp.

"The door is shut. What now?"

"Those of us on the ground have gotten hold of some tricks." She smacked the lock panel three times and kicked the latch, and the door swung out just a tiny bit.

"That's ridiculous. What kind of shoddy security protocol is that?"

"Only works on the older ships. Lucky for you, you picked a real shitty one to hide out on."

Henry groaned as she lifted the door enough for the hydraulics to snap into gear and carry it the rest of the way. Georgie's arm throbbed just thinking about lifting anything heavy, and yet here they were about to either be in for the fight of their lives, or attempt to smuggle a few dozen people off-world. The odds weren't good.

"Grab as much as you can carry. We need it to look convincing. Or it needs to be enough to blow half their forces' guns to smithereens."

"How are we going to get people out?"

"Carmen and I dug an emergency escape hatch, it was the first thing we did. It's going to be hell and a half getting everyone out without a patrol noticing, but we have to try."

"Where will we go?"

Georgie heaved a sigh as she loaded her pockets with bags of solvent. "Another building? We'll just have to keep buying time. If they think we're all dead, we'll at least have until the next birdbrain gets caught stealing shit off a ship."

"A foolproof plan. Just don't get caught."

"It's my life motto, I'll have you know." Georgie tugged at the drawstrings on her trousers to pull them tighter with the weight of her pockets weighing them down. "I really missed you, Henry. There were some days I thought I couldn't carry on, especially once they took Emeline." Even saying her sister's name made her heart ache. "I kept hoping that I just... wouldn't wake up."

"From now on, you wake up next to me. No exceptions."

"That will make it all the easier. Now come on, we have a building to blow up. You ready?"

Henry peered over the stack of solvent boxes in her arms. "As ready as I'll ever be," she gasped. "Let's go set fire to stuff."

CHAPTER THIRTY-SIX

"Too bad we don't have a wagon or something." Georgie didn't like that rasp in Henry's throat. She needed real treatments for her lungs. She'd seen enough people from the factories drown on dry land to know the signs.

"I'm fine, let's go!"

Georgie dumped the remaining bags from the crate onto the metal grate flooring of the ship's loading bay, and pulled a match from the inside of her boot and struck it against the sole, dropping it into the crate along with the wrappings from the solvent. She smacked the emergency close button on the wall and sidled out underneath the door. "That ought to do it. Come on, it's not far from here." The warm glow of the street lamps pooled on the street below, casting long shadows behind the trees that hid the back entrances of office buildings and warehouses. Her heart pounded in her chest with every pained step; she was sure that a military police officer was going to leap out of a dark doorway any second and drag them both back to the Administration building basement. Or worse, send them straight to the incinerator.

The back hatch of the secondary building was concealed with vines and crumbled old bricks. Georgie kicked them away and wrenched open the gate. "It's me!" she hissed down the uneven stairs molded from dirt and sod. "Don't shoot!"

"GEORGIE!" Carmen bellowed, pulling her down to safety. "Gods almighty, we thought you were both dead. What the hell is going on? Why are there explosions at the Administration building?" She cocked her head. "And why in all the gods' names do you have piles of cleaning solvent?"

"We have a plan. We're going to fake our deaths."

"Have you completely lost your marbles? Where would we go? What about the gardens?"

"We can rebuild."

Carmen scoffed and shook her head. "It's better than the plan of hiding and taking pot shots that we've got now," she sighed. "People are terrified. And you look like hell."

"I feel like it, too," Georgie admitted, trying not to focus on the growing pain in her thigh. At least her arm seemed less inflamed.

"Oh, it's so good to see you alive," Carmen said, wrapping her in a hug. "And you, too," she said to Henry, embracing her, too. "When Cole said he left you on your own, I nearly punched his lights out. It's a damned miracle you made it out in one piece."

"Barely," Henry muttered.

"Tell everyone to start gathering near this exit. Once the fire catches, we won't have long to get them out before the blast."

Carmen nodded. "What about patrols?"

"We took care of that," Georgie said with a grin. "Let's just say, we created another diversion for them."

Henry took a deep, ragged breath and smirked. "This whole damned city is going to be on fire."

CHAPTER THIRTY-SEVEN

"That's everyone," Carmen said, ushering the last refugee from the exit. In the distance, the docks burned, small explosions popping every few moments. "Cole is taking them to another building across town, near the city limits."

"We're ready for the explosions, then," Georgie said, nodding.

"Those MPOs at the entrance are going to start pushing in soon. If we don't hurry, they'll never think we're all dead. We need to get in there now," Henry pressed. "And it would be best if the whole building went down. Harder to look for bones amid several tons of rubble."

"My roof garden..." Carmen trailed off, and then shook her head. "No matter. We'll try again. Next time it will be better."

Georgie clapped a hand on her shoulder. "Next time we fertilize your crops with what's left of the Coalition. Let's do this."

The trio scrambled down into the basement, now empty but still reeking of human terror and mildew. Henry bit back a retch and put her face into the crook of her elbow. It was getting harder and harder to breathe with all the smoke in the air, and it would be weeks before it dissipated. Terraformers weren't equipped to filter out particulates or toxins, and Skelm was already a smoggy place.

"Put the solvent by the support beams, right on top of the base. Once this stuff starts to corrode, we need to light the fire and get the hell out of here."

"How many times have you done this, exactly?" Carmen asked.

"Enough to know how to be effective."

Henry dumped a bag of solvent out, and the particles that floated into the air burned her lungs. After this, if she never saw another container of cleaning solvent, it would be too soon. Assuming they all survived, which was unlikely, given the Coalition's strength. They'd send in more troops once Allemande's body was discovered at the bottom of that shaft, and there would be nowhere in the city to hide. Still, first things first. She emptied another bag and stepped back to where the makeshift dirt ramp to the exit was.

"Here we go," Georgie said, setting a bundle of newspaper alight and setting it atop a box full of sawdust. "Won't be long now. Let's go. We should meet the others at the new safe house."

Henry interlaced her fingers with Georgie's and squeezed gently. "We need to get that infection seen to."

"Neither of you are leaving beds for at least three days, if I have anything to say about it," Carmen chided. "Otherwise *you'll* be the fertilizer for the new garden whether you want to be or not."

"Alright, alright," Georgie said, sealing the exit hatch and covering it with ivy and rocks again. "If we're lucky, we won't run into any trouble."

Gunfire sounded in the distance.

"Oh, no," Henry breathed.

Carmen grabbed her skirts in one hand. "Run."

* * *

"Run!" Carmen screamed again.

"This way," Georgie said, gesturing towards a narrow alleyway. "We need to stay off the main roads."

"I'm not injured, I can create a diversion."

Henry shook her head. "Absolutely not. We should stick together."

"The two of you are in no shape to outrun anything," Carmen protested. "We can't lose you both."

"No!" Georgie shouted, grabbing Carmen's arm. "No. For all we know,

CHAPTER THIRTY-SEVEN

there are MPOs gunning people down. We're stronger together."

"I'm scared," Carmen admitted.

"Yeah. Me too." Georgie massaged the front of her thigh and grimaced. "You're right that I can't run, not like this. But if there's anyone who did make it to the new safe house, we need to be sure they're okay."

Behind them, the basement hatch began to leak tendrils of thick, black smoke.

Henry wheezed and covered her mouth with her elbow again. "One way or another, we need to move."

More gunfire from the docks, barely audible over the growing roar of the basement fire, and the explosions from the storage container. What they needed was a miracle, but what they had was a lot of explosions. It was better than cowering in a basement, at least.

There were screams from nearby buildings, and alarm bells began to sound all across the city. The din of the angry clanging made it easier to move undetected, their footsteps on the cobblestones muffled by citizens trying to alert the military police to the danger of the flames.

When they came to an intersection of alleyways, yellow light from the street lamp flooded the pavement. A rat squeaked as it ran from one empty crate to the next, looking for its next meal. The sky was an unsettling orange, the light from the fires at the Administration building, the original safe house, and the ship at the docks all glowing in the acrid clouds. A figure in the alley opposite pulled out a gun and pointed it.

"Identify yourself," she said.

"We're just trying to get home," Carmen said quickly. "Please, Officer, we just want to get home to our families. We were on the way home from our jobs at the factories, and—"

"The tenements are in the opposite direction," Georgie hissed.

"Er, that is, we need to—"

"Stop bullshitting me," the voice said. "Are you Coalition or not?"

"Wait!" Henry shouted. "Alice?"

The gun's silhouette dipped. "… Henry?"

Relief flooded through Henry. "Oh my gods, Alice!" She stumbled across the street and wrapped the mechanic in an embrace. "What are you doing here? Where are the others?"

"It's just me and Kady. We took the small shuttle, Vi didn't want to risk setting the ship down because half the godsdamn dock is on fire."

"Yeah, we might have had something to do with that."

Something whirred in Henry's ear and she waved her hand at it. "What the hell is that?"

"It's a pilot droid," Alice said proudly. "We found it during a scrap job, and Kady reprogrammed it. It has radar embedded into its circuitry, as well as information recording for later examination. I also added in some additional capabilities that might come in handy."

"That's neat as hell," Georgie said, stepping out of the pool of light and into the dark alley. She reached out for it, but the droid swerved.

Alice holstered her gun. "It's good to see you both alive."

"Not for long if we don't get out of here," Carmen mumbled.

"Where is Kady?" Henry asked.

"She went in the opposite direction, she's probably out near the city limit by now. We ran into some trouble on the docks, a small firefight. I think we managed to scare them off."

Carment breathed a sigh of relief. "So it was you! We thought the rest of our people got caught up in it."

"Your people?"

"We have a few dozen people, some families, some refugees from Fort Gelad, some rebels from here in the city. We have four guns between us."

Alice gave a low whistle. "We thought we were just coming in for you two. There's been no news from Skelm in the public broadcasts about refugees. The Cricket can't take on that many people, and it can't land at the docks."

"How many can you fit in your shuttle?"

"Besides the pilot? Two. Three, at a push."

"That's going to take too long, no way will you get back and forth that many times without them noticing."

"Do you have somewhere high up? I might be able to get the droid to send a message up to the ship. We don't want to leave anyone behind."

CHAPTER THIRTY-SEVEN

Carmen pointed further down the alley. "We have a new safe house on that side of the city. You might be able to get a signal on the roof."

"What about the people in the factories?" Georgie interjected. "They need our help, too. Things are only going to get worse here once we're gone. And what about Emeline? Without the governor's input, they may well sentence her to public execution—"

"Whoa, whoa," Alice shushed. "One thing at a time. Tell me on the way. By the sound of those explosions, it won't be long before MPOs are swarming near here." Alice tapped a remote embedded into a wide cuff on her wrist, and the droid bleeped and began circling them higher. "I've told it to alert any heat signatures that aren't ours."

"It's this way," Georgie said, leading the way. "They took Emeline weeks ago after the union demonstration. Allemande said she could intervene and make sure she's sent to a school instead of the gallows, but…" she trailed off.

Alice stepped around a pile of broken bricks. "What happened to Allemande?"

"I pushed her down an elevator shaft," Henry answered.

"Good riddance."

"So now Emeline might end up dead, and we're still here, and we might not even make it out alive, and—"

"We'll find your sister. Do you know where they took her and the others?" Georgie shook her head. "No."

"Let's focus on getting out of here first, okay? We need some help."

"The safe house is just ahead," Carmen said. "Let me go first, Cole and I traded a secret knock. I'd be surprised if they even have any ammunition left for those guns, but better safe than sorry." She stepped forward and knocked five times in a rhythmic pattern on a weatherbeaten, dirty door. When no one responded, she whispered, "Asshole, it's me!"

With a loud creak, the door eased open, and the four of them scuttled inside. There were several dozen terrified, tired faces staring back at them.

"Who's this?" Cole asked, evaluating Alice with a critical eye.

"She's with me," Kady said, stepping from the shadows. "The one I told you about."

"Kady!" Henry said.

"Glad to see you're not dead."

"How did you get here so soon?"

Alice snorted. "Vi insisted on heading closer as soon as Kady told her what your plan was. She was worried. *Is* worried."

"What's the plan here?" Cole demanded. "There aren't even any places to set up a fire here, no running water... people are scared."

"I need to get up to the roof," Alice said. "To send a message." The droid whirred gently above her head, flashing red and orange. "Yes, yes, I know," she said, tapping at the wrist cuff again. "Now, scan for active MPO chips."

"Are you... talking... to that thing?"

"Its name is BEEP."

"Of course you bloody named it, you'd pack bond with a cheese sandwich," Kady grumbled.

"It's short for bio-electromagnetic emulator pod."

"I know what it's short for, I programmed it!"

"BEEP and I are going to try to get word to Vi. That shuttle is too small, but the Cricket will never be able to land in the docks, not with..." Alice gestured around. "Everything."

"We'll come with," Henry said, grabbing Georgie's hand. She couldn't bear the thought of being away from her again, not even for a moment. It had been a hard lesson to learn that one moment could change everything, and the memory of Georgie standing alone on the docks as they left last time would haunt her forever. How many horrors had she endured as a result?

The stairs to the roof were half rotted and creaked noisily with every footfall. It was a good thing that the adjacent buildings were only used as offices during the day, or it would be painfully obvious that people were hiding out in here. It wasn't somewhere dozens of people could hide for very long. It was a ticking time bomb.

An orange haze hung in the air when they propped open the door to the roof, a thick smudge that bit at Henry's throat. When Georgie wrapped an arm around her waist, she leaned in and rested her head on Georgie's

CHAPTER THIRTY-SEVEN

uninjured arm.

"Alright, BEEP, send the message." The little droid hovered a few feet above Alice's head, lights flashing. It chirped and then lowered back to Alice's level. "Good. Thank you, BEEP."

"Hang on," Georgie said, "how did you send that message? Was it encrypted? We haven't been able to get anything out without Coalition monitoring, they're listening on all frequencies."

Alice shook her head. "Don't need encryption. It was a direct link to the Cricket, we got hold of some rhodium to allow comms even through stealth. It means that it's slightly limited in range, and I can't connect to other conduits, but—"

"Alice!" Henry shouted.

"Shh!"

"Alice, what if that's how they're controlling storms? What if the reason you never found anything on the terraformers that would direct the strikes, is because it wasn't on the terraformers at all?"

"Gods." Alice's eyes grew wide. "It might be the same technology."

Henry wriggled from Georgie's grasp and reached out for the droid. "I'd be willing to stake one wild idea on it, would you?"

"Hang on, what are you talking about?" Georgie asked.

"What if we use BEEP to turn their own weapons against them? What if we're able to completely disrupt operations here in Skelm?"

Georgie squinted and then rubbed her eyes, red-rimmed from the smoke in the air. "They'd just rebuild."

"Of course they would, but it might buy us some time."

"How does destroying the terraformers buy us time? By my math that just creates another countdown to deal with."

"No, Georgie, we don't target the terraformers. We target the Administration building. We target the data centers in the city, we target the factories once they're empty. We have continuous strikes, around the clock. What better chaos is there than that? It would keep the military busy enough to resist blockading the docks, and if we target the communications tower, they won't be able to get word for backup."

"I don't want BEEP getting destroyed," Alice said firmly. "It's a valuable piece of tech."

"It won't," Henry assured her. "We just need to figure out what's up there that their tech communicates with."

"Reverse polarity ray," Kady said, easing out from the doorway. "I saw one, once, before I left the Coalition science labs. Never thought I'd see them make it useful for their aims. It was initially meant as a way to redirect lightning strikes away from areas that would have problems with brush fires." She sighed and leaned back against the brick. "I never thought about it for this because they're so huge. You can't miss them. We never saw anything at any of the storm sites that would be large enough to house it."

"I bet they're hiding it in a satellite."

Alice tapped at the cuff on her wrist. "BEEP, scan for anomalies in the satellites currently in orbit." The droid rose up and circled gently, chirping quietly. "It looks like something, maybe. BEEP, try to connect remotely."

"There's no way that's gonna—" Georgie started.

"Done," Alice said with a smirk. "We're in."

"They can't have made it that easy."

"When I reprogrammed it for Alice, I left in all of the base operations," Kady explained. "As far as that satellite knows, BEEP is still operating as designed, to ferry communications from settlement or ship to satellite without risking detection on radio waves."

"Target the communication tower first," Henry said. "We have to get the jump on them, if this is going to work."

The droid beeped. "Vi said if we can clear the docks of both fire and military, they might be able to get a transport down here to take most of these folks to safety."

"This might actually work," Henry said, squeezing Georgie's hand. "We might actually make it out of this alive."

* * *

When the communication tower was attacked, Skelm became detached from

CHAPTER THIRTY-SEVEN

the rest of the Near Systems. No wire or radio transmissions in or out, no way to contact nearby bases for reinforcements or to request an immediate team of specialized technicians. The engineers in the city would give it their best shot, but with strikes occurring at irregular intervals, they couldn't even get close.

The timing of the strikes at the Administration building couldn't have been better. The fire Henry had set had long been extinguished, judging by the temporary increase in military police presence on the streets. When the first bolt struck the rod at the tip of the building, alarm bells rang out across the city, the chaotic, atonal clanging of people panicking that the storms had breached the terraforming barrier. It would be a time before the strikes damaged the building, but it also meant that everyone inside was trapped there until the strikes ceased.

"Alice, you'd better start on the factories before people start piling in," Henry said.

"BEEP seems to be overloaded. It would need a faster processor, it's barely keeping up with both locations as it is, and with all this godsforsaken smog its solar panels aren't drawing in enough power."

"What about trying to disable the city?" Georgie challenged. "What about helping the people trapped in this shithole?"

"I'm doing my best! If I had known the BEEP was going to be the way out of this mess, I'd have upgraded all that, but I didn't, did I? We're working on getting these people out, it's the best we can do!"

Georgie's eyes began to fill with tears. "The best isn't good enough! How long before someone else gets swept away in some military transport, with no way to know where they're being taken or how to get them back?"

"We'll get her back, you know," Alice said, laying a hand on her shoulder. "We won't stop until Emeline is back on board."

"I wish we could burn this city down, for good."

"Maybe someday, we will."

Through the thick haze, lights in the buildings flickered. "They're trying to reboot the systems," Henry said. "I wonder why they think that will work?"

"Shit." Kady sprang forward and balanced at the edge of the roof, surveying what she could in the smoke. "Alice, what if they have another one of those droids? Rebooting could potentially clear their cached commands." She whipped her head around. "Georgie, how long would a full city reboot take?"

"Uh... an hour? Maybe less? Possibly more if any part of the grid had been damaged by the electrical currents."

"Alice—"

"No way," Alice interrupted. "Redirecting the ray to where the power grid is most vulnerable would mean targeting the tenements."

"Of course not the tenements, I'm not a monster," Kady spat. "I was going to say, direct everything you've got to the lab wing of the Administration building. Those labs—"

"If you overload the grid there, half that equipment is going to get fried," Henry finished. "It's brilliant, really."

Georgie rubbed her leg and winced. "Is that going to be enough to draw attention from the docks, though? Captain Violet needs a clear landing or we'll never get all these people out."

"Trust me, there're enough credits invested into those back-end experiments that I'm sure it will be top priority soon enough." Henry coughed, the acrid air burning her throat. What she wouldn't give for a few days in one of the large eco-domes back on Gamma-3. Enough trees to make that air the purest you'd ever find in the Near Systems. "I say it's a good shot. Delay any reboots as long as necessary, and get everyone out."

"What about the communications tower?"

Henry shook her head. "They'll send technicians in to fix the array the second the strikes stop. If they call for backup, we're not going to make it out of this."

"I don't think we have any other options."

"Then we'd better make sure we hurry the hell up," Kady said, standing straight. "I'll prepare the others to move for the docks."

"Agreed," Alice said, tapping at the buttons on her wrist. "BEEP, focus everything on the Administration building. Switch focus. Contact Vi for a

CHAPTER THIRTY-SEVEN

pickup."

"Move out, you two," Kady said with a playful poke at Henry. "Get to the docks. We didn't come all this way to not save your asses."

"Wait—" Henry said. "What about Alice?"

"I have to stay here with BEEP. It's range is too short to do this from street level, and—"

"You do realize the captain is going to actually kill me if I get on board without you, right?" Kady asked. "How long will it take you to get to the ship?"

Alice chewed at her lip, her one good eye calculating the distance from the safe house to the docks. "Not long. Five minutes?"

"That's cutting it close."

"It will have to do, won't it? Have Vi send a message via BEEP when everyone's on board and I'll make one hell of a run for it."

"Come on, Georgie," Henry said, pulling at her gently. "Let's go get saved."

"It feels wrong to be doing this without Em."

Henry smoothed a hair from Georgie's face. "I know." They limped back down the stairs, past the desperate, exhausted refugees and unionized rebels that were already heading for the door. Carmen and Cole, slumped against each other in the corner, exhausted. Around them, the city burned.

CHAPTER THIRTY-EIGHT

"That's everyone," Kady said, ushering the last refugee onto the Cricket.

"It's not *everyone*, we have to wait for Alice," Captain Violet snapped. "I can't believe you let her stay on that roof alone. You should have stayed with her."

"You know what she's like. She wasn't about to listen to me. Besides, they needed me to get these people safe on board. How the hell are you planning on flying this rig with this many people on board, anyway? I'll be surprised if it manages to lift off the docks."

"Shh!" the captain hissed. "Don't scare these people, they've been through enough. We dumped all extra weight, and we're not taking the shuttle back with us. We have a rendezvous with Tansy as soon as we're clear of Coalition space, we'll divide up the refugees and head back to Bradach right away."

"Alice isn't going to like that you're getting rid of her shuttle."

Captain Violet sighed. "No, she won't. I'll have to buy her a new one." She checked her pocket watch. "Here's hoping she runs faster than she usually does when she's got crate duty."

The speaker on the wall crackled. "Boss, radar is detecting some anomalies. Looks like maybe incoming vessels, but it's nothing we've seen before."

"Gods be damned. How long?"

"Maybe a few minutes, tops. Where's Alice?"

"Still on her way."

CHAPTER THIRTY-EIGHT

"Going to be close, then."

"I'm sure she's almost here," Henry piped in hopefully. "I'm sure she'll be here any second now." Despite her optimistic words, fear lodged in her gut. To be so close to freedom, yet still in danger of losing it, was terrifying. She clutched the extra fabric of Georgie's coveralls. There was more than there had been the last time they'd seen each other. Skelm had never been kind to the Paynes.

"Hurry up, Alice," Kady mumbled under her breath, pulling at the frayed threads at the cuffs of her hooded jacket. "I shouldn't have left her on that roof. Someone should have stayed."

"Then we'd just have two people running for the ship," the captain said. "Like you said, she's stubborn. She'd better also be fast." She tapped the radio at her waist. "Ned, what's the update on those incoming hostiles?"

"The signatures are unknown. Some look like Coalition, but the others..." he trailed off.

"Gunships or transports?"

"Few of each, plus these unidentifiable ones."

"Do you think they're using a new cloaking technology?"

"No, we can see them plain as day, it's just they don't make any sense." The speaker popped in the tense silence. "Boss, we've got incoming projectiles!"

"Everyone, brace for impact!" the captain screamed into her radio, and her voice was echoed through the speakers.

Henry grasped for Georgie and squeezed her in her arms. At least they'd die together.

"I'm here!" Alice gasped, stumbling onto the ship, BEEP rotating lazily over her shoulder. "Go!"

"Get us the hell out of here, Ned!"

"Gonna need you up on the bridge captain, autopilot isn't going to be enough to dodge this shit!"

The captain tore off through the crew airlock, and the ship began to shudder and shake as it lifted off the docks.

"Alice, how much extra juice can you give us?" Kady shouted over the noise of the boilers. "We need anything you've got!"

"Ivy!" Alice shouted into her radio. "Ivy, redirect power from pilot console to the thrusters!"

"Is that a good idea?" Kady asked, bracing herself against an empty crate.

Alice shrugged. "She's not using autopilot anyway, it's fine!"

"Where the hell have my controls gone?" Captain Violet screeched through the speaker. "Alice Green, you know I prefer the autopilot maneuvers!"

"Just fucking fly, darling!" Alice shouted back. "Get us out of this, and I won't even be angry that *you left my shuttle in that piece of shit city*!"

"Argh!" came the frustrated reply, and the ship lurched left, and then right as it approached the atmosphere, narrowly avoiding the missiles that then exploded in the air, rocking the ship off its course.

Henry ran to the tiny porthole window and rubbed away the condensation with her sleeve. Dozens of ships lay just past the atmosphere, hanging in space, waiting. It was going to be the fight of their lives. Before she could turn around, Georgie encircled her waist and propped her chin on Henry's shoulder.

"If this is how it ends, at least I got to see you one more time."

Henry turned to face her and kissed her softly on her cracked, feverish lips. "This won't be how it ends. We didn't come this far to be outwitted by a few—"

They were thrown into the wall with the force of the ship catching the side of a missile explosion. "Report!" came the captain's voice through the speaker.

"We're fine!" Kady shouted through the radio.

"Buckle in, it's about to get nasty!" the speaker screeched.

Kady motioned for them to enter the airlock. "It will be safer in the main part of the ship if the loading bay gets breached!"

They piled in and stumbled out on the other side onto the metal grate. Georgie gasped in pain, clutching at her leg. "You'd better get that checked out," Kady warned. "I'm heading to the bridge. You two, get to the med bay."

CHAPTER THIRTY-EIGHT

"I'm fine," Georgie said through gritted teeth. "With all those refugees, they'll have their hands full."

Henry helped her to her feet. "We'll follow you," she said to Kady. "But don't wait for us."

* * *

The ship jerked, and Henry almost tripped onto the bridge.

"Dammit, Ned, what's the reading on those ships?" the captain shouted. "I don't even know who I should be shooting at!"

"I'm working as fast as I can," Ned growled, tapping feverishly at the screen in front of him. "It's definitely not Coalition."

"So are they friendlies?"

"I can't tell, the signature is scrambled—"

"Let me see," Kady said, leaning over his shoulder. "It's something new. Our system can't determine the origin."

"That's what I said!"

Captain Violet jerked at the throttle, tossing them all to the side again. "Whoever they are, get us a route out of here that keeps us the hell away!"

"Boss, we've got hostiles coming in hot on port side."

"I see them, I'll try to bank—"

"BOSS!" Ned repeated, shouting now. "There's at least a dozen, you have to get us out of here or we're done for."

"This fucking rig can only go so fast with so many extra people on board!"

Henry braced herself against the doorway, helping Georgie back to her feet. She stood, laboriously, the pain from her infection evident on her face. "You should see Hyun," she said gently.

"If we don't die in the next five minutes, I'll consider it."

The wide window that spanned the width of the bridge flashed with the bright light of missiles smashing into each other, and ships firing superheated projectiles at close range. Georgie's eyes narrowed as she studied the battle. "Captain," she said quietly, "I think those unidentified ships are shooting at the Coalition."

"Good, let them blow each other up while we hightail it out of here," she shot back.

"Boss, about a dozen more of those scrambled signatures coming in starboard," Ned shouted. "Their weapons are powered and ready, but they aren't firing at us."

"Who the hell are these people?" the captain yelled, yanking the ship from side to side again. "We're barely going to—"

A missile exploded into the ship, sending the bridge into darkness with no light other than the flashing red warning from their consoles and the firefight from outside. "Alice!" the captain shouted into the radio. "We're losing power!"

"That hit took out half the junction wiring, we've got sparks all over the place down here!"

"Can't you patch it back in?"

"Not without about twenty spools of copper wiring and a peaceful eight hours I can't!"

The ship began to slow, crawling along, lazily wobbling away from missiles, despite the captain pulling hard on the throttle. "I can't keep this up forever," she said, a bead of sweat rolling down her face. "We need *power*!"

The radio crackled. "I can reroute all available power from the shields, but it's gonna be messy. We'll have to get somewhere fast, and I mean *fast*. This hack job isn't going to hold for long."

"How long?"

"Let's just say if we come across any delays, uh... it won't be pretty. Fly fast, Vi."

The captain gritted her teeth. "I'll fly faster as soon as you get me the juice I asked for."

"Juice? In this economy?"

"Alice!"

"Alright, alright. Give me three minutes to patch."

"You get ninety seconds."

CHAPTER THIRTY-EIGHT

"Boss, we've got more Coalition hostiles coming in fast from their space base nearby," Ned said, running his huge hands through his long ginger hair, which fell loose around his shoulders. "Two gunships and a transport."

"What the hell are they bringing a transport for—" Captain Violet started. "Oh, no. They mean to take back these refugees." A dark look fell over her face, and she gripped the throttle so tight, the knuckles bulged from her fist. "Over my dead body."

"Patched!" Alice's voice shouted from the radio. "Get us out of here!"

"Ned, chart us a course to the trading beacon, monitor for hostiles."

"Aye, Boss."

The ship lurched forward, and Henry almost didn't catch Georgie when she stumbled. "It's alright, I've got you," she whispered in her ear, and Georgie responded by squeezing her hand gently.

"I know."

"What in the hell?" Ned muttered, tapping at his screens. "Boss, those unidentified vessels are forming a ring around us, well, some of them anyway. Mid-size ships. The rest have stayed and are flanking the Coalition ships." He studied the displays. "I think they're... protecting us?"

"Whoever they are, let's just be grateful, shall we?" the captain replied. "And hope they aren't just getting us on our own to board and loot." She sighed. "Not that we have anything to loot on this ship other than people."

"To some, that's enough," Kady said quietly.

"Ned, how far to the beacon?"

"At current speed, we should be there shortly, barring any decline in power."

"Alice," the captain called through the radio, "how is it looking?"

"Holding, for now, but one good hit from a projectile and things won't be looking very good."

"Understood. Over and out." The captain sat straighter in her chair, which didn't even seem possible given her already ramrod-straight posture. "All we can do is wait and hope they're friendlies, now."

* * *

"The pods towards the rear of the station are open, Boss," Ned said, examining his console. "Not too busy today. Looks like Tansy and her ships are already here."

"Good. We'll want backup if these mystery ships are up to no good."

Henry and Georgie had stayed on the bridge for the flight to the beacon; it would have felt strange to be anywhere else. The med bay was already filled with desperate refugees, and what use would going to Henry's room be? "Georgie, we're almost there," she whispered. "Maybe the station has somewhere you can get treated?"

"Mm," she replied, snuggling in closer.

"Pod bay seven, locked," the captain said, guiding the ship silently past the standard warning signs pasted on the concrete walls of the station which read, 'No Murders or Gunfights Allowed' and 'Violators Will Be Airlocked.' The threat of death was the only thing that kept these stations peaceful, and even then, occasional duels still took place. Some station owners could be convinced to look the other way, if you had enough credits.

"Okay, people, be on your guard. We're across the station from where Captain Tansy and her ships are parked, but these mystery ships are right in the surrounding pods."

"Georgie, come on," Henry said, gently jostling her. "We need to go find you some medicine."

"Mmkay." She staggered to her feet with a grimace. "I'm tired, Hen."

"I know you're tired. Soon you can sleep." Maybe it was best if Georgie stayed on the ship - after all, Henry was confident she could find medicine on her own. It wasn't her first time bartering. "Do you want to stay in my room?"

"Yes." Georgie stumbled. "Can you carry me?"

"I don't think I can carry you," Henry whispered.

"May I?" Ned asked, leaning his cane against the desk. "I'll take her. I have to stay on the ship anyway, promised the boss I would keep an eye on things."

"But your leg—"

"I may need a cane, but I can still do this," he said, wrapping Georgie's

CHAPTER THIRTY-EIGHT

arms around his neck. "It's not far."

Henry chewed at her lip. "I don't want to leave her."

"I'll be fine," Georgie mumbled, half asleep and delirious. She needed medicine, and the med bay was fresh out, between dropping more supplies with affected rebel bases and treating the refugees. Hyun and Jasper were busy enough. It would have to be her.

"Alright, George, I'll be back before you know it, okay?"

"Mmhmm."

"Ned..."

"Yeah, I know. I'll keep an eye on her until you get back."

"Thanks."

"Captain, we have some people approaching the loading bay," Kady said, craning her neck to look out the window. "We should go."

"Let's go meet our rescuers, shall we?" the captain said, untucking her shirt to cover the gun holstered on her hip. "And hope to hell this doesn't get ugly."

Henry followed the captain and Kady through the ship, smoothing her skirts nervously as she slipped through the open airlock into the loading bay, the huge steel door creaking open. She just wanted this to all be over. She wanted to sleep, to let Georgie heal, to spend at least a week doing nothing except lying next to her and ordering food to be delivered to their door, to drink her in and forget all the time they were apart.

When they stepped off the ship, there was a group of people, all in matching, ugly, chartreuse uniforms with mauve epaulets at the shoulder. Captain Violet's jaw dropped open, and then she smirked. "Nice uniforms, Josie."

"That's *Captain* Josie to you, *Violet*."

"I can only say thank you for what you did back there," the captain said, extending her hand. "After all our bad blood, it was a kindness."

Captain Josie spat on the concrete floor, the wad of saliva oozing along the gentle slope of the station. "Give me my people, Violet."

"What?"

"Do you really think I'd do anything to help you? After everything you've done?" Captain Josie laughed and slapped her knee sarcastically. "What a joker you are. No, you have some of my people on that boat, and I want them back."

"The refugees? But—"

"We were mounting our own rescue mission. Every one of those ships out there has people they're looking for, people who have been scattered across the Near Systems by these Coalition pricks. We have a list of—"

"YOU CAME!" a girl screamed, pushing past Kady to get off the ship. "You actually came!"

"Of course I came, you silly little monkey!" Josie squealed, picking the girl up in her arms and spinning her around. "Mommy will always come for you."

"I didn't realize you had a daughter," Captain Violet said.

"Why else would I be risking my ass all across the damn solar system? It's all for her, to make sure she can grow up safe, not scrounging out of garbage cans like I did." She sighed. "I left her somewhere I thought she'd be safe, and I'll bet she would have been if you morons hadn't started poking around there. You better not have harmed a hair on her head, Violet, or I'll—"

"They were nice to me, Mommy. The doctor lady gave me a pink bandage over my scrape. It's her favorite color, too!"

"Kady, let the refugees know they might have people out here. Take the rest to Tansy across the station, find out if they've got places they need to be. I assume Captain Tansy will take the rest back to Bradach."

"Sure thing, Captain." Kady swept back onto the ship, the tails of her tailored black jacket swooshing behind her.

"You're damned lucky you had refugees on board, Violet," Josie sneered. "I'd have let the Coalition have you, otherwise."

"Like I said, we're all very grateful—"

"Next time I catch you without any innocents on board, I'm going to blast you out of the sky." She shifted her daughter from one hip to the other. "And we both know that busted up rig of yours can't be ferrying folks across the Near Systems."

Captain Violet shifted her weight from one foot to the other. "Captain

CHAPTER THIRTY-EIGHT

Josie, I know I can't undo the past. I can't take back what I've done, I can't bring your captain back to life, but—"

"Cut the crap, Violet. I said what I said."

"But it haunts me every day," Captain Violet finished. "And that's the honest truth."

Josie rolled her eyes. "Sounds like bull—er, sounds like garbage to me," she said, smiling at her daughter. "Don't let me catch you coming after us, either."

"Why would we, if you're tracking down people who need rescue?"

"Because you want all the glory for yourself, I know you, Violet. You play this game of high and mighty, but all you really want is to be everyone's hero, for people to feel indebted to you. It's sick."

"That's not—"

"Goodbye, Violet." She turned to the rest of the uniformed people behind her, tears in her eyes. "Thank you all for your help. I hope we are all reunited as happily as I am right now. You heard Violet, refugees will be taken across the station. I wish you all luck in finding those you've lost. We'll regroup in Bradach in one week's time." They all shuffled off, talking amongst themselves, some of them cooing over Josie's daughter in her dirty pink dress.

"That was unexpected," Captain Violet said with a beleaguered sigh. "She's getting smarter, more organized. If we run into her again, we won't get off so easy."

Henry cleared her throat. "I didn't expect to meet the infamous Josie today, that's for sure. Larkin told me all about the feud. Who'd have thought we had her daughter on board?"

"I didn't even know she had a daughter. People are going to start getting more desperate to find their loved ones if things don't change soon." She cast a sideways glance at Henry. "As you well know."

"I do appreciate you coming after me," Henry admitted. "I don't know what might have happened if you hadn't."

"If you're going to stay on this ship, and we'd like you to, with Georgie of course, you can't go running off like that ever again. Do you have any idea

371

how worried we were? Gods, when Kady told me, I nearly hit the roof."

"I'm sorry, I just had to get to Georgie, and—"

The captain laid a hand on her shoulder. "I know. If it was Alice, I'd have done the same thing in half a heartbeat."

* * *

"Georgie?" Henry called, nudging the door open with the toe of her boot, her arms piled high with medicines and bandages. "Are you awake?"

The door swung open to reveal Hyun sitting at the edge of the bed with a thermometer, a welcome sight.

"How is she?" Henry asked, casting an eye over the drowsy Georgie.

"She'll be better once we get these antibiotics into her system," Hyun answered, standing up to hook up an IV to the needle in the crook of Georgie's arm. "Do you know if Jasper managed to get to the med shop before they closed?"

Henry nodded. "I ran into him there. He had three pallets of stuff he was roping some kids into dragging back to the ship."

"Good," Hyun said, breathing a sigh of relief. "We were down to the bare cupboard in there." She took three bottles at the top of the heap in Henry's arms and examined them. "She won't need all this, you know."

"I just wanted to make sure she got it as soon as possible. Her fever—"

"Isn't as high as I feared. Once the infection calms down, she'll heal up just fine. Why don't you set those supplies down and take a seat?"

"Me?"

Hyun gave her a stern look and gestured towards the bed, the glass beaded fringe that fell from her arm tinkling gently. "Yes, you. I'll bet you need the same treatment her mother did, and if we're lucky, you won't need it the rest of your life like she will."

"You should save medicine for others, I—"

"Shh." Hyun narrowed her eyes and tilted her head, listening to Henry's breathing. "You're lucky you didn't die, you know. If they hadn't found

CHAPTER THIRTY-EIGHT

you—"

"I know."

"Everyone was so worried."

Henry gave a heavy sigh that turned into a rasping cough. "I had to go after her." Georgie was somewhere between sleep and dozing, her breaths becoming more even and slow. She was exhausted. Hell, Henry was exhausted too, the immense weight of the past days dragging at her.

"Here," Hyun said, handing her an odd brassy contraption that began to blow clouds of silvery blue smoke. "Inhale, exhale, keep doing that until it stops smoking. And then please, for the love of all the dead gods, get some *rest*." She laid a hand on Henry's shoulder and smiled. "We missed you. I hope you take the captain's offer to join us on a permanent basis."

The door creaked as it closed, and Henry inhaled and exhaled until the contraption fizzled out with a soft hiss. She crept into the bed, nestled herself next to Georgie, and fell into a deep and dreamless sleep.

CHAPTER THIRTY-NINE

When Henry awoke in the middle of the night and reached out for Georgie, her hand only met the soft, wrinkled cotton of the bedsheets. It was the third time that week she'd sneaked out of their shared bed on the ship, desperate to find some information or lead about her sister. If Henry went looking for her, she'd find her in the kitchen, poring over old star charts and maps of all the known work camps in the Near Systems, playing and replaying the public broadcasts looking for some clue as to where she might find Emeline.

Georgie wouldn't talk about her sister, though. Every time Henry tried to bring it up, she got shut down; the conversation shifted. She wouldn't let the captain send a message to her mother telling her that Emeline was missing, either. She said she had to tell her mother herself.

Henry rubbed the sleep from her eyes and tugged on her boots. She'd be thrilled when they got back to Bradach and she could get some new clothes, including a new nightdress. She was sick of sleeping in the same thing she'd worn all day. At least it would only be a few more days until they landed in the port.

The ship was quiet this time of night, with Ned up on the bridge, Ivy down in the boiler room, and everyone else asleep or in their quarters. Everyone except for her... well, whatever they were, it seemed serious now. There didn't need to be a discussion. After spending months apart, Henry was just happy to be near her again.

"Hey," she whispered when she approached Georgie. She laid her hands

CHAPTER THIRTY-NINE

on her shoulders and massaged gently. "I woke up alone again."

"Sorry," Georgie replied, snapping the file shut. "Just researching. I didn't mean for you to get out of bed."

"We will find her, you know."

"Yeah."

Henry bent and kissed Georgie's cheek. "I mean it. We will."

"Go back to bed, I'll be there soon."

"You're not doing yourself any favors by running yourself ragged, Payne." Henry reached down and felt her head. "No fever, at least."

Georgie waved her away. "I'm fine! Hyun even said the medicine did its job."

"She *also* said you need to *rest*."

"How am I supposed to rest, when Em is out there somewhere?" she asked, tears welling in her eyes. "I just feel like if I stop for even a second, it's one more second that could have been spent finding her."

"Captain Tansy has multiple crews out looking," Henry soothed, perching on the table. "You're allowed to sleep."

"What if they've got her in some awful work camp? What if..." she trailed off. What she'd left unsaid was what had been worrying them all - the possibility that Emeline Payne was already dead, executed along with dozens of others accused of sedition. Anonymous.

"Or she might be at that fancy pants boarding school, infiltrating the Coalition."

"That's the best-case scenario, hardly likely."

Henry smoothed a hair back behind Georgie's ear. "It's as likely as the others."

"Maybe you're right," Georgie blew out a sigh that turned into a yawn. "I'm tired."

"Let's get you back in bed, then. I don't like waking up alone."

"Will you hold me until I fall asleep?"

"Always."

* * *

Georgie nearly sobbed the moment they stepped off the Cricket's ramp onto Bradach cobblestones. They'd made it. They'd survived. She barely remembered the days they spent at the trading beacon, having slept through them deeply and gratefully, with the love of her life at her side. "Ma!" she shouted, wobbling on her leg. "Lucy!"

"Oh my gods, Georgina, I've missed you something awful!" her mother cried, reaching up to put her arms around Georgie's neck. "We were so worried, weren't we, Honey Bee? Spent every evening listening to the public broadcasts listening for news." She patted Georgie's hand. "Never heard anything, though."

"Nice wheels, Ma."

"Oh Georgie-Bean, I haven't felt this good in years. I don't have to spend all my energy getting from one place to another, I've been helping the new refugees when they arrive, giving out rations, and information packs, and helping them either get settled or move on somewhere they want to go. Georgina, I feel alive for the first time since your pop died."

"That's great, Ma."

A tall man with jet black hair peppered with silver cleared his throat. "Georgie, I, uh..." he started.

"Mama's got a *boyfriend*!" Lucy screeched with a giggle. "He's real nice, and he buys me ice cream sometimes!"

Georgie blinked.

"Georgina, don't be angry with me, I've been lonely for so long, and—"

"Mrs. Payne, that's wonderful!" Henry chimed in, shaking her finger. "I knew there was something going on between you two."

"Georgie, your mother means the world to me," the man said, holding his cap in his hands. "I know this can't be easy, but—"

The floodgate keeping in all the emotions she was swallowing back threatened to breach. "You'd better take care of her!" she shouted, more abrasive than she'd intended. She cleared her throat. "What I mean is, that's great, Ma."

"José spoils me," her mother whispered. "He cooks! He loves Lucy, he couldn't wait to meet you, and—" she stopped. Georgie knew what was

CHAPTER THIRTY-NINE

coming next, and she nearly bit through her lip trying to hold in her tears. "Where's Emeline?"

Henry squeezed her hand, and Georgie tried to blink back the tears, but they spilled down her cheeks, anyway. "Ma, I tried so hard, I'm so sorry that I failed you, I—"

"Where is she?"

Georgie knelt on the ground, ignoring the dull throb of pain in her leg, and laid her head in her mother's lap. "I don't know. You'd have been so proud of her, Ma, she was the lifeblood of that unionization, a spark for the rebellion, but they... they took her away." She couldn't bring herself to say what she feared most - that she'd been killed. But if what Allemande said was true, they'd never bury that down, they'd use her sister as an example. They'd put it on the public broadcast, just like Mr. Jackson.

"No, no! Not my Emeline," her mother cried. "What happened?"

"It was a big raid. They took her and everyone else demonstrating. It was probably a hundred different folks. They brought in new people, rebels they'd picked up from all over the place."

"We're just going to have to find her, won't we?" her mother said, a sob catching in her throat. "Promise me you'll find her, Georgina. Promise me you won't give up on Emeline."

Georgie shook her head. "I would never."

Lucy threw her arms around her. "We have to get Emmy back," she whimpered. "What have they done with Emmy?"

"I don't know, Honey Bee," Georgie admitted. "But our new friends will help us find her, won't they, Henry?"

"Of course they will," Henry nodded, kneeling on the cobblestones behind her and opening her arms to give Lucy a hug. "We might already have some leads, in fact."

"Some work camps that other rebels have been spotted at. There's another group breaking people out, so I bet we see her any day now." The words sounded hollow in Georgie's ears, and her mother's weak smile confirmed that she wasn't buying it, either.

"You'd better rest up first," her mother said, smoothing a stray hair from her face. "You won't be rescuing anyone if you don't take care of that leg." When Georgie stood up, her mother took her hands. "I'm not angry at you, Georgina. I know you'll have done everything you could. But I also know that we need to get her back."

"I know, Ma. We will. We're working as fast as we can."

"And you, Ms. Weaver, I assume you're in on this as well?"

Henry stood and nodded. "I wouldn't dream of leaving you to it on your own. I care about Emeline, too."

"Planning to meet at the Pig in five minutes," Kady said, bounding off the ramp. "Mrs. Payne, the captain wants to talk to you about the search and rescue plans."

"I can't believe no one sent a wire beforehand," Georgie's mother said, and the guilt cascaded down into her chest.

"I told them not to, Ma. I wanted to tell you in person. It didn't feel right to tell you over a message."

"Oh, Georgina," her mother sighed. "Come on then, let's hear what the captain has to say, shall we?" She held onto José with one hand, and directed her wheelchair with the other. Georgie couldn't help but feel guilty for bringing this profound sadness back into her mother's life, just when she was finding a little bit of happiness.

The Purple Pig was empty, except for them, with two large circular tables pushed together, with heaping piles of steaming food set in the middle of each table. "Henry, thank fuck, it's so good to see you," Larkin said, wrapping her in a firm embrace. "We've been so worried."

"And Georgie!" Evie cried, nearly dropping a plate of tiny cupcakes as she exited the tavern's kitchen. "Georgie Payne, gods alive! I'm so glad that you made it back safely. I'm just sorry we couldn't be there to break you out ourselves."

"I can't thank you enough for holding up your end of the bargain," Georgie said, hugging her once the cupcakes were safely set down. "When I helped you two get out of Skelm last year, part of me thought I'd never lay eyes on you again."

"Well, almost. We've got to get your sister back."

CHAPTER THIRTY-NINE

Tears sprang to Georgie's eyes again, and she fought to blink them back. "I don't know why y'all are helping us so much," she managed to choke out. "All I did was throw one of you into a garbage bin."

"Well, you also caused an explosion big enough to get us out of there," Larkin joked. "And who knows, we might need your pyrotechnics again, one day. We stick together. We help people. We don't go back on our word." She thrust a bright green drink at her. "Here, try this, it's a new recipe."

Before Georgie could put the glass to her lips, Henry snatched it and set it on the table. "Larkin, she was shot twice a week ago. It's probably too soon to be experimenting with hard liquor."

"Ah, bullshit," Georgie said, snatching it back and downing it in one gulp. The fiery warmth radiated from her lips down into her stomach, and she breathed deep. "It's nice to finally have something that's not watered down. The Twisted Lantern has nothing on this place."

"You've got that right," Roger said, clinking his cocktail glass against Carmen's frosty mug of ale.

"Excuse you," Cole said acerbically. "We did the best with what we had. I actually think this place is rather ostentatious."

"Everyone, take your seats, please," Captain Violet called from the doorway. When they'd all settled, and begun to pile food on their plates, she continued. "As some of you know, Captain Tansy has multiple crews actively searching for any sign of Emeline. The rest of our contacts have ears to the ground, including Jhanvi Jhaveri at central command in the Capital."

"I always knew Jhaveri was solid," Henry said, her mouth full of food.

"As I was saying, we have multiple streams of information we're looking into. We have allies across the Near Systems, ready to mobilize if we ask them to. This crew has its work cut out for it, but hopefully with our two newest permanent members, Georgie and Henry, we will be able to increase our efficiency with medical supply drops, refugee ferrying when needed, though Captain Tansy's fleet is more outfitted for that, and scrapping every godsforsaken Coalition ship, satellite, and shuttle we come across."

"Friendly reminder here, Vi, but you still owe me a shuttle," Alice said with a grin.

"Yes, darling, you will get your shuttle, I promise." The captain cleared her throat. "If we all agree, I propose two days of shore leave, enough to restock our ship, and we get back to it."

"Uh, Boss," Ned said, wiping ale foam from his beard, "I think we need to reckon with the fact we're possibly more rebels than pirates, now."

"Good," Captain Violet said. "Fuck the Coalition."

Epilogue

Henry flipped a pancake from the iron skillet onto the faded floral pattern of the plate's porcelain and spread a dollop of fresh butter over the top while Georgie snored softly in the bed of their rented room. All the late nights had finally caught up with her, and she hadn't even stirred when Henry got up, or started making breakfast, or when she nearly dropped the little glass container of syrup that had cost more than its fair share of credits. Maple trees were difficult to grow outside Gamma-3 and thus was a popular thing to steal in pirate raids.

She poured more batter into the piping hot pan and watched it bubble as it cooked. After months of constant chaos, it felt like bliss to just fix some pancakes before they'd get sucked back into the fray tomorrow. Captain Violet had alerted all rebel colonies to the technology being used to direct storm strikes, and already the satellites had all been deactivated and scrapped, once they were located. People were safe from lightning strikes and electrical storms, at least for now.

"Hey," Georgie said blearily, sitting up in bed. "That smells good."

"It better, I'm using the good stuff."

"Did ya make any for me?"

"No, I thought I'd let you starve," Henry said with a smirk. "Of course there's some for you, but only if you get your cute little ass in here now, otherwise I'm eating yours."

"Alright, alright," Georgie said, throwing off the covers. "I hear you." Her footsteps thudded heavily on the bare wooden floor, the thin shirt she had worn to bed nearly transparent.

Henry raised an eyebrow as she set the plates on the table. "You're looking... well rested."

"Yeah. First night without nightmares in months." She sat in the pine wood chair and scooted into the table. "Thanks for making breakfast."

"Someone had to," Henry said, and then added, "I'd make breakfast for you every day if it meant that I didn't have to be away from you again."

"I missed you. I don't know if I said that enough with... everything, but I did. Desperately. You were on my mind every single day that we were apart."

"I missed you too."

"Hen, there were some days I thought I might not be able to go on without you. Everything just kept getting worse and worse, and—"

"Hey. Let's just be in this moment, okay?"

Georgie nodded. "Yeah. Okay." She took a bite of the pancakes and closed her eyes. "These are fantastic. Where did you learn to cook like this?"

"Finishing school," Henry grimaced.

"You? No!"

"Cooking was about the only part I did well, they kicked me out after the third time I set fire to the dorms doing unauthorized experiments."

"I guess some things never change."

Henry reached across the table and traced her fingertips over Georgie's bare skin. "I'm pretty confident this won't change."

"Hell no," Georgie replied, and leaned closer to kiss her on the neck. "You've got me forever. Especially if you keep making pancakes."

Henry sighed happily at the feeling of Georgie's soft lips against her skin. It had been so long. "I almost wish I'd waited to make them, now. I wish I was back in bed with you."

"My lady!" Georgie shouted, heaving herself from the chair and wobbling on her bad leg. "Your wish is my command!" She took one last bite of the pancakes and pulled at Henry's arm. "Back in bed, let's go!"

Henry didn't hesitate. To hell with pancakes and maple syrup, the only thing she was hungry for was the hot feeling of skin on skin with the woman she'd fallen in love with the moment she laid eyes on her. She stripped off her new nightdress and jumped into bed, the wooden frame creaking from the effort. She pulled gently at Georgie's shirt, tugging it off over her head to expose her breasts.

"Gods be damned, Georgie, I never wanted anyone as much as I want you."

"Good," Georgie growled, kissing down Henry's breasts and across her hips. She kissed, and teased, and gently bit Henry's thighs, and every breath brought her closer to the edge.

"Fuck," Henry whispered, grasping the bed sheets between white knuckles. She reached down and felt Georgie, slick and ready, and moaned with anticipation.

They made love for hours, long after the pancakes had grown cold. When they were finally sated, they laid wrapped in the crisp white sheets, their arms draped around each other. Henry had never felt so at peace. It was right, and it was forever.

"The public broadcast is about to start," Georgie said, leaning over to flick the radio on.

"We can listen tomorrow, can't we just have tonight—"

"Shh, it's starting."

"Good evening, I'm Delia Dodson, taking over for your previous nightly anchor. It's good to be here with you, my syndicated audience."

"Oh gods, it's her," Georgie breathed, and began to dig through the drawer, pulling out bits of loose paper and a pen.

"Who's her?"

"Shh!"

"We have a very special announcement tonight that I am thrilled to present to you - the unveiling of the new overseer for Sector Five, after weeks of intense and secretive deliberation from the High Council. After a narrow escape from a band of brigands and thugs, and overcoming incredible adversity in her role as Governor of Skelm..."

"No," Henry said. "It can't be."

"Amaranthe Allemande is here with us tonight to formally accept her new position, along with her daughter."

"She's fucking dead. I saw you throw her down a damn elevator shaft," Georgie said, gripping the pen in her hand so tightly that the veins in her arm were clearly visible.

"Since when does she have a daughter?"

"My dear Coalition citizens," oozed Allemande's voice from the radio, "I cannot express how humbled I am to have this honor bestowed upon me. It is true that I have overcome many challenges in my roles serving our wonderful empire, from a lowly military police officer, to Inspector, to Governor of Skelm, where I put down a violent and dangerous insurrection single-handedly, and narrowly escaped death only through my own cunning and the training I received from my first day as a Coalition employee. If I can do it, you can do it, if you just work hard enough."

"Thank you, Overseer Allemande, and I for one can't wait to see what your plans are for Sector Five. Now, for your nightly—"

"Actually, Ms. Dodson, my wonderful and enlightened daughter has something to say."

"Oh! Well, this is a treat! Go on dear, introduce yourself!"

The microphone rustled, sending crackles and pops through the radio. "Hello, Coalition citizens," came a horrifyingly familiar voice. Henry's blood ran cold. "I am Emeline Allemande, first daughter to the Overseer of Sector Five. I wanted to say that any rebellions will be hunted down and wiped out, in accordance with the law against treason and piracy."

"Er— thank you, Emeline. Now, for the nightly news."

Georgie snatched the radio and hurled it across the room, where it smashed into a million shards of brass and glass, sparkling in the dim light from the street lamps that crept into the room from under the curtains. "We're going to fucking kill that bitch," she snarled. "Again. And then we're going to get my sister back."

End of book three

Keep reading for a sneak peek into the next novel in the series, **Sewing Deceit**.

Sign up for my newsletter and get information about convention appearances, book launch parties, new releases, and more! Get bonus content for the Cricket Chronicles series like deleted scenes and extended cuts. You can unsubscribe at any time with no obligation.

http://eepurl.com/gOQBaP

FOLLOW ME

You can follow me on Twitter at @IMRyannFletcher, on Facebook @RyannFletcherWrites, Instagram @RyannFletcherWrites, or email at RyannFletcherBooks@Gmail.com. It's always great to hear from you!

Sewing Deceit preview

"And don't forget, it's your turn to scrub out the loading bay," the captain of the ship shouted after her.

"Yeah, yeah, Marshall, I know," Bailey replied, shifting the weight of the heavy crate in her arms. "Don't worry, the work always gets done."

"Make sure you tell that lousy good-for-nothing crew mate Rosa that if she's late back again, we're leaving without her, I don't care what her godsdamned navigating credentials are."

"Mhmm," she agreed, stepping off the ramp, rolling her eyes. The captain was a good man, as far as she could tell, but she missed the freedom that Hjarta had given her. Making a living as a rum runner was fine, most of the time, but between the heartache of losing her family, friends, and the woman she loved and the constant fatigue, she was merely drifting through consciousness. Detached. Apart.

The uneven cobblestone streets of Bradach wound their way from the port to the Purple Pig tavern, where her delivery was scheduled. Three heavy as hell crates full of top shelf illegal liquor sloshed in her hands. She'd make the delivery and head straight back to the ship. The Pig wasn't somewhere she wanted to linger for too long.

The rough wood and the ragged nails of the crates bit into her hands. It wasn't the weight so much, she was used to carrying heavy loads, but the old, splinter-ridden boxes that made this part of the job almost unbearable. It was worse in some of the more rural settlements, where the roads were unpaved, mounds of dirt tripping her up. Or that one place where she'd had to carry the delivery for miles because the roads were so bad that no cart could carry the shipment. In Bradach, it was a shorter, more manageable walk, even if her hands were already throbbing in pain.

Bailey dragged herself up the slight incline to the tavern, a little pleased with herself that it was easier now than it had been when she'd first taken this job. It paid not to skip leg day, literally. The faster she delivered shipments, the more likely it was that she'd get a second of rest before the next one. The Pig was the only tavern they delivered to in Bradach, after that embarrassing altercation with the Bronze Bell at the other end of the city. She'd never seen Captain Marshall so angry before or since.

Slipping through the open back door, she stacked the crates on the floor near a mound of potatoes. "I just need a signature," she called, craning her neck.

"Bailey!"

She jumped. "Larkin, you scared the hell out of me. Why do you always have to sneak around like that?"

Larkin shrugged. "Old habits."

"I just need a signature for your shipment, and I'll get outta your hair."

"Why don't you stay a minute? Have a drink, catch up—"

Bailey waved her off. "Can't. Got more deliveries to make," she lied.

"You and I both know that's bullshit after what happened at the Bell. What, do I smell, or something? You don't like Evie's food here? What is it?"

"No, no, nothing like that. Just... busy."

"Busy. Sure."

"The job keeps me occupied, that's all I can say."

"How long has it been, now?" Larkin asked, signing the invoice with a tiny, scrawled signature that was illegible. Old habits, indeed. "Six months?"

"Seven."

"No complaints?"

Bailey shrugged. "No more than any other job, I guess. Rum running pays the bills."

"Any word about your people?"

"No." The word burned like bile in her mouth, the shame of not being the hero they'd all needed that day. "No word."

"I'm sure Eves will hear some intel soon, she's cracked a new code, you know. With the help of—" she stopped short.

"Yeah. I heard."

Larkin cleared her throat nervously. "Right, right, of course you did. I'm just being a grapefruit."

"Mm." Bailey held out the clipboard. "You have to sign here, too."

"Come on, you should stay, just for a minute. Catch up. I'll fix you one of my new specialties, it blends some very interesting botanicals that really brings out the woodiness of the whiskey, and—"

"I can't, I'm sorry."

"They're not here, you know. Not even in port, and only left last week. It's not like she's going to swan in here and rub it in your face."

Bailey sighed, the clipboard dropping to her side. "She wouldn't do that anyway. It's not in her nature to be cruel."

"Yikes. Still got it bad, huh?"

"Like not even a day has passed."

Larkin grimaced. "Shit. I'm sorry. Listen, if you'd rather just go, I'll just sign that copy and let you be on your way. Hell knows I wouldn't stick around here if I was you. Probably would have tossed the crates through the back door and forged the signature. Would have run all the way back to the ship. When I thought I lost Evie to that - *woman*... well. It wasn't a fun time."

"Captain says anyone caught forging invoices spends the next month on dish duty. I have terrible handwriting and hate dishes, so..." She looked at the scrawled signature. "Although, I reckon I'd have gotten away with yours."

"Oh, piss off," Larkin said with a laugh. "Now, are you staying for a drink, or not?"

The afternoon light glowed at the door, the shadows growing longer with every passing minute. She didn't have plans that night, not really. Eating cold leftovers by herself in the ship's crappy old kitchen didn't really count as plans. "Yeah, alright then. Let's have this new drink you've concocted." Bailey set the clipboard on the counter and sauntered through the backroom door into the main room of the tavern, a beautiful establishment with gilded accents on the walls, thick velvet upholstery, and the delicate dance of lantern light at each little table.

"Did you hear we started having live music on the weekends, now?"

"No, that's..." Bailey felt her fingers itch for the strings of a fiddle. How long had it even been, since she had stomped and shredded some notes with her friends? "That's really great."

"It's nice to give something back to the community, you know? With all the refugees coming in from all over the Near Systems, the pool of talent has grown exponentially. Besides, it keeps the regulars happy, and it's better than the alternative."

"What's the alternative?"

Larkin wrinkled her nose. "Comedy."

"What, you don't like to laugh?" Bailey punched her lightly in the arm.

"A bunch of drunks telling old jokes is hardly worth laughing at. Here, take a seat, I'll fix you up that new cocktail."

"Seems like you're really settling into this mixology thing."

"Yeah, well, when you spend most of your life knowing the delicate ins and outs of hiding poison, it's not a far jump to finding yourself in the kitchen with your old mortar and pestle, grinding up some new herbs and spices for some seriously good drinks."

Bailey eyed the glass in Larkin's hand suspiciously. "Old mortar and pestle? As in, the one you used for poisons?"

"Oh, please, I washed it, *obviously*."

"Maybe I should pass on that drink, actually—"

Larkin burst out laughing. "Hey, *relax*. It's one Eves bought me special when we got this place. My old one is in a trunk somewhere." She winked. "Probably." She ground some leafy stems into the marble bowl, and turned to crack the wax seal on a new bottle. "See? Breaking out the good stuff for you."

"Why? I'm just your courier."

"Let's just say I want to make sure that my connection to the top shelf stuff stays intact." Larkin shook the green pulp with a healthy shot of amber liquid and strained it. "Anyway, I like you. You're much nicer to talk to than the last asshole who had your job."

"I think he got fired."

"Not surprising, given that attitude. I almost socked him in the jaw one day. Here," Larkin said, pushing the drink across the bar, "try this."

Bailey sipped at the drink, savoring the simple yet satisfying flavors. Mint cooled her tongue, while the smoky liquor warmed her throat. "It's good. What's it called?"

"Dunno. Doesn't have a name yet."

"When's this one going on the menu?"

Larkin wiped down the bar. "As soon as it has a name, I guess."

"Where's Evie?" The short, bookish barkeep was always a welcome sight to Bailey, especially as she was usually offering her food.

"Out. Down at the research tent, I expect."

Bailey tensed and sipped at the drink. "Oh?"

"I told you, she's not in Bradach. Her lab partner is, though, I think he's starting to take on more down there. Something about weather pattern predictions, I don't know. After they figured out how all that was happening, and disabled those satellites, it sounds like they're trying to figure out how to turn it back on the Coalition." Larkin shrugged. "I dunno. I'm an assassin and a bartender, not a scientist."

"I bet those damn scientists couldn't mix a drink this good, though."

"You're godsdamned right, they couldn't," Larkin said proudly. "You're not bothered by the lab partner, are you? If you are, I can make sure—"

Bailey waved her away. "No, no. Roger's fine. Glad to hear he's healing up."

"He seems to be happier on the ground than in the sky. The Cricket can be a bit of a maze inside."

"Yeah." Bailey's heart ached at the memory. She'd never set foot on that ship again. It would be too painful. "It can." She drained her glass and slid it across the polished, freshly-lacquered wood. "Thanks for the drink."

"If you want to stay for dinner, I can see what Evie is making—"

"Nah. Thanks though. I've gotta scrub the loading bay before bed tonight, some lemon sold us a crate of unsealed gin. The pressure change in the bay meant they leaked everywhere."

"What a waste."

"Marshall was pissed."

Larkin rinsed the glass under a tap and dried it. "I would be too. Good gin is hard to come by, everyone across every backwater settlement thinks their undistilled bathtub swill is worth selling." She set the glass back on the shelf. "It isn't."

"You can say that again," Bailey said with a snort. "Gods, there have been some seriously gross taste tests over the past few months."

"So, where to next?"

"Dunno. Could be anywhere. Marshall tries not to let things get too routine, no circular shipment patterns. Coalition is getting too smart, too many patrols all over the place."

"Sometimes I forget how frantic it gets out there. I'm getting soft now, all snuggled up with a cushy job here."

Bailey nodded. "It's worse than before, too. No rest for the weary."

"Don't be a stranger, okay? You're always welcome here."

"We'll see. There's only so much torture a woman can bear, you know?"

Larkin looked at her sadly. "You'll meet someone else."

"Not like her, I won't."

"You will." The bartender flipped her long, shiny braid over her shoulder and tucked the bar rag into a belt loop. "Now go on, get out of here. Don't you have work to do? I swear, you rum runners are all the same, kicking back when you have swill to deliver."

Bailey snorted. "Be nice, or yours might just accidentally get dumped into a storm drain."

About the Author

The Cricket Chronicles would be nothing without my wife and captain of continuity. She inspires me to keep writing, even on days where I'd rather hide under the covers. Her tireless enthusiasm is a refreshment for my writer's soul.

A big thank you as well to the Sunday morning writing group - y'all have brought laughs and giggles to a year that felt terrible in so many ways. I look forward to seeing your faces on my screen every week.

Another huge thanks goes out to all my beta readers, who offered their time willingly to help shore up the edges of this book. You're the best, and I mean that.

And finally, I want to thank YOU, the reader, for using your precious time to read this book. I hope you will join all of us in book four, Sewing Deceit.

Ryann Fletcher is a writer who lives with her wife and too many craft supplies. She writes sapphic science fiction and fantasy, and likes to cook.

You can connect with me on:

- https://ryannfletcher.com
- https://twitter.com/IMRyannFletcher
- https://facebook.com/RyannFletcherWrites
- https://instagram.com/RyannFletcherWrites

Subscribe to my newsletter:

- http://eepurl.com/gOQBaP

Also by Ryann Fletcher

Sewing Deceit

https://books2read.com/SewingDeceit

Bailey is still heartbroken, working as a rum-runner, desperate to find her people and save them from a life of indentured servitude to the Coalition. When she's sent on a lucrative delivery contract to the Capital, she's pulled into a swirling vortex of conspiracies, impersonating a high-ranking general.

When Mae's parents summon her back to Gamma-3, she is reluctant to leave her successful seamstress business behind in Bradach. Will she fit into her new role in the family business, or will she ignore her father's threats to expose the pirate city?

Overseer Allemande is pulling the strings in the Capital - how far will she go in quest for power?

Printed in Great Britain
by Amazon